DEBT OF WAR

Professionally Published Books by Christopher G. Nuttall

The Embers of War

Debt of Honor
Debt of Loyalty

Angel in the Whirlwind

The Oncoming Storm
Falcone Strike
Cursed Command
Desperate Fire

The Hyperspace Trap

ELSEWHEN PRESS

The Royal Sorceress

The Royal Sorceress (Book I)
The Great Game (Book II)
Necropolis (Book III)
Sons of Liberty (Book IV)

Bookworm

Bookworm
Bookworm II: The Very Ugly Duckling
Bookworm III: The Best Laid Plans
Bookworm IV: Full Circle

Inverse Shadows

Sufficiently Advanced Technology

Stand-Alone

A Life Less Ordinary
The Mind's Eye

TWILIGHT TIMES BOOKS

Schooled in Magic

HENCHMEN PRESS

First Strike

DEBT OF WAR

CHRISTOPHER G. NUTTALL

Text copyright © 2020 by Christopher G. Nuttall
All rights reserved.

No part of this book may be reproduced, or stored in a retrieval system, or transmitted in any form or by any means, electronic, mechanical, photocopying, recording, or otherwise, without express written permission of the publisher.

Published by 47North, Seattle

www.apub.com

Amazon, the Amazon logo, and 47North are trademarks of Amazon.com, Inc., or its affiliates.

ISBN-13: 9781542019552
ISBN-10: 1542019559

Cover design by Mike Heath | Magnus Creative

Printed in the United States of America

DEBT OF WAR

PROLOGUE I

The interior of the space yacht was luxurious to a degree that even Lady Constance Turin, a distant relative of Duchess Turin, found staggering. No expense had been spared to ensure that interstellar travel was as comfortable as staying at home on the family estates. The cabins were huge, the food was delicious, and the companionship—composed of trusted family retainers—was excellent. She'd even been told that she could take a handful of travel companions with her, despite the secrecy of her mission. But she had the feeling that she was ultimately regarded as expendable. She was high-ranking enough to speak for her distant aunt, but too lowly for her missteps to rebound badly on the family. Her *next* voyage might be a far less comfortable flight into exile.

She poured herself a drink as the yacht dropped out of hyperspace a reasonably safe distance from Caledonia. It felt odd to be taking extreme care when approaching a world, but the starship's captain had made it clear to her that there *was* a war on . . . as if he'd expected her not to understand the implications. Constance—Connie, to her friends—had to admit she *hadn't* realized some things that should have been obvious. If the yacht came out of hyperspace too close to the planet, she might be blown away by the planetary defenses before they realized who she was . . . and, if they did realize who she was, they might blow her away deliberately. There were so many rumors about who was actually in charge on the planet below that it was hard to tell just what she should expect, from the king greeting her with open arms to the colonials arresting her and putting her on trial for crimes against the colony worlds. In hindsight, Connie rather thought her aunt should have made arrangements for Connie's reception before ordering her to leave Tyre.

But that wasn't an option, she reminded herself as she stood and posed in front of the mirror. *They didn't dare risk making contact with the king . . .*

Her reflection looked back at her, her body and face almost painfully young. She *was* young, by aristocratic standards. A mere child of twenty-five, barely old enough to be taken seriously in a universe where the senior figures were rarely less than three or four times her age. And while they looked young too—human vanity was an unchanging constant even in a universe gone mad—they had an experienced glint in their eyes she knew she lacked. A year ago, she'd been spending her trust fund and sowing her wild oats before she matured and took her place in the family business. Now she was an ambassador on a deniable mission who could be disowned at a moment's notice. She kicked herself, mentally, for not holding out for more solid rewards. Her aunt had put her out on a limb and was busily sawing off the branch behind her.

And the universe has gone crazy, she thought morbidly. *Who expected an actual civil war to break out?*

She shook her head. She'd never paid much attention to politics. The role of the colonials in the Commonwealth, the Theocratic War, and—most importantly—the balance of power between the king, the House of Lords, and the House of Commons had never much interested her. They'd never really *touched* her. She'd had no real prospects of making something of herself, certainly not like Kat Falcone or some of the others who'd thrown their titles aside and plunged into the military. It still seemed insane to her. If you had so much, why throw it away?

Her aunt had been very clear during their one and only private meeting. Officially, as far as anyone knew outside the family itself, the family and the giant corporation it controlled were firmly on the government's side. They were working as hard as they could to ensure a victory, to put the king firmly back in his box and slam the lid closed. But unofficially, they were hedging their bets. There was no guarantee the king would lose the war. If he won, if he got into a position where he could compel the government to surrender, it was vitally important that the family ended up on the right side. And *that* was the side that won.

"If the king wins," Duchess Turin had said, "I will be in some trouble. But the family itself must be spared, even if I have to fall on my sword."

Connie hadn't understood, not then. But she thought she did now. The family was double-dealing, saying one thing to its allies while pledging covert loyalty to its enemies. The entire affair still staggered her every time she contemplated what she'd been sent to do. She'd be disowned if the king lost the war, the mission branded as nothing more than a crazy child's desperate bid for power. No one would believe Duchess Turin, Connie was sure, but they'd all *pretend* to believe her. The Duchess had said as much herself, citing hints and tips that their family wasn't the only one playing a double game. They *had* to emerge from the war on the winning side.

Her terminal bleeped. "Your Ladyship, we've received orders to await inspection before we enter orbit," Captain Turin said. He was family—barely. If he wasn't, he wouldn't be trusted to command the yacht. "We can still turn and run if you wish, but we're rapidly running out of time."

Connie felt a hot flash of irritation mingled with grim understanding. Before the war, no one would have dared inspect an aristocratic yacht. Their IFF codes would have been enough to get them into orbit and heading down to the surface without even a cursory inspection. But now . . . She supposed she couldn't blame them. The yacht was harmless, yet the locals had no way of *knowing* this. A modern warship could do a great deal of damage if it closed to point-blank range before opening fire, if it were camouflaged and no one realized it might be a threat.

She sighed. She'd endured indignities, such as being snubbed by society hostesses, in the past. She could endure having her ship searched from top to bottom. At least the gesture meant they were taking her seriously.

"We can deal with it," she said tiredly. "Make arrangements for me to meet the king as soon as possible."

She let out a long breath as she picked up her datapad. Her aunt hadn't given her any *written* instructions—that would have been far too incriminating, if they'd fallen into the wrong hands—but she knew what she had to do. Talk to the king, open lines of communication . . . without making promises that would come back to haunt the family when the war was over. And she knew it wouldn't be easy. The king would want promises—cooperation—that she couldn't offer, not without being immediately disowned. The family didn't dare choose a side for good until they were sure the other side wouldn't be able to destroy them.

"Because we don't know who will win," Duchess Turin had said when Connie asked why. "If we knew, we'd support the winner. Right now, all we can do is keep our options open and hope we can pick a side when we still have something to bargain with."

A low quiver ran through the ship, the background hum of the drives fading away as the yacht waited to be boarded. Connie looked up, feeling oddly uneasy. She'd never had to contemplate the prospect of death before, death or disgrace. High Society was quite forgiving, if you had the right name and connections. But now . . .

If I fail, I will be disgraced, Connie thought. She had no illusions. Failure would mean permanent exclusion from the inner circles. *I must not fail.*

I will not fail.

And she waited.

PROLOGUE II

"We've got to stop meeting like this," Captain Sarah Henderson said as she poured herself a mug of coffee and took her seat at the table. "People will talk."

"People will always talk," Governor Rogan said. He smiled at her, the expression never touching his eyes. "We've gone to some trouble to ensure we can speak privately."

Sarah nodded, taking the opportunity to look around the table. There were seven people in the room, counting herself, all movers and shakers within the Colonial Alliance. They came from seven different worlds, all colonies. None came from Tyre. She had the nasty feeling it boded ill for the future. The Colonial Alliance had sworn to support the king to the bitter end. Just by being here, by meeting behind his back, they were breaking their word.

And the king may already know, she thought grimly. Caledonia's government was so close to the king it had practically ceded authority to him. The king's security forces were growing larger, pervading the spaceport and the surrounding facilities like nits in hair. *If he knows, what will he do?*

Governor Rogan didn't mince words. "You know what happened at Tarleton," he said. "The king's man arrested and imprisoned the entire government on charges of treason. If Admiral Falcone hadn't intervened, they might well have been executed by now and the planet under permanent martial law."

"The king was within his rights to be angry," Ambassador Yang pointed out. She looked young, but Sarah knew she'd been an ambassador longer than Sarah had been alive. "The planet *did* surrender."

"The planet had no choice," Sarah said flatly. She was the only military officer at the table. She was the only one who could point out the truth and make them believe it. "The Tyrians had complete control of the high orbitals. Resistance would have been . . ."

"Futile?" Ambassador Guarani asked. "Or useless?"

"I was going to say *impossible*," Sarah said. "They could not have so much as scratched the paint on the warships while the Tyrians reduced the planet's surface to radioactive cinders. There comes a point, sir, when further resistance is pointless."

"That wasn't the attitude we had when we fought the god-botherers," Guarani snapped. "We fought to the bitter end!"

"If a planet surrendered to the Theocrats, the people knew what to expect." Sarah met his eyes, evenly. "The planet would be forcibly reshaped. Planetary leaders would be executed, military and police personnel would be put to hard labor, women would be forced into the home, and children would be raised in their poisonous religion. The Theocrats wouldn't honor whatever terms they offered the planet in order to induce the locals to surrender. Once we knew that, we didn't surrender.

"Tyre is different. This war has been marked with a notable lack of atrocities. There was no mass roundup of traitors on Tarleton, let alone any of the other worlds and settlements they've occupied over the last six months. The Tyrians have been clever enough to ensure that we *can* surrender without baring our necks for the executioner's blade. They've made it clear they intend to be decent, and so far they've honored their word. I cannot blame the local government for surrendering when they had a flat choice between a reasonably harmless occupation and complete destruction."

"It wouldn't have been harmless," Yang pointed out. "The House of Lords has made it clear that they intend to recoup their investments, somehow."

"Somehow," Guarani repeated. He laughed, harshly. "I wonder what they have in mind. The money to repay them simply doesn't exist. And if they levy heavy taxes, they're going to kill the goose that lays the golden eggs."

"More like iron eggs," Yang said. "And there are cheaper, easier, and safer ways to get iron."

Sarah looked from one to the other, keeping her thoughts to herself. Guarani had a point. The Colonial Alliance wasn't that rich. The concept of careful development had been tossed out the airlock when the Theocratic War had begun, destroying all the plans for the colonial worlds to repay Tyre for its massive investment. Sure, they could recover all the industrial plants and productive nodes they'd built over the last ten years, but it would cost them more than it was worth to transport everything back to Tyre. And, at the same time, they'd destroy a sizable market for *their* goods. Her lips twitched, humorlessly. No one would be buying anything from Tyre if they didn't have money to buy it *with*.

"We're getting off topic," Governor Rogan said. "Can we trust the king?"

The words echoed in the chamber. Sarah shivered despite the warm air. She'd sworn an oath to the king when she'd donned her uniform; she'd betrayed her then commanding officer to take control of her ship when the king and his former government had finally come to blows. She knew she would be executed for mutiny if she fell into enemy hands. And yet . . . she felt uncomfortable, as if she were betraying a *second* master.

"He shouldn't have passed judgment on Tarleton so quickly," Guarani said flatly. "But—"

"It isn't the first time he's acted without our agreement." Yang cut him off, her expression grim. "Right now, he's running the war like an autocrat."

"He may not have a choice," Sarah said. "There's no time to debate when the missiles are flying."

"That's not in doubt," Governor Rogan said. "But the missiles *aren't* flying."

"Yet." Sarah hadn't seen any tactical or strategic projections, but she was no fool. The House of Lords had to be planning an offensive against Caledonia itself in the hopes of capturing the king and his loyalists in a single blow. It wouldn't be long before they amassed the power to launch a major offensive. "If we don't hang together, we'll hang separately."

"And what will we do," Governor Rogan asked, "if the king doesn't keep his promises after the war?"

Sarah looked down at her hands. She had no answer.

"So . . . what do we do?" Yang smiled, humorlessly. "Which of us will volunteer to bell the cat?"

"There's already discontent on the streets," Governor Rogan said. "It's only going to get worse as news of Tarleton spreads from one end of the Alliance to the other. The StarCom network will make sure of it."

The House of Lords will make sure of it when they realize what sort of propaganda tool has fallen into their laps, Sarah thought. *They'll go out of their way to make the news as harmful for the king as possible.*

"Yeah," Guarani said. "Who'll tell the king he needs to back down?"

"There aren't many of us who *can*," Governor Rogan said. "We're being frozen out of the innermost circles. His closest supporters are unlikely to go against him."

"Kat Falcone might," Sarah said quietly.

"She lost status when she lost the Battle of Tyre," Guarani pointed out. "And the king's already pissed at her."

"There's another point," Yang said. "If we talk to the king, and the king refuses to listen to us, what do we do? And, if we do something drastic, what will happen to us?"

"The king is not all-powerful." Governor Rogan indicated Sarah. "A sizable chunk of his military is composed of colonials."

"Yes," Sarah said.

"That's not the point," Yang said. "If we start disputing with the king, if matters start heading downhill rapidly, the House of Lords will take advantage of it. We could lose the war. And what will happen then?"

Sarah winced. She had no answer. But she knew that others did.

PROLOGUE III

Ambassador Francis Villeneuve of Marseilles was finding little to impress him on his incognito tour of Caledonia. His experienced eyes noted the places where the colony world's natural development had given way to rushed industrialization to fight the greatest war the galaxy had ever seen, followed by the planet's hasty incorporation as the capital of a government-in-exile. Or semiexile, he supposed. His intelligence staff had made it clear that King Hadrian and his staffers were exchanging hundreds of messages with friends, supporters, and possible contacts on Tyre. For a war that both sides had pledged to fight to the last, there was an astonishing number of people making official, semiofficial, and blatantly unauthorized attempts to bring the two sides to the negotiation table. He supposed it wasn't too surprising. There were hundreds—perhaps thousands—of families that found themselves torn in two by the war.

Which gives them a chance of coming out on top no matter who wins, he thought as the aircar finally landed on the embassy's roof. *Or at least of making sure whoever winds up on the losing side gets nothing worse than a slap on the wrist.*

He kept his thoughts to himself as he clambered out of the aircar, exchanged salutes with the guard on duty, and stepped through the security field. There were so many intelligence and counterintelligence operations underway on Caledonia that he would have been surprised if he *hadn't* been stung with a nanotech bug or two . . . dozen. Marseilles was bending the laws on interstellar relationships to a breaking point, although Tyre hadn't bothered to do more than lodge a formal complaint. It was only a matter of time, Francis knew, before that changed. The legal fiction that allowed his government to establish an embassy on Caledonia wouldn't stand up to scrutiny, although *that* didn't matter. The only thing that mattered was military power and the will to use it. If Tyre ever found out what his government was doing, they'd get very willful indeed.

Another guard passed him a datapad. Francis glanced at it, noting that the security field had killed fourteen bugs. He had no way of knowing who'd stung him or why, although there was no shortage of suspects. One complication of a civil war was that both sides used the same equipment and technology, their forces interchangeable in a manner the galaxy hadn't seen since the Breakdown. Francis shrugged, returned the datapad, and made his way down to the makeshift office. Admiral Giles Jacanas was waiting for him.

"Mr. Ambassador," Jacanas said. "I trust the mission was successful?"

"The king is running out of time to stall," Francis said with heavy satisfaction. "He must decide, soon, if he wants to do more than flirt with us."

He sat down, mentally composing his report. In one sense, Marseilles didn't care who came out ahead in the Commonwealth Civil War. The war wasn't going to really alter the balance of power unless both sides took the gloves off and started slaughtering entire populations on a scale that would make the Theocrats blanch. But, in another way, it was important to keep the fighting going as long as possible. The Commonwealth had been a growing threat to Marseilles simply by blocking interstellar expansion away from the remnants of Earth even before it had fought and won a war with the Theocracy. In the short term, the war had been incredibly costly and destructive; in the long term, it had positioned Tyre to make a bid for galactic power. Marseilles had been relieved that Tyre had stopped the Theocracy but wasn't blind to the threat Tyre represented. The combination of a powerful military, an experienced officer corps, and the need for a distraction from serious structural weaknesses might have pushed Tyre into considering a second war. Francis wasn't so sure, but it wouldn't be the first time a government had done something outsiders had considered insane even without the advantages of hindsight.

"The king will have to give up the technical specifications soon if he wants to win," he said dryly. A maid brought him coffee, bowed, and retreated as silently as she'd come. "Or he can stay here and wait for his enemies to come knocking."

"Time is not on his side," Jacanas agreed. "The House of Lords will be ready for a decisive offensive within twelve months, if not less."

"And so we must time it carefully," Francis said. He sipped his coffee. "And make sure he pays us while he *can* pay us."

He smiled coldly, then sobered. The Commonwealth had developed enough newer and better weapons technology to give it a decisive advantage if it went to war against a peer power. Marseilles was working desperately to catch up, as were all the *other* interstellar powers, but the Commonwealth had a window of opportunity. Francis and his superiors weren't blind to the implications. The longer they took to catch up, the greater the chance of Tyre turning expansionist and punching Marseilles out before they could mount a reasonable defense. If they could get their hands on pieces of hardware to study, let alone the blueprints themselves, it would be a great deal easier to catch up.

And put us in the position to contemplate some expansion for ourselves, he thought. *Or even to gain unfettered access to unexplored stars.*

Marseilles was in an odd position, geopolitically speaking, hemmed in on all sides by other interstellar powers that could block its access to the rim of known space. Blockading hyperspace wasn't easy, but it could be done.

He sat back in his chair, schooling his thoughts into calm. There was no point in contemplating a future that might not come to pass, not when everything depended on a king who was under immense pressure. The poor bastard was caught between multiple factions, all of whom could be relied upon to react badly if the king seemed to be favoring their rivals. Perhaps it was no surprise that the king was already making mistakes. His friends and allies—his true friends and allies—were few and far between. Everyone else wanted something. And woe betide the one who failed to supply it.

It doesn't matter who wins, Francis told himself. *As long as we get what we want out of the bargain, the king can win or lose and we still come out ahead.*

CHAPTER ONE

CALEDONIA

There had been a time, Kat Falcone recalled with a bitterness that surprised her, that King Hadrian would have welcomed her to his palace. There had been a time when he would have instantly dismissed petitioners when she arrived, doing whatever he had to do to make time to see her. There had even been a handful of times, when they'd been planning the final stages of the Theocratic War and, later, the occupation, when they'd even just kicked back and been nothing more than friends. Her lips quirked at the thought. They hadn't been lovers. They'd been friends who'd wanted, who'd needed, nothing the other could supply. They'd been free to be *themselves*.

She sat in the waiting room, tapping her fingers in impatience. The room was strikingly luxurious, designed to give an image of limitless wealth and power, but there was nothing to do while waiting. Whoever had designed the chamber had set out to convey the impression that everyone who waited to be seen was nothing more than an insignificant petitioner, someone who didn't matter. She'd seen the pattern before, back on Tyre. It had never impressed her. Anyone who had a reason to be in the waiting room, anyone who was important enough to see the *king*, wouldn't be impressed. They'd probably even be aware of the manipulation, which wouldn't amuse them in the slightest.

And we're wasting time, she thought, looking at the door on the far side of the room. She could walk through it and then . . . and then what? The king was in negotiations with *someone.* Her sudden appearance might make things worse if they thought she heralded bad news. She snorted, bitterly. In a sense, she *did* herald bad news. The war was still trapped in a stalemate. And the last engagement had been a tactical victory but a strategic defeat. *We need to find a way to tip the balance in our favor.*

She rose and paced the room, wishing she'd thought to bring a book or an e-reader with her, something—anything—that could distract her from the war. She'd read the reports, both the official ones submitted to the makeshift Admiralty and the unofficial ones from a bewildering network of influencers, pollsters, and outright spies who reported to the king. There were people who blamed her for everything, from losing the Battle of Tyre to the recent engagement, insisting that she was secretly working for the House of Lords—an idea so absurd she honestly couldn't wrap her head around it. If she'd wanted to betray the king, all she would have had to do was arrest him the moment he set foot on her starship. There would have been no need to fight a civil war when she could have ended it in a second.

A mirror hung in the corner, glinting oddly as it caught the light. She stood in front of her reflection and studied herself. Blonde hair fell over a heart-shaped face, the hair really too long for military service. She'd cut it short when she'd joined the navy, even though she probably could have gotten away with bending the regulations that far. The navy made accommodations for people, provided their accommodations didn't get in the way of military efficiency. And she was an aristocrat . . . She frowned as she noted how tired her blue eyes looked, how pale and drawn her face was. She looked tired—tired and beaten. She rubbed her eyes, wondering if the king's PR specialists would recoil in horror the moment they saw her. She didn't look like a great heroine. No doubt the pictures and videos would be carefully tweaked before they were released to an unsuspecting public. The laws against manipulating content, everything from smoothing out one's skin to outright deepfakes, had been tossed aside long ago. She wondered, sourly, if anyone truly believed the lies. There were just too many independent news producers, scattered across the Commonwealth, for a largely fictional narrative to take root.

Which might make crafting such a narrative possible, she thought grimly. *If everyone thinks faking a story is impossible, they might not realize that it can be done.*

The door opened, revealing a dark-skinned man in a simple suit and tie. Kat turned to face him, noting how he stood. His hands were never far from his belt. A bodyguard, she thought. Probably someone with genuine military training. The king's paranoia had only grown in the days and weeks since the Battle of Tyre, when it had sunk in that the war wasn't going to end in a single vicious engagement. He'd recruited so many guards that wages were going up right across the planet. Plus, half the population seemed convinced it was only a matter of time before the planet was invaded and brutally put to the sword.

"Admiral." The bodyguard inclined his head, his eyes never leaving her. "His Majesty will see you now."

Kat nodded, allowing him to lead her through the door. The body-guard's act was good, although she could see the weaknesses. He always kept himself a certain distance from her, as if he feared she'd put a knife in his back. Kat rather suspected he didn't really trust the guards on duty outside the palace, the ones who'd scanned her right down to the nanoscopic level before they'd allowed her to pass the first checkpoint. There was literally nowhere she could have concealed a weapon, not from that level of security. And yet, the bodyguard was paranoid. His master was probably the foremost target in the entire galaxy.

She kept the thought to herself as the bodyguard showed her into the king's private office. It was surprisingly comfortable compared to his more formal office or the council chamber where his closest advisers and supporters met. There were comfortable armchairs, welcoming sofas, and, to her dismay, a sizable drinks cabinet. She'd helped him to bed only a few short days ago after he'd drunk enough to challenge even *his* genetically enhanced biology. She was not pleased to see him pouring himself a rather large drink.

"And thank all the gods *that's* over," the king said as he held up an empty glass. "Will you join me in a toast?"

"No, if you don't mind." Kat kept her voice even, although she knew the king might mind a great deal. "I need to keep my wits about me."

"Always a good idea, in this place." The king waved her to an armchair, then sat himself to face her. "Everyone has a plan to win, and everyone *else* doesn't want to hear it."

He lifted his drink. "Cheers."

Kat frowned as he drained the glass. The king was as handsome as ever, the combination of genetic engineering and cosmetic sculpting gave him a mature look, with an angular face, short dark hair, and a smile that didn't quite touch his eyes. But he also looked . . . *sloppy*, as if he'd been liquefied and practically poured into his outfit. He wore a simple black suit with a single golden rose pinned to his breast. Yet . . . it looked ill-fitting. Kat felt a flicker of concern mingled with a grim awareness that clothing was the least of their concerns. The war could still go either way.

"I concluded preliminary a deal with Ambassador Villeneuve of Marseilles," the king said. "If things go well, they'll be filling the gaps in our roster and supplying everything we can't make for ourselves."

"That's rather a lot of things," Kat said. She would be astonished if Marseilles sent actual starships to fight beside the king. The House of Lords might turn a blind eye to diplomatic missives, and even the establishment of an embassy, but they'd hardly ignore a foreign fleet defending Caledonia. It would be a de facto declaration of war. "What do they want in return?"

"Nothing much." The king reached for the bottle and poured himself another glass. "They want some minor border concessions, where the Commonwealth brushes against their territory, and access to detailed technical specifications for our latest weapons."

Kat's eyes narrowed. "They want us to give them advanced weapons?"

The king snorted, as if she'd said something stupid. "How *else* are they going to supply us with modern weapons?"

"It will take them months, at the very least, to gear up their plants to put the latest missiles into mass production," Kat said. She'd never taken any interest in the production side of things, but she knew the basics. Months was an optimistic estimate. "In that time, Your Highness, the war may be won or lost. They may never supply us with a single missile."

"They flatly refused to supply us with *their* missiles," the king said. "They claimed it would be impossible for us to fire them from our ships."

Kat frowned, uneasily. There was a certain amount of truth in that, she supposed. Foreign missiles weren't configured for Tyrian missile tubes. Their control links would have to be reprogrammed to allow their new owners to target and fire them. And yet, it was possible to overcome such problems. She'd had no trouble capturing enemy hardware during the Theocratic War and pointing the systems right back at them. But then, the Commonwealth and the Theocrats had already been at war. Marseilles probably didn't want to risk pushing the House of Lords to the point where their provocations couldn't be overlooked any longer. The king's ships firing Marseillan missiles would be something they'd *have* to respond to. The Marseillans might as well have sent the House of Lords a calling card attached to an insulting note.

And that might draw some of the heat off us, she thought. *But . . .*

She shook her head. Widening the war would be utterly disastrous, no matter who came out ahead. If Marseilles won a decisive victory, they might claim Tyre itself and then advance to swallow the remainder of the Commonwealth. The king would count for nothing if the throne was lost beyond all hope of recovery. And if the House of Lords recovered, they'd have all the proof they needed that the king was a tool of a foreign power. His reputation would never recover, whatever happened. He would certainly never be allowed to rule unchallenged, even in the colonies. The Colonial Alliance would be reluctant to swap one master for another.

Which makes me wonder if they know what the king is doing, she mused. *And what they'll do if they find out they're being kept in the dark?*

She put the thought into words. "How many people know about the negotiations?"

"Here?" The king looked down at his glass. "Only four . . . five, counting you. We conducted the discussions under immense secrecy. No point in letting everyone know. It would only upset them."

"It would galvanize the House of Lords to throw caution to the wind and attack us here," Kat warned. "And not all of your supporters would go along with trading information for missiles."

"They won't have a choice." The king corrected himself, sharply. "They *don't* have a choice, do they? If we lose this war, we lose everything."

"Yeah." Kat couldn't disagree with that, even as she wondered at his methods. "But we also have to think about the future. We could win one war only to blunder straight into another."

"We'll worry about that when it happens," the king said. He put his glass aside, somewhat to her relief. "If we win the war, we can renegotiate terms with our suppliers. If we lose, they're not going to get paid anyway. And anyone who finds out ahead of time will have to think about the future too."

Kat frowned. "Do you really think you can keep this setup a secret until the time is right?"

"Yes," the king said. "Only my most trusted advisers know the truth."

"Really." Kat wasn't so sure. Caledonia was infested with spies. She would be astonished if there weren't at least a million spies on the surface, ranging from long-term sources to information brokers and opportunists keen to make their fortunes before the war came to an end. Someone would be monitoring the palace, the embassies, and everywhere else that had even the tiniest shred of importance. And someone else would be tying it together into a single picture. "I doubt the House of Lords will remain in the dark forever."

"As long as they remain in the dark long *enough*," the king said. "And who would believe them?"

"Too many people," Kat said. "They don't have a reputation for outright lying. Not yet."

She leaned back into her chair, feeling grimly unsure of herself. The House of Lords could certainly *claim* the king was allying himself with foreign powers . . . and discover, later, that they had been telling the truth all along. So far, they'd been remarkably restrained. That would change, she was sure, as attitudes hardened on both sides and all hope of a relatively peaceful return to sanity faded away. Or when it finally dawned on them that they didn't need to lie to do immense damage to the king's reputation. All they had to do was tell the truth about everything that had happened on Tarleton. The king's man had tried to arrest the colonial government. The Colonial Alliance wouldn't be pleased when it learned that Justiciar Montfort had acted under Hadrian's orders.

If a somewhat loose interpretation of his orders, Kat thought sourly. She wasn't blind to the simple truth that Justiciar Montfort's defense *was* quite reasonable and would have been sufficient, if there hadn't been so much outrage at him. *If they decide the king knew what was going to happen, or gave the order, they could do anything in response.*

"We have to win the war," the king said. "Whatever . . . *questionable* . . . decisions we have to make will be handled then, once the war is over. Or put aside forever, if the war is lost."

"Yes, Your Majesty," Kat said. "I understand."

"Very good." The king poured himself yet another glass. "I have a meeting with my inner council in twenty minutes. Do you have a plan to win the war?"

Kat's eyes narrowed. She hadn't been invited to the meeting, even though she'd been one of the king's strongest supporters. An oversight or . . . or what? The king might have chosen to exclude her to please the idiots who suspected her of treason, or . . . or chosen to exclude her because she disagreed with him openly. Or . . . Was she overthinking the problem? She was a military officer, not a political leader. She'd never tried to hide that she found nonmilitary matters boring when she'd first been invited to the privy council. The king had gone along with it.

And being hundreds of light-years away didn't help either, she reflected. She'd been so far from Tyre that she couldn't even attend via hologram. Nor did she have the time to read the highly classified transcripts that had been forwarded to her. *No time to do more than read the summaries and cast meaningless votes.*

She put her concerns aside. "Your Majesty, we need to continue to wear them down, in hopes of creating an opening we can use to win the war in a single blow."

"Quite," the king said. "And how do you intend to achieve this?"

"I don't know, not yet." Kat scowled. "If we deploy our entire fleet in hopes of making the diversionary operations convincing, we run the risk of giving *them* a clear shot at Caledonia."

Or of making the House of Lords too unsure of themselves to deploy their fleet away from Tyre, she added, silently. *The trick is to offer them a shot at victory without actually giving them a shot at victory.*

She watched the king stand and start to pace, a mannerism they had in common. He knew as well as she did that they couldn't hope to win a long, drawn-out war, no matter what assistance they received from Marseilles. The House of Lords was bringing the reserve fleet online, training up new officers and crewmen, and building newer and better weapons. It would be just a matter of time until her brother and her best friend—her *former* best friend—felt strong enough to hit Caledonia without leaving Tyre exposed. And that would be the end. The king couldn't keep his cause alive once his capital had been captured and his fleet scattered beyond hope of resupply. He'd have to throw himself on the House of Lords' collective mercy, a trait Kat knew to be in very short supply.

"I'll look for options," she said calmly. "We may have to gamble."

"We can wait until we receive the newer weapons and supplies," the king said. "Marseilles isn't the only interstellar power interested in supporting us."

"They're interested in keeping the Commonwealth off-balance," Kat said, sharply. "They're not interested—"

The king rounded on her. *"Don't you think I know that?"*

He calmed himself with an effort. "I apologize," he said stiffly. "The stress is getting to me."

"I quite understand," Kat said. She did, although she wasn't inclined to forgive people who shouted at her. At least he'd had the grace to apologize. "Perhaps you shouldn't be drinking so much."

"There's little else I can do," the king said. He snorted, humorlessly. "I'm a prisoner of events."

"Then we'll try to find a way to take control," Kat said. She knew that wouldn't be easy. The king was rapidly running up against the limits of his power. His fate wouldn't be decided on Caledonia, or at least Caledonia alone. All their plans might come to nothing if the House of Lords put its own plans into operation. "There are always options."

"Yes," the king said. "And sometimes we need to stake everything on one throw of the dice."

CHAPTER TWO

CALEDONIA

"Justice for Tarleton," the voices bellowed. "Justice for Tarleton!"

Captain Sarah Henderson shivered, despite herself, as the protest march hove into view. It was as spontaneous as any large protest could be on a planet under martial law; she'd heard the local government had only granted permission after it had been pointed out that the march was probably going to go ahead with or without the government's blessing. The protest was already growing rapidly in size and shouting power. She felt something deeply primal within her, both luring her into the crowd and urging her to run. She'd had two days of shore leave and . . . She shuddered. She hadn't had the chance to do much of anything for herself before the shit hit the fan.

She lifted her cup to her lips and took a sip. She'd spent the last few hours exploring the city, trying to get a sense of local feeling. The time hadn't really been informative. There had been grumbles about shops selling out of imports from Tyre and the rest of the colonies, but nothing that hinted at a change of public opinion. And anger about the problem of Tarleton had been mounting steadily as the king and his closest supporters failed to do anything to quell the unease. She had the grim feeling that it had finally burst into the open.

The mob advanced, shadowed by a handful of policemen in riot gear. The march was both threatening and remarkably well behaved, shouts echoing off the tall skyscrapers even as the protesters stayed within the road and allowed pedestrians to walk down the street without harassment. Several teenagers handed out paper leaflets, running in and out of the crowd as if they expected to be cited by the policemen if they stood still for more than a few seconds. Sarah took a leaflet from a young girl and scanned it quickly. The paper charged that the king had given the justiciar private orders, which he'd attempted to carry out. Sarah frowned, concerned. Secret orders were not unknown in the navy, but they were of questionable legal value. Justiciar Montfort would probably have had more latitude than anyone outside the establishment would realize. It didn't absolve him of his crimes, even if it did land the king in hot water.

She gritted her teeth as the shouting grew louder. Her eyes swept the mob, noting people who were clearly spacers along with industrial workers and immigrants who'd moved to Caledonia in the hopes of finding newer and better jobs. The latter would be in some trouble, she suspected, if the protest turned violent. Caledonia had never been as welcoming to immigrants as Tyre—the planetary infrastructure and security forces were less capable of handling potential disruptions—and the locals would demand their immediate deportation if they appeared to be more trouble than they were worth. She frowned as the noise grew worse, trying to ignore the handful of police flyers hanging menacingly in the distance. All along the road, doors closed and heavy shutters slammed shut. Caledonia had seen too much political and social unrest for anyone to believe the mob would disperse peacefully. The leaders might hope for a peaceful resolution, for a simple march to show local feeling, but there would be troublemakers in the crowd yearning for violence. Rumor claimed the House of Lords was funding every loudmouth with a lack of common sense.

The waiter materialized at her side. "We're closing," he said bluntly. The politeness he'd displayed when she'd entered the café was gone. She had no trouble recognizing his fear. Mobs were terrifying, even if one had enough firepower to crush an army. They had no brain and no fear, at least until the bullets started flying. "Do you want to come inside or leave now?"

Sarah considered his words, then shrugged. It went against the grain to allow fear to dominate her life, even though she *was* nervous. The shouting was growing louder, pressing against her eardrums. She wanted to run, to turn and flee for her life. She knew she couldn't give in to the fear or it would forever overshadow her. She reached into her pocket and produced a handful of royals, the planet's local currency. Caledonia had never embraced e-currency to the same level as Tyre and the other first-rank worlds. The locals were justifiably suspicious of money they couldn't hold in their hands.

"I'll go." Sarah paid him, adding a midsized tip. The coins weren't worth their face value. She was grimly aware that inflation was rising, despite the king's pleas for calm and the government's best efforts. It was only a matter of time before the government started to fix prices, blowing the bottom out of the economy. "I'm sure I'll be back. It was very good coffee."

"If we're still here," the waiter said. He'd tried to flirt with her when she'd entered, but now . . . he looked too worried to muster even a single tedious quip. He seemed torn between the urge to tell her to run and inviting her to take shelter inside the café. "Good luck."

Sarah nodded as she stepped through the tiny gate and onto the street. The mob seemed to be good about not pressing onto the pavement, but that would soon change. She caught sight of a handful of children amid the crowd, grinning as they chanted as if it were just a special day out. Shouldn't they be in school? She laughed at herself a moment later. She was thinking like a Tyrian, not someone who'd grown up on a piss-poor planet in the middle of nowhere. School? Kids couldn't go to school when there was work to be done on the farm. But Caledonia had schools, didn't it? The government had worked hard to catch up with the first-rank worlds.

She kept moving as a line of policemen marched past her wearing armor that would have been intimidating to uninformed civilians. She shuddered, wondering just how uninformed—and unarmed—the civilians in the mob actually were. They could have all sorts of weapons, from makeshift tools to actual guns and ammunition. Caledonia had no gun laws, a legacy of the days when the police didn't exist and a horde of religious fanatics might fall out of the skies at any moment. If the mob turned into an insurgency . . .

"Justice," the mob howled. "Justice!"

A man pressed another leaflet into her hand and hurried on before she could get a good look at him. She crumpled the paper and shoved it into her pocket, then resumed her walk towards the road linking the city to the spaceport strip. The mob seemed to swell, as if half the city was on the march. She spotted a stream of spacers, some wearing naval uniforms, flowing out of the spaceport and joining the crowd. They'd be in hot water if they were caught . . . or they would have been a few short months ago. The military wasn't supposed to get involved in politics, but . . . She snorted. The Royal Navy had been dominated by politics. Pretty much all of her former commanding officers had been selected by their patrons for political reliability rather than demonstrated competence. A number had been killed off during the opening days of the war. The last war. The remainder had stayed at their posts until they'd been reassigned or pushed into resigning.

You can't count on the Theocrats for anything, she thought wryly. *You can't even count on them to rid us of incompetent officers.*

The noise rapidly dwindled as she made her way through the spaceport strip. There were guards everywhere, locals and marines, looking wary as they glanced towards the distant gates. A number of shops and entertainment facilities, even brothels, were closing, something she'd thought impossible. The spaceport was normally open every hour of every day, even on planets that observed the Sabbath or their local counterpart. Now . . . She saw spacers hurrying around, their eyes nervous as they took in the lack of crowds. The handful of people who sneaked through the gates, mainly youngsters intent on visiting facilities that were rarely available outside the wire, were gone.

It felt like the end of the world.

She reached the terminal and stepped inside, noting just how few shuttles were prepped and ready for immediate departure. The frantic push to get as many military and former civilian ships online as quickly as possible was putting huge demands on the planetary infrastructure, demands that it couldn't even begin to meet. She knew things were going to get worse before they got better, if they ever did. The king had no shortage of trained manpower, but he was very short on materials and support infrastructure. The only upside, as far as she could tell, was that the Tyrians appeared to have the opposite problem.

"Captain," the dispatcher said, "I can have a shuttle for you in twenty minutes."

"There's no hurry," Sarah lied. She wanted to get off the planet, back onto her command deck. She'd be happier up there, even though she knew there would be people trying to kill her. At least such potentially deadly dynamics would be nice and understandable. The politics on the surface left her cold. "I'll wait."

She took a chair and dug through her pockets until she found the leaflet. It looked like something that had been run off by hand, rather than mass-produced in a printer. She snorted, wondering if that was deliberate. Caledonia had never fallen *that* far in the years since she was cut off from Earth. But printed matter did tend to be taken more seriously than electronic text. There was something about it that carried more weight. She smiled at the thought—all of her tactical manuals were electronic—as she unfolded the leaflet. The text warned the reader, all readers, that they'd better not be caught with the document. The results might be disastrous for their employment, their reputation, and even perhaps their freedom.

Her eyes narrowed as she skimmed the remainder of the leaflet. The writer seemed to believe the king was on the verge of imposing a tyrannical regime across the entire Commonwealth, threatening the freedoms of every last world . . . regardless of which side it had taken when the dispute between the king and his government turned to civil war. The justiciar's decision to try to arrest the entire government on Tarleton was only the beginning. Soon, the writer warned, the king would move to take control of the entire government. The colonials were already being frozen out.

Which might be true, Sarah thought. Governor Rogan had said the same, back when they'd held their meeting. The king's government was torn between his clients, many of whom hoped to return to Tyre if proper terms could be arranged, and the colonials, who knew they wouldn't have a future unless Tyre was brought to heel. *And who knows what will happen then?*

She crumpled the leaflet, then dropped it in the bin as her shuttle was called. The unknown writer might be right, although it was hard to separate cold hard truth from demented ravings. Princess Drusilla, the king's wife, might have come from the Theocracy, but blaming her for the crimes of her father, brothers, and everyone else was simply unfair. She'd had no power whatsoever. Besides, by the same logic, the king himself was a traitor. He'd been born and bred on Tyre.

The House of Lords would probably agree with that logic, she thought. *They think he's a traitor too.*

◆ ◆ ◆

There was no shortage of irony, Governor Bertram Rogan considered, in establishing the Colonial Alliance headquarters in a skyscraper that had once belonged to the Falcone Corporation. The building was the kind of place where the Colonial Alliance's representatives had never been welcome, where anyone who dared mention words like "union" or "political rights" was shown the door as quickly as possible. Bertram had always loathed the corporations for their arrogance, but he'd hated the simple truth that they had a reason to be arrogant. They'd sewn up political power on Tyre, and by extension in the Commonwealth, decades before he'd been born. What they said *went*, and if there was even the faintest chance that a colonial would come out ahead, they'd change the rules to make sure he couldn't and didn't.

Bertram stood at the window, watching the protest march as it strode down the boulevard and past the House of Worlds, where the king's makeshift government was taking shape. The king had said all the right things as the Commonwealth had lurched towards civil war, but now . . . Bertram had his doubts. The king and his closest supporters were too intent on returning to Tyre, too determined to recover what they'd lost to build something new. Bertram wasn't blind to the simple fact that they held most of the power, controlling most of the fleet and the ever-growing planetary security forces. The colonials would need to launch a second round of mutinies to get rid of him if they felt they had no other choice. That wouldn't be easy. The first set of mutinies had been largely unprecedented. Indeed, there had only been one mutiny on a naval vessel before the civil war. But now . . .

He rubbed his forehead, feeling a dull ache behind his temples. There were dozens, if not hundreds, of armed soldiers on each and every starship, save perhaps for the lowliest gunboats. A mutiny might be quashed before it could take the starship out of commission, let alone turn the vessel against the king. And even if they *could* mutiny . . . He felt his headache grow worse as he considered the dangers. The House of Lords might move to take advantage of the chaos and smash the Colonial Alliance, and the king's faction, before they could get back on their feet. No, there was no might about it. So many spies lurked on Caledonia that it was hard to believe there was room for civilians. The

House of Lords would know if the king fell out with his supporters, and they would take advantage of it. And that would be the end.

"We don't have a choice," he muttered tiredly. "We have to work with the king."

All had seemed so simple, once upon a time. The House of Lords, the Tyrians, were exploiting the colonies. Even calling them *colonies* was a mark of disdain. It wasn't as if any of the worlds Bertram represented had been founded from Tyre. And the king had seemed their protector, the one willing to make investments that would eventually turn them all into first-rank worlds. Bertram didn't regret allying with the king, not after the recession had thrown millions out of work and kicked off a series of economic collapses. There was no way he would have worked with the House of Lords, even if they'd wanted to work with him. He'd always be aware that they were measuring his back for the knife. And yet . . .

He knew the war hung in the balance. The Battle of Tyre had been lost. Elsewhere, the king had made gains, only to lose them again when the House of Lords struck back. Bertram wasn't blind to the simple truth that they had to hang together or be hung separately, yet . . . he knew, all too well, that they couldn't allow themselves to become too dependent on the king. What would Hadrian do with absolute power? He'd already shown signs of losing control of himself. The decision to send the justiciar to Tarleton might not have been a misstep—Bertram knew there were factions in the colonies who would have loudly cheered if the entire planetary government had been sentenced to death—but trying to arrest the government without the Alliance's consent had been a disaster. The king owed Kat Falcone more than he could ever repay. His allies were now worried about the future. If the king was prepared to throw his weight around when he wasn't all-powerful, what would he do when he *was*?

We don't know, Bertram thought. *And that's the problem, isn't it?*

The intercom bleeped. "Sir, the petition has been presented to the House of Worlds," his secretary said. "They're going to pass it to the king tomorrow."

"I'm sure they are," Bertram said with heavy sarcasm. He wasn't sure the king would take any notice. His advisers probably wouldn't give a damn. Most of them simply wanted to go home, back to Tyre. Bertram was morbidly sure they'd betray the king in a heartbeat if they thought they could get away with it. "Inform them I'll take it to him myself."

"Yes, sir."

Bertram frowned as he turned back to the window. The crowd was steadily dispersing now, streams of people flowing away in all directions. He allowed himself a moment of relief, though it was combined with the grim awareness that next time the protest might well be different. He'd sought to steer the groundswell of public opinion, but he hadn't originated the outrage. He was all too aware the king had started it by doing something that alarmed and horrified the public. And if he failed to meet their demands for change, for a concession, they'd seek newer leaders. And . . .

"And we could lose the war," he muttered. Out on the streets, he could be arrested for defeatism if he dared say those words out loud. Here . . . he had to face up to the possibility of defeat. The Theocracy had lost, at least in part, because its leaders refused to admit they could lose. "It could be the end."

CHAPTER THREE

TYRE

Peter's private office was very quiet.

Duke Peter Falcone sat at his desk, watching as Admiral Sir William McElney worked his way through the investigator's report. The admiral was in his seventies, same as Peter himself, but he looked and *felt* older, a kind of maturity that Peter privately felt he lacked. His father, Duke Lucas Falcone, had ruled the family corporation for decades, long enough to know where all the bodies were buried and form a cluster of allies who'd back him against the remainder of the family. Peter . . . felt young and untried, even though he had adult children who were inching towards kids of their own. The sheer scale of his responsibilities weighed heavily on his mind.

He studied McElney thoughtfully, wondering what was going through his mind. The admiral would never be considered classically handsome, although his rugged face did have a certain kind of charm, with his dark hair shading to gray despite a handful of rejuvenation treatments. But he looked like the kind of person who could be relied upon. Kat had relied upon him, once upon a time. His sister had many flaws, Peter admitted in the privacy of his own thoughts, but she was a good judge of people. Sometimes. Kat had no way to know the contents of the report. Only a handful of people knew even a *glimmering* of the truth, but she'd missed the hints that she should be wary. She'd allowed her determination to do her job to override her common sense, leading her into treason.

And why does treason never prosper? Peter would have smiled if circumstances hadn't been so tragic. *Because if it prospers, none dare call it treason.*

His mood darkened. He knew, through his spies, that the other families were playing a double game. They were sending agents to the king, openly swearing to fight to the last while covertly opening up lines of communication just in case the war didn't go their way. Peter understood their logic—having friends on both sides of the political divide was good for a corporation's long-term health—but he couldn't help taking such tactics personally. He'd had to practically disown his youngest sister, even though she'd declared her side openly. The others had been much sneakier. And the worst of it was that he couldn't blame them, not really. They had to consider what might happen if they lost the war.

And it's only a matter of time before the king pushes them into outright treason, he mused as McElney—Sir William—finished reading the file. *And then they'll have to decide which side they're really on.*

"Your Grace." Sir William sounded stunned. "Is this true? I mean . . . Is it?"

"The evidence suggests so." Peter kept his voice calm, somehow. "The king murdered my father."

"Kat's father," William said.

"A man can have more than one child," Peter said waspishly. "My father had *ten* children."

He stared at the wooden desk, once again feeling the weight of the world pressing down on him. He understood, now, why so many middle managers had their desks covered with distractions, with things that might keep them from thinking about what they were really doing. He would almost have welcomed a time-wasting device to keep him from dwelling on the truth. His father, the man who'd raised him to be his successor, had been murdered. And his sister—damn her!—had sided with the murderer. The king might not have pulled the trigger himself, but he'd still given the order. And if Duke Lucas hadn't been killed . . .

Murdered, he thought angrily. He felt his hand threatening to shake as the sheer immensity of the crime started to dawn on him. Any death was tragic, but Duke Lucas . . . killing him had thrown the government into chaos, allowing the king to make a bid for power and depriving the House of Lords of a strong leader, someone who could smooth over the cracks and unite the aristocracy against the king. *The king murdered my father so he could have his war.*

He tried to comprehend just what the king had done, but it was beyond him. Hadrian had been mad. *Was* mad. Deliberately starting a war with the Theocracy . . . No, giving them an opportunity to launch an unprovoked attack with considerable prospect of success. The gesture had united the entire Commonwealth behind him at the cost of millions of lives. And murdering everyone who might have stood in his way. The investigators had noted at least five other deaths that might be tied to the king. Peter believed the allegations, for what it was worth. He was no fool. The king wasn't the only person who benefited from their deaths, but he was certainly the one who came out on top. And . . . and . . . and . . . he just couldn't understand. The king was mad. He had to be mad. What if the Theocrats had won the war?

He thought he couldn't lose, Peter thought. In hindsight, he'd seen that kind of arrogance before. The king wasn't just any aristocrat, but he *was* an aristocrat. *And he was incredibly lucky.*

William was saying something. Peter dragged his attention back to him with an effort.

"I'm sorry," he said. "Can you please repeat that?"

"If this is true, it would shake the king's government to the core," William said. "But can you prove it?"

Peter felt a hot flash of anger. "We have the files," he said sharply. "We can hand them over to anyone who wants to check them."

"Files can be faked," William pointed out. "The king would certainly argue so."

"It's difficult to fake such files." Peter felt his heart sink. "We hacked them out of the king's private bunker for crying out loud!"

"But not impossible." William met his eyes, evenly. "The king would claim the files are nothing more than fakes. He'd argue that all the independent analysts on Tyre were actually in the pay of one faction or another. Even the most truthful news outlet would be suspect, particularly under martial law. And, if the files are not accepted as evidence, all you have is a chain of inferences that might be just coincidences. The vast majority of the Commonwealth knows that Duke Lucas was murdered by the Theocracy. They'd be slow to believe any alternate facts."

Peter scowled at him. "Let me ask you a question," he said bluntly. "Do *you* believe the files?"

"I know the king," William said. He didn't show any offense at the question. "And yes, I believe he could have come up with such a plan. And yes, he has the nerve to make it work."

He paused deliberately. "But I also know that the truth will not be believed. People will not *want* to believe it. And the king will play that angle up as much as possible."

"He'll have some problems disproving it," Peter said stiffly.

"He doesn't really have to disprove it," William said. "We're the ones who have to prove his guilt, Your Grace, and that will not be easy. The king will argue that we made the evidence up out of whole cloth, and we will not be able to prove him wrong. It will come across as yet another smear campaign, one that will be as absurd as any of the others. Frankly, a great many people who *do* believe the accusations will wonder if the king was actually right."

"To kill my father?" Peter shook his head. "Impossible."

"To lure the Theocracy into war," William said. "The colonials *know* the Theocracy was a deadly threat. Their worlds were occupied, their people brutalized until they were liberated . . . they may see the king as having done the right thing, as someone who was forced to be covert because the establishment here was too shortsighted to see the growing threat. And they may not care that much about your father. Your Grace, the big corporations are not popular. Kat's the only aristocrat who has any genuine popularity, the only one they might listen to, and she's on the wrong side."

"She doesn't know the king murdered her father," Peter said. He wasn't sure of much, but he was sure of that. "She would never have sided with him if she'd known."

"Not when she thought Duke Lucas would have found a way through the postwar chaos," William agreed. "But, right now, she isn't going to be easy to convince either."

Peter sucked in his breath. "I have a meeting in an hour," he said. "We have to decide how to push ahead with what we've discovered, maybe even start formal impeachment proceedings against the king."

William barked a harsh laugh. "I think we're far beyond that now, Your Grace."

"Yes," Peter said. "But we do *need* to formally impeach him"—he waved a hand at the datapad—"for that, if nothing else. And if he refuses to appear and present a defense, we can move to summary judgment against him."

"Which won't impress his supporters," William pointed out. "They'll say you were trying to entrap him. They'll claim you had no intention of letting him go, whatever defense he presented. They'll say you created a situation where you couldn't possibly lose. And they'd be right."

"It would force them to decide between declaring their support for an impeached monarch, which would let us formally strip them of their titles and positions, and abandoning the king," Peter said. "And it would give us legal cover."

"Which won't matter in the slightest if the king wins the war," William said. "Why would he honor a court judgment that will certainly go against him?"

Peter shrugged. "We don't want anyone to say, later, that we didn't give him a fair chance to defend himself," he said. "And if we remove the legal ground beneath his feet, and his supporters, we can charge them with treason if they refuse to surrender."

"None of which will matter if the king wins the war," William said again. "We need a plan for victory, not legal cover."

"And devising that plan is your job," Peter said. "How do you suggest we proceed?"

William considered his response for a long moment. "You could start by making it public that the king gave the Theocracy a clear shot at us," he said. "You can explain how the king patronized Admiral Morrison, with orders to keep readiness levels low . . . You could even imply the king gave Kat private orders to do whatever she had to do to preserve the fleet—"

Peter cut him off. "Do you believe there's any truth in that?"

"No," William said. He sounded as if he wanted to say something ruder. "I was her XO. I don't believe she expected anyone, except perhaps Duke Lucas, to come to her aid if she was put in front of a court-martial. She expected her career to end if the Theocracy *didn't* attack. If she had any reason to think otherwise, she never showed it to me. And . . . I don't believe she was ever that good a dissembler. I was beside her for years. She always wore her emotions on her sleeve."

He paused, waiting for comment. Peter said nothing.

"I think you can focus on the charge the king started the war, or at least did everything in his power to ensure the Theocracy started the war," William continued, after a moment. "You can put together a fairly simple narrative, one that can be easily fact-checked. Plenty of details are in the public domain now, even off-world. And there are plenty of former resistance fighters in the king's forces, people who saw their friends killed, their wives raped, their children . . ."

Peter held up his hand. He'd heard the liturgy of horror. His father had made it clear to him, before his death, that the Commonwealth could not afford to forget how evil the Theocracy had truly been. Evil on an unimaginable scale, where millions of people had suffered and died . . . millions upon millions, nothing more than a statistic with no more emotional impact than a corporate annual report written by bureaucrats so far from the front lines that they might as well be working for another corporation. The death toll was bloodless. His father had insisted they had to put a human face, as many human faces as possible, on the Theocracy's crimes. It was the only way to make it clear that the Theocracy could not be allowed to rise again.

"I take your point," he said. "You think it might turn them against him."

"I think it might cause some discontent," William said. "And it is more believable than claiming the king has a personal body count. These are not the days when kings could kill their enemies in single combat."

"It would make things a great deal easier," Peter said. "But we *could* charge him with murder . . ."

"The allegations would come across as far too good," William said. He let out a shaky breath. "When I was younger, I had to work with the redcaps . . . ah, with various levels of the military police. They always said they were suspicious of perfect alibis because they'd clearly been prepared well in advance. There were always gaps, chinks of suspicion, in stories that hadn't been planned in advance. Spacers would have to explain things that looked suspicious even if they were completely innocent.

"You're telling the truth. I believe it. But it looks like a smear job to anyone who *doesn't* know you and the king. And they're not going to believe the charges. Politicians accuse each other of stupid shit all the time."

"Yes," Peter agreed. He found Sir William's informality refreshing. "But they generally accuse each other of *really* stupid shit, not outright murder."

"Yes, Your Grace," William said. "But there was always a layer of . . . believability about it. Back home, politicians would be accused of being poor children of the kirk, of minor immoralities that were inherently impossible to disprove. They were always wary about leveling more serious charges, charges that might be impossible to prove even if they were true. People might believe that a senior politician fiddled his expenses or took unsubtle bribes. They're not going to believe outright criminal or treasonous charges without a *lot* of evidence.

"And in this case, you'd need some pretty solid proof. The king could just deny the allegations. And it would be impossible to prove them beyond reasonable doubt."

"I hope you're right," Peter said. He clenched his fist. "What do you suggest we do with the remainder of the report?"

"Nothing, as yet." William frowned. "Can I think about all of this, Your Grace? If we deploy the report too soon, it could be turned against us."

"And if we deploy it too late, it could be useless," Peter snapped. He leaned back in his chair, calming himself. He'd hoped to have months, if not years, to settle into his role. His father had promised as much, a promise he'd been unable to keep. Peter felt a surge of red-hot hatred for the king. He'd stolen Peter's father from him and his family and . . . he'd tricked Peter's sister into treason. "I . . ."

He gritted his teeth. "We have a council meeting in thirty minutes," he said. "I'd like you to sit in. We may need your expertise."

"It would be my pleasure," William said. If he was telling the truth, Peter would have been astonished. Peter hated those meetings and he was a duke, with all the wealth and power the title implied. "However, I do have to return to my post . . ."

"Unless the king attacks in the next few hours, you can leave everything in the hands of your staff," Peter pointed out. "Or don't you think they can handle it?"

"I have every faith in them," William assured him. "But I am always nervous when I leave them alone for too long. I don't have time to deal with political games."

"Tough," Peter said. "Politics taint everyone who reaches high rank, you included. Sorry."

He smiled at Sir William's downcast expression. The man had never made any secret of his disdain for politics. It was almost a shame he hadn't stayed with Kat when the Theocratic War had come to an end. He could have done much for her instead of wasting his time on Asher Dales. William had never taken the king at face value. If he'd talked Kat out of following him . . .

There's no point in woolgathering, he told himself as he tapped his terminal and ordered a quick snack. No one would notice if he ate during the meeting, thanks to the wonder of holographic filters, but it was a bad habit. He had to remain focused. He had no doubt his inexperience was already working against him. *We have to deal with things as they are, not as we wish them to be.*

He keyed the display, bringing up a starchart. A cluster of stars glowed red, a mocking reminder of just how many worlds had sided with the king. Their decision would cost them . . . it *would*, if they had anything with which to pay. A shortage of postwar investment was hardly a death sentence, yet . . . it wasn't as if they had anything worth *taking*. The effort involved in snatching what few resources they had would be more than the reward.

They think they don't have anywhere to go, he mused. *And the hell of it is that they might be right.*

CHAPTER FOUR

TYRE

William knew, without false modesty, that he was lucky as hell to be in a position of power on Tyre. He was, after all, a colonial, with no family or connections worthy of the name. Indeed, the only person he did have any ties to, Kat Falcone, was firmly on the other side. But he wasn't blind to the simple fact that that did give him some advantages. He couldn't build a power base of his own, not without sacrificing his independence. The House of Lords and the inner council could use him without fearing he'd turn against them.

And that would be a bad idea, he mused, listening to the inner council debate with half an ear. *The king is mad.*

He sighed inwardly. He'd never really liked or trusted the king. He smiled too much. No, it was a little more serious than that. The king had always come across as a junior officer, dangerously promoted out of his competence zone. Too much rank, too little actual *experience* . . . Yes, William could believe the king had worked hard to trigger a war at the time and place of his choosing. In hindsight, his maneuverings had worked out very well for him. And yet, he'd been very lucky. William knew he'd probably be among the Theocratic POWs worked to death—if his ship hadn't been simply blown out of space—had Kat not devised a plan to save the fleet. No wonder the king had worked so hard to get her on his side.

She doesn't know, William told himself again and again. *She doesn't know what he did.*

He turned the thought over and over as the debate raged on, trying to determine a way to make use of the truth. He hadn't lied to Duke Peter. The truth was too easy to discredit, particularly when it was just a little too good. And yet, there had to be some way to use what they'd learned against Hadrian. How many of his supporters would stick with him when they learned the king had murdered a duke? How many would allow themselves to be dragged through the mud? None, if they knew. And if they believed what they'd been told . . .

"If the reports are accurate," Duchess Zangaria said, "the king has been receiving missions from a dozen different powers. They may start forwarding help."

"It will take them time to supply anything," Grand Admiral Victor Rudbek said. The grand admiral shot William a sharp look, daring him to say anything that might be taken as contradiction. The navy's uniformed head wasn't William's biggest fan. "The king needs help and supplies now."

"Indeed," Duke Peter said. Kat's brother made a show of looking at William. "Sir William?"

"Outside powers are unlikely to risk aiding the king too much unless he seems the clear victor," William said. Interstellar politics seemed to have a great deal in common with the schoolyard. "Whatever help they give will be very limited, and deniable. I don't think they'll be giving him superdreadnoughts."

"Unless they think they can split the Commonwealth in two permanently," Duke Tolliver grumbled. "Our ability to retaliate will be very limited."

"We *are* bringing the remainder of the fleet back online," Grand Admiral Rudbek said. "They may have been building up their forces since the war, but they don't have our advanced weapons or our experience."

"And both of those gaps can be closed," Duke Tolliver warned. "The king could be promising them anything, if he wins the war. He might even sell out the border stars."

"That won't go down well with his allies," Duke Peter pointed out. "They'd turn on him in an instant."

"Unless they see it as the only way to win," Duchess Turin said. "I swear, the king will do anything to keep his power."

"And if he does put himself in debt to outsiders, he will weaken his power," Duchess Zangaria countered. "If he surrenders the border stars . . . he'll move the border a great deal closer to Tyre."

"It isn't as if those stars are worth much now," Tolliver said. "They could be retaken at any moment."

"They'd move Marseilles closer to the rim," Duchess Zangaria said. "Giving them reasonably clear access to the Jorlem Sector and the worlds beyond . . ."

Which means less than you might think, William thought as the debate raged on. *If those worlds cannot be defended, or cannot defend themselves, they'll be utterly irrelevant to any future war.*

"The point remains, we need to win quickly," Duke Peter said. "Grand Admiral?"

Grand Admiral Rudbek scowled. "Your Grace, we do in theory have enough superdreadnoughts to punch through Caledonia's defenses and land an assault force," he said, his tone heavy. "However, we would be drawn into a long planet-wide campaign to take down the PDCs while *they* might be causing trouble elsewhere. Someone as . . . determined as Kat Falcone might even take the risk of *letting* us attack Caledonia, while she swoops in here and takes Tyre off our hands. It could shorten the war."

Duchess Zangaria snorted. "Are you saying we could not hold out here, even without the fleet? Planetary Defense . . ."

"The king's fleet would be in a position to do immense damage to our industrial base, even as it landed troops," Grand Admiral Rudbek said. "We'd have to come to terms with him pretty quickly, and those terms would not be in our favor. He'd win the war in a single blow."

"Assuming the timing worked out," William said quietly.

"Really?" Duchess Zangaria sounded disbelieving. "Are you *sure* we couldn't beat him on the ground?"

She looked at William, inviting him to answer. They wouldn't want to hear the truth, but . . .

"There haven't been *many* attempts to land troops and take a planet by force since the Breakdown," he said. "The only real large-scale landing force was on Ahura Mazda, which ended the Theocratic War. The planet was poorly defended, the population was sick of war and being lied to by its leaders, and yet both sides, along with civilians, suffered huge casualties. We don't really know how many of *their* people were killed. And Ahura Mazda was not a particularly well-defended world."

"The Theocracy landed troops too," Duchess Zangaria pointed out.

"The Theocracy never invaded a heavily defended world," William countered. "Cadiz and New Southport were the most heavily defended planets to be attacked during the early stages of the war, and both had flimsy defenses compared to Caledonia or Tyre itself. If they land here, Your Grace, they will inflict immense damage even if they're eventually kicked back into orbit. And even if they lose, they may win the war simply by destroying our will to resist."

He met her eyes, evenly. "In many ways, Caledonia will be a harder target. The civilian population is heavily armed. The Caledonians are more used to deprivation than Tyrians. The king wouldn't have so much at risk . . . not at first, anyway. He could easily slip away from the planet, even if we control the high orbitals. I'd be surprised if he doesn't have plans to do just that."

"So what do we do?" Duke Peter addressed the chamber. "We cannot wait for the remainder of the fleet, and we cannot move now."

William frowned as the debate raged back and forth. None of them, even the Grand Admiral, had any real military experience. Duke Peter had been raised as corporate royalty, not a navy brat. They were used to talking about numbers, statements on a balance sheet, not about lives and starship hulls and the intangibles that might make the difference between victory and defeat. William had studied war throughout the ages. He'd also lived it.

He waited until they asked his opinion, then leaned forward. "There is a good chance the king's faction is already threatening to split," he said. The spies claimed as much, although long experience had taught him to be wary of anything the spooks said unless it was independently confirmed. "He's failed to produce immediate victory. He's doomed to lose unless he finds a new source of ships and weapons, and anything he does find will come with a heavy price tag. There will be factions who want to fight to the death and factions who will abandon him if offered a chance to back out. Perhaps we should offer them an easy way out."

"At the cost of losing our investment in their infrastructure," Duchess Zangaria snapped. She tapped the table in front of her sharply, the sound faithfully reproduced by the holographic projectors. "Do you know how much it *cost?*"

Enough money that the investment can only be explained by resorting to imaginary numbers, William thought wryly. *More accurately, enough money to rebuild the entire fleet from scratch.*

He dismissed the thought with a shrug. "Your Grace, the money is lost. I don't think there's any way you can force them to pay, not when they literally don't have the money to repay their debts. All the prewar financial assumptions went out the airlock after Cadiz. I think you'd be better off accepting that you're not going to get the money back and moving on from there. If you offer to forgive the debts owed by every world that comes back to you, you might get a few takers. You might even offer to let the king go into exile on the other side of the Wall."

"Poor bastard," Duke Tolliver muttered.

Duke Peter shook his head. "You want to let him get away with murder—multiple murders—and starting a fucking civil war?"

"It will be harder for him to keep the civil war going if he has a way out," William said. He understood the duke's outrage, but ending the war came first. "And his supporters will drift away from him when they realize he could have gotten out but didn't."

"We'll consider it," Duke Peter said in a tone that added *over my dead body*. "We can certainly *try* debt forgiveness."

"And who is going to pay?" Duchess Zangaria scowled. "There's no such thing as a free lunch, young man! The money has to come from somewhere."

"We could always strip the king's corporation to pay," Duke Tolliver suggested, nastily. "Let him pay for the lost facilities."

"And do immense damage to ourselves in the process?" Duchess Turin looked utterly unwilling to compromise. "We couldn't afford it. Not now, not ever."

"I had my people run projections on the assumption those monies would never be repaid," Duke Peter said. "It will be painful, I admit, but not disastrous. There's a good chance we'll never get the money, regardless of what we do. I don't think we have much to lose because"—he smiled thinly—"we've already lost it."

"So you say," Duchess Turin said. "Can I remind you that your father advocated for making those loans?"

Duke Peter flinched. William felt a stab of sympathy.

"My father did not know, at the time, that we'd be fighting a war that would require us to abandon all our careful planning and throw money in all directions," Duke Peter said, his voice sharp enough to cut stone. "We believed the loans would be long-term, yes, but that they'd be repaid over the next few decades. There was no reason, then, to believe otherwise. In hindsight, those loans were a mistake. My father did not have the advantage of knowing then what we know now."

"We're not blaming your father," Duchess Zangaria said.

Good, William thought. He felt a flash of vindictive amusement. *Because you sat on those council meetings too, didn't you?*

He smiled. Duke Peter and Duke Jackson Cavendish—who hadn't been invited—were the only dukes who hadn't taken part in those discussions, let alone voted for and against the planetary infrastructure project. They could claim innocence, quite rightly. They could blame their fellows, as unfair as it was . . . He chuckled. Duke Peter wasn't the kind of person to rub their noses in their mistakes. And Duke Jackson Cavendish had other problems. His entire corporation was teetering on the brink of disaster.

"Then it's time to admit that the loans will never be repaid," Duke Peter said. "We can launch a two-prong offensive. One, to discuss how the king manipulated events to start the war and plunge a number of worlds into enemy hands. Two, to offer debt forgiveness and general amnesty to any colonial world that forsakes the king and returns to the Commonwealth. We can agree to let bygones be bygones if they do the same."

"And so the guilty get away," Duchess Turin pointed out. "They won't be brought to justice."

"They can bow out of public life," Duke Peter added. "People don't fight to the death, Your Grace, if they think there's a chance of surviving defeat. Just think how many Theocrats surrendered after they realized we weren't going to gun them down on the spot! Let them go. It costs us nothing and gains us much."

"Not all the time," Duke Rudbek mused. He'd been silent until now, content to let the younger aristocrats debate. "I've studied history. There have been times when the former rulers of defeated states, states that thoroughly deserved their defeat, were able to regain power and convince their people that they'd been on the side of right all along."

"How stupid those people must have been," Duchess Zangaria said. "To believe lies is foolish at the best of times, but to believe liars after their untruths have been exposed is truly absurd."

Duke Rudbek chuckled. "What have the Romans ever done for us?"

William smiled. He got the reference but doubted many of the others did. Kat Falcone was the only aristocrat he'd met who'd been particularly interested in prespace movies . . . The others, as far as he knew, had had little time to develop such tastes. Perhaps Kat had been rebelling against her parents and social class. He wondered, absently, what was Duke Rudbek's excuse.

"The scene is a joke," Duke Rudbek explained. "The Romans have actually done a lot of good things for the locals. But they're Romans, and thus outsiders and thus untrustworthy by definition. They represent power without local accountability and could turn nasty at any moment. And so, distrust of the Romans makes perfect sense even though the Romans really *have* done a lot of wonderful things."

"Brought peace," William muttered.

"Quite," Duke Rudbek agreed. "Point is, the former rulers were able to spin a narrative that made them the good guys and the outsiders the bad guys. And it wasn't as stupid as it sounds."

"It doesn't matter," Duke Peter said. "We can and we will make sure the former rulers go into exile. Or stay out of politics, as a quid pro quo for their survival. And if we reconstruct the governments properly, with *sensible* economic opportunities for those willing to take advantage of them, they won't be a problem even if they try to return to power."

"I admire your optimism," Duchess Turin said. She looked at Grand Admiral Rudbek. "Do you have a military plan to keep up the pressure?"

Grand Admiral Rudbek looked at William, who nodded. "Yes, Your Grace. We intend to continue pressing against their territory, forcing them to either concede entire star systems to us or expend their resources defending them. Either way, we put wear and tear on their equipment that will make it harder for them to continue the war. We're also looking at ways to hit their industrial base and damage it, but . . .

there are concerns of mass casualties if we launch hit-and-run raids. We don't want to be responsible for a slaughter."

"I'd have said we were already well past that point," Duchess Turin said. "What about launching minor raids on Caledonia itself?"

"Doable, but ineffective unless we launch a major offensive," William said. A thought was nagging at the back of his mind. It might be possible . . . He made a mental note for future consideration, then redirected his attention to the councilors. "They'll see them as little more than harassment, until we really push them."

"At least the raids will keep them off-balance," Duke Peter said. He sounded as if he was looking for an excuse to end the meeting as quickly as possible. "And keep them from searching for weak points in our defenses."

William agreed. The basic equation hadn't changed since the war had begun. The side that gambled everything on a single throw of the dice would either win a complete victory or suffer the most disastrous— and avoidable—defeat since Midway. Even the Theocracy had limits to how far it was prepared to gamble, despite being certain God was on its side. He couldn't see Kat taking the risk unless she was desperate. And yet, the hell of it was that she would be desperate. Either she won the war quickly, or she conceded eventual defeat.

And the king will know this, he mused as the meeting finally came to an end. He'd have to find an excuse to avoid the next one. Being a few hundred light-years away should suffice. *And he will be ready to gamble . . .*

William shuddered. The king had gambled, and so far he'd been winning. Even when he hadn't won outright, he hadn't lost either. He had talent, William conceded, although it was largely untrained. He'd built enough fallback positions into his plans to save himself from certain defeat, enough redundancies to keep his enemies confused about what he'd actually done. And that meant . . .

William let out a breath as the holographic images vanished. He'd just had an idea.

CHAPTER FIVE

CALEDONIA

From a distance, the fleet looked formidable.

It *was* formidable, Kat told herself as she studied the holographic display. Five squadrons of superdreadnoughts surrounded by more than four hundred smaller ships—battlecruisers, cruisers, destroyers, frigates, and gunboat carriers. It represented a force that could take on the entire Theocratic Navy and crush it effortlessly, perhaps even without so much as getting its paint scratched. The crew would have more problems with hangnails than enemy fire. She would have loved to have such a fleet under her command at Cadiz. The war would have lasted less than a day.

But the weaknesses were all too apparent to one who knew what to look for. There was no shortage of manpower—the king had recruited thousands upon thousands of merchant spacers and retired naval crewmen—but nearly everything else was in short supply. Kat knew, with a sickening certainty that could not be denied, that she couldn't risk engaging the enemy in a long-range missile duel. She simply didn't have enough missiles. She might win one engagement and find the enemy had smashed her to atoms the next because she could neither return fire nor close the range. And the shortage of spare parts was growing worrying. Her engineers were working overtime to modify older components sourced from god-knows-where, but they couldn't be brought up to frontline standards. A competent Inspectorate General inspection would probably have resulted in her being relieved of her command, if she didn't get thrown in the brig for willfully endangering her personnel. Her fleet was not ready for a full-scale engagement, not yet. She was starting to wonder if it ever would be.

She allowed her eyes to track over the holographic display, noting the hundreds of modified civilian ships that had joined the fleet. The colonials had no shortage of bravery—she'd seen *that* during the last war—but there were limits to what bravery could overcome. They *might* be able to take on a destroyer and henpeck her to death. A superdread-nought would cut most of them down in seconds and never notice it had been in a fight. She'd seen a hundred tactical sims suggesting the colonials might be able to take down a naval squadron, but she didn't believe them. They represented a triumph of wishful thinking over cold reality.

Unless our forces get very lucky, they'll all be killed for nothing, she thought as she watched a team of engineers bolting missile pods to a bulk freighter. Perhaps the plan was to make the enemy die laughing. The trick would be effective against pirates, who needed to close the range to take their targets intact, but a warship would simply blow any suspect freighter away from long range. *And their deaths won't even be noted in the ship's log.*

She rubbed her tired eyes as she reached out and clicked off the holographic display. It vanished, revealing a string of reports waiting for her. She glared at them, cursing once again the shortage of personnel officers and other bean counters. The irony would have made her laugh if there were an ounce of humor in it. She'd always joked, as had every other frontline officer, that the key to making the navy more efficient was to put the bureaucrats out the nearest airlock, but the truth was they *needed* bureaucrats. Too many bureaucrats could spoil the navy, sure, yet so could too *few*. And the vast majority of experienced bureaucrats had sided with the House of Lords. She simply didn't have enough staff officers to make everything work.

We don't have enough time to smooth things out, she mused. *And they're probably already overcoming their problems.*

The doorbell chimed. She looked up. "Come."

Lieutenant Kitty Patterson stepped into the compartment. "Admiral, I have the latest updates from the spooks."

"Great." Kat told herself, firmly, not to take her bad mood out on her subordinate. "Did they discover anything important? Anything we could *use?*"

"No, Admiral," Kitty said. "But they seem very sure the House of Lords is planning a major offensive."

I didn't need them to tell me that, Kat thought crossly. She knew the score. The tactical situation might be constantly changing, but the strategic aspects of the civil war were unchanged and effectively unchangeable. *If they want to win the war, they have to come here and capture or kill the king.*

She keyed her terminal, bringing up the starchart. It still felt odd to be struggling with a strategic problem that, only a few short months ago, would have seemed unthinkable. The king *had* to recapture Tyre or lose the war; the House of Lords had to capture Caledonia or . . . or, perhaps, *not* lose the war. She snorted at the thought. The stalemate couldn't continue. No, it wouldn't continue. The House of Lords would keep bringing older ships into service and churning out new ones, readying the force they needed to crush the king's fleet and invade every colonial world. Kat had no illusions about what would happen to her ships once they were cut off from all succor. Even if they managed to evade the enemy fleet, they'd rapidly run out of supplies and wind up choking as their life support died. She'd read the reports on the handful of captured Theocratic ships. They'd been so badly maintained that they'd been more dangerous to their crews than their enemies.

"We need a way to take the offensive ourselves," she mused. "And that isn't going to be easy."

She brought up the intelligence reports from Tyre. The planet had always been heavily defended but now was practically impregnable. Planetary Defense had belonged to the House of Lords, which hadn't stinted on building up the strongest defenses known to man. The planet was ringed with everything from orbital battlestations to automated weapons platforms and even minefields, backed up by a sizable fleet. Kat knew it was just a matter of time before the House of Lords worked up the nerve to cut the fleet loose, confident their fixed defenses could handle any reasonable threat. And they might be right. The king could do immense damage to Tyre, if he risked an attack, but he couldn't reoccupy his homeworld without taking massive losses. He could win the battle and yet lose the war.

And destroying the planet's industrial infrastructure would make it worthless, she thought grimly. The colonial officers had suggested as much, pointing out that weakening Tyre would help *them* in the long run. Kat could see their point, but she hated the thought of killing trained people and destroying installations her family, among others, had worked so hard to build. *And the engagement would weaken us if one of the outside powers comes calling.*

"We could try to pinch off a section of their fleet," Kitty suggested. "If we could weaken them, they might come to the table."

Kat scowled. On paper, the ploy might have worked. In practice, it would be a little harder. Grand Admiral Rudbek was known for being about as imaginative as a barmy bureaucrat—competent at bureaucratic power games, incompetent at actual strategy and naval combat—while William was hardly a fool. Her heart twisted in bitter pain. William should have sided with her, not the House of Lords! He wasn't a client who had no choice but to follow where his patron led. He should have stayed on her ship, stayed with her . . . She would have given her right arm for someone who could be relied upon to do a good job.

"They wouldn't let us lure them out of place that easily, not if we demonstrated in front of Tyre itself," Kat said. "They'd stay near the planetary defenses and force us to engage them there."

Or devastate the asteroid settlements, she mused. *And that would cost us missiles we cannot afford to lose.*

She shook her head. "Do we have an update on missile resupply?"

Kitty switched subjects without missing a beat. "The first-rank supplies are practically tapped out," she said. "The various industrial nodes are churning out more as we speak, but supplies will be very limited for the next few months. The second- and third-rank supplies are on the way, but they're not frontline missiles. And sooner or later they'll be tapped out too."

"Of course," Kat said. "They're not in production any longer."

And they'd be worthless if they were, her thoughts added. The Royal Navy had improved its missiles remarkably over the last few years, always looking for another edge over its enemies. The missiles they'd stockpiled before the war were little more than glorified fireworks now, at least when deployed against frontline forces. She supposed the technological gap was why the House of Lords had left the stockpiles in place. *The colonies couldn't use them against the Royal Navy.*

She eyed the reports with a sense of growing dread. The king might have a point, when he said they needed to seek help from outside. They needed modern missiles or . . . they'd lose. The local industries simply couldn't meet the demand for missiles, not when they were being expended almost as soon as they were produced. And Hadrian's forces were putting immense strain on their productive nodes. It wouldn't be long before they started to have *serious* problems.

And once production starts breaking down completely, she reminded herself, *we'll be within shouting distance of losing the war.*

She looked up at her subordinate. "How's morale holding up?"

Kitty's face went blank, suggesting she was trying to decide how best to present bad news. Kat winced inwardly. She wasn't one of the officers who had a reputation for shooting the messenger, but . . . it was never easy to predict how an admiral would respond to bad news. They tended to develop a certain level of insulation from reality, which often led to a belief that their will alone was enough to reshape reality into a more agreeable form. And the longer they stayed off the command deck, the harder it was to remember that shit happened. One could do everything right and *still* lose the battle.

"Mixed, Admiral," Kitty reported, finally. "There's still faith we'll win the war, but . . . it's starting to sink in that the war isn't going to be over by Christmas."

"If it was, that would probably not be good news," Kat commented dryly. "The House of Lords would have won."

"Yes, Admiral." Kitty gathered herself. "There have also been some clefts opening up between the colonials and . . . well, *us*. The Tyrians. The former think we should be pressing the war against Tyre, the latter think we should continue to fight a limited war . . ."

Just as I thought, Kat reminded herself.

". . . And what happened on Tarleton didn't do wonders for morale," Kitty said. "On one hand, Admiral, they know we won a battle we couldn't possibly have lost. On the other, they see the justiciar as a villain and think the king massively overstepped. But . . . it's hard to be sure how many people believe that. They don't always talk to staff officers."

Because staff officers are regarded as sneaks, Kat thought. She'd done a mercifully short stint as a staff officer, something that, in hindsight, had been clear preparation for a later promotion. *They think Kitty will take anything she hears to me.*

She tapped her terminal, calling for coffee. There was no time to sleep. There was no time to do anything that might have passed for relaxation. She'd ordered her crew and officers to rotate through the planet's shore leave facilities, to make sure they had some rest before they had to go back to the war, but she couldn't. Not now. Perhaps not ever. Her lips quirked as she remembered the joke about the junior officer who'd gone to a crewman's brothel. They might have discovered that the poor bastard actually had balls, but . . . it hadn't been good for discipline. Officers were supposed to be a cut above their crews. Their crews were certainly not supposed to see them relaxing.

Which is stupid, she told herself crossly. *We don't become robots when they pin rank badges on us.*

"Try to keep an eye on the situation," she said, looking at Kitty. "And try to reassure them that I won't hold their opinions against them."

"Right now, there aren't many people who'll talk outside their departments," Kitty warned. "Our departments are fairly stable, Admiral, but our crews are not. We keep switching too many people around."

"I know," Kat said. "Do you have any better suggestions?"

"No, Admiral." Kitty bit her lip. "I am aware of the problems facing us. But it is my duty to make you aware of the downsides . . ."

Kat nodded, once. "I don't hold that against you either."

She studied the display for a long moment. The hell of it was that she *could* have done something to upset the balance, if she was prepared to take risks. She *was* prepared to take the risks, but the king . . . might have other ideas. Kat understood his problem—if he lost a sizable chunk of his fleet, he would lose the war along with it—yet she also understood the overall problem. A long, drawn-out war would end with the House of Lords winning outright. Her fellow Tyrians were unimaginative—Kat knew her brother wasn't remotely imaginative, and the others weren't much better—but one didn't have to be particularly smart to wield the largest hammer in the known galaxy. As long as her forces avoided basic mistakes, they'd come out ahead.

And William will make sure we don't, she thought. Her heart twisted again. He really was on the wrong side. *He's got the imagination they lack.*

She felt her sprits sink as she contemplated the problem. The colonials told themselves that what they lacked in war materials they made up in élan. They had the fire and determination the Tyrians lacked. They had the experience to see opportunities and take advantage of them, winning victories against seemingly overpowering force. And yet, Kat knew that wasn't true. Tyre wasn't short on manpower. It might take months or years for competent officers to rise to the top, but they would. And then the combination of superior firepower and skilled officers would spell doom. And then . . .

"Have the analysts take a look at Perfuma," she said slowly. The twin planets weren't that important, in the grand scheme of things, but they belonged to the Rudbek Corporation. The Grand Admiral would come under immense pressure to do something if the two worlds were seriously threatened. William would recognize the feint but wouldn't have the political clout to override his uniformed superior. "Have them draw up an attack plan."

"Yes, Admiral," Kitty said. "What limits?"

Kat frowned. There was no way she could convince the king to let her take the entire fleet, not when doing so would leave Caledonia exposed to enemy attack. The fixed defenses were strong, getting stronger all the time, but they would not be strong enough to stand off an all-out attack. She considered using Caledonia as bait to lure the enemy fleet out of place, which might work, but the king would have a heart attack if she dared suggest it. Her lips quirked. They had a chance to win outright, but . . . if they lost, they'd lose everything.

"Two superdreadnought squadrons, perhaps three," she said. "We'll use decoys to convince any watching eyes that the main body of the fleet remains here."

"Aye, Admiral," Kitty said. She cocked her head as if she was about to make a suggestion she knew would be rejected. "We *could* cut off the StarCom."

Kat shook her head. Kitty was quite right, from a tactical point of view, but there was no way anyone would go for it. The StarCom network was still up and running, right across the entire Commonwealth.

She was morbidly certain enemy spies were using the StarCom to send messages to Tyre, and vice versa, but there was nothing anyone could do about it. The advantages of keeping the network online outweighed the disadvantages.

And besides, they'll have mounted watchful eyes on ships coming and going within the system. The king's call for smugglers and civilians, even pirates, despite her objections, had turned the system into a very open system indeed. *There's no way to keep spies from spreading the word.*

"Right now it doesn't matter," she said. "We can use the StarCom to spread disinformation. Speaking of which"—she smiled coldly—"have the fleet alerted that we'll be carrying out more tactical exercises in a week or so. That should give us cover for slipping a couple of squadrons right out of the system."

Unless they've filled hyperspace with pickets, she added silently. Theoretically possible, if one had the ships. *But even they would find that difficult.*

She stood, feeling more optimistic than she had since the last engagement. "I'm going to take a walk," she said. She felt as if she was skipping out on her duties, but there was nothing she could do until the tactical plan was ready. "Alert me if anything changes."

"Aye, Admiral," Kitty said. She looked ready to carry out her orders. "I'll keep you informed."

The intercom pinged. "Admiral, this is Gavin in Communications," a voice said. "You've received an immediate summons to the surface. There's an encoded datapacket attached for you."

Somehow Kat wasn't surprised. "Forward the packet to my terminal," she ordered as she reached for her jacket. "I'm on my way."

CHAPTER SIX

TYRE

"You wanted to see me?" Peter raised his eyebrows as William was shown into his office. "That's unusual."

William didn't have the grace to look embarrassed. Peter found it hard to care. He had too many subordinates who couldn't be relied upon to do anything without receiving written orders in triplicate and then having their hands held throughout the entire process. Peter didn't have the time to micromanage one subordinate, let alone the millions who reported directly or indirectly to him. And he certainly didn't have time to educate himself in matters outside his direct control; better to have reliable subordinates who could be trusted to handle things for themselves.

"Yes, Your Grace." William took the chair he was offered and rested his hands in his lap. "I wanted to discuss a potential . . . *option* . . . with you, one that cannot be discussed with anyone else."

"A potential option?" Peter felt a flicker of concern. "And one I have to keep to myself?"

"Yes, Your Grace." William met his eyes. "If *anyone* gets wind of this before we try to do it, the plan won't work."

Peter frowned. "And you want me to keep it from the rest of the council," he said. He'd already spent far too long reassuring Israel

Harrison that he hadn't been deliberately excluded from the last meeting, although that wasn't entirely true. He certainly didn't want to risk Harrison discovering the truth about the king until matters were well in hand. "I think you'd better explain."

"Yes, Your Grace," William said. "I'll be blunt. Kat doesn't know the king ordered her father killed. She wouldn't have gone along with him if she did."

"No." Peter regarded his youngest sister with curiously mixed emotions. He'd been a grown man when Kat had been born and they'd never had a stable relationship, but he was sure Kat wouldn't have gone along with a plot to murder their father. Kat had always been Duke Lucas's favorite, although he'd hidden it well. "And you propose to *tell* her?"

He smiled, humorlessly. "I thought *you* were the one who pointed out that it would be positioned as a smear campaign."

"Yes, Your Grace." William nodded. "If we made the allegations public, they *would* be treated as a smear campaign. Kat would have every reason to disbelieve the charges. She simply wouldn't *want* to accept that she sided with the man who killed her father. And if we made our discovery public, it would be impossible to prove that we're telling the truth. It isn't as if we managed to capture the assassins, or secured footage of the king ordering the hit and cackling."

"No." Peter ignored the forced levity. "And what do you have in mind?"

"A covert approach," William said. "We arrange a meeting—a face-to-face meeting—between Kat and myself. I tell her the truth, in a manner that will make it harder for her to simply dismiss."

Peter studied him for a long moment. "I don't think the king will let you meet her," he said quietly. "Not once the news broadcasts start hitting the StarCom network. He has to be aware of what *else* could have fallen into our hands."

"No." William looked back at him evenly. "My brother has been opening lines of communication to the king as a smuggler with much to offer. I thought I'd ask him to take the message, then see what we could work out. Kat would have problems slipping away . . . on Caledonia, at least. We'd have to figure out the details, Your Grace, but the basic idea is sound."

"And we haven't impeded your brother, because . . ." Peter lifted his eyebrows. "Is there a *reason*?"

"He did useful work for us, during the war," William said. "And he's been trying to go legit, something that hasn't been easy since the war came to an end. And the spooks figured it might be useful to have a pipeline into the king's circles if we needed to mount a covert operation or two. The time is now."

Peter looked down at the desk. "Family ties always make things complicated, don't they?"

"Yes, Your Grace," William said. "But, in the end, family should always be there for you."

"Hah," Peter muttered. His younger sisters ranged from very competent and helpful to wastrels who seemed to be doing their level best to exhaust their trust funds. And an outright traitor, if one counted Kat. It was a minor miracle his uncles and aunts hadn't tried to force him to disown Kat completely. But they were looking to the future. If the king won, Kat would have to plead her family's case to him. "Did your brother look out for you?"

"He did, sometimes," William said. "We didn't have an easy childhood."

"I read your file," Peter said. William hadn't had a *remotely* easy childhood. He'd lost his parents at a young age, and everything had gone downhill until he'd joined the navy. "I'll have to read his before I sign off on anything."

"Quite." William nodded. "I do understand."

Peter met his eyes. "Tell me," he said. "Suppose you do meet. Suppose you do convince her that the king is a murderer. What then?"

"It depends." William didn't try to lie or dissemble. "She might simply surrender rather easily, the next time her fleet meets ours. And that would weaken Hadrian to the point we can end the war within the week. Or she might smuggle troops to Caledonia, ensuring they get a clear shot at the king. Or . . . there are a multitude of options, Your Grace. They depend pretty much on *her*."

"And then we'd have to decide how best to put an end to the war," Peter mused. He'd already started putting out covert feelers to the colonials, but it would be a while before he received any results. Changing sides was always a tricky business. Anyone who wanted to do it had to make sure they jumped when their former side couldn't harm them any longer, yet, at the same time, ensure they were still useful to their new side. "Or is that getting a bit ahead of ourselves?"

"Yes, Your Grace," William said. "Right now, the plan is just a plan. It might misfire completely."

"Yeah." Peter considered the strategy for a moment. Kat wouldn't deliberately lure William into a trap, he thought, but the king would do it in a heartbeat. Worse, perhaps, he might seek to kill William, and Kat, if he suspected the true purpose of the mission. His sister might be branded a martyr who'd given her life for the king. The thought made Peter want to retch, but it couldn't be denied. Hadrian would turn on Kat if he thought she was a danger to him. "And everything you know might fall into their hands."

"I know the risks," William said. "And I'll deal with them."

"I'm sure you will," Peter said. "But I have to plan for the worst."

He kept his thoughts to himself as he pulled up the file and scanned it. William wasn't *that* important, not in the grand scheme of things. He was a competent officer, true, but that wasn't unique. A dozen other officers were already being marked and groomed for future greatness. They had the disadvantage of having families that would press their case, for better or worse, but . . . perhaps their advantages outweighed their disadvantages. Still, he wasn't sure what would happen if William fell into enemy hands. A little conditioning and he'd make speeches condemning the House of Lords and praising the king . . .

Kat would know there was something wrong with him, Peter told himself. *And she'd do something about it . . . wouldn't she?*

He shivered. Perhaps Kat *would* do something about it. There were limits to what one could rationalize away. Kat wasn't the sort who'd accept a friend being brainwashed and turned into a propaganda tool. But the king would be laying the groundwork to deal with her if she turned into a problem. Kat was a naval officer, not a politician. She wouldn't expect a knife in the back. If she hadn't suspected the king had murdered her father . . .

"None of us did," Peter muttered. "It was blamed on the Theocracy."

William blinked. "Your Grace?"

"Just woolgathering," Peter said. He cleared his throat. "You have my permission, my *verbal* permission, to attempt to open a line of communication and arrange a covert meeting with my sister. However"—he held up a hand—"I want you to make certain there are no records of the meeting, *and* I expect you to make very sure you don't fall into enemy hands. Take a suicide implant and be ready to use it."

"Yes, Your Grace." William didn't flinch. Peter supposed the naval officer was used to the prospect of death. "I'll make sure of it."

"Take all possible precautions," Peter said. "And . . . if you see a chance to kidnap her, take it."

William shook his head. "She'd see it coming," he said. "And that would destroy all hope of getting through to her. Of having her work on our behalf."

"There are ways to get around any precautions," Peter pointed out. His voice hardened. "And taking her off the board would be very useful."

"Perhaps," William said. "Though we'd be unable to have her to take out the king."

Peter let out a breath. "Do as you see fit," he said. "Bear in mind that she *is* the best he has."

"That may be true," William said. "But she's a double-edged sword in the right hands."

"True." Peter met his eyes. "Good luck."

William looked back at him. "I can't promise results, Your Grace. But we can at least try."

Peter glanced at the terminal. "I know," he said. "Like I said, good luck."

◆ ◆ ◆

William was mildly surprised Duke Peter had accepted his proposal without a real argument. The risks were considerable, perhaps more than the civilian duke realized. William liked to think he was prepared to commit suicide if there was a reasonable chance of falling into enemy hands, but he'd been raised to consider suicide a mortal sin. He knew he might hesitate before triggering the implant, he knew he might be stunned before he got over his hesitation and did his duty . . . Kat wouldn't betray him willingly, he was sure, but the king wouldn't hesitate to take advantage of the meeting if he caught wind of it.

He kept his face under tight control as Yasmeena, the duke's secretary, led him through a maze of corridors and up the stairs to the rooftop landing pad. His shuttle was waiting there, looking oddly fragile against the roof-mounted tractor beam projectors and heavy weapons emplacements. The entire city was bristling with weapons, despite the simple fact the king couldn't mount an all-out attack unless he took down the PDCs and their shield generators first. William peered at the giant complex in the distance. Planetary Defense had gone through its personnel with a fine-toothed comb, rooting out anyone who looked even remotely suspicious, but it was impossible to be sure there was no one with ties to the king. The king had had access to all files and records, enough to make sure that his people looked perfectly legitimate. Hell, they *were* legitimate. Their paperwork could pass for legitimate paperwork because, in one sense, that was exactly what it was. It would be tricky, very tricky, to poke holes in their stories.

The hatch opened as he approached, his pilot already powering up the drives. William took his seat, trying to ignore the way his datapad was blinking alerts. There was never any shortage of work that required his personal attention, even though he had more staff officers than he knew what to do with. Half of them couldn't be employed elsewhere. The remainder knew their work, but . . . He shook his head. Admiral Greg Kalian's empire building had left a baleful legacy. It didn't help that William's staff officers were fairly sure he wouldn't be sticking around after the war.

Which might well be true, he mused. He loved the navy life to the point he still kicked himself for leaving after the Theocratic War. Perhaps things would have been different if he'd stayed in the navy. But he'd lost two starships under his command, and that looked bad on *anyone's* record. *They might not want to keep me when the missiles stop flying.*

He leaned back in his seat as the shuttle climbed into the air. A pair of armored flyers fell into position beside them, providing an escort that was more appearance than substance. The civilians might be awed—or intimidated—by the paramilitary aircraft flying over their city, but William knew better. A handful of HVMs would be enough to clear the skies, wiping out the police flyers before they knew they were under attack. He scowled as he realized, not for the first time, what Duke Lucas's final moments must have been like. The duke had probably had just enough time to realize he was under attack before being blown to atoms. Maybe he'd been lucky. Maybe death had come too quickly for him to know he was doomed. And then . . .

William forced himself to relax as the shuttle banked over the city, following a preauthorized flight path that would eventually take them into orbit. The city looked as pretty as ever from high overhead, but he knew that a sizable majority of the population had either left or was trying to leave. They were fortunate, he supposed, that the city wasn't *that* large. And yet . . . He shook his head. Tyre wasn't ready for all-out war. The citizens were lucky the king wasn't gambling everything on a desperate invasion.

He might still have people on the ground, William warned himself. *And they could be a real threat, if they came out of hiding at the right time.*

The shuttle rose into space, heading straight for William's flagship. The massive superdreadnought slowly came into view, the hammerhead hull bristling with weapons, looking completely unstoppable. William knew better. The superdreadnought was heavily armored, but even *she* could be destroyed. In theory, no one would be able to pick the command ship out of the fleet; in practice, Kat and the king might already know where to aim their missiles. God alone knew how many people were spying for the king. William was morbidly certain the counterintelligence sweeps hadn't netted all of them.

And the king was smart enough to keep some of his clients concealed from the others, William thought. If the king had patronized, in all senses of the word, Admiral Morrison, he could easily have built up a covert network of clients. In hindsight, it was the sort of thing no one would have thought to look for. The patronage system was so deeply embedded right across the Commonwealth, with patrons drawing their power from the number of clients under their control, that no one would seek to conceal their clients. But the king had, and, William admitted, the move had paid off for him. *Clever murdering bastard.*

"Admiral." Commander Tom Thomas met him at the airlock. "I have the latest set of reports for you."

"Forward them to my terminal," William ordered. Commander Thomas was young, too young to realize the difference between reports his superiors needed to see at once and reports that could wait for a spare moment. "Inform my staff. I want a full meeting at 1700."

"Aye, sir." Thomas saluted. "I'll see to it personally."

William smiled as he stepped into his office, the hatch hissing closed behind him. The compartment was huge, easily two or three times the size of his cabin on *Uncanny*. And it was his office, not his suite. He wondered, sourly, how some of his former commanders had found time to enjoy the palatial suites the navy gave them. William was aware he wasn't getting anything like enough sleep, let alone anything else. The cabin should probably have been assigned to the reporters. They might be useless oxygen thieves, but at least they'd make some use of the space.

He sat down at his desk and activated the privacy shields, then opened a locked drawer and retrieved a single datachip. Scott McElney had given it to him years ago, when he'd been trying to lure William into leaving the navy and joining him. William had never used it, not even when Scott had been working for the Commonwealth. The time had never seemed quite right. It had been something for *him*, not for the navy.

"Well," William said, "let's see what we can do."

He plugged the chip into the terminal, then cleared his throat. "We need to meet," he said, keeping his voice calm. "On Tyre. Let me know the place and time."

The message glimmered in front of him as the chip automatically encrypted it, then uploaded the compressed data into the StarCom queue. Someone *might* try to decrypt it, but . . . William shook his head. The message itself proved nothing. It wouldn't be the only encoded message flowing through the network, automatically booting itself to its final destination. Scott had sworn blind the encryption scheme was unbreakable. William doubted that was true, but no matter. Scott was the only one who'd know William had sent it and how to get back in touch with him. And even if someone traced it back . . .

We have to win the war quickly, William thought. *Compared to that, nothing else matters.*

CHAPTER SEVEN

CALEDONIA

Kat could feel the tension in the air as she followed Sir Reginald Grantham into the House of Worlds. The building had been designed for Caledonia's aristocratic assembly, a gathering that had never really taken shape before the civil war had seen its proposed home handed over to the Colonial Alliance and turned into its representative parliament. Fifty boxes were crammed with ambassadors from all over the Commonwealth, while on the floor below it was standing room only. Kat quietly groaned as she realized she'd be sharing a box with Sir Reginald. The king's fixer wasn't someone she liked, and he knew it. She wouldn't have cared for him even if he *hadn't* tried to interfere with the navy.

She took a seat and calmed herself with an effort, listening to the angry muttering running through the hall. The datapacket she'd read during the flight to the surface made it clear that the House of Lords had launched a new propaganda offensive, branding the king a mass-murderer who'd deliberately started the war with the Theocracy. Kat hadn't studied the claims in any great detail, but she had to admit they sounded pretty unlikely. The king could have started the war by ordering an offensive, if he'd wished, not lowering his guard and waiting to be hit. The plan sounded as if it had too many moving parts to be particularly workable. She'd been a naval officer long enough to truly understand the wisdom of "Keep it simple, stupid."

The datapad buzzed against her hip. She glanced at it, noting how stories were trending right across the Commonwealth. The House of Lords was sparing no expense to make sure the stories poured into Caledonia and the rest of the alliance, pushing their version of the truth and the supplementary documents everywhere they could. The Alliance's PR specialists were returning fire, but they looked to have been caught on the hop. Their early responses looked too defensive to be believable, at least outside their bubbles. They'd need time to assess what the House of Lords was saying, then devise a counterplan. And it looked as if they weren't going to be given that time.

"It isn't good," Sir Reginald said. "There are people around us who are looking for an excuse to dump His Majesty."

"They're politicians," Kat said. The level of venom in her voice surprised even *her*. It hadn't been that long since politicians had been breaking promises right, left, and center, forcing her to abandon people they'd promised to protect. She had no doubt that, for once, Sir Reginald was right. There were people in the chamber who'd abandon the king in a heartbeat if they thought they'd come out ahead. Very much like home. "What do you expect?"

Sir Reginald leaned closer, as if he thought she was flirting with him. "Can His Majesty count on your support?"

Kat glared at him. He flinched. "I think *His Majesty* has no doubts about where my loyalties lie," she snarled. "And constantly questioning them is *not* helpful."

She kept eye contact until he looked away, then turned back to survey the crowd. She didn't really feel proud of herself for intimidating him . . . if, of course, she *had* intimidated him. Sir Reginald was utterly dependent on the king, unlike Kat and many of his other supporters. If push came to shove, Sir Reginald would be booted out the airlock to appease the king's doubters. *Scapegoat* was probably part of his job description.

The chamber was much less decorous than the House of Lords, she had to admit. There was no order, no patience . . . different factions bickered with their enemies, ignoring the elephant in the room. The king had had as little to do with the House of Worlds as possible, she'd heard; looking at the chaos, she understood why. The House of Worlds would have *no* future if it lost the war, if the *king* lost the war, and yet, it was bickering over obviously fake charges while its advantages, such as they were, slipped away. Kat had no doubt the House of Lords intended to take full advantage of the bombshell. They probably had a fleet inbound already.

And even if we do disprove the charges leveled against the king, she mused, *we'll never get rid of the stink.*

A low rustle ran through the chamber as the king marched into the room, striding down the walkway and taking his place at the podium without looking either left or right. He looked impressive, Kat noted. He'd traded his usual suit for a simple colonial uniform, a single gold star at his breast. Someone had put a great deal of thought into his appearance, she decided. His dresser had mixed and matched from a dozen sources to ensure the king represented them all, rather than wearing something that belonged exclusively to Tyre or the Colonial Alliance. She wasn't entirely sure that was a good idea. The House of Worlds *was* exclusive to the Colonial Alliance, for all intents and purposes. The boxes that should have represented Tyre had been reallocated long ago.

Sir Reginald cleared his throat, nervously. "Will they listen to him?"

Kat ignored the comment as the king reached the podium and waited for quiet. The giant complex had no noise-damping systems, nothing that could impose quiet. She wondered if that was deliberate or an oversight, the former suggesting, perhaps, that the colonials didn't trust the systems. She didn't really blame them. It was quite easy to mute criticism by simply making sure no one actually heard negative remarks. And no one would be entirely sure they weren't alone in their doubts and fears.

It felt like hours before the room stilled, before the king tapped his throatmike to turn the device on. The entire chamber seemed ready to commend or condemn the king.

"I will not deny," the king said calmly, "that I believed we, the Commonwealth, would eventually have to fight the Theocracy. The Theocracy was clearly an expansionist power steadily taking world after world as it advanced towards the Wall, Cadiz, and, beyond Cadiz, the Commonwealth itself. I believed—and I was right to believe—that the Commonwealth had to prepare for war. I pushed for everything from the development of newer and better weapons to the outright annexation of Cadiz to ensure that, when war came, we were ready to fight it."

He paused, allowing his words to sink in. Kat kept her expression under tight control. The annexation of Cadiz was a two-edged sword. The colonials would understand the need to make hard choices, sometimes, but they'd also be grimly aware that the same logic could be used to annex almost *any* world. There were colonies that had joined the Commonwealth because they believed, rightly or wrongly, that they'd never be allowed to remain outside the Commonwealth. Mentioning Cadiz might have been a tactical error, even if it had truly been the king's brainstorm. Kat didn't think that was true. There had been strong bipartisan support for the annexation.

"I make no apologies," Hadrian continued. "I pressed for everything because I believed there was no choice. And I was *right*! The Theocracy *did* attack. It *did* launch a full-scale invasion of the Commonwealth. Their forces killed millions of people and ruined the lives of millions more. The Theocracy even rendered an entire planet effectively uninhabitable! If I hadn't taken a stance against them, where would we be now? Still fighting the war? Or worshipping their god of blood and slaughter?"

His voice rose. "If you feel I did the wrong thing in planning for war, you are free to feel that way. And the *reason* you are free to feel that way is because we *won* the war! We fought for the principles of freedom and self-determination, of free speech and economic freedom and all the other things the Theocracy would have destroyed. I worked for *your* liberty. And I—we—won the war!

"But a charge has been leveled against me, by the very same House of Lords that has fallen into enemy hands and become a burden on our people. They charge that *I* started the war, that I lured the Theocracy into launching an offensive that, they claim, could not possibly have led to our total defeat. They have collected a series of incidents and woven them into a grandiose conspiracy theory that credits me with coming up with a plan that worked so perfectly that not a single thing went wrong. They say I deliberately started the war.

"And I ask you"—he grinned boyishly—"did I even need to *bother?*"

Kat had to smile. She saw others smiling, heard chuckles echoing around the chamber. Beside her, Sir Reginald let out a breath.

The king had carried the day. Probably.

"I ask you," the king repeated. "You know as well as I do that the Theocracy was an expansionist power. You know as well as I did that it was only a matter of time before the Theocracy did something we couldn't ignore. There were dozens of incidents along the border before open war broke out. Tell me . . . why would I risk everything, from my crown to millions upon millions of lives, when I could rely on the Theocracy doing it for me? Why would I come up with a scheme so complex when it would happen anyway, with or without me? And why, I ask you, would I come up with a scheme that was almost bound to fail?"

He shrugged expressively. "I'm sure your answers will make more sense than anything they come up with, eh?"

There were more chuckles. Kat frowned, wondering if there was some truth to the story. Admiral Morrison's patron had never been conclusively identified, although the smart money rested on Robert Cavendish, who'd vanished with *Supreme*. There had been quite a few news programs arguing the vanished liner had taken Robert Cavendish to a new life well away from the Commonwealth, before his family's debts started to catch up with him. Kat shook her head slightly at the absurd thought. It was unlikely that anyone would risk fleeing on one of the most recognizable ships in the galaxy, one that every navy would be watching for when the news finally broke. Besides, what had happened to the *other* wealthy and famous passengers?

And the king wouldn't have found it so easy to hide his involvement, once Father started looking, she thought. *The charges can't be true.*

The king waited for quiet, then continued. "This is just a tedious and utterly unimaginative attempt to weaken the bonds holding us together," he said. "It fails almost all of the tests one might hurl at it, starting with the simple fact that there are easier and safer ways to smear someone like myself. The House of Lords, long a hive of scum and villainy, has no conception of the world outside their hallowed halls. They cannot imagine what it's like to live without wealth and power and a social safety net. They hold you, and those who take your side, in abject contempt. This piece of utter . . . *bullshit* . . . is merely proof of how little they think of you. Of us!"

Kat smiled again, despite herself. On Tyre, anyone who used a swear word in the House of Lords would be severely censured at the very least. The appearance of decency was more important than the reality. They'd expect the king to say *bovine excrement.*

"They ask me to respond, as if they have the right to put me on trial. But how can I respond to a charge that cannot possibly be taken seriously? What will they do next? Accuse me of rigging the Miss Teen Tyre competition? Masterminding the Breakdown? Triggering the Breakaway Wars? Exterminating the dinosaurs? Once this level of absurdity is permitted, it knows no limits. I do not *choose* to pretend to take it seriously. I do not *choose* to pretend that they take it seriously. Instead, I roll my eyes"—he matched action to words—"and I promise them that, when I reclaim my own, I will make sure that those who lie about me face the consequences. This war started because they played petty power games instead of doing their fucking jobs. I will not let them get away with throwing hundreds of thousands of lives into the fire because they'd sooner fiddle with themselves!

"There will be no response. And I ask you all to join me in shunning their lies, in telling them that we will not *tolerate* their lies. No more. I say to you, no more! We can no longer afford to deal with lies. We will fight for our rights and win. They would not have lied to us, not so blatantly, unless they felt we were on the verge of defeat."

He stepped back from the podium. Kat nodded, watching in approval as representatives from all over the Commonwealth rose to acclaim their ruler. Below her, the journalists got it all on video. There weren't any live broadcasts—thus avoiding telling would-be assassins where to aim their missiles—but word would probably already be sneaking out. A few hours from now, Peter and the rest of the House of Lords would be watching the king's defiance. She wondered, absently, what they'd make of his speech. They didn't expect him to be immediately stripped of power and executed, did they? Not likely.

But people will wonder, Kat thought as the clapping grew louder. *Or . . . they may find it useful to believe it. Who knows?*

◆　◆　◆

It had been a good speech, Governor Bertram Rogan admitted stiffly. The king's presentation had just the right combination of careful planning and scripting, mingled with an attitude that suggested the whole thing had been delivered completely off the cuff. Indeed, the king and his staffers had responded very well to the challenge. Bertram wondered if they'd had a contingency plan for something like it all along. Hadrian had to know his enemies were ready to slander him in any way they could, hurling mud in the hope some of it would stick.

He joined in the clapping and cheering, barely devoting any effort to it while he considered the possibilities. The king had a point, Bertram conceded; any plan to deliberately lure the Theocracy into war would be difficult, dangerous, and, worst of all, unnecessary. If one was sure war was inevitable, why waste time trying to start one? It would happen, sooner or later, without leaving damning evidence that would eventually overshadow one's future career. Bertram was honest enough to admit that he would have understood the king's point, if he'd really entrapped the Theocracy, but Tyrians wouldn't have been so accepting. The war had barely touched them.

Not that cold logic would have meant anything to the people who lost relatives to the war, he told himself. *They'd have been mad as hell at the king.*

He put the thought aside as Hadrian left the chamber. He'd chosen not to stay and answer questions, something that was technically within his rights . . . Bertram wasn't sure what to make of that. The king clearly had no intention of answering the charges—he refused to admit there was *anything* to the charges—but still, he should have answered questions. His avoidance suggested . . . What? A certain level of arrogance? A refusal to risk being questioned in public? The king still hadn't managed to put a lid on the Tarleton affair. The problem would never be solved, unless . . .

Bertram dismissed the thought as he surveyed the chamber. The king's closest associates were already leaving, having cheered their fill. Bertram knew they were probably seeking more private reassurance, given the threat to their legal status . . . He dismissed the thought. They were fucked, unless the king won.

He heard the door opening behind him and turned just in time to see Sir Reginald enter the box. Bertram felt a flicker of disgust mingled with contempt. The man was a bottom-licking crawler, one with nothing to recommend him beyond a truly disgusting level of obsequious sycophancy. Rumors already existed about precisely *what* Sir Reginald did for the king—nasty rumors. Bertram didn't believe them, but . . . they stuck.

"Governor," Sir Reginald said. He bowed deeply. "His Majesty would be pleased to see you in the inner council chamber, twenty minutes from now."

"And he'd be somewhere else?" Bertram couldn't resist the jab at Sir Reginald. "Or will he be waiting for me there?"

"I believe he will be chairing the meeting," Sir Reginald said stiffly. If he had a sense of humor, no one had ever seen it. His smiles were as false as the rest of him. "And he requires the presence of the entire inner council."

But not the inner-inner council, Bertram thought. He knew the king didn't handle *everything* through the inner council. *And there might even be an innermost council.*

He stood. "I'll be there," he said. He was a councilor, after all. "And I have many questions for His Majesty."

CHAPTER EIGHT

CALEDONIA

"Before we start, there are two things I should make clear," the king said. He sat at the head of the table, Princess Drusilla sitting beside him. "First, as I said earlier, the charges leveled against me are total nonsense. There will be no formal reply and no suggestion, now or ever, that we will cooperate with impeachment proceedings."

Because they'd never let you go afterwards, Kat mused. *They'd be fools to just let you slip away if you attended in person.*

"Second, I made a mistake. Tarleton was a mistake. I overreacted to what I saw as betrayal and chose a representative who grossly exceeded his orders. I apologize for that without reservation, and I hope we can put it behind us."

"I'm sure we can," Earl Antony said. The hawkish minister glowered at the colonial representatives. "There is, after all, a war on."

"We will be happy to put it behind us as long as the question of treason and betrayal is firmly laid to rest," Governor Rogan said bluntly. "The planetary government had no choice. It did what it had to do. And I want that clearly understood before the *next* enemy fleet appears in our skies."

"Understood," the king said. "Justiciar Montfort has been demoted and reassigned to somewhere harmless."

"I want him to stand trial," Governor Rogan insisted. "The matter *has* to be laid to rest."

"We don't have time," the king said. "Let his demotion serve as punishment."

Kat frowned, wondering just what was really going on. There was no disputing that Justiciar Montfort had exceeded his authority and the bounds of common sense, but it was hard to know what he'd been thinking. Had he been trying to carry out orders or . . . or what? It could be a simple case of empire building or something more sinister. A trial would make sense, she thought, if only to establish the truth. But the proceedings could also prove hopelessly divisive.

"Then it is to be clearly understood that he is not to wield authority again, *ever*," Governor Rogan said. "Nothing less will suffice."

"Very well." The king threw his servant under the shuttlecraft with practiced ease. "He'll never serve in a position of power again."

Kat felt her frown deepen as she sensed the mood shifting around the table. On one hand, Justiciar Montfort really had stepped over the line. On the other, the casual demotion and dismissal of one of the king's loyal servants wouldn't sit well with the others. Even the ones who wanted Justiciar Montfort put on trial and shot weren't comfortable with summary justice. They might be the next person to be unceremoniously dismissed for becoming politically inconvenient. Hadrian's councilors would be doing a *lot* of second-guessing over the next few weeks.

The king cleared his throat. "It has become clear, unfortunately, that there are agitators on Caledonia and many other worlds. The House of Lords has no shortage of money to reward traitors prepared to raise the rabble against me, against *us*. The protest marches over the last few days and the riots on other worlds are clear proof of outside interference. We already have evidence pointing to influencers who took money from the House of Lords."

"And yet," Governor Rogan said tartly, "it's hard to tell how influential the influencers actually were."

Kat nodded. She'd read enough influencer reports to know they had a nasty habit of claiming they'd been decisive, even if there hadn't been a solid link between the results, whatever they were, and the influencer campaign. They had a strong incentive to claim victory even if they'd had nothing to do with it just to keep the money flowing in their direction. Her father had been profoundly cynical about the whole issue. The vast number of credits expended on advertising and propaganda during the war might have been completely wasted.

It wasn't as if the colonials needed a reason to be pissed, after Tarleton, she thought coldly. *They had all the incentive they needed after the justiciar exceeded his authority.*

"Worse, there are clear signs of discontent on our warships," the king continued, ignoring the governor's injection. "There have been whisper campaigns and suggestions that crews should consider mutinying against me in support of the House of Lords. These actions represent a serious threat. We cannot risk a series of mutinies when we're battling for our very survival. It could cost us the war."

"Action must be taken," Earl Antony snapped. He thumped the table. "We cannot let traitors bring us down!"

"Action *will* be taken," the king assured him. "I am already building up special security forces. They will be responsible for securing warships, orbital fortresses, and the rest of our facilities against enemy action. They will have full authority to monitor our personnel for discontent and take corrective action, from publishing the actual truth instead of enemy propaganda to . . . *removing* enemy assets. They will even have authority to override a starship's captain . . ."

"No." Kat spoke before she could stop herself. "Not during combat. Not *ever.* The captain's authority must not be brought into question."

"The captain might be a traitor," Earl Antony said.

Kat took a long breath, composing herself. "If you believe that," she said with as much biting sarcasm as she could muster, "you may as well admit defeat, surrender now, and save time."

"His Majesty wants to secure the fleet," Earl Antony snapped. "And you . . ."

"If you convince the majority of crewmen and commanding officers that you view them as untrustworthy," Kat said, "you'll *make* them untrustworthy. If you give someone else authority over the captain, on her own ship, you'll destroy the chain of command. And if that person knows less about naval affairs than you do, they'll make mistakes, and mistakes during combat can be fatal. I will *not* have someone trying to override my orders in the middle of a battle."

She met the king's eyes. "That's precisely what happened to the Theocracy. Their smarter officers were overridden, constantly, by clerics who thought they knew better. Such behavior cost them the war."

"The Theocracy was ruled by a bunch of idiots," Earl Antony pointed out. "We . . ."

"Should refrain from repeating their mistakes," Kat said. She saw his face darken and knew she'd made an enemy for life. She found it hard to care. "I will not have someone trying to override my orders in a combat situation."

"Perhaps we can compromise," Lord Gleneden said. "The security officers—"

"Political commissioners," Kat injected.

". . . will have very tightly restricted powers," Lord Gleneden continued. "They will not be authorized to override the captain during battle."

"They will need more restrictions than that," Kat said tersely. "Spacers grumble. Military officers and personnel have been grumbling about everything from the day mankind first learned to make war on itself. They grumble about the food, they grumble about the mud, they grumble about senior officers who clearly don't know what they're doing . . .

Sir, half the military's jokes revolve around the dangers of giving maps to junior officers! And if you put security officers on ships, officers who cannot tell the difference between letting off steam and actual discontent, you are going to *spread* discontent!"

"Then that's all the more reason to have the officers on the ships," Earl Antony said.

"There isn't a single man on the fleet who didn't volunteer to fight for the king," Kat said. "They joined because they were loyal. If you treat them like enemies, they will *become* enemies."

She looked at the king. "And then it will be just a matter of time before it all falls to pieces."

"Their authority will be tightly restricted," the king assured her. "Admiral Ruben has been supervising their training. He'll ensure they don't impede operational efficiency."

Kat frowned. Admiral Ruben had been a thorn in her side from day one, but . . . she had to admit he was competent, if something of a fire-eater. She was mildly surprised he'd been given the task of preparing the security forces, if only because it was something of a demotion for him. He'd been in command of the planetary defenses ever since Kat had been semidemoted after the Battle of Tyre. He knew his job, she supposed. But something about the appointment felt ominous to her.

The king doesn't have many officers he can depend upon, she reminded herself. *And just about everyone has their own agenda too.*

"My people are known for speaking their minds," Governor Rogan said. "We won't let that become a crime."

"No," the king agreed. "But anything that impedes the war effort *will* be a crime."

He paused, resting his hands on the table. "Lord Gleneden, how do we stand . . . economically speaking?"

Lord Gleneden looked displeased. "Right now, Your Majesty, we are caught between the need to churn out more supplies for the fleet and the need to expand our industrial base."

"So nothing has changed," Earl Antony sniped.

The king shot him a sharp look. "Lord Gleneden. Continue."

"Missile production is as high as it's going to get, at least for the foreseeable future." Lord Gleneden's expression darkened. "We're fortunate to have a considerable number of engineers working for us, men who can repurpose civilian gear for military uses, but it's created a string of issues. I'd be surprised if we didn't start running into all sorts of problems within the next few months, from one piece of equipment being incompatible with the others to simple wear and tear on components that cannot be replaced in a hurry. Really, if we're forced to rely on our own production facilities, we're going to grind to a halt in a year."

"And sooner," Kat put in, "if the enemy concentrates its attacks on our industrial nodes."

"Correct, Admiral." Lord Gleneden nodded to her. "We *are* buying as much as we can from outside, but there are limits on how much they can and will send to us. Bluntly, we have little free cash and poor credit. The only thing keeping us from being cut out altogether is the simple fact we might win, in which case we'd have all the money we needed to pay our debts. However"—he took a breath—"there are limits we cannot surmount. The House of Lords is in a position to threaten war if anyone supplies us too openly. We cannot counter their threat until we win the war, whereupon it won't matter any longer."

"So we need to take the offensive," the king said. His voice was very calm. "And quickly."

He smiled at Kat. "Admiral?"

Kat took a breath. "The core of the problem hasn't changed," she said. There was no need to go over it again. She'd explained the matter time and time again to people who were slow to realize that bravery and stark determination counted for nothing in the face of overwhelming firepower. "We cannot hope to punch out Home Fleet, not as long as it remains intact. Nor can we fight a war of attrition. Therefore our tactics must be to bite off a chunk of Home Fleet and crush it. This is not going to be easy."

"Because of the damnable traitor in command of Home Fleet," Earl Antony snarled.

He isn't a traitor, Kat thought, feeling a flash of savage anger. *He didn't betray us . . .*

She kept that thought to herself. She was probably the only person on Caledonia who *didn't* consider William a traitor. The king saw him as someone who served the House of Lords, the colonials saw him as a turncoat . . . It wasn't fair or just, but it was very human. William was a colonial. He should be fighting for the colonials. But instead he was fighting for the House of Lords. Kat suspected she knew why, although she'd kept that thought to herself too. William had never liked, let alone trusted, the king. And yet . . .

"I have devised a plan to lure a chunk of Home Fleet out of place," Kat said, putting her doubts aside. "Ideally, we'll be able to intercept and destroy two enemy superdreadnought squadrons by bringing overwhelming force to bear on them. The only way to do that is to offer them a chance to bring overwhelming force to bear on *us*."

She briefly outlined the plan. "They will have to take the bait," she finished. She was sure of it. A chance to take out one of her squadrons would be almost irresistible. She'd break any officer who let the chance go, even though, in this case, the decision would be the right call. "If they do, we have a shot at their hulls and a chance to retreat if they dispatch a force we can't handle. If they don't, we'll do immense damage to the corporate economy and make them look like losers. Again. They'll find themselves compelled to either do something desperate or try to come to terms with us."

Which isn't likely to happen, she added silently. She'd read some of the messages being exchanged between Caledonia and Tyre. The distance between the two sides was just too great. One side would have to beat the other into submission if they weren't willing to make concessions that would anger most of their supporters. *They won't accept a return to the status quo ante bellum, and that's the very least we'd accept.*

Lord Gleneden tapped the table lightly. "Are you *sure* the plan will work?"

"There are no guarantees in war," Kat said. She resisted the urge to point out, sharply, that history was *littered* with brilliant plans that had failed spectacularly the moment they'd come face-to-face with reality. "They may grit their teeth and refuse to take the bait. They may send overwhelming force, ensuring we have to retreat rather than fight. They may even *miss* our provocation, to the point they won't react because they don't know they *have* to react. I cannot promise you victory. All I can promise you"—she met Gleneden's eyes evenly—"is that we'll do our best to ensure the odds are stacked in our favor."

She kept her thoughts to herself. William was *smart*. He'd know she was trying to bait him . . . probably. And he'd see through any simple trick. She knew, all too well, that there was a good chance the plan wouldn't work perfectly. There were just too many moving parts. But the very complexity of the scheme worked in her favor. William wouldn't suspect her of violating the KISS principle too openly.

And even if he does, he'll be pushed into action, Kat thought. Grand Admiral Rudbek wasn't just a Rudbek client, he *was* a Rudbek. His family would be furious if he let Kat get away with hitting Perfuma and retreating without losses. They'd bring immense pressure to bear on him if he didn't order William to chase Kat out again before they realized what was happening. Kat knew the Grand Admiral. He had much to recommend him, but a solid backbone wasn't one of them. *William might not be able to talk him out of dispatching the fleet.*

She smiled as the discussion continued to rage. The plan promised victory no matter *what* the enemy did. If she shot hell out of the installations and vanished, she'd make the enemy look like fools; if she had a chance to take out a couple of superdreadnought squadrons, she'd be on the way to winning the war. And if she had to retreat without firing a shot, even for the honor of the flag, she would still have made them look incompetent. The House of Lords would demand immediate action, whatever the risk. Who knew? Maybe they'd throw their entire fleet at Caledonia. It might just give her a chance to pull off a major victory.

Assuming we win, she mused. Engagements could be dangerously unpredictable. She had no doubt the House of Lords was working frantically to put new weapons and technologies into deployment. Something that changed the tactical equation, again, would be decisive. *If they crush us instead, game over.*

"I trust we are all in agreement," the king said. "Admiral Falcone, when do you intend to depart?"

"I believe we should be ready to leave in a week, barring unforeseen developments," Kat told him. "The squadrons will have to be primed for departure, Your Majesty, and a deception plan put in place to convince them that only one squadron has left."

"See to it," the king said. "And make it clear to your personnel that victory is the only acceptable outcome."

Kat gritted her teeth. "I told you," she said. She hated repeating herself, but there was no choice. "There are no guarantees in war."

She lifted her eyes to the holographic display, silently weighing the odds. If the House of Lords did nothing over the next three weeks, the plan should succeed. But if the House of Lords did something . . . whatever their plan was, it could accidentally prevent them from responding to Kat's provocation. *That* would be ironic. William and his superiors would have saved themselves from an embarrassing if not disastrous defeat without ever knowing what they'd done.

"Do what you can," the king said. He smiled at her, a reminder of happier days. "I have faith in you."

"As do we all," Governor Rogan said. "It's high time we reminded them that we're resolved to fight till the bitter end."

"Good," the king said. "Now, about the planned deals with outside powers . . ."

CHAPTER NINE

CALEDONIA

"Captain, the last set of supplies has been delayed," Commander Clinton Remus reported, shortly. "They couldn't give us an updated delivery date before departure. I . . ."

Captain Sarah Henderson resisted the urge to say something cutting. Her last two XOs had been reassigned on short notice, one to take command of his own ship and the other to fill a hole on someone else's command roster. Commander Remus was really too young, even by aristocratic standards, to be XO of a heavy cruiser. His record was good, but he'd have been lucky to make lieutenant in the days before the war. Now . . . On paper, he looked good. But inexperience was already taking its toll.

"Inform them we require the supplies within three days," she said instead. "And remind them that we're attached to Falcone Squadron."

"But they're saying . . ." Remus stopped himself. "Aye, Captain."

"The chances are good that they're trying to resist stripping themselves bare," Sarah said, taking pity on him. It seemed to be a law of nature that supply departments turned into bureaucratic hellholes, even in the middle of a war. She could understand why a supply officer might hate the thought of not having something in stock, but it was bloody stupid to refuse to empty his shelves when there was a fucking war on. "And if they continue to argue, remind them that we have priority."

Remus saluted, another sign of just how green he was, and turned away. Sarah watched him step through the hatch, the airlock hissing closed behind him before she let out a sigh. He really *was* too young. Her crew had been a mixed bag even before the last string of battles. Now half her crew was young enough that her officers were joking about kindergarten and the other half was composed of merchant spacers who ranged from being very competent to having disciplinary problems. She was lucky to have kept a handful of her original officers, she'd been told. There were just too many ships that needed experienced personnel for her to keep them all.

She glared at the latest series of reports, wishing, again, that they had time to catch their breath. The engineers said that they'd been putting immense wear and tear on their ship, wearing out everything from air filters to internal compensators. They could smooth things over for a while—the ship had been overengineered to the point where she could take one hell of a beating and keep going—but there were limits. Some failures would be harmless, if irritating. Others would be lethal. And they didn't have time to fix them all before they had to depart.

At least we can swap out some components in transit, she told herself. *But there are sections we cannot repair or replace without a proper shipyard.*

She studied the report on the fusion cores for a long moment, cursing under her breath. Two of her four fusion cores were showing signs of strain. They were designed for long-term service, but . . . She shook her head. Her crew wasn't experienced enough to take chances with the fusion cores. Ideally, she'd have them removed and replaced, but that would take the ship out of service for months. A rush job could end up costing them the entire ship. And yet, she knew the maintenance wasn't going to happen. The facilities for such a job were in short supply.

Her intercom bleeped. "Captain, Mr. Soto would like to see you."

Sarah rubbed her eyes, tiredly. Soto was a pain in the ass, to put it mildly. He was very much the *last* person she wanted to see, not when there were a hundred and one other problems that demanded her immediate attention. God knew she couldn't rely on the XO to keep the ship running smoothly. Remus's ignorance scared her. Hell, her *own* ignorance scared her. She knew every last inch of the ship, but there were aspects of her systems that Sarah didn't pretend to understand. They were just too complicated for anyone who didn't specialize in the right departments.

"Tell him . . ." Sarah caught herself before she could say something more suited to the lower deck than a commanding officer's ready room. "Tell him he can attend upon me in my office. And have coffee sent in."

"Aye, Captain."

She leaned back in her chair, resisting the urge to pick up a datapad and pretend to be busy. She'd known and loathed officers who'd played petty little power games, but now . . . now, she thought she understood. Pretending that she was doing something more important than heeding a subordinate was more than just a sign of insecurity.

The hatch hissed open. Mr. Soto—technically, he was a *commander*—stepped into the office. He was a tall man with blond hair and stern features a little *too* perfect to be real. Sarah had tried to access the man's file when he and his team had been assigned to her ship, but it had been too highly classified for her clearance. She doubted that was a good sign. A man who could be a model, combined with an attitude that suggested he'd never served on a warship . . . boded ill. She'd filed a request for the information, but so far nothing had been provided. The request, like everything else that wasn't urgent, had probably been put on the back burner.

"Captain," Soto said. He had a warm, trustworthy voice that grated on her ears. It was just a little *too* warm. "Thank you for seeing me."

"My pleasure," Sarah lied. She waved him to a seat as a steward entered, carrying a pot of coffee and two mugs. The steward was as ill-trained as the rest of the crew. He hadn't thought to bring a tray or a box of cookies or anything . . . Sarah put such trivialities aside. She didn't really want to offer Soto anything. "What can I do for you?"

"Your crew doesn't seem to want to talk to my people," Soto said. His voice seemed disarming, as if he were inviting her to share intimate confidences. His smile was charming, and yet it didn't quite touch his eyes. "It's really quite awkward."

"My crew is currently scrambling to meet a deadline," Sarah said bluntly. She was damned if she was wasting politeness on a commissioner. She'd heard enough grumbling about them over the last few days to know she couldn't let him take her for granted. "They don't have time to talk to you about anything."

"But I have my orders," Soto said. He sounded shocked at her remark, as if he'd expected her to order her crew to put his demands first. "I have to carry them out."

"So do I," Sarah said. She reached for a random datapad and held it up. "I have hundreds of things I have to do, personally, before departure. We're leaving in three days. Really . . ." She sipped her coffee meaningfully. "I'm wasting time just talking to you now."

Soto's eyes went wide. "Then why are you talking to me?"

"Because I also have orders to cooperate with you as much as possible," Sarah said. Admiral Falcone had given her officers plenty of leeway, but Sarah had a nasty suspicion that Admiral Falcone wasn't calling the shots. Not after Tyre. "But I cannot deal with you wasting my time. I simply don't have it to waste."

She picked up another datapad. "Ammunition shortages. Crew shortages. Half my departments are significantly undermanned, to the point where we'll have real trouble coping with any unexpected engagements. A lack of shore leave for the vast majority of my crew . . ."

"There *is* a war on," Soto said mildly.

Sarah felt her temper flare. "With all due respect, *sir*, a military force cannot remain at full alert indefinitely. The longer a crew goes without a chance to decompress, to relax and enjoy themselves, the greater the danger of mistakes. And some of those mistakes can be lethal. We are putting immense demands on a relatively small number of people, and they are suffering for it. We've got to realize that before one of those people makes a mistake and someone gets killed."

Soto spoke as if he hadn't heard her. "And I am responsible for tracking morale throughout the ship," he continued. "A number of crewmen"—he produced a datapad of his own—"have been complaining about . . ."

Sarah took the pad, glanced at it, and shook her head. "They're some of my best people."

"They're damaging morale," Soto said. "You cannot allow a high-performer to go unpunished because he's a high-performer."

"Really?" Sarah snorted. "People complain all the time. They complain about *everything*, from navy-issue slop to navy-issue rags to fanatical bastards in starships hurling missiles at them! There's a difference between complaining loudly and being ready to mutiny."

"But their complaints harm morale," Soto insisted.

Sarah looked him in the eye. "When I was a young officer, there were complaints about navy-issue underwear. Do you think *that* harmed morale?"

She went on, not giving him a chance to answer. "Either the complaints are just mindless complaints, which are generally ignored as nothing more than whining, or they come from something real. If the former, they are ignored; if the latter, silencing the people complaining isn't going to fix the problem. It's better to know what people are bitching about rather than letting their discontent fester in silence.

"Now, if you have a problem with that, you can take it to Admiral Falcone," she said. "I'm sure she'll be very pleased to hear from you. If not, stay out of the way. This ship is going to depart in the next three days. If we're not ready to go, we'll all be for the high jump."

Soto reddened. "Aye, Captain."

"And don't do anything stupid," Sarah said as Soto rose to go. "I'll make damn sure you regret it."

She watched him leave, then finished her coffee. The communications datanet was already full of complaints and rumors about the commissioners—no one called them security officers—ranging from suggestions they were in enemy pay to claims they'd been putting surveillance monitors in bathrooms and sleeping racks. Sarah hoped that wasn't true. She knew there was scant expectation of privacy in the military, but there were limits. If that were true . . .

I'd have to kick him off the ship before he accidentally walked out an airlock, she thought. *And that would open a whole new can of worms.*

She wished, just for a moment, that she could go back to Caledonia and discuss the matter with Governor Rogan. Had *he* signed off on the commissioners? Or had he found himself presented with a fait accompli? Or . . . or what? He couldn't be blind to the problems they would cause, could he? She made a face as she considered the implications. Steps taken to prevent a future mutiny might accidentally wind up causing one.

At least Admiral Falcone understands the problems, she thought. *But who's really calling the shots?*

◆ ◆ ◆

"The last intelligence report states that Home Fleet is engaged in heavy exercising, but otherwise hasn't left Tyre," Kitty reported. "They've actually redeployed another squadron from the border stars to Home Fleet."

"They must be concerned about a sneak attack," Kat mused. "And less worried about the border than we hoped."

She frowned as she studied the chart, weighing up the travel times between the border and Tyre itself. The border colonies weren't exactly *friendly* to Tyre, but they were grimly aware that their choice was between the Commonwealth and Marseilles. They'd done everything in their power to avoid taking a side, speaking sweetly to both the king and the House of Lords without actually committing themselves to anything. Kat didn't blame them, but she knew their studied neutrality was likely to come with a price. Marseilles might want those worlds in exchange for their support.

And that's going to cause problems when it finally dawns on the inhabitants, Kat thought. The debate about seeking help from Marseilles had raged on for hours, with people torn between taking what they could get and fearing the price for outside support. Governor Rogan had been flatly against trading planets and systems away, as if the will of the locals meant nothing. *If they don't support us, why should we support them?*

She put the thought to one side as she ran through the calculations again. Her tactical staff had turned the vague concept into a workable plan, running hundreds of sims in hopes of predicting the possible outcomes. The good guys had won more than they'd lost, in simulation. Kat was all too aware that sims tended to leave out everything from newer and better enemy weapons to simple random chance. William wouldn't let her lead him by the nose. And, if he was ordered to take her bait, he'd try to find some way to subvert it.

"Admiral?" Kitty caught her attention. "Ah . . ."

Kat flushed. "I was light-years away," she said. "What were you saying?"

Kitty looked down. "I was wondering if they were planning an offensive of their own."

"I'm sure of it," Kat said. "They can't let the war go on forever, even if time is on their side."

She frowned. William would understand the risks of assaulting a heavily defended star system, but sooner or later he'd have to do it anyway. Given time, the House of Lords could build up the firepower to crush Caledonia's defenses and . . . and then what? If they captured the king, they could end one problem, but what about the Colonial Alliance? They could end the war yet lose the peace. Or . . . She shook her head. If that happened, it wouldn't be *her* problem. She might die in the final engagement of the war.

"We have time," she said, although she wasn't sure that was true. William was careful, not given to rash moves, but his superiors would be breathing down his neck for action. He'd probably be planning more raids into colonial territory, targeting industrial nodes even if he didn't land troops. "And we have to keep them off-balance."

"Yes, Admiral," Kitty said.

Kat glanced at the engagement ring on her hand, feeling a pang of grief and guilt, then shook her head. "Are there any concerns about meeting the deadline?"

"Nothing serious, Admiral," Kitty said. "There has been a string of complaints about supplies, as usual, and the commissioners . . . ah, *security officers*. The latter have been quite annoying. One of them got punched out, and the entire crew closed ranks."

Kat groaned. "I knew they'd be trouble," she said. "I wish . . ."

She bit the comment off sharply. Kitty was her aide, but she couldn't badmouth the king in front of her. She understood his reasoning, yet she thought the appointment of the so-called security officers was fatally flawed. It would provoke discontent, if discontent was already there. The colonials would bitterly resent their presence. The Tyrians would feel the same way.

"Tell them to behave themselves," she said finally. There was little else she *could* do, not unless she wanted to damage morale herself. "And remind commanding officers that they have the power to brig any commissioner"—she used the word with a flicker of amusement—"who causes problems. I'll take the heat."

"Yes, Admiral." Kitty sounded concerned. "Is that wise?"

"Perhaps not," Kat said without heat. "But it has to be done."

She changed the subject. "Did the out-system sweep turn up anything?"

"No, Admiral." Kitty looked puzzled. "I . . . I thought they didn't have a hope of finding anything."

"I would have been astonished if they had," Kat said. She didn't mind the question. They were alone. She could take the time to explain her reasoning without weakening her authority. "The sweep serves two purposes. First, it does make it harder for the enemy to sneak a ship into the system and therefore forces them to keep their distance. And second, the sweep helps our crews build up cohesion. They're going to need it when they come under fire."

"Yes, Admiral," Kitty said.

And they'll be coming under fire very soon, Kat thought stiffly. *We'll be departing in three days.*

She picked up a datapad and checked the reports. The fleet would be ready on schedule, as ready as it would ever be. The shortages were starting to bite, and bite hard. The king was probably going to have to come to terms with Marseilles soon, if he hadn't already. She rather suspected he was a lot closer to making the formal agreement than he'd claimed during the council meeting. He'd likely frozen out most of his own government from the discussions.

Which isn't a good thing, she reminded herself. She was surprised the king hadn't assigned someone to handle the discussions in his place. *It's easy to disown an ambassador. It's a lot harder to disown a king.*

She put the thought aside as she turned back to the simulations. The king was right about one thing. If they won, they could renegotiate. Marseilles wouldn't be able to do anything about a "creative" interpretation of the agreement. And if they lost, it wouldn't matter.

Of course not, her thoughts mocked her. *If we lose, we'll be dead.*

CHAPTER TEN

CALEDONIA

It was a curious fact, Captain Gianni Yolinda had discovered over the last few weeks, that whoever had opened Caledonia's immense asteroid belts and gas giant orbits to exploitation hadn't bothered to impose any rules or regulations. There were thousands upon thousands of mining facilities, from simple one-person operations to huge corporate facilities fully the equal of anything to be found near Tyre. The whole scene was something out of a movie about the early days of space exploration, not something from the modern universe. She was puzzled and galled in equal measure to find that Caledonia was so *lax*. It was oddly offensive to her.

And yet, she had to admit, the setup worked in her favor.

Her ship looked, from the outside, like one of the thousands of tramp freighters pottering their merry way through the asteroid belt. She appeared to be nothing more than a free trader, someone who sold simple goods to asteroid miners who rarely have more than a handful of credits to rub together. And yet, if the locals ever inspected her ship, they would be more than a little upset. Her passive sensor array was so sharp she could monitor activity on the other side of the system as long as she accounted for the time delay; her communications system was capable of inserting a message into the StarCom network without giving anyone a chance to freeze the signal, let alone trace it back to her. They'd have to shut the StarCom down completely if they wanted to keep her from sending messages, something that would alert Tyre that Caledonia was up to something. Gianni snorted at the thought. That wouldn't be their only problem. StarComs were flimsy things. If they shut the device down, they might not be able to start it up again.

She relaxed in her chair, watching more and more data piling up in front of her. The locals didn't really monitor the asteroid belt, not even now there was a war on. She had plenty of contingency plans for making her escape, if they demanded she prepare to be boarded, but it was starting to look as if she'd *never* need such plans. Surely they should have noticed that she'd *never* made port anywhere. But then, a tramp trader wouldn't make port at any of the bigger installations either. The local authorities would be more likely to serve Gianni conscription papers and demand she present herself and her ship for military service.

Which would be awkward all round, she mused as she studied the display. *Better to make my escape if they demand my presence.*

The data kept flowing into her display, her tactical computers crunching the numbers and turning it into something she could use. The king's fleet had been working its way through a fairly simple exercise, grinding out the kinks before he had to take his fleet into battle. Gianni wasn't too impressed by their efforts, but she had to admit they were working hard to overcome their weaknesses. She'd seen worse, back during the *last* war. The Theocracy had rarely bothered with exercises, scripted or unscripted. God would provide, they'd reasoned. But God hadn't obliged . . .

She leaned forward as she saw a pair of superdreadnought squadrons altering course, making their way out of the system. A thrill ran through her. An attack fleet, about to set course for one of a hundred possible targets? Or a decoy, intended to flush her—or someone like her—out of cover? She was all too aware that they had to know they were being watched. The system was practically designed to allow outsiders to spy on them. And yet, if they were watching . . . Her gaze slipped to the near-space display. There was nothing there, as far as she could tell. That was meaningless. A cloaked ship could be sneaking up on her, and as long as her crew were careful, she might pass completely unnoticed until she was well within firing range. Gianni felt another thrill. She'd always liked the thought of sneaking around, embracing the risk of being caught, which was why she'd accepted the role when it had been offered to her. The thrill more than outweighed the risks.

An alarm flared as the superdreadnoughts opened vortexes, waves of FTL energy rippling through space before fading back into the vacuum. Gianni leaned forward, breathing a sigh of relief mingled with irritation as the superdreadnoughts continued onwards. They'd opened vortexes, briefly, but they hadn't slipped into hyperspace. They were already reversing course, heading back to Caledonia. Gianni let out a cross breath as a third superdreadnought squadron, millions of kilometers farther away, vanished into hyperspace. A single squadron had left the system . . .

Unless it's trying to get into position before dropping out of hyperspace, she reminded herself. Her sensors were sharp enough to detect a vortex two light-years distant, according to the techs. The longer the squadron remained undetected, the farther away it was . . . and the more likely it was on a mission rather than carrying out pointless exercises. *They might have something clever in mind.*

She waited, silently counting the seconds. Each minute felt like an hour. The superdreadnought squadron didn't reappear. She ran through the sensor records, trying to identify which ships had left. The king's forces seemed to switch IFF signals on a daily basis, presumably to confuse watching eyes like hers, but the trick had its limits. She knew their ships too well to be fooled for long. HMS *Violence*, Kat Falcone's command ship, had led the third squadron as it vanished. And that meant . . . they were up to something.

Good, Gianni thought. *It's been too quiet recently.*

She composed a message, then encoded it. The king's inspectors would be alarmed if the code was unbreakable, so she was careful to use a civilian encryption program that wouldn't stand up to a military-grade decryption system. They'd be reassured when they saw the message, perhaps taking a day or two to review, unaware it meant something totally different. And they'd send it on without hesitation. Her lips quirked as she reread the message, just to be sure it was perfect.

And now we wait and see, Gianni told herself as she sent the message. *Who knows? Maybe they'll figure out the target and have a reception committee waiting . . .*

◆ ◆ ◆

"Admiral," Kitty said. "We've reached the RV point."

Kat looked up from her console. She'd watched, carefully, as two superdreadnought squadrons slid into hyperspace, leaving behind a cluster of drones and modified freighters, but there was no way to know if their deception had been successful. Someone was certainly watching. She'd stake her entire trust fund on it, if she still had one. And if they were close enough to spot the deception, the entire plan would be worse than useless. They might realize that half the king's superdreadnoughts would be on their way to an unknown destination, completely out of contact until they reached their target. Who knew what sort of mischief someone could do if they realized the truth?

Too much, Kat thought. The king had agreed to the plan at once, understanding that they needed to gamble, but some of his supporters had objected strongly. *We're taking a serious risk here.*

She met Kitty's eyes. "Download their tactical records, then set course for the second waypoint," she ordered. "Deploy sensor drones and watch for prying eyes."

"Aye, Admiral," Kitty said. "Long-range sensors are clear."

"Of course they are," Kat said. "Don't take that for granted."

She sighed as she leaned back into her chair. Hyperspace was a rolling sea of energy, a seething mass of sensor distortions and reflections that made it impossible to be sure something was out there until it was right on top of the fleet. The ninety ships under her command were flying in close formation, and even *they* had problems keeping track of each other's location. Hyperspace was more than usually agitated today, as if someone had been detonating nukes and antimatter bombs only a few short light-years away. She wondered if someone *was*. Disrupting hyperspace was dangerously unpredictable, a tactic of desperation, but . . . someone might be willing to try. Impeding transit between star systems might be very helpful to someone who wasn't dependent on interstellar trade.

But someone could be trying to keep an eye on us, she reminded herself. *And if they figure out our target and get ahead of us . . .*

She shook her head. There was no way to be certain they weren't being followed. They'd have to carry out the exercises to make tracking difficult, all too aware that they might be wasting their time or . . . or simply wasting their time in another way. She was almost tempted to drop a bomb or two herself, just to confuse any watching eyes, but she knew it was too dangerous.

A dull quiver ran through the superdreadnought. "Admiral, we're on course to the next waypoint," Kitty reported. "We should be there in ten days."

"Give or take a few hours," Kat said. It was impossible to be sure precisely how much time they would need to reach the waypoint, let alone Perfuma. She'd planned on the assumption the fleet would take longer than simulations suggested. "Inform the crew that we'll remain on low-level alert until we reach the waypoint, unless something enters our sensor displays."

"Aye, Admiral," Kitty said.

Kat nodded. They weren't following a straight-line course to Perfuma, which meant spending a few extra hours in transit. But the longer route minimized the risk of detection. The spacelanes between Caledonia and Perfuma were quiet these days, yet the risk of detection was higher than she was prepared to tolerate. Taking a few extra hours to reach their target was worthwhile if they remained undetected. The odds of being detected were quite low.

She stood. "We'll continue tactical exercises tomorrow," she said. "Until then, order the tactical crews to get some sleep. You too."

"Aye, Admiral," Kitty said.

Kat stepped through the hatch, nodding to the marine on duty as she passed him and made her way down the corridor. The superdreadnought felt odd, both home and yet not home. Kat felt a twist in her heart, knowing what it meant. *Violence* might be under her command, but she wasn't her ship. Kat wasn't her mistress. She couldn't legally give orders to anyone on the vessel save for her tactical staff. Not, she supposed, that an ensign would stand up to her if she tried to give him orders. He'd wind up in deep shit even if he was standing on firm legal ground.

Although Captain Procaccini would be irked if I did give some poor bastard orders, Kat thought sardonically. It was an oddity of the chain of command that a lowly ensign might outrank an admiral under the right circumstances. *On the other hand, he might realize the ensign didn't have much choice.*

She reached the cabin and stepped inside, feeling tiredness threatening to overwhelm her as she sat on the sofa. She wanted—she needed— to sleep, but she was too keyed up to sleep. The last few days had been busy, too busy. There'd been too many headaches she had to resolve, headaches that wouldn't have been a problem sixth months ago. She could have left such matters in subordinate hands, if she'd ever heard of them at all. Admirals didn't *have* to know the gory details. She would have been quite happy if her staff had taken care of them . . .

She looked at the golden band on her hand and scowled. What would Pat Davidson think of her now? He'd always been loyal to the

Commonwealth, but . . . what side would *he* have taken, when push came to shove? Would Kat herself have even taken a side? They'd talked about buying a freighter and setting off on their own, building a life for themselves that would have been free of obligation . . .

She felt a bitter pang, knowing she should take the ring off and make a new life for herself. The headshrinkers had said as much, in the weeks and months after the end of the last war. Kat hadn't cared one whit for their words. The ring was all she had left to remember him.

And yet, William took the other side, she reminded herself. *Would Pat have been on the other side too?*

She didn't want to think about it, but she had no choice. The war might be remarkably civilized so far, yet it was also terrible. She knew the men and women on the other side. Her brother was practically leading the other side. Her best friend was fighting for it. Her . . . She shook her head. She and Hadrian knew practically everyone on the other side. Yet they were fighting, and things were likely to get worse before they got better. The king might want a limited war, but some of his supporters thought otherwise. The colonials wanted to be free of Tyre and didn't much care who got hurt, as long as they broke free.

The intercom bleeped. Kat cursed. "Yes?"

"Admiral," Commander Jenkins said. "I've arrested a crewman for sedition. He's appealed to you."

Kat blinked. "You've arrested a crewman? Did you clear it with Captain Procaccini?"

"No, Admiral," Jenkins said. "My authority from the king—"

"Does not supersede the captain's authority on his ship," Kat snarled. They'd gone over this. They'd gone over it again and again and . . . she wanted to wrap her hands around Jenkins's neck and squeeze. Damn him. Captain Procaccini was not going to be pleased. His crew was going to be furious. "Bring him to my cabin. And inform the captain, if you haven't already."

She sat upright, brushing down her uniform. She supposed she should have ordered them to her office, but she was just too tired to care. She reached for an injector tab, then shook her head. The stimulant would wear off quickly, and then she'd be in a far worse place. The tab was only to be used if there was no other choice.

The hatch bleeped, then opened on her command. Jenkins entered, escorting a middle-aged man in cuffs. Two more security officers followed, shockrods tightly clutched in their hands as if they expected to need them. Kat wondered, sardonically, if they thought their prisoner was enhanced to the point he could break his cuffs and take them down before they could draw real weapons. Shockrods were nasty, if used properly. But a trained man could avoid them long enough to fight back.

"Admiral," Jenkins said. "I present to you Senior Chief Watterson, who was caught spreading sedition . . ."

A senior chief. The idiot had arrested a senior chief. There were few NCOs more respected than senior chiefs. In many ways, they were the backbone of the navy belowdecks. Captain Procaccini was going to be pissed unless there was very clear proof of sedition. She took a long breath, wishing she knew Watterson. The days when she'd known everyone under her command were long gone.

She met Jenkins's eyes. "What did he do?"

Jenkins looked back at her, warily. "He was questioning the Colonial Alliance's decision to continue to support the king."

"I see," Kat said. She felt a sudden urge to scream in frustration. It wasn't sedition. It couldn't be sedition. "That isn't sedition."

"Admiral." Jenkins paused, then started again. "Admiral, there is a legal definition of sedition . . ."

"And merely questioning the king doesn't meet it," Kat snapped. She put firm controls on her temper. She wanted to sleep. No, she wanted to do something—anything—to burn off her frustration before she lost control. "Commander, plotting a mutiny would be sedition.

Encouraging others to plot or carry out a mutiny would be sedition. Anything else . . . rather less so."

"Admiral, he was undermining the social order," Jenkins said. "It isn't his place to question the king's position . . ."

Kat sucked in her breath. From one point of view, Jenkins was right. A senior officer, or senior chief, shouldn't have a public opinion. But, from another, Jenkins was dead wrong. A citizen had every right to question his government's decisions, in hopes of either changing them or being educated in the underlying reasoning. And, on the gripping hand, the commissioners were already unpopular. If they started arresting people for expressing opinions, they'd simply drive those opinions underground.

And then people really will start plotting, Kat thought. She knew that such silencing had helped the king, back when he'd put out a call for supporters. *And then we'll come apart at the seams.*

She met his eyes. "You will release him. You will apologize to him. You will report to Captain Procaccini, and you will apologize to him too. And if you have grounds for arresting anyone else, for any reason at all, you will clear it with me and the captain first. Is that understood?"

"Admiral," Jenkins began. "I . . ."

"Is that understood?" Kat repeated. Her anger started to bubble out of control. The urge to do something thoroughly unpleasant was almost overwhelming. "Or do I have to have you all imprisoned?"

"No, Admiral," Jenkins said. "I understand."

"Good," Kat snapped. She calmed herself with an effort. "Release him, then go. Now."

CHAPTER ELEVEN

CALEDONIA

"The message is clear, Admiral," Flag Captain Lucy Cavendish said. "The king dispatched a single superdreadnought squadron from Tyre."

"So it seems," William said. A single superdreadnought squadron could cause a great deal of harm, but . . . it couldn't materially affect the balance of power. "When was the message sent?"

"Nine hours ago," Lucy said. She made a show of looking at her wristcom. "It was only forwarded to us now."

William nodded. The message wasn't very informative. There was no raw sensor data, something that couldn't be sent over the StarCom network without raising eyebrows, but it was enough. An enemy superdreadnought squadron had departed Caledonia, destination unknown. The observer hadn't forwarded the squadron's vector, not that it mattered. Any captain worthy of the name would know to change course once they were in hyperspace. It was page one of the tactical manual.

"I daresay we'll see them soon enough," he mused. Nine hours . . . The squadron couldn't have moved *that* far from Caledonia. It would be days before the enemy ships reached their target, days . . . He shook his head. There was scant hope of mounting an ambush. The squadron would probably reach its destination before any reinforcements from Tyre. "Alert the fleet bases to expect attack."

"Aye, Admiral," Lucy said.

William put the matter aside as he turned his attention back to the endless series of reports. Home Fleet was growing stronger every day as more and more starships came out of the reserve and joined the fleet. There were still crewing shortages, a problem made worse by power games among his well-connected officers, but he was fairly confident they'd be overcome sooner or later. And then . . . He looked up at the starchart, silently calculating the distance between Tyre and Caledonia. Home Fleet could reach the king's base in less than two weeks. The king could surrender, fight to the death, or flee. And then the war would be effectively over.

"Order the tactical department to start drawing up plans for raids into enemy territory," he said calmly. He was losing his reluctance to target colonial infrastructure. The loss of life would be bad enough, but the economic damage would almost be worse. And yet, there was no choice. If he wasn't allowed to challenge the king's fleet directly, he'd have to take out the industries that kept the fleet alive. "I want operational plans on my desk by the end of the day."

"Yes, sir," Commander Isa Yagami said. "I'll see to it personally."

And the plans probably already exist, at least in draft form, William thought. Tactical staffers spent half their time doing the prep work, often before they were ordered to prepare the operational assessments underlying the tactical plans. They seemed to like imagining wars that would leave half the galaxy in ruins, if anyone had the resources and will to fight them. *They shouldn't have any trouble updating the plans and bringing them to me.*

His wristcom bleeped. A private message had arrived. He opened it and frowned, skimming the handful of lines. His brother was on Island One, waiting for him. William swallowed, his mouth suddenly dry. He had no qualms about what he was doing, but . . .

He dismissed the thought. "Commander, alert my shuttle," he ordered. "I'm going to Island One."

"Aye, sir," Yagami said.

William went back to his cabin, changed into a civilian outfit, and made his way to the shuttlebay. His personal craft was already waiting, the drives humming . . . He was still taken aback by the luxury of having his own shuttlecraft, even though it came in handy from time to time. He would have been happy using a standard shuttle whenever he needed one. Admirals had all kinds of perks, but . . . a personal shuttle was just absurd. He put the thought aside as the pilot flew him to Island One, William's codes allowing him to pass through the security screen as though it wasn't there. William made a mental note to raise the issue with his superiors when he had a moment. A lone shuttle, packed with antimatter, could vaporize Island One, or another habitat, if it was allowed to dock without being inspected.

And yet, the checks we'd need to ensure it could never happen would annoy people, he mused as he disembarked and headed for the bar. *No shortage of complaints to contend with during the war.*

He made his way through the crowd. Island One was the oldest habitat in the system, old enough to predate most of the settlements on Tyre itself. Immigrants had gone through Island One to be processed before they'd been allowed to land on the planet below. Even now, Island One was still a gateway to the stars, as close to Tyre as someone could get without passing through an intensive security check. The lower decks were crammed with immigrants, people hoping to get a work visa before they were deported back home. William had heard the immigration rate hadn't changed even though there was a war on. Somehow he wasn't surprised.

The sound of loud music greeted him as he stepped into the bar. He looked around, rolling his eyes at the erotic dancers on stage. The bar had clearly had its day a long time ago. He noticed only a handful of patrons, all of whom seemed more interested in their drinks than the dancers. William ignored a wave from one of the performers as he peered into the cubicles. Commodore Scott McElney, his brother, was sitting in the semidarkness, nursing a pint of beer. William hoped it was beer. The bar was seedy enough that it was hard to be sure.

"Bill," Scott said as William slipped into the cubicle and sat down. "I got your message. I also got a string of shipping contracts. Do I have you to thank for that?"

"No," William said. He was damned if he was abusing his position, even though everyone knew everyone did it. He wasn't an aristo with a family that would back him if he was caught by the IG. "Dare I ask who hired your crews?"

"Probably better you don't know," Scott said. "You might have . . . issues with it."

The king, William guessed. Scott had been playing both sides of the field. *And you know I know . . .*

He put the thought aside. "How's business?"

"Wars are good for business," Scott said. "But then, I guess you know that."

"Peace is *also* good for business," William countered. An old argument. "But then, I guess you know that too."

Scott laughed. "People don't ask so many questions during wartime," he said. "They're so grateful you're prepared to work for them that they don't put barriers in your way. In peace, on the other hand, there are taxes and tariffs and tedious morality and all the other things that get in the way of free trade."

"And if there weren't, you'd be out of a job," William said lightly. "What sort of gratitude is that?"

"Hey, I'd be legit if I could," Scott said. He shrugged. "I daresay you're not going to come and work for me. And you don't need to come in person to make a deal with me. So . . . why did you want to *see* me?"

William met his eyes. "I want you to do me a favor."

Scott looked back at him, his voice dead serious. "What do you want?"

"I need you to take a message to Caledonia," William said. "And it absolutely, positively *cannot* be intercepted."

"I see," Scott said. "And do you want me to take a side in this war?"

William allowed his irritation to show. "Scott . . . I get it. I really do. I understand precisely why you're so sour on governments in general and ours in particular. But right now . . . if you wind up on the wrong side of the war . . ."

"The one that loses," Scott quoted.

". . . Then you'll be in deep shit afterwards," William said. "I know you don't want to choose a side until there's a clear winner, but by the time a clear winner is visible they're not going to need you any longer, are they? This is your chance to earn one hell of a lot of gratitude from the Commonwealth."

"Gratitude is insubstantial," Scott pointed out. "I need something a little more solid."

"You can go legit," William said. He knew his brother. He'd taken the time to lay the groundwork for a reward, if Scott wanted it. "Whatever you did, in the past, would be left in the past."

"The past has a habit of turning rotten and stinking the place out," Scott said. "As you know perfectly well."

"Our past is a radioactive wasteland," William snapped. "It's time to look to the future."

"True," Scott agreed. "You want me to take a message. To Kat Falcone, I presume."

"Quite." William wasn't surprised Scott had figured that out. His brother was smarter than he acted. Besides, there weren't many people William would send a covert message to. "I want to arrange a meeting."

Scott lifted his eyebrows. "And how do you intend to meet her?"

"I haven't worked that out yet," William admitted. He'd had several ideas, but they all depended on a degree of cooperation from Kat. His superiors wouldn't let him visit Caledonia, even if he could sneak onto the planet without setting off alarms when he passed through the security checkpoints. "The first step is to let her know I want to meet her."

"Really, now." Scott's voice was sardonic. "Missing her that much, are you?"

William felt anger rise. "This isn't the time to be snide."

"You never think it's a good time to be snide," Scott said.

"This is a particularly bad time," William said. "There's a war on."

"A war that's quite profitable," Scott pointed out. "Why would I want it to end?"

"The king started the war that left our homeland a radioactive nightmare," William snapped coldly. "He has to be stopped."

"Our homeworld sold girls into sexual slavery to save themselves from pirates," Scott countered. "Do you think I *care* what happened to the bastards?"

"Did they *all* deserve to die?" William resisted the urge to reach across and slap his brother as hard as possible. "The children? The teenagers? The adults who were teenagers and kids when *we* were young? Did they *all* deserve to die?"

He held up a hand before Scott could say something unforgivable. "I understand. Really, I understand. But the assholes who sold your girlfriend and treated us like shit are dead. They were dead before the war. Things were getting better, before the Theocracy nuked the planet with dirty bombs. And that happened because of the *king*! He's got to be stopped."

Scott raised a single eyebrow. "And you expect me to help?"

"Yes." William calmed himself. "If the king wins the war, things will get harder for you. He won't be able to help himself. If the king *loses*, the government here"—he waved a hand at the deck—"will not be inclined to see you as anything other than a traitor. They won't have any incentive to do you favors. They'll throw the book at you."

"There's always work for smugglers," Scott said.

"Are you sure?" William smiled thinly. "You might find yourself frozen out of shipping lanes, if the big corporations get their way. God knows they resented competition, even before the war. They'll have all the incentive they could possibly want to hit you with a legal hammer! They'll have enough of an excuse for doing it, because you did help the king, that people who might otherwise be friendly to you will say *fuck you*. Yeah, maybe common sense will reassert itself, but . . . I wouldn't count on it.

"And where would you go? You could take your ships to Jorlem, but the pickings there aren't great. You could go into the former Theocratic worlds, yet . . . they're too poor to pay you. Not enough to keep your ships going, at least. There aren't many places in the human sphere that will tolerate you, let alone pay you. You'll be reduced to skulking around the fringes of human society, shipping goods from black colonies to primitive rim worlds. In the end, you might even become a pirate yourself. And wouldn't *that* be ironic?"

He leaned forward. "This is your chance. You can go legit. You can get a place in the postwar universe with shipping contracts that'll give you a chance to make a life for yourself and your people. All you have to do is carry a simple message to Caledonia."

"And get it into the hands of someone who is presumably being watched and guarded," Scott said. "What's the difference between bodyguards and wardens?"

"I'm fairly sure Kat is not commanding the king's fleet at gunpoint," William said sardonically. "And she doesn't like being surrounded by bodyguards."

"There's a whole list of people who want to kill her and do unspeakable things to her dead body," Scott countered. "And not all of them are from the Theocracy."

William grimaced. Scott had a point. There was no shortage of people who regarded Kat as a traitor or, worse, an aristo in a position that should be held by a colonial. The spooks kept predicting that the king's alliance would fall apart, sooner rather later, as it became impossible to smooth over the cracks in the coalition. William wasn't holding his breath waiting for it. The king's supporters knew they had to hang together or hang separately. They'd be insane to start fighting each other, at least until the war was safely won.

"I trust you to find a way to talk to her," he said curtly. "You already spoke to her once, didn't you?"

"Yeah." Scott shrugged. "But that was before things started to go wrong for both sides."

"Then you can do it again," William said. "I'm sure if you turn up with a hold full of supplies, they won't turn you away."

"They'd be sure to look a gift horse in the mouth," Scott said. "I'd be surprised if they didn't examine everything thoroughly before installing whatever I brought in their ships."

"Me too." William smiled. A handful of his staffers had suggested sending the king's forces booby-trapped supplies. The engineers had vetoed the plan, pointing out that the king could easily check for surprises and, when they were uncovered, remove them. They'd be giving the king a boost for nothing. "Besides, we want them to trust you."

Scott grinned. "Does anyone trust me?"

"Far be it from me to dispute that," William said lightly. He *did* trust his brother, at least to some extent. Scott might refuse to do what William wanted, but he wouldn't betray him. He was a smuggler, operating outside the law. A reputation for keeping his word was the only thing that kept him in business when his clients couldn't seek redress through the courts. "I want you to take her a message. Tell her I want to meet. And that we can figure out a way to meet if she's open to it."

"She may want to know something more," Scott said. "Like why should she meet you when all you can do is recite your position papers at her?"

"I can't tell you, not now," William said. "You don't want to know."

"So you're not going to confess your love to her?" Scott teased. "What a shame. I'm sure she'll be very disappointed."

"Shut your mouth," William said tartly. "This is important."

"Important to *you*, maybe," Scott said. "I don't know, yet, if it's important to *me*."

"You're being paid through the nose," William said. In truth, Scott was being *overpaid*. The fee was enough, he was sure, to convince his brother that more rested on the meeting than William had said. "I'd say that makes it important to you."

"True enough," Scott said. "Jokes aside, how dangerous is this likely to be?"

William shrugged. There was no way to know. The king, or more likely his supporters, would be foolish to come down hard on a smuggler, not when he needed smugglers to keep his fleet running. Scott could be kicked off Caledonia without causing too much of a fuss, but anything worse . . . He told himself, firmly, that the king wasn't that foolish. And yet . . . If the king knew the real purpose of the meeting, he'd act ruthlessly to ensure it could never happen. William had no doubt of this. The king had gone too far to risk making mistakes now.

"I think you'll be fine, as long as you're careful," he said finally. "And don't expose yourself too much."

"I think I was exposed from the very first breath I took," Scott said. He picked up his glass and drained it in a single long swallow. "I'll let you know how things go."

William produced a datachip from his pocket. "There's a network address here," he said, handing it over. "Perfectly civilian, I've been told. She won't draw any attention if she sends a message there. But ideally, we'd prefer you to carry messages between us."

"*We,*" Scott repeated. "Very well. For the money, of course."

"Of course," William echoed. "Tell me, have you ever considered doing anything out of the goodness of your heart?"

"Yep." Scott snorted. "And then I remember how many people worked themselves to death, doing things without pay or reward. And then I decide, once again, to only take cash."

"You'll be paid," William assured him. "And I wish you joy of it."

Scott stood. "Money doesn't buy happiness," he said. "But you know what? Life's a lot nicer with it."

"Money can't buy everything," William commented. "Just ask the king."

CHAPTER TWELVE

TYRE

"Your Grace," Yasmeena said. "Ah . . . *Ambassador* Grison is here."

Peter stood. "Show him in, please," he said. "And bring us both coffee."

He watched with studied interest as his aide escorted Ambassador Grison into the office. The colonial was a tanned man, someone who would have been handsome if his lower jaw hadn't looked ghastly. It was covered by a mass of scars from a botched operation during the war, scars that could have been removed in an instant by modern bodysculpting surgery. But Grison had chosen to keep his wounds. Peter suspected there was a message there for Grison's voters rather than his friends and enemies on Tyre. Grison was too confident in himself to need cosmetic surgery.

And the scars are striking enough to ensure he's remembered, Peter thought as they shook hands, *without looking ugly enough to draw contempt.*

"Your Grace," Grison said. His accent was strong enough to be noticeable without making him hard to understand. Another part of his act, Peter guessed. Grison didn't want to give his supporters the impression he was no longer one of them. "Thank you for seeing me."

"It's my pleasure," Peter said. He was less than amused by Grison's attempt to see him personally, rather than going through the Foreign Office, but the whole situation *was* unprecedented. Legally, the Commonwealth wasn't foreign. "However, you understand that I am a busy man."

"I quite understand." Grison took the proffered seat, then accepted his coffee with a flourish. "I am a busy man myself, these days."

Peter wasn't sure that was true but let it pass without comment. He'd taken the time to read Grison's file when the ambassador had arrived and asked for the meeting, only to discover that Grison was seen as a moderate in a climate where extremists were regarded as being a little too soft. The intelligence officers had speculated that Grison was considered expendable by his superiors even though they'd given him an ambassadorial role. He would certainly be easy to disown if things went badly wrong. His superiors might even claim Grison had acted without orders . . .

Except the king isn't likely to believe them, Peter thought. Ambassadors generally had a great deal of leeway, but there was no way any of them would travel to another world without at least some degree of official backing. *I wonder if he'll pretend to believe them.*

He sat, sipping his coffee. "Let's get straight to the point," he said. It wasn't very diplomatic, but *he* wasn't very diplomatic. "What do you want to say to me?"

"My homeworld is deeply concerned about the recent . . . discoveries about the king's role in starting the war," Grison said. "There is some fear that they may have been sold a bill of goods. If there were to be clear proof the king *did* start the war . . ."

"We gave you all the proof we had," Peter said truthfully. He knew the king had chosen what was, perhaps, the best possible way to undermine the truth. The story *did* sound absurd, to someone who knew the Theocracy. "If that isn't good enough, I don't know what we can do for you."

Grison eyed him for a moment, then took the plunge. "My superiors are considering withdrawing from the war," he said. "If we did so, what terms would you offer us?"

Peter looked back at him. "How serious are your . . . superiors?"

"Opinion is divided," Grison said. He didn't seem to resent the unspoken implication that he was acting without permission from higher authority. "I believe a majority of them would prefer to leave the war rather than switch sides, if terms could be agreed on."

"And if we were to say you *had* to switch sides?" Peter pressed his advantage, curious to see what happened. "That you *had* to join us?"

"We don't want to break our word," Grison said. "And we gave the king our word we wouldn't turn on him."

And yet, you're prepared to leave the war if it goes against you, Peter thought. There were always limits to how far one government was prepared to support another, but breaking one's word too openly tended to cause blowback. *You'd leave the king, yet . . .*

He frowned. Grison probably couldn't commit his homeworld to waging war on the king. It might be hard enough to convince his fellows to step back from the war, to leave the king and his enemies to settle their disputes. And yet, Peter felt his stomach churn at the thought of simply letting them get away with joining the rebels. He'd be setting a ghastly precedent for the future.

"Our terms are simple," Peter said flatly. "You would be expected to rejoin the Commonwealth. You'd repay the loans made to you, but, as a gesture of goodwill, we'd cancel the interest. If you've already repaid the original loan, we'll count it as the end of the payments. After that . . . as long as you abide by the Commonwealth treaties, we won't seek any further retribution."

Grison cocked his head. "And if we insist on *all* payments being canceled?"

"Then we'd have to insist on the infrastructure being returned to us," Peter said calmly. "We either operate it within your system, as laid down by the treaties, or relocate it somewhere else."

He met Grison's eyes. "We are aware that you have reason to be . . . annoyed at us," he added after a moment. "But there are limits to what we're prepared to allow you to do in response."

Grison said nothing. Peter watched him, wondering what thoughts were flickering behind the scarred face. Grison had to know his home-world was being offered a very good deal indeed, if it quit the war before the king lost, but . . . he also knew he risked exposing his world to the king's retaliation. And Hadrian *would* seek to retaliate. Kat might hesitate to bombard a rebel world, as Peter was *sure* she'd refuse orders she considered illegal, but she wasn't the only officer under the king's command. There were a handful of his supporters who would happily throw an entire planet into the fire if they thought it would please their monarch.

"I will have to discuss it with my superiors," Grison said finally. "With your permission, I will withdraw and communicate with them."

"You have full access to the StarCom," Peter assured him as Grison rose and bowed. "I look forward to hearing their reply."

He smiled, thinly, as Yasmeena escorted Grison out of the office. It was unlikely Grison would trust the StarCom network, *whatever* assurances Peter offered. The temptation to try to decrypt the messages would be overwhelming. And the king might be trying to intercept the messages as well. It was far more likely Grison would send a courier, ensuring that it would be weeks, if not months, before his superiors sent a response. Peter wondered, as he turned his attention to the latest set of reports, if Grison would have time to get a reply before the war was over, one way or the other. The poor bastard would have to fall on his sword if the king won.

We'll do our best to keep our files from falling into his hands, Peter thought morbidly. *But he'd be a fool to believe us.*

Yasmeena pinged him thirty minutes later. "Your Grace, Admiral Sir William is requesting a meeting."

"A face-to-face meeting?" Peter knew perfectly well that William disliked attending meetings, particularly physical meetings. "Really?"

"He's on his way," Yasmeena said. "He was very clear he wanted a private meeting."

Peter didn't have to look at his schedule to know what he had to do. "Send him in as soon as he arrives," he ordered. "I'll be here."

He read the endless series of economic reports, feeling his head start to pound as he worked his way through the buzzwords and the general tendency not to use one word when the writers could use an entire paragraph. The economic slowdown seemed to have been halted, for the moment, but he couldn't say how long things would go on before something collapsed, triggering another economic decline. The big corporations had helped by placing large orders for war material, yet . . . He shook his head in annoyance. When the war ended, the orders would be canceled. Again. He made a mental note to see if they could find someone who wanted to buy warships and war material, but doubted it would get very far. They didn't want to sell ships to someone who might turn on Tyre.

Yasmeena opened the door. "Sir William is here, Your Grace," she said. "Do you want me to bring more coffee?"

Peter glanced at his mug, unsure when he'd finished it. "Please," he said. "And then hold all my calls."

He waved William to a chair as he entered, then put the datapad to one side. "I take it something's happened?"

"I spoke to my brother two hours ago," William said. "He's agreed to carry our message. At a price, of course."

"Of course." Perversely, Peter was oddly pleased about that. People who acted out of simple greed were more understandable, and predictable, than people who claimed to be acting out of principle. The latter tended to be more inclined to find newer and better ways to warp the rules out of shape, twisting them into a complex mess without ever quite breaking them. "I'm happy to keep our side of the bargain."

William nodded curtly. Peter understood, better than he cared to admit. William wasn't the only one with awkward relations. Peter had several dozen relatives who were little more than oxygen thieves, drinking and gambling their trust funds away instead of making something of themselves. It wasn't as if they were short of things to do. Peter had plenty of positions within the family corporation that really needed to be held by a relative, someone he trusted to have good reason not to screw the family. But some of his relatives were so irritating that he would almost have sooner taken the risk of hiring an outsider.

And Kat is fighting for the king, he thought tersely. *The only person who made a life for herself outside the family is fighting on the wrong bloody side.*

He sipped his coffee, controlling his irritation with an effort. He should have come to terms with it by now. God knew, he and Kat had been at loggerheads for most of her life. He wanted to go back in time and kick his younger self in the bum, telling him that he should be patient with his baby sister rather than regard her as a childish nuisance. And yet . . . He couldn't overcome the sense that Kat had betrayed her heritage. There were plenty of other ways she could have rebelled without putting the family itself at risk. He put the mug aside, telling himself he was being stupid. Kat was a grown woman. She'd made her choice.

But she didn't have all the facts, he thought, again and again. *She didn't know what she was doing.*

"I hope your brother does come to the light," he said shortly. "We're prepared to welcome him."

"Scott spent most of his life battling against an unfair system," William said. "He's been fighting for so long, he cannot tell when he doesn't *have* to fight."

Peter nodded. "It can't have been easy, growing up there. Both of you rebelled, did you not?"

"Perhaps we wouldn't have rebelled if they'd accepted us," William said slowly. "But that's air out of the airlock now."

"True." Peter changed the subject. "Is the fleet ready for deployment?"

"We could give Caledonia a very hard time *now*," William said. "But the Grand Admiral doesn't want to take the risk."

"Losing Home Fleet would make life difficult for us," Peter said dryly. "I don't like the rumors from the border."

"Me neither," William said. "Do you think the king will sell them out?"

"I think he's considering it, if intelligence is to be believed," Peter said. "Of course, he could be just stringing the Marseillans along . . ."

"Perhaps." William didn't sound convinced. "And if they do gain possession of the border worlds, they'll be thirty or so light-years closer to Tyre."

Peter nodded, stiffly. In one sense, it wouldn't matter. The border wasn't a physical barrier. The Marseillans could send a fleet from Marseilles to Tyre and, as long as they were careful, remain undetected until they emerged at their destination. But, in another, it was quite serious. Narrowing the gap between Marseilles and Tyre would give them a chance to pre-position a fleet within striking range in the short term, while allowing them to absorb the border worlds would enhance their population and, in the long term, their industrial base. It couldn't fail to affect the balance of power. And who knew what would happen then?

We might face a foe tougher and smarter than the Theocracy, Peter thought. In theory, there was no reason for Marseilles and Tyre to go to war. In practice, it was impossible to be sure. Wars had started by accident before, triggered by an incident that sparked off a series of responses and retaliations until neither side could back down without weakening itself. *Or face demands for more concessions further down the line.*

"If we fought them," he mused, "could we win?"

"Their fleet is supposed to be smaller, and less advanced," William said. "Of course, they'll have been working on their own weapons ever since they saw us deploy newer and better weapons systems in combat.

I'd be surprised if they haven't already matched us, when we faced the Theocracy. There's no way to know until we see their ships in battle."

He waved at the holographic starchart. "The Theocracy based its tactics around smashing enemies and grabbing their territory in a series of single-engagement wars," he added. "They weren't prepared for a multistar enemy when they realized they'd have to fight us, sooner or later. They never really laid the groundwork for supporting their fleet. We can't count on the Marseillans making the same mistake. I'd be astonished if they haven't been studying the war. *We've* been studying the war."

Peter frowned. "You don't sound pleased about it."

"It's easier to learn from defeat than victory," William explained. "If you're defeated, you cannot hide behind victory. You cannot allow yourself to believe that you won because you deserved to win, let alone that victory is the natural state of affairs for you. Right now there are people arguing that our victory was practically certain. They don't bother to look at the factors that let us win because, *hey, our victory was assured*. And that's dangerous because victory is *never* assured. Overconfidence is just as much a weakness as fanaticism."

"The Theocracy *did* have an unbroken string of victories until Cadiz," Peter mused.

"Yes," William said. "And they never stopped to ask why those victories were so easy."

"Point," Peter conceded. "As you can see, we cannot risk lunging at Caledonia. Not yet. Even if we win, we might lose."

"If the Marseillans stab us in the back," William conceded. "Are they likely to try?"

"We have to assume the worst," Peter said, after a moment. "And they *do* have good reason to want us weakened, or gone."

"It seems to me we should be able to come to some kind of agreement," William mused. "What do they want?"

"They wouldn't accept anything we could reasonably offer," Peter said. "And that's the hell of it." He shrugged. "Not that it matters, right now. I had a meeting only an hour or so ago."

"Interesting," William said, when Peter had finished outlining the meeting. "Do you think they'll drop out of the war?"

"I don't know," Peter said. "What do *you* think?"

"I think they'd drop out if they thought they could do it safely," William said. "But it would be difficult."

"Quite," Peter said. "The sooner we win, the better."

William laughed. "We could win now if we took a risk," he said. "But it could end badly."

"So you've said," Peter reminded him. "When do you think you can move without a major risk?"

"Several months, at least," William said. "But we can keep putting pressure on them."

"And hope they fragment under the strain," Peter said. "Unless we fragment first."

William looked alarmed. "Is that likely?"

"It's unclear," Peter admitted. "It depends on factors beyond our control. The economy is weaker than we'd like, right now. Even conceding that we're never going to see those loans and investments again hurts us, if only because we have to basically pay ourselves. And that will hurt the taxpayers, when it gets out. They'll be unhappy if they're forced to subsidize the corporations."

He ran his hands through his hair. "And the king wants to *come back*," he added. "I wonder if he'd want to stay away, instead, if he knew what sort of mess he was going to inherit."

"He'd come," William said flatly, a hint of hatred in his tone. "A person like that never sees the downside, never really understands the risks. And when it catches up with them, the consequences take down everyone else as well."

"And they say I'm lucky," Peter said.

"You *are* lucky," William pointed out. "Do you know how many people on Tyre, just *Tyre*, would trade places with you?"

"Not with me," Peter corrected. "With my family. With the ones who do nothing but fritter away their trust funds. If they knew how much weight rested on my shoulders . . ."

He shook his head. "They wouldn't want it at all," he said. "And I couldn't blame them."

CHAPTER THIRTEEN

In Transit, Perfuma

Kat had hoped to spend the voyage gathering herself, resting, and considering the future. There *was* a war on, after all, and it was her duty to figure out how to fight it. But there had been too many problems aboard her ships for her to relax. The commissioners had rapidly made themselves more hated than anyone else, even by the Tyrians. They'd suffered all kinds of little discomforts, from "accidentally" having their life support reconfigured so it produced irritating noises to nearly putting their lives in very real danger. One commissioner had practically walked out an airlock, his hide only saved by his mystery assailant getting cold feet midway through the deed. Kat found it hard to be angry, even though she knew she couldn't tolerate someone trying to murder the commissioners. It didn't help that the commissioners seemed to like finding new ways to be annoying.

"Admiral," Kitty said. "We have reached the RV point."

Kat studied the display. The fleet rested in hyperspace, a single light-year from Perfuma. They should be well out of detection range, although she'd been careful to make sure they kept a wary eye out for pickets and freighters that might—might—catch a sniff of their presence. Logically, any passing freighter should assume that the fleet was nothing more than a cluster of sensor ghosts, but it was impossible to be sure. A picket ship watching for possible intruders would sound the alert first and ask questions later.

"Order *Merlin* to detach herself from the fleet and survey the target system," Kat said quietly. She would have preferred to go herself, but the superdreadnought was far too noticeable. "And then to return as quickly as possible."

"Aye, Admiral."

Kat sat back in her chair, feeling the familiar tension before an engagement. *Merlin* should be able to get in and out without being intercepted, although the enemy could realize they were being watched and sound the alarm. It shouldn't matter, unless the defenses had been radically strengthened in the last two weeks. After all, the grand admiral was a Rudbek. He'd be expected to pull strings to defend his family's interests. She'd be more surprised if he *hadn't* done everything in his power to make sure his family didn't lose the war.

"*Merlin* has left the fleet, Admiral," Kitty reported.

"Hold us here," Kat ordered. "We'll wait."

She checked the tactical plan one final time. Ideally, the defenders would only see *one* superdreadnought squadron. If the House of Lords reacted as she hoped, they might not realize there were two more lurking in hyperspace. Even if they didn't . . . they'd still have to make some hard choices. She smiled at herself. The plan had seemed perfect—almost impossible to screw up—when she'd been safely on Caledonia. Now, it seemed a little less perfect.

"They should be back in an hour," she mused. She wasn't sure what she'd do if *Merlin* didn't make it back. The heavy cruiser might have suffered an accident or . . . might have run into something big and powerful enough to eat her. There really was no way to know. In theory, *Merlin* could run from anything she couldn't fight. In practice, she might get very unlucky. Coming out of hyperspace within point-blank range of a superdreadnought would be very unlucky—and fatal—indeed. "And then we'll know."

She closed her eyes for a long moment, gathering herself. "It won't be long now."

◆ ◆ ◆

"Captain," Lieutenant Honshu said. "We'll be leaving hyperspace in five minutes."

Sarah nodded, watching as the countdown ticked mercilessly towards zero. It felt good to be going into action after the travails of the voyage, even though she knew there was a significant chance they might wind up dead in the next few minutes. She would have preferred to leave hyperspace a great deal sooner, but that would have ensured they were unable to convince the defenders they were friendly. Sarah hadn't liked the idea when it had been explained to her, although she understood the logic. The whole strategy struck her as more than a little underhanded.

She resisted the urge to glance at Mr. Soto—*Commissioner* Soto—as the last few seconds ticked away. The commissioner looked as if he made combat jumps every day, although Sarah was fairly sure that wasn't true. She'd spent a lot of time teasing her way through the files, trying to find something on the commissioner's past, but had drawn a blank. He seemed to have appeared from nowhere. She rather suspected there was more truth in that than she cared to admit.

"Vortex opening now," Lieutenant Honshu reported.

Merlin shuddered as she slid back into realspace, her sensors scanning for any potential threats. The display updated rapidly, showing Perfuma I and its cluster of orbital habitats and industrial nodes in close proximity. A handful of starships moved near the planet, traveling between the rocky world and the distant gas giant. Perfuma II, in the distance, looked rather less inhabited. Sarah reminded herself that it was an illusion. They were just too far from the secondary world for real-time sensor data.

"Transmit our modified IFF, then request permission to use the StarCom," she ordered. The fake IFF *should* work, according to the hackers, but she had her doubts. Her ship's characteristics were on file back on Tyre. They wouldn't be able to keep up the pretense if someone thought to check sensor readings against the file. "And keep us ready to jump out if they come after us."

"Aye, Captain," Lieutenant Honshu said.

Sarah nodded, watching as the display continued to fill with data. Perfuma was heavily defended, as she'd known all along, but the House of Lords appeared to have withdrawn most of the mobile units it had assigned to the system. They were possibly under cloak, she supposed, but that made no sense. The enemy would prefer to intimidate attackers rather than risk a battle that could go either way. Her stomach twitched at the thought. Perfuma was immaterial, in the grander scheme of things. But Admiral Falcone's fleet was not. If the enemy knew Admiral Falcone's fleet was coming, they might have baited a trap.

"Captain," Lieutenant Yu said. "I'm picking up a demand for real-time conversation."

"They know," Commander Remus said.

"They guess," Sarah corrected, although it didn't matter. The planetary defenses wouldn't have asked for real-time conversation unless whoever was in command already smelled a rat. Her eyes narrowed as she saw the enemy defenses starting to come online, limited only by the desire not to cause a panic. The enemy commander had messed up. If he'd tried to lure her into point-blank range, he might have succeeded. "I think it's time to take our leave."

She smiled as a flight of gunboats appeared, charging towards her ship. "Helm, take us out of here," she commanded. "Back to the fleet."

"Aye, Admiral," Lieutenant Honshu said.

"You don't want to engage them?" Mr. Soto glanced at her. "They're just gunboats?"

"Our orders are clear," Sarah reminded him tartly. She couldn't remember *anyone* questioning Captain Saul on his bridge. The old man would have thrown them in the brig so hard they'd probably smash their way through the bulkhead. "We're not here to pick a fight."

She felt the vortex generator cycle up as the gunboats swooped closer, their tactical sensors locking on to *Merlin's* hull. Too little, too late. Sarah wondered, absently, if the pilots would be in trouble when they returned home. They hadn't had a chance of getting into firing range, and they would have had to throw themselves into her point defense if they wanted to *really* hurt her, but their superiors might not realize it. Perfuma was a Rudbek world. They might not have an experienced naval officer in command.

Which would be foolish, she thought, as her ship slipped back into hyperspace and headed for the fleet. *They must have plenty of officers under their command.*

She dismissed the thought. It didn't matter. All that mattered was alerting the admiral, then joining the offensive. The alert would already be racing to Tyre. It just wouldn't get there in time to matter. Or so she hoped.

And if the alert doesn't get there at all, she told herself, *the remainder of the plan will be worse than useless.*

◆ ◆ ◆

"They've drawn down the mobile element, Admiral," Kitty observed. "Where did they send it?"

"Somewhere else?" Kat shook her head. The long-range sensor records showed no warships within the system, save for the handful of ships defending Perfuma I and II—more than enough ships to convince pirates to go elsewhere, but nowhere near enough to deter a superdreadnought squadron. "Order the fleet to advance, as planned. We'll come out of hyperspace at Point Alpha."

"Aye, Admiral," Kitty said.

Kat studied the display, turning the raw results and the hasty reports from the analysts over and over in her head. Perfuma *was* supposed to be heavily defended. She was surprised the Rudbek Corporation hadn't protested, loudly, when their mobile defenses had been drawn down. Grand Admiral Rudbek should have been able to block it. Perhaps they'd realized that losing Perfuma would be irritating but losing Tyre would be an utter disaster. Or perhaps they'd assumed the fixed defenses would be enough to deter attack. Under other circumstances, they might have been right.

"We'll be out of hyperspace in five minutes, Admiral," Kitty said. "Do you want to address the fleet?"

"No," Kat said. Her crews knew what they had to do. They wouldn't be impressed by grandiose speeches, not now. She promised herself, silently, that she'd find a way to convince the king to withdraw the commissioners, or at least make them behave themselves. Her crewmen didn't deserve to be regarded as potential traitors. They'd had a chance to go back to Tyre, or withdraw from the war, and had chosen to stay and fight for Hadrian. "Take us out as planned."

She braced herself as the vortexes opened, allowing her fleet to steer its way back into realspace on a direct course towards Perfuma I. The planetary defenses were coming to life, hundreds of gunboats flying towards the ships as they hastily formed a line of battle between Kat's squadron and the planet itself. Kat groaned in disgust as the enemy ships prepared to make their stand. They had nothing larger than a heavy cruiser. They should either fall back on the planet, combining their point defense with the orbital defenses, or open vortexes and retreat into hyperspace. It wasn't as if she could have stopped them.

"Signal the planet, as planned," Kat ordered. "And inform me the moment they respond."

"Aye, Admiral."

The range closed rapidly. Kat watched, torn between a grim certainty the enemy commander was an inexperienced idiot and a nagging feeling she was flying into a trap. No sane board of inquiry would punish the enemy commander for retreating. Her lips quirked. No *sane* board of inquiry, which probably meant the poor bastard would be shot when they faced a panel composed of officers who hadn't seen combat in years. The navy was generally good about ensuring that experienced officers handled court-martial proceedings, but there were limits . . . particularly, she acknowledged silently, if someone wanted to ensure the board came to the right decision.

"Admiral, they're tightening their targeting locks," Kitty warned. "I think . . ."

The display sparkled with red icons. "Missile separation! Multiple missile separations!"

Clever, Kat thought. *Very clever indeed.*

She smiled, humorlessly, as the range continued to close. In theory, the enemy had fired at dangerously extreme range. Modern missiles had more range than the missiles she'd used at Cadiz, years ago, but they had their limits. She was, technically, right at the edge of their range. Practically, however, she was impaling herself on their missiles, her own closing speed bringing her within their range. And they'd had missiles floating in space, increasing the weight of their opening salvoes . . .

"Open fire," she ordered. "And bring up the point defense."

She watched, coolly, as the enemy missiles slipped into her point defense envelope, the gunboats following them in. That was clever too, she acknowledged. The missiles were still operating at extreme range, unable to either evade her fire or hide their exact location, but they were providing cover for the gunboats. And she couldn't ignore the missiles, either, unless she wanted to let them have a clear shot at her hulls. She wished, suddenly, that the navy had managed to work the kinks out of the starfighter concept. The gunboats wouldn't have been so great a pain in the ass if she'd had gunboats, or starfighters, of her own.

The missiles started to evaporate, a handful surviving long enough to throw themselves against her shields. A shudder ran through the superdreadnought as she took a direct hit, shrugging the blast off with casual ease. Kat tensed, wondering if the enemy had figured out that *Violence* was her flagship. It shouldn't have been possible, but the enemy knew everything about her ships. Neither the king nor the colonials had had time to start churning out new ships of their own. The enemy might just have figured it out.

She nodded to herself as the enemy ships scattered, firing a handful of shots as they cut and ran for deep space. That was smart too. They'd given the battle their best shot, their gunboats having done a bit of damage, and then retreated, cutting their losses while they were ahead. Kat was almost relieved she wouldn't have to kill them, even though she knew she was likely to see the ships coming back at her when Tyre dispatched reinforcements. She glanced at the display, noting that the enemy StarCom was sending message after message in all directions. Tyre already knew she was here. They just needed some time to respond.

Unless they've sent their fleet to Caledonia already. That would be rather awkward.

"Admiral," Kitty said. "The planetary defenses are opening fire."

Kat gritted her teeth. "Target the fortresses only," she ordered. "Fire at will."

The superdreadnought heaved as she unleashed a full broadside. Kat frowned as the missiles raced towards their targets, hoping and praying that none of them slipped past the orbital defenses and struck the planet itself. The fortresses could barely move—their station-keeping drives were puny—but they crammed more point defense into their hulls than a superdreadnought. It was quite possible she *wouldn't* manage to take them out before she ran out of missiles . . .

Although we could complete the plan without taking the planet itself, she mused. *And that might actually work out in our favor.*

She nodded, coldly, as one of the fortresses vanished from the display. She tried, hard, not to think about what the winked-out icon actually meant. The lucky crewmen would be dead, vaporized before they knew what hit them. The unlucky crewmen would die slowly, gasping for breath or freezing to death as the atmosphere streamed into the vacuum. Even the ones who managed to get to the lifepods wouldn't be out of trouble. Kat had made it clear that her forces weren't to engage lifepods directly, but automated targeting systems might mistake them for deadly threats. Hell, *friendly* targeting systems might mistake them for deadly threats.

"Admiral," Kitty said. "I'm picking up a signal. It's from Commissioner Kevin Rudbek."

The planetary governor, Kat thought. She'd met him, in happier days. He was old enough to be her father . . . he and her father had been schoolmates, if she recalled correctly. The thought made her heart twist in pain. The war was going to destroy a great many friendships and families before it was over. The Rudbek Family would never forgive her. *Poor bastard.*

"Put it through," she ordered.

A grim-faced man appeared in front of her. He was older than she recalled. For a moment, she honestly thought she'd made a mistake, that it wasn't the man she remembered. And then she kicked herself. She'd been a child when they'd met, more than twenty years ago. Of course he'd gotten older.

"Kat," Kevin Rudbek said. He'd always been kind to a young girl when he'd visited the estate. "Your father would be very disappointed in you."

Kat clamped down, hard, on her emotions. "Kevin. You will surrender your orbital installations and military stockpiles at once, without further delay. If you do so, you and your personnel will not be harmed, and my fleet will retreat from the system in good order. If not, I will take the high orbitals by force."

Kevin Rudbek met her eyes. "Do you think you're doing the right thing?"

Kat ignored him. "Surrender now or face the consequences."

"As you command," Kevin Rudbek said. He sounded calm for someone who'd be disgraced when—if—he got back to Tyre. The Rudbeks would be looking for scapegoats. Kevin would fit the bill nicely, particularly if he'd been in command of the engagement as well as the planet itself. "I wish you joy of it."

"Thanks," Kat said. "My staff will take care of the details."

She tapped the console, closing the channel. Kevin Rudbek's image vanished. She'd won. She knew she'd won. And the second stage of the plan was underway. She'd been careful not to order him to give up or power down the StarCom. She needed him to scream for help.

I won, she thought, suddenly feeling as old as her father. The battle was over, and the plan was well underway . . . She had good reason to be pleased. *So why do I feel so terrible?*

CHAPTER FOURTEEN

CALEDONIA

The terminal bleeped, loudly.

Peter started, half convinced that something was badly wrong. He'd been so deeply asleep that he'd been dreaming, before the first bleep. He sat upright, his head spinning as he groped for the terminal. Yasmeena's face appeared in front of him, looking as perfect as ever. Did she sleep? He was suddenly very aware that he'd never seen her sleep . . .

"What?" His voice sounded thick in his ears, as if he were still asleep. "What's happening?"

"We just picked up a priority signal from Perfuma, Your Grace." Yasmeena's voice was brisk, efficient. "The system is under attack."

"Perfuma?" It took Peter a moment to place the system. Perfuma. A Rudbek world, only a handful of light-years from Tyre. "How badly?"

"The report stated that the system was likely to fall at any moment," Yasmeena said. "I don't have a direct link to the naval communications network."

Peter swung his legs over the side and stood. "Bring me some coffee," he ordered. "I'll be in my office."

He grabbed his robe and pulled it on as he half stumbled towards the door. It wasn't *fair*. There was nothing he could do, not now, about Perfuma . . . but he had to be up and active anyway, pressing the flesh and reassuring people that everything was going to be fine. The enemy was light-years away, a few days from reaching Tyre even if they set out at once. He caught his breath as he walked down the corridor, pacing himself as best he could. He couldn't afford to look agitated once the communications network started pinging. Everyone and their maiden aunt would want to have their say, damn it. And most were too important to be told to go back to bed and sleep it off.

And too many of them would be insulted if I refused to speak to them personally, Peter told himself as he walked into his office. A mug of steaming coffee was waiting for him. Peter practically snatched it off the desk and poured the hot liquid down his throat. The concoction tasted foul but jarred him awake. *They all expect me to do something, and I can't do anything.*

He put the mug down and took his seat. The first messages, all marked *urgent*, were blinking on his terminal. He glanced at the headers, then put them to one side as he brought up the latest reports from Perfuma. They were coming in real time, more or less. The oddity puzzled him. Surely, any attackers worth their salt would shut down or destroy the StarCom. Hadrian was as dependent on the network as the loyalists, but there were limits. Sending real-time tactical data to Tyre surely pushed those limits to a breaking point.

Yasmeena entered, looking as perfect as always. Peter eyed her warily, wondering how she managed to look so elegant, not a hair out of place, when she *had* to have been woken in the middle of the night. He glanced at the timer, kicking himself for not looking earlier. It was 0436. He'd only had five hours of sleep, more or less. He scowled, wondering if going back to bed would be worth the political fallout. Didn't he have someone who could press the flesh, hold hands, kiss babies, and do all the other pointless things he had to do to maintain his position?

Could be worse, he told himself. *I could be an elected representative.*

"You have forty-seven communications requests," Yasmeena informed him. "Seven of them are from outside the priority list. Reporters, mainly."

"Ignore them," Peter ordered curtly. The media had probably hacked the live feed from Naval HQ if they hadn't been tipped off by some staffer on base. They'd be in trouble for that when the dust settled. Reporters weren't treated like tin gods during wartime. "Who's on the inner priority list?"

"So far, no one," Yasmeena said. "That'll change."

Peter nodded.

"What do we know so far?" The first reports would be vague, probably wrong, but they were better than nothing. "Who's in command of the enemy fleet, and what have they done?"

Yasmeena frowned. Peter knew the answer before she put it into words. "Your sister, Your Grace," she said. "So far she seems to have occupied Perfuma I and started to loot it."

"Ouch." Peter smiled, thinly. "And Perfuma II?"

"No word as yet," Yasmeena said. "I daresay it's only a matter of time."

"I daresay," Peter echoed.

He studied the starchart for a long moment, torn between irritation and amusement. The Rudbeks would look like idiots if they just let Kat loot their supply depots instead of destroying the supplies before surrendering. He could probably use it for political advantage at some later date. But, at the same time, it would make them all the more determined to push for immediate action. If nothing else, Kat couldn't loot the entire world in a day. She'd need weeks to transport most of the captured supplies back to Caledonia. And if she moved on to Perfuma II, she'd need more ships, more time . . .

And she'd force us to act fast, Peter thought. Perfuma I belonged to the Rudbeks. Perfuma II was a colony world settled directly from Tyre, with a population that had representatives in the House of Commons.

She might leave Perfuma II alone in the hopes we'd just let her get on with the looting.

He shook his head. That wasn't going to happen. Kat had to know it. The supplies alone would make the king a far more deadly threat, if—when—Kat managed to get them back to Caledonia. Peter would be delighted if she left Perfuma II alone, but that wouldn't keep him from insisting the navy take immediate action. If nothing else, the chance to undo her victory within a week could hardly be passed up. She'd made the loyalists look weak. Peter didn't dare let that impression take root.

Not as long as we're trying to convince the colonials to abandon the king, he told himself as Yasmeena's datapad started to bleep. *They don't want to switch sides as long as it looks like the king can take revenge.*

Yasmeena peered over at him. "Your Grace, Duke Rudbek is on line one," she said. "He wants to speak to you."

"And he's on the topmost priority list," Peter muttered. There was no point in trying to deny it. "Put him through, then bring me more coffee. I'm going to need it."

"Yes, Your Grace." Yasmeena's fingers danced over the datapad. "I'll put him through now."

Duke Rudbek's face materialized over the desk. Peter wasn't too surprised to see the telltale signs of an image filter. Duke Rudbek looked a little too good for someone who'd probably been woken only a few short minutes ago. It was possible the Grand Admiral had woken him first . . . no, probable. Peter made a mental note to insert more of his clients into the naval bureaucracy. It was imperative that he be among the very first to be informed of anything that might impinge upon his interests.

Which is pretty much anything and everything, he thought as he cleared his throat. *I'll be bombarded with alerts every moment of every day.*

"Your Grace," he said. "Thank you for calling."

"Your Grace," Duke Rudbek said. He made a slight motion to dismiss the formalities. "We have to recover Perfuma."

"Indeed," Peter agreed. There was no point in disputing that, although the temptation to play power games was overwhelming. "However, right now it isn't a major problem."

"The world is ours," Duke Rudbek said. "And it must be recovered before its seizure causes more economic troubles."

And that's a very good point, Peter conceded. *If Rudbek weakens and goes down, it'll take a lot of others down as well.*

"Very well," he said. "I won't oppose a push for immediate military action."

"Good," Duke Rudbek said. "And I think it's time we started to take action against Caledonia ourselves."

"Nothing has changed since our last discussion," Peter said. "Or has it?"

"I don't believe so," Duke Rudbek said. "But we have to win this war before it kills us all."

As everyone keeps saying, again and again, Peter mused. He rubbed his forehead. *We have to win quickly, and it's the one thing we can't do.*

"I look forward to discussing your tactical concepts at a later date," he said briskly. An alert popped up in front of him. The remainder of the dukes and the senior political leadership were awake. Their staffers were laying the groundwork for a holographic conference. "Right now we have too many other problems to deal with."

"I won't stand still and let the king destroy us," Duke Rudbek warned. "If I have to take unilateral action myself, I will."

Peter ran his hand through his hair. It wasn't *easy* being the youngest duke, even though he'd been an adult for nearly forty years. In hindsight, he should have pushed to be treated as a co-duke . . . as if that were possible. He couldn't have been treated as anything other than the heir until his father had died . . . until his father had been *murdered*. He felt a hot flash of anger at the thought. Sir William's brother was supposed to be on his way to Caledonia. If he reached the planet, if he spoke to Kat, if . . .

He put the thought aside and leaned forward. "We must fight this war as a body," he said firmly. "We wouldn't have gotten into this mess if we'd brought the king to heel long ago."

"The king wanted power," Duke Rudbek said. "And we didn't realize it in time."

Of course not, Peter thought sarcastically. *You had so much power that you didn't understand what life was like to someone who had position, but not power.*

"It doesn't matter, not now," he said. "All that matters is winning the war."

◆ ◆ ◆

"Admiral," Grand Admiral Rudbek said. "I trust you slept well?"

William frowned, resisting the urge to rub his unshaven chin. He'd been fast asleep when the alert had arrived and, thankfully, his officers had resisted the urge to wake him until Grand Admiral Rudbek and the Admiralty needed him. William hadn't taken part in the preliminary planning sessions, and thus the government would have decided what it wanted to do without his input.

"Well enough," he said. His body was urgently reminding him that he wasn't a young man any longer despite a string of rejuvenation treatments. It wanted him to go back to bed and sleep. "I assume you didn't call to ask about my health?"

"No," Grand Admiral Rudbek said. "The House of Lords wants you to recover Perfuma."

What, personally? William smiled. *Don't they want me to take the entire fleet with me?*

He sobered as he pulled up the latest report. They were still getting reports in real time, something that worried him. *Kat's too experienced a naval officer to leave the StarCom online unless she wants us to know where she is.*

"I think they're trying to lure us out of position," he said slowly. One enemy superdreadnought squadron and escorts . . . a serious threat, yes, but not to Tyre. Perfuma wasn't that important, not in the grand scheme of things. "If we dispatch ships to Perfuma, we run the risk of weakening our defenses here."

"That may be true," Grand Admiral Rudbek said. "However, you have your orders."

William frowned as he pulled up the fleet lists and scanned them. The king couldn't expect him to throw everything at Kat, could he? That was the sort of plan that even the rawest of greenie officers wouldn't devise, unless they thought the sheer insanity of the strategy would make it work. But . . . William didn't *have* to dispatch the entire fleet. Two superdreadnought squadrons and escorts would be enough to make short work of Kat's force.

Unless she's planning to run before we arrive. It would put a lot of wear and tear on our equipment and *make us look like idiots.*

He examined the starchart. It was practically a *given* that Tyre and Home Fleet were under close observation. The king didn't need pickets and stealth ships to monitor William's fleet. He had no shortage of supporters scattered throughout the naval bureaucracy. The security services swore blind they'd rooted them out, but William didn't believe the propaganda. If no one had realized that Hadrian had been Admiral Morrison's secret patron, how could they pick out a lowly clerk in Planetary Defense who might take money from the king? Hell, it might be something as *simple* as money. It would be difficult to spot someone who hadn't taken visible advantage of a patron's patronage. Someone who simply took a bribe . . .

"We have to move now," Grand Admiral Rudbek said. "She *cannot* be allowed to hold the system."

"She won't hold it forever," William pointed out. "If we wait a few days, she'll probably withdraw and allow us to retake the system with a single destroyer."

Grand Admiral Rudbek purpled, as if William had made an obscene suggestion. "We cannot afford to look weak," he snapped. "And this looks like the perfect chance to smash a fraction of the king's fleet!"

"I know," William said. "That's what bothers me."

"Take two squadrons and liberate Perfuma," Grand Admiral Rudbek ordered. "If you can destroy her fleet, do it. I don't want her to get away with this."

"Neither do I," William said, ignoring the twist in his heart. Scott was en route to Caledonia. God alone knew what he'd do if Kat was killed before he could meet her. "I'd prefer to take *three* superdreadnought squadrons . . ."

"That would leave us exposed here," Grand Admiral Rudbek said. "Two. Two only. And don't ask for more."

William swallowed the response that came to mind. Grand Admiral Rudbek wasn't incompetent, but he lacked a backbone. His family had probably spent the last few hours making it very clear to him that Perfuma had to be recovered or else. And *or else* could be something as unpleasant as being dishonorably discharged from the navy and then disowned from the family. The poor bastard was caught between a rock and a hard place. He'd have no choice but to do as his family wished. And William could hardly go to *his* patron and ask for help. That would make it impossible to work with the grand admiral in the future.

Assuming my career survives, William thought dryly. *Perhaps I should have stayed on Asher Dales. Would have been so much simpler . . .*

"I'll see to it personally," he said. "Two of my squadrons are on quick-reaction duty. I'll take them and . . . liberate Perfuma. If you ready the rest for action elsewhere . . ."

Grand Admiral Rudbek frowned. "We have to cover Tyre."

"Yes," William said. "But Kat might easily take her fleet elsewhere before we can reach Perfuma."

He looked at the starchart, weighing the odds. Kat would need to resupply her fleet before a major engagement, if she genuinely intended to wait to be hit. That was odd, so odd he resolved to be *very* careful when he entered the system. Kat wasn't the sort of person to make obvious mistakes. She was up to something, but what? Kat wanted—needed—to pinch off a section of Home Fleet and destroy it, just as he had to do the same to the king's fleet. And yet, the king hadn't let her take more than a single superdreadnought squadron to Perfuma. He couldn't uncover Caledonia any more than the House of Lords could uncover Tyre.

"If they keep the real-time reports flowing . . ." He shook his head. "We'll check the reports just before we enter the system, just in case Kat intends to go elsewhere before we can arrive. If not, we'll close with the enemy ships and destroy them."

"See that you do," Grand Admiral Rudbek said. "You know how much is resting on this, Admiral. We cannot afford a defeat."

"Then we need to commit additional ships to my fleet," William said. He tried to sound convincing, even though he suspected it was pointless. "A third superdreadnought squadron . . ."

"Is unavailable," Grand Admiral Rudbek said crossly. He sounded as if he wasn't happy himself. "We need to keep the ships here."

"Yes, sir," William said tiredly.

"I understand your concerns," Grand Admiral Rudbek said, "but you have your orders. Good luck."

His image vanished. William stared at the blank display for a long moment, then tapped the intercom and called for coffee. Thankfully Home Fleet had spent enough time training over the past few months that everyone knew what they had to do. The superdreadnoughts were bringing their drives online, ready to depart. Their escorts would have to be organized . . . William worked his way through the fleet lists, ensuring that his formation would have plenty of scouting elements. If Kat was planning a surprise, hopefully he'd see it coming before it got into range.

And if I don't, things are going to get interesting.

CHAPTER FIFTEEN

PERFUMA

Kat felt uneasy as she jerked awake, unsure what had woken her. Her dreams had been dark and shadowy, mocking reminders of everything she'd lost over the last few years. Life had been so simple, once upon a time. She'd commanded a starship, she'd fought in a war, she'd had a lover and friends and a father . . .

She sat upright, feeling sweat beading on her brow. The dozens of messages from Kevin Rudbek, damn the man, were getting to her. She knew she'd done the right thing. She told herself, time and time again, that she'd done the right thing. But they were still wearing her down.

She rubbed her forehead, feeling a headache starting to pound behind her temples. There was something reassuringly simple about military life, for all the complexities of modern warfare. The gods of the copybook headings could not be cheated. One either won or lost, with little room in between. She liked the simplicity of naval life—a far cry from the aristocracy, where someone could argue that black was white or that up was down, and rules were nothing more than suggestions to the right connections. She'd met enough people who could twist arguments out of shape, who were very imaginative when it came to finding reasons she should do something and they shouldn't do something . . . It was easy, terrifyingly easy, to rationalize just about anything if one tried. And she *hated* such people. Kevin Rudbek was too clever to realize he wasn't being very smart, or that his people might suffer for his sharp tongue.

Just like all the civilians in the occupied zone, who suffered when the House of Lords started pulling ships and marines out of the territory, Kat thought. *The bastards let them suffer to make a political point.*

She stood on wobbly legs. She hadn't felt so bad since her first and last experiment with serious drinking, something that had taught her a lesson she didn't need to experience time and time again. The mirror seemed too bright, almost, as she stood in front of it and glared at herself. Her body was perfect, but her eyes were tired and worn. She looked as if she could go on forever, yet . . . she needed a rest. She needed . . .

Pat would say I needed something else, Kat thought. *And he'd offer to provide it . . .*

A wave of despondency rose up, threatening to overwhelm her. She felt tears prickling at the corners of her eyes. Pat was dead. Her father was dead. Many of the people she knew and loved were on the wrong side. They thought *she* was on the wrong side. And that hurt, more than she wanted to admit. She knew she was right. She knew Hadrian was right . . . And she knew there was no way she'd ever be able to convince them of that. People who had power and privilege were prepared to do anything, as long as they didn't have to give up their status. They never realized they might be part of the problem.

And they never truly realize that other people don't have their advantages, Kat thought sourly. She'd never realized it herself until she'd gone to Piker's Peak, which was the first time she'd spent any time with commoners, people who'd grown up outside the aristocracy. She'd never even *thought* about their lives until she'd met them. *A minor inconvenience to them might be a serious problem to someone else.*

She stumbled into the washroom and climbed into the shower. The hot water jarred her awake but didn't do anything for her headache.

She washed herself quickly, wishing she had time for a bath. There *was* a bath, but . . . normally, she made a point not to use it. The rest of the crew had to make do with showers. She knew they wouldn't know if she used it or not, but . . . it didn't matter. *She'd* know. She wouldn't feel *right* about enjoying something the remainder of her crew couldn't share.

Not that you'd willingly go back to the wardroom, her thoughts mocked her. *There are limits, aren't there, on how much you're prepared to give up too.*

Kat snorted at the thought as she dressed. It was a law of nature, or something, that wardrooms were always tiny, no matter how big the ship. Midshipmen didn't have enough room to swing a cat, let alone anything else. They practically slept in each other's bunks. Privacy was nonexistent. She supposed it was as good a way as any other to encourage the midshipmen to strive for promotion. Lieutenants got tiny cabins, but at least they were private.

The intercom chimed. "Admiral," Kitty said. "A picket just returned. They're claiming to have spotted a hyperwake approaching Perfuma."

"Really." Kat would have been more concerned if there hadn't been a dozen false alarms over the last few days. "Do they have hard data?"

"The analysts are processing it now," Kitty said. "The timing does fit though."

Kat nodded. The report from Tyre had been grim. Two enemy superdreadnought squadrons had departed on a least-time course for Perfuma. They could have changed course and gone somewhere else . . . Possible, but unlikely. The Rudbeks would be calling in every favor they were owed to make sure Kat was quickly chased out of the system. They might even forgo the chance to destroy her ships in their desperation to get rid of her. And there might even be *more* enemy ships. William was devious. He might have unknowingly copied her trick . . .

Because I did it, she mused, *I have to assume that they did it too.*

"Raise the alert level," she ordered as she got dressed. "But don't sound battlestations. Not yet."

"Aye, Admiral," Kitty said. "Should I alert the freighters?"

"Yes," Kat said. "I want the loaded ships ready for departure as soon as possible. There's nothing to be gained by keeping them here."

And the odds of them being intercepted are fairly low. She glanced in the mirror and nodded curtly to herself. She looked professional rather than someone on the verge of bursting into tears. *But I'll have to make sure they're escorted anyway.*

She keyed her terminal, bringing up the near-space display. Interstellar traffic to and from the system had dried up over the last few days as word spread through the StarCom network. A number of interplanetary ships were still moving between the asteroid settlements and Perfuma II, but most had shut down their drives and gone into hiding rather than risk drawing her attention. Kat understood, even though she also knew they probably didn't have anything worth stealing. The asteroid mining stations weren't producing anything unusual, and there was no point in trying to capture the interplanetary ships. She'd have problems taking them back to Caledonia.

Unless I wanted to impede industrial development, she mused as she headed out of the cabin and down to the CIC. *And they'd certainly have reason to be scared of that.*

She stepped into the compartment and looked at the display. "Report."

"The analysts think there's a reasonable chance the enemy fleet is nearing the system," Kitty said calmly. "But they're not completely sure."

"Of course not." Kat took her seat, resting her hands on her lap. "The enemy fleet could still be a few light-years away."

But she knew, all too well, that might not be true.

◆ ◆ ◆

"Admiral," Commander Isa Yagami said. "The scouts have returned. They've confirmed the presence of the enemy fleet holding station near Perfuma I."

"I see," William said. He frowned, stroking his chin as he studied the reports. He'd assumed Kat would have left days ago, thumbing her nose at the fleet the House of Lords had sent to retake the system. But instead she was still looting the planet. Was she *that* desperate for supplies? Or was she baiting a trap? "And only one superdreadnought squadron?"

"Yes, sir," Yagami said. "That's all we saw leaving Caledonia."

"Appearances can be deceptive," William muttered. He'd done everything he could to disguise his fleet as it left Tyre, even though he knew he was probably wasting his time. "If I was worried about uncovering a system"—which he was—"I'd go to some trouble to convince watching eyes that the system was still heavily defended."

He let out a breath. His orders didn't give him much wiggle room, even if he was an admiral with a powerful patron. He had to recover the system quickly. Someone was probably going to complain he'd wasted time sending scouts instead of relying on the real-time data from Perfuma. The whole thing just didn't make sense. Kat wouldn't have left the StarCom alone accidentally, which meant it was part of a trap . . . and yet, the scouting reports suggested the real-time reports were accurate. He didn't understand it. The king might not want to set a precedent for destroying StarComs, but they could have easily shut the bloody thing down.

"Alert the fleet," he ordered. "We'll go with Tango-Three."

Yagami looked puzzled even as he carried out his orders. "Yes, sir."

William chose to explain. "The enemy commander is up to something," he said. "Maybe she just intends to run as soon as we show our ugly faces, leaving us shaking our fists helplessly after her. Maybe she's up to something nastier. Either way, I want some room to maneuver if the shit hits the fan."

"Yes, sir." Yagami didn't sound reassured. "The fleet is ready to move on your command."

"Then let's go find out what's waiting for us," William said. "Take us into the fire."

"Aye, Admiral."

◆ ◆ ◆

Kat looked up as red icons blossomed to life on the display. Vortexes. Twenty-seven vortexes. Her eyes narrowed as a sizable enemy fleet flowed into the system, its escorts fanning out and launching probes to scan for cloaked ships. She'd hoped they'd drop out of hyperspace closer to Perfuma itself, even though current circumstances did work in her favor in some ways. She'd have more time to prepare her fleet for the coming engagement.

"Send the ready signal to Task Force Hammer," she ordered calmly. Perversely, she felt better. The universe had just become a great deal simpler. "And then tell the freighters to leave. They can meet us at the first waypoint."

"Aye, Admiral," Kitty said.

Kat nodded, then returned her attention to the enemy fleet. Two superdreadnought squadrons, unless one of them was composed of sensor decoys and drones. Not impossible, although it would be difficult to fake superdreadnoughts pumping out so many targeting pulses. The fleet was shaking down rapidly, as smoothly professional as it had been during the war. Kat felt her heart twist, knowing who was in command of the enemy fleet. William might not be facing her directly, not now, but his influence was clearly visible. *He* wouldn't have let aristocrats into high positions without making sure they knew what they were doing.

And he would have been right, Kat thought. She wished William had stayed on Asher Dales, where he'd be out of the civil war. *If he wasn't on the other side . . .*

"Admiral, they're demanding our surrender," Kitty said. "They want a reply within five minutes."

"I'm sure they do," Kat said. "Signal the fleet. We'll depart as planned."

She ran through the tactical problem one final time. William, or whoever was *really* in command, would try to trap her against the planet. Good tactics, except he'd come out of hyperspace too far from the planet to make that possible. She had more than enough time to power up her vortex generators and jump out of the system before he pinned her down. She wondered, idly, if he'd done that deliberately or if he'd merely decided to be careful. He had a two-to-one advantage, as far as he knew, but that wasn't enough to guarantee victory.

Our shortage of missiles might be a far more dangerous problem, she thought as the range continued to close. *And if he knows how little ammunition we have, he'll bring his ships into sprint-mode range.*

A low quiver ran through the superdreadnought. "Admiral, the fleet is ready," Kitty reported. "We can depart on your command."

"Then take us out," Kat ordered. "Let them see us leaving."

She waited, feeling the seconds ticking away. The enemy commander wouldn't expect her to stand and fight. He'd have smelled a rat if she'd tried. But he'd understand her launching missiles at long range for the honor of the flag, if nothing else, before she ran for her life. Funny how civilians thought it was cowardly to retreat if one was seriously outgunned. They wouldn't be amused if Kat simply retreated at once without firing a single shot.

And neither will the king, Kat thought tiredly. The smarter or more experienced representatives would understand, but the remainder would insist she'd *let* the House of Lords recapture Perfuma without a fight. *We need a victory or two before the coalition fragments completely.*

Her heart started to pound as the enemy fleet adjusted course. They'd be heading her off from open space if she didn't have access to hyperspace. A civilian might not realize that the trap was about as insubstantial as a politician's promise, but any military officer worthy of the name would. And that would make him a little overconfident, or desperate to bring his guns to bear on her before she escaped. William, or his subordinate, might not realize it, but she was luring him onto a predictable course.

"Missile range in seven minutes," Kitty reported. "Admiral?"

"Hold the course," Kat ordered. If things worked as planned, the enemy ships would get a bloody nose. If they didn't . . . she could always launch a barrage and jump into hyperspace before they retaliated. The move wouldn't sit well with her, but at least they'd know they'd been kissed. "Send the activation signal in five minutes."

"Aye, Admiral."

◆ ◆ ◆

William wasn't particularly surprised that Kat *hadn't* retreated into hyperspace the moment she'd got a good look at his hulls. Kat was no coward. She'd hate the idea of running without firing a shot, even though it was the logical thing to do. And her only real option, if she didn't want to run without firing a shot, was to force him into a long-range missile duel, one that offered her the greatest chance of hurting him without taking serious damage herself. William wasn't blind to the political aspects. If Kat had left a day ago, no one would have cared. Now she had to fight.

And yet, the thought—the certainty—that something was wrong kept nagging at him. Kat wasn't a predictable commander. She would understand his ships and their weaknesses as well as he did. She'd know how to take advantage of them. And that meant . . . either she was doing something she'd been ordered to do—unlikely—or she was up to something. But what?

He turned his attention to the near-space display. He'd launched hundreds of probes, enough to give the bean counters a heart attack when they realized how few units could be refurbished and put back into service. All worth it. The probes had quartered space, watching for cloaked or powered-down starships. They'd found nothing, save a pair of stealthed sensor platforms. William had taken sardonic pleasure in destroying both of them. And yet . . . he would almost have felt better if they *had* found something. It would have been better than the growing sense of unease . . .

"Admiral," Yagami said. "We'll enter missile range in one minute."

"Hold fire until they open fire, then launch a single salvo," William ordered. He doubted Kat would stick around, not when she was outgunned so badly. "Bring up the point defense and clear it to fire when the enemy missiles enter engagement range."

He frowned as the range fell, the last few seconds ticking away. Kat could have fired *now*, if she wished, relying on his ships to close the range for her. She could have snapped off a couple of salvos before he could have replied, then vanished . . . She wouldn't do much damage, but she'd make him look stupid.

I could talk to her, he thought as the display sparkled with red icons. *But who knows who else would overhear?*

"The enemy has opened fire," Yagami reported. "Missiles firing . . . now!"

The superdreadnought shuddered as she fired a single salvo, aimed into the teeth of enemy fire. William watched, morbidly certain that Kat was going to run. She had no choice, not unless she wanted to risk being run down and destroyed. She hadn't even fired a full salvo of missiles. Her stocks had to be low . . .

Alarms howled. "Admiral," Yagami snapped. Red icons appeared on the display, growing brighter and brighter as newcomers flowed into realspace. "Vortexes! Multiple vortexes! Behind us!"

William swore. "Rotate the fleet," he snapped. Suddenly *he* was outgunned. The enemy fleet was real. Had to be. There was no way to fake vortexes, not unless the king's people had somehow made a breakthrough that had been concealed from the rest of the navy. "Bring us about and open fire!"

But he knew, even as he issued the order, that it was too late.

CHAPTER SIXTEEN

Perfuma

Gotcha, Kat thought with a flash of vindictive glee.

The timing hadn't been quite perfect—she'd been a naval officer long enough to know that a plan that called for perfect timing was doomed to fail—but it had been close enough. The enemy fleet was suddenly caught between two fires, between her retreating fleet and two *more* superdreadnought squadrons that had appeared behind them. And the newcomers hadn't just come out from behind. They'd come out of hyperspace with enough speed to close the range within minutes. The crews would be vomiting on the decks, but that wouldn't matter. Their automatics could handle the engagement long enough to for them to recover.

"Reverse course," she ordered. "Bring us about and prepare to continue firing."

"Aye, Admiral," Kitty said.

Kat watched as Task Force Hammer slammed into the rear of the enemy fleet. The range was continuing to fall, making it harder for the enemy ships, their point defense focusing on her fleet, to react before it was too late. They'd deployed their ECM to deal with a threat from her, not from a threat *behind* them. They were well trained, she admitted coolly. They'd reacted well without a trace of panic, but it wasn't going to save them from a very bloody nose.

And an energy weapons engagement if they let the range fall too far, she thought. A low quiver ran through her superdreadnought, followed by a shudder as she emptied her missile tubes at the enemy fleet. *They can afford to replace their losses. Do they know it?*

She frowned. The enemy fleet had lost its edge, but could still do immense damage to her fleet if it was prepared to soak up the losses and risk total destruction. Cold logic suggested it should do just that, despite the cost. And yet, she doubted anyone on the other side would be comfortable with fighting a war of attrition. She chuckled at the thought, feeling another quiver running through the ship. It didn't matter what they were comfortable doing. They *were* fighting a war of attrition.

"Our missiles are entering their engagement envelope," Kitty reported. "They've improved their point defense from our last engagement."

Kat watched as the enemy fleet pushed its escorts forward to absorb the missiles. Their point defense had definitely improved, the result of better training and drilling rather than new technology. She *hoped* it was the result of better training. She knew enough about the more fantastical ideas the engineers and researchers had devised to be seriously worried about the prospect of some of them coming out of their heads and into the real world. The House of Lords would be throwing all the money they could at the Next Generation Weapons program. They needed a silver bullet as much as anyone else.

And you have a choice, she thought, addressing the enemy commander as his missiles started to tear into her formation. *Are you going to risk a close-range encounter, are you going to widen the range, or . . . are you going to do nothing and let me make the choice for you?*

She waited. She'd been careful to allow the enemy room to retreat, to *run*, if they were smart enough to see it. The king would complain if he realized what she'd done, but he'd understand that she didn't dare risk a close-range engagement if it could be avoided. The enemy commander had to see this, didn't he? Or would he be afraid to run?

He might think I've mined that section of space. Unlikely—she hadn't bothered to even try, given how useless mines were outside planetary orbits and shipping lanes—but she'd already pulled off one surprise. *Or his superiors might be very un-understanding.*

Her eyes narrowed. *And if he doesn't move soon, he'll be doomed whatever he does. And he might take me down with him.*

♦ ♦ ♦

William felt as if he'd been punched in the belly, hard. All made sense now. The enemy had brought three superdreadnought squadrons to the party, not just one. And they'd hidden two of the squadrons until they could catch him with his pants down. They'd caught him . . . He thought he heard Scott making an obscene remark, a scatological observation that encompassed just how badly he'd been tricked. If Admiral Rudbek had given him the third squadron . . .

He shoved the thought to one side as the range continued to close. His point defense crews were working wonders, but the damage was starting to mount rapidly. Through sheer luck, the enemy was concentrating on his superdreadnoughts, ignoring the smaller ships unless they got in their way. The superdreadnoughts could take the battering for the moment. That would soon start to change. Alerts were already flashing up in front of him.

And they're going to close the range until they're practically touching us, William thought. An engagement at point-blank range would probably end in mutual destruction . . . or it would if he wasn't outgunned. *They used our own goddamned StarComs against us.*

"Order the fleet to alter course," he said as he traced a line on the display. He'd made a second mistake when he'd reversed course, surrendering the chance to run the first enemy fleet down. There was no point in trying to regain the position now. The incoming ships had a huge speed advantage. "We're breaking for deep space."

Yagami swallowed. "Aye, Admiral."

The superdreadnought rocked as two missiles punched through the point defense and slammed into the shields. William caught his breath, noting that the enemy ships were firing antimatter warheads. They must be desperate. Using nukes so close to a planet was bad enough, but antimatter. *Perfuma I didn't have any defenses left, damn it.* A single antimatter-tipped warhead striking the planet could do untold damage. Kat had to be mad to take the risk. Or maybe the king ordered it.

He braced himself as the fleet slowly started to alter course. The enemy ships altered theirs too, but for once his fleet had a slight advantage. The enemy ships would find it harder to alter course before they rushed past his fleet and the range started to open again. He briefly considered powering up the vortex generators and popping back into hyperspace, conceding a defeat he knew had become inevitable unless reinforcements appeared out of nowhere, which he knew wasn't going to happen, but there were some advantages to prolonging the engagement. Forcing the enemy ships to shoot themselves dry would make the *next* counteroffensive far more likely to succeed.

Another missile struck the ship. "Rear shields weakening," a voice snapped. "Rotate shield harmonics to compensate!"

"Admiral," Yagami said. "This ship appears to be being targeted specifically."

"That could be a problem," William said. Command ships weren't supposed to be easy to spot, but many of his enemies had served in the navy, the *same* navy, as long as he had. They'd probably know which ships were configured as flagships, if they couldn't pick out the subtle point defense patterns that suggested some vessels were more important than others. "Warn Commodore Green that command may devolve on him at any moment."

155

"Aye, Admiral," Yagami said.

William nodded, watching grimly as the range closed . . . and then, slowly, started to open again. The three enemy squadrons looked as if they planned to concentrate their forces before trying to run him down, although he knew that might be an illusion. Kat's original force was well behind the other two, chasing William with slightly less enthusiasm. William had to smile, even though he knew the situation wasn't funny. Kat didn't want to chase him too enthusiastically, or she might wind up catching him. That would be awkward if she really was short of missiles.

He kept his thoughts to himself as the tactical situation gradually became more predictable. The range was starting to steady, allowing both sides to engage with missiles and, at the same time, swat enemy missiles out of space as they made their approach. He was tempted to retreat now, but his calculation hadn't changed. As long as losses remained fairly even there was something to be said for making them expend their missiles. Or dragging them out of position. He kept a wary eye on the near-space display. Had Kat run out of tricks? She certainly wasn't trying to do more than drive him back out of the system.

"The enemy ships are falling back," Yagami reported. "I think they're running out of ammunition."

". . . Maybe," William said. He knew better than to believe it, not completely. Any naval officer worthy of the name would be careful to keep some missiles in reserve. "Let the range continue to open."

The enemy fire started to slacken, as if they'd given up hope of running him down. They probably had, unless they were willing to risk using hyperspace to dodge around his position and come at him from the front. It *was* possible, but coordination would be a pain in the ass, and there would be no way to keep him from seeing the maneuver coming. And then he'd either detonate warheads in hyperspace or simply flee himself. He already knew there was no prospect of completing his orders, not until he received reinforcements. The battle was, at best, a draw.

And we'll be leaving her in possession of the system, he mused. That was irritating, even if he knew she'd never get to keep it. *The PR guys are going to have to work hard to spin that into a victory.*

He pushed the idea aside—coming up with lies to tell the population was their problem, not his—and started to assess his options. There was little point in lurking around the system, harassing shipping and generally making life difficult for the inhabitants. Perfuma had never joined the Colonial Alliance, even when it had been a perfectly legitimate political organization. Harassing the locals would be worse than merely petty and pointless. It would be targeting people who were supposed to be on his side. He was sure the Rudbeks would have a lot to say about that, when they found out . . . That was their problem too. He had other concerns.

"Order the fleet to jump into hyperspace on my command," he said. "We'll regroup at Point Sigma."

A low rustle ran around the giant compartment as the operators heard the command. They didn't like the thought of retreating, even though there was little choice. They'd assumed all the precautions he'd worked into the operational plans were nothing more than paranoia, professional ass-covering by an officer who knew few would come to his aid if he fumbled an engagement or lost a battle. They'd been wrong. All contingencies had to be considered, at least. Even outright defeat . . .

War is a democracy, he reminded himself sternly. *The enemy always gets a vote.*

"Aye, sir," Yagami said. There was a pause as he keyed commands into the console. "The fleet is ready to jump."

William nodded, stiffly. He hated to admit defeat, even though . . . No, there was no point in lying to himself. A man who believed his own lies was a man doomed to certain defeat when reality—inconvenient reality—finally had its day. He'd lost the engagement. He'd have to wait and see if he'd lost his post and career as well.

"Take us into hyperspace," he ordered quietly. "And then to Point Sigma."

"Aye, Admiral," Yagami said.

◆ ◆ ◆

"Admiral," Kitty said. "The enemy fleet is leaving the system."

"So it seems," Kat mused. She'd united her fleet, but she was painfully aware just how close she was to running out of ammunition. "Order the fleet to return to the planet."

"Aye, Admiral," Kitty said. "They'll be back, won't they?"

"I have no doubt of it," Kat said. William, or whoever was in command of the enemy fleet, would have brought supporting elements, if not an entire fleet train, with him. They'd be lurking a light-year or two from Perfuma, completely undetectable. William would repair and reload his ships, then return for round two. "Once the fleet has returned to the high orbitals, order them to complete stripping the planet of anything useful. I want all freighters, save for the fleet train, to be loaded and ready to go within twelve hours."

Kitty looked unsurprised by the command. "Aye, Admiral."

And we'll be lucky if we have time to take everything we need, Kat thought sourly. Kitty didn't realize it, but twelve hours wasn't anything like long enough to loot the planet of everything she wanted. *We barely have time to take the stockpiled supplies, and they're already in orbit.*

She leaned back in her chair, thinking hard. The king *had* ordered her to take prisoners, important prisoners, if possible. He'd probably be delighted if she snatched Kevin Rudbek and transported him to Caledonia. But . . . She shook her head. She didn't want the bastard on her ship. And the part of her that remembered him being kind to her didn't want to hand him over to Hadrian either. God knew what would happen if she carted him to Caledonia. The king probably didn't know himself.

"We'll pull out in twelve hours, even if the freighters aren't loaded," she said. She essayed a joke. "I think we've outstayed our welcome."

She pulled up the first reports and skimmed them, noting what had worked and what hadn't. She'd hoped to do more than merely damage a handful of enemy superdreadnoughts, but whoever was in command had done a good job at taking the opening she'd offered him and retreating in a timely fashion. She knew she should be grateful, even though there were people on Caledonia who'd accuse her of letting the enemy ships run. There'd be enough truth in their statements that she'd have real problems refuting them. It didn't matter. They'd won a planet, looted the planet, and chased away an enemy fleet. Not a complete victory, but it wasn't an utter disaster either.

Her fleet had coped well, she noted. She'd lost a handful of smaller ships, but the superdreadnoughts remained intact and largely undamaged. The real problem lay in ammunition supplies. They were terrifyingly short of missiles. The fleet train would resupply one of her squadrons, just one. And then . . . she'd have to go back to Caledonia to rearm. A major headache. She was morbidly sure the House of Lords was working on plans to take out the king's supply depots and industrial nodes.

They've probably already written off the industrial nodes, Kat thought. She knew her people. The sunk cost fallacy had probably run its course. There was no way they'd recover the nodes or the money used to build them, not now. And if they realized it, they'd set out to *destroy* the nodes. *They'll probably hit us as soon as possible, just to knock our morale back down after this victory.*

"We're returning to orbit," Kitty said. "Governor Rudbek is trying to call you."

"Ignore him," Kat said curtly. She didn't want to talk to Kevin Rudbek. She wanted to enjoy her victory as long as possible. And the more she talked to him, the more she'd want to arrest the older man and take him to the king. "And make it clear to his subordinates that resistance will draw severe punishment."

She felt a flicker of pity for the midlevel managers, caught between the guns and the will of their superiors, then shrugged. Duke Rudbek was a tight-fisted bastard, if rumor was to be believed, but he wasn't *stupid*. Very few of the high-ranking aristocrats were stupid, although they were self-interested. She didn't think he'd punish his people for surrendering when surrender was the only viable option. They'd turn on him if he did. Hadrian might find supporters in the oddest of places.

Or they'll try to seek work somewhere else, she mused. *It doesn't really matter.*

Kat studied the starchart for a moment, thinking hard. There was no way she could try to keep Perfuma, not now. The next offensive would kick her out, if it didn't destroy her. She was tempted to head straight back to Caledonia but hated the thought of just leaving without taking advantage of being so close to Tyre. A fleet of superdreadnoughts in their backyard would concentrate their minds on her, rather than plotting war against Caledonia. And yet, where should she go?

She stroked her chin. There were several possible options for her next target, of varying levels of economic importance. The *really* big targets were too heavily defended for her to hit, not unless she was prepared to soak up immense damage herself as she pressed the offensive into the teeth of enemy fire. She couldn't, not unless she wanted to shorten the war. There was only one real exception, and they'd know it as well as she did. Rosebud. It would make a suitable target, but . . . they'd know it would make a suitable target. They'd expect her. And even if they didn't, they'd react fast once they knew where she was. That would bring their fleet after her as surely as . . .

Her lips curved into a smile. She could use that, if she was careful. And even if they refused to take the bait, she might just come out ahead.

CHAPTER SEVENTEEN

Interstellar Space, Near Perfuma

"You failed in your duty."

William stood in the holochamber, hands clasped behind his back, and listened to Grand Admiral Rudbek's rant. Behind him, Duke Rudbek and Duke Peter's images stood and listened too. They looked slightly blurry, as if the StarCom link was too weak to sustain a proper image. William wondered if someone was quietly arranging a communications breakdown. There should be enough bandwidth, even here, to hold a real-time conversation.

"You allowed yourself to be tricked and driven back out of the system," Grand Admiral Rudbek said. "And now you dare ask for *reinforcements?*"

William said nothing. It was a law of nature that shit rolled downhill. The duke had probably given Grand Admiral Rudbek a bollocking to end all bollockings, which the admiral was now passing down to his subordinate. William kept his face impassive, even though it was irritating to be lectured like a naughty boy. Grand Admiral Rudbek was, in many ways, more vulnerable than William himself. He had a great deal more to lose.

"You lost the engagement," the Grand Admiral continued. "The king is laughing at us, even now! We look like fools!"

"I doubt it," William said. Kat had probably sent word back to Caledonia immediately, but it was unlikely the king and his PR specialists had had time to turn a minor skirmish into the greatest naval victory in history. They'd need a few hours, at least, to come up with a narrative that sounded convincing. The House of Lords had plenty of time to devise a counternarrative of its own. "The king knows it was just a limited victory."

"But we were still defeated," Grand Admiral Rudbek snapped. "Why should we not relieve you of command for gross incompetence?"

William felt his temper flare. Accusations of everything from procolonial sentiment to outright treason he could ignore, but accusations of naked incompetence were something altogether different. He had to protect his reputation as an experienced naval officer, particularly if he wanted to remain in the service after the war. Asher Dales might not want him back if he resigned a second time . . .

"First, our intelligence stated that there was only one enemy superdreadnought squadron at Perfuma," William said coolly. Kat had clearly played a shell game with her limited squadrons, ensuring that any watching eyes didn't realize she'd taken three squadrons to Perfuma. "And second, I *did* request a third squadron of my own. If the postbattle analysis is accurate"—he picked a random datapad off his desk and held it up dramatically—"three superdreadnought squadrons on *our* side would have tipped the odds in our favor."

"You don't know that," Grand Admiral Rudbek said. His voice was icy. William had shifted the charge of incompetence squarely onto his shoulders. "Your forces and *hers*"—he glanced at Duke Peter—"would have been evenly matched."

"I think we would have had the edge," William said. "Kat—Admiral Falcone—was careful to leave us a way out, a way to escape, rather than closing the range dramatically and seeking to utterly destroy us. I think she didn't want to risk running out of ammunition in an engagement that would have ended very badly for her, if she actually *did*. She wanted to give us a bloody nose, not go for our throats."

"Which she did," Duke Peter observed neutrally. "Whatever the realities of the situation, the truth is that the defeat will make us look weak. Again."

Public perception doesn't matter, William thought, although he knew it wasn't true. The colonials wouldn't—couldn't—desert the king as long as it seemed possible he'd claw a victory from the jaws of defeat. *We're still holding our own.*

"Right now, my ships are rearming," he said, putting the thought to one side. "Given a few hours, my crews will be rested and ready to return to Perfuma. This time we know what we face. We can engage Admiral Falcone in a long-range duel that will force her to either expend missiles she cannot afford to lose or retreat at once, surrendering the system without a fight. Either way, sir, we win."

"Unless she has a *fourth* squadron lurking in cloak," Grand Admiral Rudbek said. "We cannot risk another defeat."

"Then we need to start discussing terms of surrender," William said. "We will not win the war unless we take a few risks. Kat took a risk, and it paid off for her."

"Yes." Grand Admiral Rudbek glared at him. "And yet, you want reinforcements?"

"A third superdreadnought squadron would be very helpful," William said. "If nothing else, it would show our commitment to Perfuma."

Duke Rudbek nodded stiffly. "One will be dispatched," he said. "And victory will be assured."

Or you'll be for the high jump, William finished. The duke shouldn't be moving starships around the galaxy like pieces on his personal chessboard. Technically, he should have given orders to Grand Admiral Rudbek, who would forward them to the squadron's CO . . . He dismissed the thought. The chain of command was already tangled beyond easy repair. Something they'd have to fix after the war. *If we lose, it won't matter.*

"We'll have equal numbers of ships and more ammunition," William said. "We should have the edge."

"And if there are *more* enemy superdreadnought squadrons orbiting Perfuma?" Grand Admiral Rudbek didn't look convinced. "You might suffer a second defeat."

"If there are, then Caledonia is dangerously exposed," William pointed out. "I'm surprised she managed to get *three* superdreadnought squadrons assigned to her fleet. The king can hardly risk uncovering his capital, not when we could attack at any moment."

"We could," Duke Peter mused. "If we attacked Caledonia instead of Perfuma . . ."

"The king would see our ships leave and know what we had in mind," William told him. "And Kat would have plenty of time to return to Caledonia to command the defense."

Duke Peter nodded. "Very well," he said. "Recover Perfuma as soon as possible."

Grand Admiral Rudbek appeared to be irked. "And when you return home, we need to discuss further offensive measures," he said. "We can't keep reacting and reacting until we run out of ships. Or they run out of targets."

"Yes, sir," William said, resisting the urge to point out that plans for taking the offensive already existed. They were just waiting for the admiral and his political superiors to give them their blessing. "We can discuss that when I return home."

"Come back with a victory or don't come back at all," Grand Admiral Rudbek said. "Good luck."

The holographic images vanished. An icon popped up, informing William that the communications link had been terminated. William let out a long breath, wondering just how long it had been since Grand Admiral Rudbek had stood on the command deck of a starship. Years, at least. He'd served during the war, but William didn't recall ever meeting him. It proved nothing, he supposed, yet . . . Grand Admiral Rudbek had clearly forgotten everything he'd known about dealing with subordinates, sounding more like a bad actor than a serving military officer.

And he is under a lot of pressure, William reminded himself. *The shit he dumped on me is probably a tiny percentage of the shit that got dropped on him. He needed to look tough in front of his superior.*

He keyed his terminal. "Commander Yagami, dispatch two destroyers to Perfuma to keep an eye on the enemy fleet," he ordered. "Inform them that they are to send a burst signal through the StarCom—if it's still in operation—if anything changes."

"Aye, sir," Yagami said.

"And order the crews to expedite the rearming," William continued. "I want to return to Perfuma as soon as possible."

"Aye, sir."

William closed the connection, then brought up the starchart. The fleet was holding position a few light-months from Perfuma. They might as well be on the other side of the galaxy, as far as Kat's sensors were concerned. She might reason, correctly, that William wouldn't have run that far, but it wouldn't matter. The entire fleet was nothing more than grains of sand drifting in the sea of stars. The odds of her finding them were so tiny that they were practically beyond calculation. She would know better than even to try.

Unless some unhelpful soul decides to spill the beans. If the king has agents on the fleet . . .

He shook his head. The fleet was in lockdown. No messages would be going back home, let alone elsewhere, until they won the battle or returned to Tyre. If the king had agents on his ship, they were impotent. They'd be keeping their heads down, waiting for a chance to do real harm or simply hoping their previous allegiance would go unnoticed. The king might have convinced most of the colonials that he hadn't started the Theocratic War, but it would be harder for any of the loyalists to cling to the delusion. The evidence was on all the major news channels.

Which are owned by the big corporations, which are owned by the House of Lords. Not everyone takes everything they say for granted.

Not that it matters, his own thoughts answered him. *There's work to be done.*

◆ ◆ ◆

"We took a single hit, Captain," Commander Remus said. "But it did considerable damage to Fusion Two."

Sarah nodded as she took the datapad. She'd taken *Merlin* out of the line of battle as soon as the enemy fleet retreated, giving her crew time to assess and repair the damage. But it looked as if the damage couldn't be repaired, not outside a major shipyard. The enemy had known precisely where to target her ship for maximum damage. A single laser warhead had sliced into her hull, blasted through the armor, and nearly destroyed a fusion core. The hell of it was that she knew she'd been lucky. If the hit had been elsewhere, the resulting explosion could have blown her ship to atoms.

"We can just jury-rig a replacement," Mr. Soto said. "Can't we?"

"No," Sarah said shortly. She skimmed the report. "There's no way we can jury-rig a fusion core. We'll be lucky if we can dismantle and remove the wreckage without taking the ship into a shipyard."

She looked at Commander Remus. "Order them to shut the remainder of the core down completely, then isolate it from the power grid. We'll have to see if we can get a replacement when we go home."

"They should have one in stock," Commander Remus said. "It isn't as if we have to worry about cutting through the armor."

Sarah gave him a sharp look. They'd patched the gash in the hull as best as they could, but . . . She gritted her teeth in irritation. The gash was too big for her peace of mind—it would be one hell of a target if the enemy realized what they'd done—and yet too small for anything helpful. They'd have to widen the gash just to transport the remains of Fusion Two out of the ship and then install the replacement before they resealed the armor plating and returned to the line of battle. The process would have been a pain even during the last war, when there'd been no shortage of replacements and repair facilities. Now . . .

"You can start drawing up repair plans," she said. "And hope we can get it done before we have to go back into battle."

Mr. Soto looked puzzled. "I thought you could fly this ship with one fusion core."

"You can, in theory," Sarah acknowledged. "But you'd be in trouble if you lost more than one."

She scowled as she skimmed the rest of the report. Thirty-seven dead, nineteen injured . . . three likely to die, unless they received urgent medical attention the moment they were pulled out of the stasis tubes. Sarah felt a pang of guilt for not knowing the dead crewmen, for not feeling anything when she scanned the list of dead, wounded, and missing names. She was their commanding officer. It was her duty to say something about them when the crew bid farewell to the dead. But what could she say?

The remainder of the fleet wasn't in any better state, if scuttle-butt was to be trusted. The enemy had concentrated their fire on the superdreadnoughts, giving them a beating that had pushed even *their* point defense and armor to the limits. Admiral Falcone hadn't lost a single superdreadnought, but four were heavily damaged and almost all were out of ammunition. Sarah knew she was short on ammunition too. *Merlin* most likely wouldn't be rearmed, not when there were so many other ships that had shot themselves dry. One more victory like that would leave the fleet practically defenseless, unable to fight. If the enemy realized how few missiles remained, surely they'd move to attack . . .

Her wristcom bleeped. "Captain," Lieutenant Honshu said. "We have our orders from the flag."

"Good," Sarah said. She resisted the urge to snap at him. "And what *are* our orders?"

A hint of embarrassment shaded the younger man's tone. "We're to escort the freighters to Caledonia, along with most of the fleet," Lieutenant Honshu said. "And we're to avoid engagement along the way."

Good thinking, Sarah thought. The fleet was in no state for a second engagement. *We have to get home and make repairs before the hammer comes down.*

Mr. Soto frowned. "We're not going to keep this world?"

"It's pointless," Sarah said. A dozen arguments rose to her lips. She focused on the simplest, the one that might make sense even to him. "When the enemy ships return, and they will, they'll kick us out and recover the world anyway. We might as well leave on our terms."

She keyed the wristcom. "Inform the flag that we'll be ready," she ordered. "I'll be on the bridge shortly."

"It still feels odd to just walk away," Mr. Soto mused. "We could stay and fight . . ."

"And then we'd lose," Sarah said flatly. She was too tired, too damn tired, to mind her words. "Our ships are damaged. We're running out of supplies. And our crews need a rest before they plunge back into battle. Morale is low"—*Partly because of you*, her thoughts added silently—"even though we won the engagement. We cannot afford another victory on such terms."

She turned away, not caring to meet his eyes a moment longer. "Commander, I'll see you on the bridge," she said. "If they realize we're leaving, they'll do something about it. I want to be ready."

"Aye, Captain," Remus said.

◆ ◆ ◆

William braced himself as the superdreadnought squadrons plunged through the vortex and appeared, once again, in the Perfuma System. The reports from the pickets had been clear—the enemy fleet had packed up and departed en masse. He hadn't been sure he believed it. Kat was smart enough to know that retreat was the only sensible move, yet it would have been out of character for her *not* to look for a way to hurt her foes. Still the display was blank. The enemy fleet appeared to have dropped into hyperspace and vanished.

Curious, he mused as the fleet launched probes in all directions. *They appear to have departed, without even bothering to bombard the orbital facilities.*

"Admiral," Yagami said. He looked up, his face stoic. "The planetary governor would like to talk to you."

I bet he would, William thought. *But do I want to talk to him?*

"Inform him that we can chat after the system is secure," he ordered. The display kept updating, revealing a handful of asteroid settlements and powered-down interplanetary transports. There were no cloaked ships, as far as he could tell. "Right now, we have too many other problems."

He frowned as more and more reports appeared in front of him. Perfuma II had been untouched, save for a single brief visit that had been aimed more at collecting intelligence and spreading propaganda than stealing supplies and looting the planet. He supposed it made a certain kind of sense: Perfuma I belonged to the Rudbeks, but Perfuma II was technically independent, although he was surprised that someone in desperate straits was prepared to leave the planet alone. Perhaps Hadrian was looking to the future or . . . perhaps Kat simply didn't have the freighters to loot the planet. She might have made a virtue out of necessity.

"Admiral, the system is secure," Yagami reported. "There's no trace of the enemy fleet. They ran."

"They left before we could return," William corrected. It hadn't been a glorious victory. It hadn't really been a victory at all. The PR specialists could lie their heads off until their pants caught fire, but propaganda wouldn't make any difference. Both sides would know the truth, no matter what spin they put on the story. "They didn't make us fight for the system."

He let out a sigh. "Inform Tyre that we have reoccupied Perfuma," he said, even though they hadn't taken the system by force. He rather suspected the official statements would be a little more exciting. "And that the enemy fleet has escaped."

"Aye, sir," Yagami said. The display brightened as the fleet stood down from red alert. "Do you want to speak to the governor now?"

I suppose I should, William thought. He didn't *want* to speak to the governor, but he didn't have a choice. The man would probably complain if William kept fobbing him off. *And I hope he won't expect me to make a courtesy call.*

"I'll speak to him in my office," he said, standing. "Give me a moment, then put him through."

"Aye, sir."

CHAPTER EIGHTEEN

CALEDONIA

Ambassador Francis Villeneuve looked around with interest as he was shown into the king's private chambers. He'd visited the palace before, during his earlier discussions with Hadrian's representatives, but it was the first time he'd been invited into the innermost sections and asked to make himself at home. He was too experienced an ambassador to take all he was seeing at face value—the king's people would do everything in their power to project the impression they wanted to project—but he knew what to look for. The real story was all around him if he could tease it out.

He kept his face impassive as they walked past a pair of holographic displays, both showing images from the front. Mighty fleets were moving through space, clashing with a thunder to shake the stars themselves . . . Red arrows glided from system to system, showing known and projected enemy movements. Francis was fairly sure most of them were fictional, planned, or predicted offensives at best, but it was impossible to be sure. The Commonwealth was the first interstellar power to fight and win a full-scale war. To have two such wars in the space of five years struck him as careless, at the very least. But then, the results of the last war had laid the groundwork for the current conflict.

The king rose as Francis was escorted into his office, extending a hand in greeting. Francis shook it gravely, noting how the king had been carefully taught to comport himself in a manner befitting a senior politician. His handshake was firm but not *too* firm, perfectly crafted to say that he was strong, that he was greeting Francis as an equal, without putting Francis down in any way. It would have been impressive if Francis hadn't known the trick. The king was good at presenting himself. Francis wondered, grimly, just how far that talent would actually go if the war went against him. There were already stresses and strains pervading the king's coalition. Francis knew, even if Hadrian didn't, that there were colonials looking for a way out before it was too late.

"You know my wife, of course," the king said.

Francis nodded, bowing to Princess Drusilla. *Queen* Drusilla now, he supposed. She was beautiful, her exotic face strikingly different. It was meaningless, in a day and age where everything from skin and eye color to gender itself was mutable, but her features were still a reminder that Drusilla wasn't from the Commonwealth. She'd escaped the Theocracy shortly before the war. Francis knew Drusilla wasn't popular on Tyre. Xenophobia or something else, something more understandable? A person couldn't grow up under a theocratic system without picking up a *lot* of bad habits.

"Charmed," he said. It didn't matter. He had his orders. "My congratulations on your recent victory."

"I thank you." The king looked and sounded as if he'd won the victory himself rather than remaining on Caledonia while Kat Falcone fought a battle on his behalf. "It is merely the first of many."

"Quite." Francis kept his opinion of *that* to himself. He had never claimed to be a military expert, but he was fairly sure that the Battle of Perfuma was little more than a minor skirmish in the grand scheme of things. The Battle of Cadiz had been fought on a much bigger scale, with much more at stake. "My government has considered your proposal."

The king leaned forward, slightly. Very slightly. Francis frowned, inwardly. Was Hadrian betraying his eagerness or . . . or was he trying to give that impression? There was no way to be sure. The king had grown up in a snake pit, where the slightest mistake could have cost him his crown, trust fund, and political power. Perhaps *that* was why he'd married Drusilla. She'd grown up in a snake pit too. And they'd both been at risk of being married off to people they hadn't chosen for themselves . . .

And yet, his people really don't like her, Francis mused. *There might be a better reason for that than simple bigotry.*

He put the thought aside. It wasn't his problem. "We are prepared to meet your demands for ammunition," he said. "In exchange, we want two sets of concessions from you."

The king's face became a blank mask, although he had to know what Francis's superiors wanted. He'd been following the negotiations very closely, even when he hadn't been personally involved. Francis would have been astonished if the king didn't know. The discussions had gone backwards and forwards for weeks, but the goalposts hadn't moved more than a millimeter in either direction. And the time for talking was nearly over.

We have to secure the concessions before the king becomes strong enough to tell us to go to hell, he reminded himself, *or weak enough that he can no longer give us what we want.*

"First, we want the technical plans and specifications you promised us," Francis said. They were less important than the king believed—knowing that something was possible was halfway to figuring out how to do it—but it might be better to keep the king thinking otherwise. He'd be more reassured if he thought the gap between the Commonwealth and its rivals was insurmountable, at least in the next few years. "We want them delivered to us within the next few days, so we can courier them to the border."

The king nodded, curtly. Francis wondered just how much Hadrian actually knew. Did he realize his government was in serious trouble? Was he thinking so hard about the future that he was ignoring the present? Or was he simply rolling the dice, again and again, convinced that it was the only way to keep ahead of his enemies? Francis believed the story about the king planning the Theocratic War, deliberately giving his enemies a chance to launch a strike against the Commonwealth. The plan was insane, but very in-character for a man who didn't think he could *really* lose.

Not that it matters, Francis thought. *All that matters is that the king prolongs the war.*

"Second, we want title to the nine border systems, as detailed in our last set of notes." Francis removed a datachip from his pocket and placed it on the table. He didn't think the king had lost the notes, but it was important to deprive him of a psychological buffer. "The systems are to be handed to us as soon as possible, once our ships are in position to take possession. They will become part of our sphere of influence from that moment."

"You think they *want* you?" Drusilla leaned forward, her dark eyes alight with something Francis couldn't place. "They're *Commonwealth* worlds."

Francis looked back at her evenly. "Does their opinion really matter?"

The king said nothing for a long moment. Francis wondered what was going through the mind behind his too-handsome face. He wasn't a fool, for all that he'd started a war to keep the power he'd obtained by deception. He had to know that conceding the border worlds would risk another conflict, either a civil war within the Commonwealth or a later interstellar war with Marseilles. And it wasn't as if he didn't already have a civil war. But he had very little choice. The enemy had most of the cards. If he didn't find a way to even the odds, he'd be in deep shit when their fleet came to Caledonia and took the remaining cards. He needed to sell out the border worlds to keep his cause alive.

"You will permit anyone who wants to leave to do so," the king said finally. "And you will make sure they *can* do so."

"Of course," Francis said. Human capital was important, but not important enough to risk starting an insurgency by preventing people from leaving. Besides, it wasn't easy to force a rebellious population to do more than sullenly tolerate outside rule. The Theocracy had found itself fighting a constant series of small wars just to keep its early conquests under control. "We want the systems themselves. The population can leave, if they wish."

He leaned back in his chair. The populace would be unhappy, but their opinions didn't matter. Their *worlds* didn't matter, not really. Marseilles wanted the systems and the resources within them, the gas giants and asteroid belts and rocky airless worlds. The inhabited worlds could be left alone, if the population refused to either leave or accept the new order. Who knew? A few decades of investment and they might become productive and loyal citizens. The Commonwealth hadn't done enough to keep them loyal.

"And you will formally recognize me as ruler of the Commonwealth," the king said. "That's the only way the territory transfer can be considered legal."

Francis schooled his face into immobility. "We cannot take that step, not yet," he said. "While we would *prefer* to see you as the ruler, the blunt truth is that you do not rule the entire Commonwealth. We cannot avoid dealing with your enemies as long as they wield power. Nor can we deny them recognition. There's nothing to be gained by pretending you wield complete authority when you don't."

The king looked displeased, a flicker of frustration glimmering through his mask. Francis didn't blame him, but he knew the score. Countless diplomatic missions had been useless—worse than useless, all too often—because they'd talked to governments that didn't wield any real power. It was frighteningly easy for someone who talked a good game to claim they were the one true government, a pretense that could suck in blood and treasure before the truth came out. Francis didn't *like* dealing with unfriendly or unpleasant governments, but as long as they were the ones in charge and no one was prepared to remove them, there was no way to avoid it.

And there are worse governments out there, he reminded himself. The king was civilized enough, thankfully, not to harm ambassadors. The Theocracy hadn't been so polite. *You could have been assigned to that hellhole before the war.*

"You will receive your plans by the end of the day," the king said. "When can we expect our supplies?"

"In two weeks," Francis assured him. "The convoy is already on its way."

The king nodded stiffly. He'd probably hoped to get the supplies at once, but . . . the realities of interstellar shipping rendered such a feat impossible, even if Francis had been willing to oblige. It wouldn't do to give the king a chance to renege on the deal. God knew the colonials wouldn't be pleased when they heard what he'd done. Francis would have preferred to insist on occupying the border worlds at once, but . . . it wouldn't do to accidentally blow the king's coalition out of the water either. A civil war within the civil war would lead to certain defeat, once the House of Lords stopped laughing. And then there'd be no hope of securing the border worlds without triggering another full-scale conflict.

"I'll formally surrender the border stars once the convoy arrives," the king told him. "I trust that will be suitable?"

"Quite suitable." Francis smiled thinly. "Our forces should be in position to take possession by then."

He had to fight to keep his concern from showing on his face. In theory, the Commonwealth, no matter who won the civil war, should be in no position to recover the border stars. In practice, there was no way to be sure what they'd do. The House of Lords might swallow the loss, taking advantage of their victory to blame everything on the king, or they might go to war to recover them. And the king himself would come under immense pressure, if he won the war, to go back on his agreement. The treaty they were about to sign might just be the start of a chain of events that would lead, eventually, to mayhem.

"The formal treaty will be signed when the convoy arrives," he said. This would give his government a chance to think better of it, particularly once the technical specifications were in their possession. "And then we'll stake our claim."

"Good," the king said.

Francis felt a flash of pity, mingled with contempt and a sobering awareness that the king had little choice. He *needed* foreign aid, even if that aid came with a whole string of—his lips quirked at the wordplay—strings attached. And yet, the price he had to pay for that aid might result in his defeat. Francis told himself that it wasn't his concern. The ultimate winner of the civil war wasn't important, not to him. All that mattered was getting what they wanted while the king was strong enough to give it to them and weak enough not to take it back.

And securing our position before the House of Lords wins the war, if they do win, Francis thought. *They're smart enough not to start a war they might lose.*

He stood. "Thank you for your time, Your Majesty," he said. He nodded, politely, to the princess. "I'll see you when the time comes to sign."

"Of course," the king said. "I look forward to it."

Francis kept his thoughts to himself as Sir Reginald Grantham showed him back to the landing pad, where his aircar was waiting. Lord Snow, the king's diplomat, hadn't been *that* closely involved in the negotiations. Francis wondered if that was a sign Snow disapproved of the planned treaty, or a simple bid by Sir Reginald to increase his power and position within the king's court. Francis had no doubt the king would destroy Sir Reginald in an instant if he failed to be as useful and accommodating as possible. Or if he needed a scapegoat. Lord Snow was too experienced a diplomat to leave his back bare to a superior who might need to put a knife in it at any moment.

Perhaps literally, he pondered as the aircar rose into the sky. *The more things change, the more they stay the same.*

He watched, dispassionately, as the streets below came into view. They were crowded with demonstrators, with pro- and anti-king mobs clashing violently despite the best efforts of policemen, security officers, and actual soldiers. Caledonia was under de facto martial law, according to the news broadcasts. Francis suspected that boded ill for Hadrian. The colonials were more used to hardship than his subjects, but they were also sensitive to assaults on their personal liberty. They'd fight to defend a person's right to be himself, even if they disliked the thought of whatever he wanted to do. And the king had impinged upon their liberties by putting troops on the streets.

The aircar landed neatly on the embassy roof. Francis stood, bid farewell to the driver, and walked through the door and through a maze of corridors until he reached his office. Admiral Giles Jacanas was already there, waiting for him. He held a small datapad in one hand.

"Perfuma has fallen, again," he said. "The official news broadcasts from Tyre claim that seventeen of the king's superdreadnoughts were destroyed and a further nine badly damaged."

Francis raised his eyebrows as he removed his jacket and passed it to his orderly. "Do you believe it?"

"I never believe anything I read in all the major news outlets," Jacanas said. "But it does seem clear that Perfuma has fallen. They wouldn't lie about something so easily checked."

"True." Francis poured himself a mug of coffee and sat down. "When did you get the word?"

"Thirty-odd minutes ago," Jacanas said. "You didn't want to be interrupted."

"Interesting," Francis said. "I wonder if the *king* knew, while he was talking to me."

"He might have," Jacanas said. He met Francis's eyes. "Do we still want to involve ourselves in this . . . scrabble?"

"We don't have a choice," Francis said. "There won't be a better chance to move the border dozens of light-years rimwards. You know as well as I do that we have to expand or die."

"You know as well as I do that our space isn't *small*," Jacanas countered. "We're not living on a single island with restricted living room. We're not living on a single world. It will take centuries to burn through our resources . . ."

Francis smiled. "I thought you understood the importance of moving the border closer to Tyre," he said. "And of making sure the Commonwealth doesn't become a serious threat."

"I do," Jacanas confirmed. "But it is also my duty to make sure you understand the implications. The *military* implications."

"Yes." Francis sipped his coffee. "Does losing Perfuma change things in any real sense?"

"Not unless the reports are accurate." Jacanas picked up a datapad. "But given that the combined navies of both sides in this war have been wiped out several times over, as far as the news broadcasts are concerned, I wouldn't put money on it."

"Probably not," Francis agreed. He waved his hand, dismissively. "It's in our interests to keep the civil war going as long as possible, as you know. And to make sure we're ready for the day when a winner finally emerges."

"And to fight a war with him," Jacanas said.

"Ideally, we won't have to fight," Francis said. "And if we look ready to fight, perhaps they'll refrain from calling our bluff."

"The king started a war with the Theocracy," Jacanas pointed out. "If you believe the news broadcasts, of course. We haven't been able to prove they're fakes, Your Excellency, nor have the locals. And if it is true . . . how do you know the king won't start a war with us?"

"I don't," Francis admitted. "But we don't have any other options. We must meddle."

He studied the chart for a long moment. "And if we do, and he does, we'll be in a much better position to fight."

CHAPTER NINETEEN

ROSEBUD

Manager Toni O'Brian knew little of the war and cared less.

The conflict didn't touch her, not really. Oh, she knew Perfuma had been attacked, and Perfuma was only five light-years from Rosebud, but she had more important concerns. The giant cluster of cloudscoops under her command belonged to the Cavendish Corporation, which was, despite being bailed out by its former peers, hovering permanently on the verge of bankruptcy. She wanted—needed—to show what she could do, if only to ensure she stayed employed if the corporation passed its interests in the system to one of its rivals. The bastards would kick her out or demote her if they thought she couldn't be useful.

She drifted in the heart of the command center, studying holographic displays as they flickered in and out of existence. She didn't really need to monitor them that closely, but she knew better than to leave her subordinates completely unsupervised. They were planning their own exits, she thought; they'd seek to find employment somewhere else, if they had a chance, or steal what they could from the corporation and go into business for themselves. There was never any shortage of demand for HE3. Everyone used it, from perfectly legal business and military installations to the underground gray and black economy. And yet, there was never any shortage of supply either. The cloudscoops under her command had rivals. She was gloomily aware that there was no way she could raise prices, not without being heavily undercut and outsold. She honestly didn't know how she was going to meet her quotas without cutting costs somewhere, but . . . where from? She'd already pared everything right down to the bone. Her crews were pulling double shifts and paying as little heed to safety regs as possible, and they were still running at a loss.

I should probably try to find a new job for myself, she thought. She hated the idea of looking elsewhere—there was no way she'd get such a high position somewhere else, not for several years at least—but there might be no other choice. She had loans to pay off if she wanted to stay legit. There were ways to hide, in the gray or black economy, but she'd never be able to go home again. *If they blame me for the losses and shortfalls, I won't get a job anywhere else.*

She rubbed her forehead, secretly glad she lived and worked in a zero-gravity environment. It made it so much easier to keep inspectors from poking around, although she'd be in real trouble if HQ realized just how scanty the inspections had actually been and sent a skilled team to conduct an audit. They wouldn't have to work hard to find an excuse to sack her, not once they saw how many regulations she'd quietly put to one side. Toni had no choice, but she knew the inspectors wouldn't understand. They were hidebound bureaucrats, idiots who had no real experience . . . or understanding of what they could and couldn't let slide. Toni did, damn it. She knew where she could cut corners without having it coming back to bite her on the ass. She'd made damn sure not to fiddle with the life-support systems or the sensor networks or . . .

An alarm rang through the compartment. Toni looked up as the displays flickered, showing the live feed from the military-grade observation platforms orbiting the gas giant. Two . . . no, *three* squadrons of superdreadnoughts were visible, one heading straight for the complex while the other two remained in high orbit. Toni blinked in shock, half convinced the sensors were seeing things. Rosebud wasn't an important system, not like the cluster of stars surrounding Tyre. They had nothing worth hitting, nothing that would draw an enemy fleet. Even the Theocracy hadn't raided the star during the early days of the war.

"Sound the alert," she yelled as the enemy ships drew closer. The superdreadnoughts were surrounded by smaller ships, cruisers and destroyers. Their powerful sensors burned through space. They were so powerful that they were disrupting her systems. "Raise them. Find out who they are."

She pulled herself to her webbing and strapped in as alarms howled through the giant complex. She had no illusions about their chances if the intruders opened fire. The complex was huge but fragile. A single hit would be enough to shatter the struts holding the nodes together and send them plunging into the gas giant's atmosphere—if it didn't kill them first. She snapped orders, commanding her crews to take the women and children—those she'd allowed to remain aboard—to the shuttles. They'd grumbled about her cutting costs by sending the remainder home a year ago, back when the universe had made sense, but she doubted anyone would be complaining now. In hindsight, it was starting to look like one of the best decisions she'd ever made.

"Order the beta crews to head to the shuttles too," she said. It was unlikely they could get away, if the attackers were truly murderous, but escape was worth a try. "And prep the remaining shuttles for emergency departure."

She tapped her console. They'd sent an automatic distress call the moment they'd seen the incoming ships—the sensor platforms would have sent a warning of their own—but no one would likely hear the warning before it was too late. By the time the call reached someone who was capable of doing something, the attackers would have done their grisly work and vanished. She wondered, sourly, why someone had aimed three *superdreadnought* squadrons at her complex. Maybe it was someone who hated her, or the Cavendish Corporation, or both. So excessive. A pair of cruisers would have more than enough firepower to smash the complex to atoms and vanish before anyone could catch up with them.

Her eyes narrowed as she studied the tactical plot. Her stint in the navy was years ago. She'd been discharged before the Commonwealth had been more than a vague idea, but she knew the basics. The enemy ships were already well within missile range. They had to know that they could smash her already, that nothing would be gained by closing to point-blank range. Her point defense was laughable. A handful of rail-gun pellets would be more than enough to take out the entire complex.

A console chimed. "Manager, we're receiving a signal."

"Put it through," Toni ordered.

She leaned forward, feeling the webbing constrict around her as a familiar face appeared on the display. Toni didn't pay much attention to politics, but even *she* had heard of Kat Falcone. Indeed, she'd found it quite amusing—after the Falcone Family had spent millions of credits on promoting her—that Kat Falcone had joined the king. Perhaps the younger woman had just gotten tired of having her ass repeatedly kissed by everyone who wanted something from her. Toni could understand *that.* Half the new recruits she'd received in the last few years seemed to have majored in sucking up. No wonder the corporation was going to the dogs. All the competent people had been pushed out long ago.

"This is Katherine Falcone, speaking for King Hadrian and the Colonial Alliance," Kat Falcone said. Her voice was very cool. "I intend to destroy your complex. You have ten minutes from this signal to evacuate. Anyone remaining on the complex after that time will be killed when I open fire. There will be no further warnings."

Toni tried to think of a response, but she couldn't come up with anything before the image vanished. Kat Falcone wasn't interested in a debate, just . . . destroying the complex. A glance at her display showed her that the warning had been broadcast to the other cloudscoops too. They were *all* launching shuttles, trying frantically to get the hell out before destruction rained down. Some stations were beaming signals in all directions, begging for mercy or begging for help. There was no response. The attackers simply wanted to destroy.

"Evacuate the remaining crews," Toni ordered. "Now."

She unhooked herself from the webbing and hurried the remainder of the crew to the hatch. There should only be a handful of people on the complex now . . . She keyed her wristcom, checking on the alpha crewers as she ran through the emergency procedures and prepped the datacore for self-destruct. The enemy wouldn't waste time vaporizing the complex when they could simply tear it to pieces instead. They probably didn't care about what was on the datacore, but she knew her job. There was information on the core that couldn't be allowed to fall into enemy hands.

Like our corporate rivals. I suppose we don't want them laughing themselves to death.

She made her way to the shuttle, silently relieved she'd worked her crews so hard. The beta, delta, and gamma crews were already off the complex. She jumped into the shuttle, slammed the hatch behind her, and let out a breath as they drifted away from the complex. Her heart twisted as the timer reached zero. Kat Falcone didn't hesitate. A spray of railgun pellets tore the cloudscoop apart.

Toni gasped, despite herself. The structure had been her *life*, her home, although thankfully she'd made sure never to take anything onto the complex she couldn't replace. She hadn't lost anything of sentimental value . . . She shook her head as the shuttle glided away from the expanding cloud of debris. She'd lost a life and a career and . . .

She cursed the king and all his followers as savagely as she knew how. Their war was leaving a trail of destroyed lives right across the Commonwealth.

"Set course for Tomas Asteroid," she ordered as the enemy super-dreadnoughts started to move to their next target. "And hope like hell those bastards don't feel like killing a few million people today."

◆ ◆ ◆

"All targets destroyed," Kitty said.

Kat said nothing for a long moment. She wasn't blind to the political implications of targeting the cloudscoops. HE3 was cheap, but the price would go up as it sank in that any further supplies to Rosebud would have to be shipped over interstellar distances . . . at least until the cloudscoops were replaced. The corporations that owned them, from the highest to the lowest, would be demanding military action, threatening all sorts of things if they didn't get justice. The House of Lords would have to act fast if they didn't want to face a political challenge.

Which means they'll have to come after us, she mused as the fleet started to reverse course. *And they have a handful of ships within a few days from our position.*

"Admiral?" Kitty sounded concerned. "The targets . . ."

"I heard," Kat said. She would have been more alarmed if the gunners had missed. Their targets were huge. Had *been* huge. A gunner who missed such a target would be summarily relieved of duty and told to practice in the simulators until his eyes were dripping bloody tears. "Order the fleet to proceed to the next target."

Kitty carried out her orders. It felt wrong to be stalking through the system, steadily picking off cloudscoops, mining settlements, and interplanetary transports and doing immense damage to the local economy. Rosebud wasn't *that* important, but . . . Kat was deliberately offering the enemy another shot at her ships. William would scent a trap, yet . . . he'd practically be forced to spring it. He'd already reoccupied Perfuma.

Her lips twitched. They'd intercepted news broadcasts as they'd entered Rosebud. The media was making all sorts of exaggerated claims, including a story insisting that her entire fleet had been wiped out. She wondered who was spreading that story and why. The media was known for lying—or, more accurately, for bending the truth creatively—but surely they had to know William hadn't killed her. They wouldn't have let *that* story pass, if they thought it was true. They'd be running sentimental stories about the tragedy of William being forced to kill his best friend, the woman who'd supported the king . . . She rolled her eyes.

Kat kept a wary eye on the timer, wondering just how long she'd have before William's fleet arrived. She'd made no attempt to hide the fleet as she burst into the system and hadn't even tried to take out the StarCom, but William would suspect trouble. After what she'd done to him last time, he could hardly help second-guessing everything he saw. And yet, she was certain he knew she was short of ammo. He might take the risk of forcing an engagement.

"Admiral," Kitty said. "The target is requesting more time to evacuate."

Kat nodded curtly. The fleet was approaching another mining asteroid. The files stated that the only inhabitants were miners, but, unless she was much mistaken, the census didn't include hundreds of transients, everything from shopkeepers and traders to prostitutes and drug dealers. They'd all have to be evacuated before she blew up the asteroid. She made a mental note to have the complex swept before it was too late, then turned to her aide. Nothing would be gained from mass slaughter.

"Give them time, then have the marines check the complex before we destroy it," she ordered stiffly. "And then move us to the next target."

She keyed her console, bringing up the system display. Hundreds of mining camps and asteroid settlements were going dark, trying to hide in the inky shadows of interplanetary space. A waste of time and they had to know it, but they were still trying. They hadn't given up. Others were running in all directions, starships opening vortexes and jumping into hyperspace. They didn't seem to believe her promises that no one would be harmed. She supposed, deep inside, that they had a point. She didn't intend to kill anyone, if it could be avoided, but she *was* tearing their lives apart. A great many people were going to be reduced to poverty because she'd destroyed their livelihoods.

No point in feeling guilty now, she told herself. *You knew what you were doing when you chose to support Hadrian.*

She stared down at her hands, trusting her subordinates to handle the grisly task. Yes, she'd known what she was doing. Yes, she'd known what she was fighting for. Yes, she believed the king was in the right. But . . . she looked at the display, watching as lights blinked out . . . each light representing a colony, someone's home, that had been destroyed. The king's forces were getting bogged down, resorting to desperate measures to win a victory that was starting to look unattainable. And they were destroying lives for nothing. Kat had no illusions about her work, or about the people she'd killed and would kill in the future, but she wanted it to be for *something*. She wanted to fight for a worthy cause. And it was growing harder and harder to convince herself that was what she was doing.

And the other side isn't much better. They made things worse for everyone too.

She stood. "Issue a system-wide evacuation order, with a deadline of three days from now," she said. They'd already taken out most of the priority targets. "Habitats will be left alone, but industrial nodes and mining camps will be targeted and destroyed. Three days. That's more than long enough."

And long enough for William to arrive, for things to become simple again. And then we can go home.

The thought depressed her. Where *was* home? Her ties to Tyre had frayed long ago, well before they'd snapped altogether. Caledonia was the king's base but wasn't her home. She didn't even think she had an apartment on the planet's surface. The king had given her rooms in the palace, but they weren't *hers*. Her only true home was her ship and even *she* wasn't hers. The ship belonged to her captain in actuality. She remembered her first real command with a wistfulness that surprised her, even though that ship had been lost in action long ago. The first thing that was truly hers.

Her terminal pinged. "Admiral," Jenkins said. "His Majesty ordered you to destroy . . ."

"I will not kill hundreds of thousands of people to make a point," Kat said. She wished, just for a moment, that Jenkins was right in front of her so she could slam her fist into his nose. "We're not here for mindless vandalism. We're here to bait a trap. Again."

She closed the channel, wondering what Jenkins would say. He didn't have the authority to relieve her of command, although . . . she had a private suspicion that his team of agents were rather better prepared for mayhem than their files—their suspiciously bland files—suggested. But he could whine to the king. *That* would be embarrassing. Kat would almost be relieved if he told her to quit his service. She grunted softly. That wasn't likely to happen. He didn't have enough decent commanding officers as it was.

And there aren't many who enjoy support from both his court and the colonials, she mused as the fleet waited for the deadline. *He simply doesn't have someone who can replace me without kicking off a whole string of problems.*

The thought wasn't reassuring. *It doesn't matter*, she told herself. *If we don't win the war, it'll all be over anyway.*

CHAPTER TWENTY

ROSEBUD

"Emergence in twenty minutes, Admiral."

William was morbidly sure he was either wasting his time while putting immense wear and tear on his fleet or flying straight into a trap. The alert had come in before he could leave Perfuma, before he could take his fleet back to Tyre and prepare to take the offensive. His orders, which had arrived within minutes of the alert, were clear. He had no maneuvering room at all. He had to take his fleet to Rosebud and stop Kat before she devastated the entire system.

He paced the CIC, hands clasped behind his back. Not the picture of calm he was supposed to present in a compartment crammed with staff officers and tactical aides who might panic if they saw their CO pacing the deck, but he couldn't stay still. He'd spent the past three days mulling over the reports, wondering just what Kat was doing. Rosebud was hardly a priority target. She hadn't even bothered to engage the planetary defense force. It looked like she was wasting her time, meandering around the system taking potshots at cloudscoops and asteroid mines. William rather suspected he was about to run into another trap. Kat had to have something up her sleeve.

And she's constantly shifting position. The reports from the recon ships had made it very clear that Kat's forces were gliding around the system, not holding position and waiting for him. *We can't drop out of hyperspace right on top of her.*

He mulled the situation over, wondering just what she had in mind. An ambush? She couldn't have borrowed more than three superdreadnought squadrons from Caledonia, could she? That would be one hell of a risk, even if it did promise an awesome payoff. William was all too aware of how close he'd come to disaster at Perfuma. Kat would have done a great deal more damage if she'd closed the range, rather than offering him a chance to escape. The analysts swore blind she'd been running out of missiles . . . William had been in the navy long enough to know depletion was possible, but Kat had been in the navy long enough to know not to let it happen.

We go to war with the navy we have, not the navy we want, he thought darkly. *And there were limits to how many supply depots the king could establish before we started shooting at each other.*

"Emergence in two minutes, Admiral," Commander Isa Yagami said. "The fleet is ready to engage."

"Good." William returned to his chair and sat down. "Remind the fleet we'll be playing it careful. There are three enemy superdreadnought squadrons waiting for us."

He sucked in his breath as the final seconds ticked down to zero. If the analysts were right, Kat's fleet had taken one hell of a pounding. They needed time to repair their ships and reload their magazines . . . time she'd chosen not to give them. It wouldn't have been that hard to return to Caledonia, rather than targeting another loyalist world. Kat's ships had to be in better condition than he thought. Or . . . maybe she was bluffing. Her ships weren't unleashing full salvos at *anything.* But there was a shortage of heavily shielded targets at Rosebud.

An odd target, he told himself. *For someone who claims to be fighting for the common man, the king is going to harm the commoners far more than the aristocracy by hitting Rosebud. Half the mining stations orbiting the star are independent . . .*

The superdreadnought lurched as the fleet powered through the vortex and into realspace. William leaned forward, half expecting to see enemy missiles flying towards him. Kat had the nerve to set up an ambush, if she had a rough idea where he intended to emerge. But her ships were still in interplanetary space, gliding around the system as if she didn't have a care in the world. Moments later, they started to alter course. She'd seen him. William glanced at the reports as more and more data flowed into his console. Kat had blown up the cloudscoops and a handful of asteroid mining stations, but she'd left the rest of the system alone. Perhaps the king thought destroying the corporate stations would win him friends and allies.

And it might, if she hadn't blown up the cloudscoops, he mused. *As it is, there's going to be a serious shortage of fuel.*

"Admiral," Yagami said. "The enemy fleet is holding position."

"Interesting," William said. The display updated, again, as his fleet launched probes towards the enemy ships. "What are they doing?"

He stroked his chin, considering his options. Kat had chosen her battleground well, if she intended to escape into hyperspace and flee. There were no gravity shadows that might impede her fleet's passage into interstellar space. And yet, she wasn't attempting to take advantage of her apparent superiority. A tacit admission she didn't have the firepower to take him on? Or was she hoping he'd impale himself on her fire? That tactic would give her a very slight edge if she was truly short of ammunition.

"Take us to engagement range," he ordered slowly, choosing the least bad option. He couldn't let Kat pin him down either, not here. Rosebud wasn't that important. "And prepare to engage."

He felt the mood on the deck grow tense as the superdreadnoughts picked up speed. William winced, inwardly. Morale had taken a beating after the last battle, although they'd more than held their own. It didn't help, he supposed, that the crews had read the press releases and grown convinced their superiors really didn't know what was going on. The media reports were true, from a certain point of view. William had to admit that whoever had devised the press releases was a master of misdirection. He'd made it sound as if William had won a great victory without ever admitting he hadn't fired a shot. The reoccupation of Perfuma sounded like the Battle of Cadiz.

"Contact in ten minutes, Admiral," Yagami reported. "They're locking weapons on us, sir, but making no move to escape."

William felt sweat beading on his forehead. Kat was up to something, but . . . but what? He could see her superdreadnoughts. The ships were surrounded by an electronic haze, making it difficult to produce reliable data, yet they *were* superdreadnoughts. He wondered, sourly, if he was looking at ECM drones, but that was unlikely unless the king's scientists had produced a breakthrough. The range was too short, and narrowing still further, for them to pull off the deception. And Kat had to know it.

"They're deploying point defense sensor platforms," Yagami warned. "Sir . . ."

William heard the question in his voice, but he had no answer. Kat was up to something . . . It *looked* as if she intended to stand and fight. But she couldn't, not unless her ships were in perfect condition. And they weren't. She simply hadn't had time to do more than reload her ships. She couldn't have repaired the damage, not in the last six days. Such a feat was physically impossible.

"Launch additional probes," he ordered. "I want to see through that haze."

His eyes narrowed as the probes flew towards their targets. There was no *point*, as far as he could tell, to Kat's actions. And that meant . . . what? She wasn't trying to hide her ships, merely their condition. But that also made her ships easy targets. She was deploying drones and sensor decoys, yet . . . she couldn't hope to hide her real ships. It was almost as if she was tiptoeing around while shouting at the top of her voice.

"We'll enter firing range in one minute," Yagami reported.

"Yes," William said. Technically, Kat *was already in* firing range. If she fired now, his ships would glide right into her missiles. And yet . . .

she held her fire, waiting for the range to close. He understood her logic, but . . . he almost wished she'd opened fire. He could have reversed course and let her missiles burn themselves out before closing the range again. She couldn't have full magazines. She *couldn't*. "Open fire on my command."

He leaned forward, studying the display as if he could draw more insight by looking closer. Kat's ships were barely moving, as if they were sitting ducks. The haze made it harder to tell. He frowned, wondering just what she was doing. The range was closing rapidly. She didn't have a hope of escaping unscathed, even if she did have full magazines. William might even risk closing the range himself, sacrificing his vessels in an attempt to smash the king's forces. It might even pay off for the loyalists in the long run.

"Fire," he ordered, quietly.

The superdreadnought shuddered as she unleashed her first barrage, flushing her external racks and internal tubes at the enemy. William watched as a tidal wave of destruction roared towards the enemy ships, enough firepower to scatter and destroy an entire superdreadnought squadron. *Three* squadrons might survive, but . . . they'd take one hell of a beating. His crews were already rushing to prepare the next salvo, hoping to land a second blow before the enemy ships struck back. William frowned, unsure what Kat was waiting for. There was no point in holding back now. She might find herself watching helplessly as her ships were vaporized, their missiles unfired. And . . .

He felt his heart skip a beat as thousands of red icons sparkled to life on the display. Thousands . . . more than there should have been, even if Kat had six superdreadnought squadrons under her command. He stared, even as his well-trained crews hurried to prep the point defense. Impossible. The king's *entire* fleet couldn't have produced such a massive salvo. And yet, it had happened.

"Admiral, I'm picking up hyperspatial distortions," Yagami reported. "A fraction of their fleet is jumping out."

William swore under his breath as the pieces fell into place. He'd thought he was facing three superdreadnought squadrons. He'd been wrong. He was facing one superdreadnought squadron and two squadrons of converted bulk freighters. Some ingenious bastard had crammed thousands of missile tubes into the freighters, covering their hulls with missile pods . . . all quite easy, if one didn't care about the freighters surviving the engagement. They didn't have point defense or shields or armor . . . He studied the live feed, shaking his head in disbelief. Kat had crammed missiles taken from Perfuma into the freighters and fired them at him. They weren't as fast or destructive as naval missiles but there was one hell of a *lot* of them.

And then she used the ECM haze to convince us she was trying to hide her fleet's condition, he mused. *She showed us what we wanted to see, and we didn't think to look for what she might be hiding.*

"Let them go," he ordered. The freighters were drifting out of formation now, probably operating on automatic. Anyone mad enough to crew them would be taking to the lifepods by now. Freighters were easy targets, even to destroyers. The hurricane of missiles bearing down on them would smash the vessels to atoms. "Rotate the fleet and stand ready to take enemy fire."

He considered, briefly, jumping into hyperspace himself. But there wasn't time to bring up the generators. The missiles would catch his fleet on the hop, exposed and vulnerable. He had to stand off the barrage, not try to run. Besides, Kat would probably have detonated a few warheads in hyperspace itself. The storms would probably fade quickly, but not quickly enough.

His fleet was effectively trapped.

And if she'd caught us like this a few months ago, she might have crushed us, he thought as the missiles came into attack range. *But I had time to work on training my crews.*

He braced himself as hundreds of missiles vanished from the display. His point defense crews really *had* improved. His eyes narrowed as he realized Kat had deployed sensor platforms, using them to coordinate her missile strike. Expensive—he wondered, with a flicker of gallows humor, if the *king's* bean counters would whine at her for expending the platforms—but crafty. The bloody things were hardly out of range, yet . . . it was too late to order his first salvo to take them out. They were busy obliterating the helpless and harmless freighters.

"Target the sensor platforms," he ordered. Kat's ships had either fled or been blown to atoms. "Take them out."

"Aye, Admiral," Yagami said. "I . . ."

The superdreadnought rocked as five missiles slammed into her shields. Alarms howled, red icons flashing up on the status display. William glanced at the stream of orders from the bridge—Captain Cavendish's damage control teams already had matters in hand—and then turned back to his display. Three of his superdreadnoughts had taken heavy damage, a fourth . . . he cursed savagely as a fourth superdreadnought exploded. The damage would have been a great deal more serious if Kat had held her fire for a few moments longer. It was no consolation to realize she'd known her deception couldn't be sustained forever.

Nor can her fire, he thought as the last of the missiles vanished from the display. *It's over.*

He sat back in his chair, studying the reports from the fleet. A dozen ships damaged . . . five of them badly enough to require weeks in a repair yard. It would have been acceptable if he'd taken out a bunch of *her* superdreadnoughts, but he hadn't even hit them. Kat had wisely fled before he'd had a chance. The news broadcasts would make her out to be a coward, but anyone who knew anything about military affairs would know better. She'd suckered him, twice. This was not going to look good.

Until the media hears about it, he told himself. *They'll make me look good.*

He turned to Yagami. "Secure the fleet, then arrange a StarCom channel to Tyre," he said. "Alert the loyalist systems. We don't know what she did with her other superdreadnought squadrons. They could be anywhere."

"Aye, sir," Yagami said.

William rubbed his forehead as he settled back into his chair. The engagement would be branded a victory. Both sides would claim it for their own. He knew better. It had been a draw, one that slightly favored the enemy. And . . . he shook his head. The House of Lords could fight and win a war of attrition, but they didn't have time. They had to take the offensive. And he was starting to come up with a plan.

◆ ◆ ◆

"We made it, Admiral," Kitty said. "There's no sign of pursuit."

"Good." Kat allowed herself a tight smile. The engagement had been so simple, even though she'd kept her ships on a hair-trigger, ready to cut and run the moment the enemy ships realized they'd been lured into a trap. It was almost a shame she hadn't been able to keep the other two superdreadnought squadrons with her. She might have been able to pull off a major victory, perhaps even a *decisive* one. "Set course for Caledonia."

She closed her eyes for a long moment. She'd left scouts behind with orders to monitor the engagement and report on the final outcome. They'd tell her, she hoped, if she'd done real damage. And then . . . She shook her head. There was no hope of reversing course, of returning to the battlefield and completing the destruction of the enemy fleet. They didn't know it, she hoped, but she'd emptied her magazines. She barely had enough missiles left to deter a destroyer let alone a superdreadnought. She couldn't risk another engagement until she had a chance to rearm.

Turning victory into defeat would be embarrassing, she mused as the first reports appeared in her display. The freighter crews had made it through the vortexes and rejoined the fleet, where they were being feted as the heroes of the hour. She'd won a victory without losing a single life. That would have been impressive, if she hadn't known she was dangerously close to losing the war without firing another shot. *We have to rearm before anything else happens.*

She brought up the starchart and studied it thoughtfully. Grand Admiral Rudbek was known for being unimaginative, but William wasn't. He'd be looking for ways to take the offensive as soon as possible. And being unimaginative wasn't necessarily a bad thing in this situation. The admiral might throw everything he had at Caledonia. That would be bad for the king, even if he won. He'd take such heavy losses that the next engagement would be his last.

Savor the victory, she told herself firmly. *You never know when you'll get another one.*

She stood. "Order the fleet to continue on course, evading all sensor contacts," she said. "I'll be in my cabin."

"Aye, Admiral," Kitty said.

The king will be pleased, Kat thought as she left the CIC. She was sure of it. Hadrian had ordered the strike on Rosebud. *But not everyone will agree with him.*

She kept her face impassive until she reached her cabin and heard the hatch hiss closed behind her. It was growing harder to convince herself that she'd done the right thing, even though she was fighting for the right side. The king was going to have problems spinning the damage she'd done into something positive. The real victims had been the little industries, not the big corporations. And *she'd* followed orders. She'd refused to commit actual war crimes before, but now . . .

They weren't war crimes. It was true. She just didn't believe it. *I hit legitimate targets.*

Sure. Her own thoughts mocked her. *And everyone is going to see it that way.*

CHAPTER TWENTY-ONE

CALEDONIA

The streets felt as if something bad was about to happen.

Sarah shivered, despite herself, as she made her way through the spaceport complex. Avenues were jam-packed with spacers on leave, desperately spending money in search of intercourse and intoxication before they had to return to their ships. The fleet's crews had been given bonuses upon their return from Perfuma, bonuses that would be worthless if they died during the next engagement. She scowled as she saw a handful of bare-breasted prostitutes staggering down the streets, half carrying spacers too drunk or drugged up to know what they were doing. They probably wouldn't be robbed blind—the spaceport strip was surprisingly safe, with plenty of ways to take someone's money perfectly legally—but they'd wake up the following morning wondering what had happened. Behind them, she heard drunken singing coming from a bar. The singers didn't seem to know the words.

She kept walking, keeping her coat buttoned up as a cold wind blew down the street. A line of rent boys waved to her, calling out enticements. She ignored them, as well as their female counterparts. She couldn't afford to waste time in a brothel, even the high-end pleasure palaces for senior officers and anyone else who could pay the fees. A line of policemen walked past, their faces grim. She tried to ignore them too, but it wasn't easy. There were policemen, guardsmen, security officers, and soldiers on every corner. It felt as if they were trying to mute the celebrations without actually *doing* anything.

I shouldn't be down here, Sarah thought. She'd left Remus on the ship, handling the repairs . . . the few they could do, in the time allocated before their next deployment. The king was already talking about hitting another world or two, if scuttlebutt was to be believed. *I really have to stay on the ship* . . .

She reached the spaceport hotel and stepped inside. Silence fell the moment the door closed behind her. Sarah relaxed and stepped over to the desk. The assistant looked her up and down, as if she thought Sarah had no right to be there. She changed the moment Sarah held up her ID card. It was almost a shame she'd switched to civilian clothes before she'd boarded the shuttle to the surface. The assistant would have been *very* polite the moment she walked in the door.

"You're in Room 101, Captain," the assistant said. "Do you need a guide?"

"I've been here before," Sarah said curtly. She'd visited enough spaceport hotels—the chain was practically omnipresent—to know it was hard to get lost. The internal security network was designed to chivvy visitors away from places they weren't supposed to go without being too obvious. "Thank you."

She turned and walked up the stairs. She'd spent enough time in intership cars to dislike the idea of taking an elevator if it could be avoided. Besides, she needed the exercise. She stepped through the door on the first floor and walked down the corridor. Room 101 was where it always was, in spaceport hotels. She privately suspected the franchise prefabricated the components on Tyre and transhipped them to whatever they wanted to install them. There was no other way to explain just how freakishly alike the spaces were . . .

The door opened as she approached, revealing a handful of others. Sarah tensed, knowing she was bending the rules as she stepped inside.

She was a naval officer, one who wasn't supposed to play politics. She'd certainly never liked watching *better-connected* officers playing politics. And yet, what choice did she have? She let out a breath as Governor Rogan held out a scanner and waved it over her body, then relaxed. It was unlikely that Soto or one of his subordinates had managed to sting her with a bug, but such subterfuge couldn't be ruled out completely. The asshole had a remarkable talent for doing things other people found outrageous and getting away with it.

"Captain," Governor Rogan said. "Welcome."

"Thank you." Sarah nodded tersely. "I'm sorry I'm late."

"It took longer than I expected to arrange this meeting," Governor Rogan said. "I assume you know everyone here?"

"Yes, sir," Sarah said. She'd only met a few of the guests, but she knew the others by reputation. Governor Rogan was taking a serious risk by gathering them together in one place. The meeting wasn't technically illegal but would raise eyebrows. It might have been better to meet outside the spaceport, but that wasn't an option. The spaceport was the only place they could all meet without definitely arousing suspicion. "I know who they are."

"Good." Governor Rogan indicated the drinks cabinet. "Fix yourself something, if you like. We'll be getting started in a moment."

Sarah poured herself a glass of water. She didn't dare risk getting tipsy, let alone drunk. She gazed around the room, quietly matching names to faces. Planetary representatives, militiamen, even a couple of other military officers. All colonials, of course, just like the last meeting. And all fairly senior within their branches. Sarah thought she was probably the lowest person among them.

Governor Rogan tapped his glass. "As far as anyone is concerned, this meeting is to celebrate the king's recent victory at Perfuma," he said, "and to discuss how we might make best use of it. Those of you who are junior have been invited to allow you to meet potential patrons, for your future careers. It may not be the most convincing story, but it's one they'll accept."

Probably, Sarah thought. Whoever had first argued *if you have nothing to hide, you have nothing to fear* had either been a naive idiot or openly malicious. The mere act of watching someone without their consent was enough to sway the observer against the observed, be it through simply violating their rights to seeing something out of context and jumping to the wrong conclusion. *If they suspect we're up to something, they'll keep us under a cloud of suspicion whatever we do.*

"On paper, the king's victory was decisive," Governor Rogan said. "That's certainly the story *he's* been putting forward. But practically . . . it was rather less so. We gave them a bloody nose, yes. We didn't kick them in the groin, stamp on their stomach, and finally crush their throat under our boot."

He looked at Sarah. "You were there. Would you agree with that assessment?"

Sarah kept her face under tight control. "Crude," she said. "But accurate."

Governor Rogan nodded. "We embarrassed them," he said. "We humiliated them. But we didn't defeat them. They *still* have their shipyards, their industrial nodes, their trained personnel . . . everything they need to fight and win a war against us. And His Majesty"—his voice was suddenly very hard—"hasn't been keen to do anything that might deprive them of those advantages."

"To be fair," Representative Quinn pointed out, "taking out their infrastructure would require mass slaughter."

"Yes," Governor Rogan agreed. "But he hasn't even considered attacks that *wouldn't* result in mass slaughter."

Sarah frowned. "Many of the targets you suggest are heavily defended," she pointed out. "We could damage them, or destroy them, but only if we were prepared to pay the price. It could cost us the war."

"And not destroying them could *also* cost us the war," Governor Rogan said. "But that isn't the worst of it. The king's behavior has grown increasingly autocratic."

His eyes were suddenly cold. "On one hand, he's ordered the appointment of . . . *political commissioners* . . . to the fleet. Officially, those commissioners have no authority to override the starships' captains. In practice, there has been a string of reports of commissioners doing just that. They have impeded operations, poked their noses where they were not welcome, and generally made themselves incredibly unpopular. I don't believe they're going to do wonders for military efficiency."

Very true, Sarah thought. *They're going to do more for the enemy than they can ever do for us.*

"And, on the other, I have been informed that the king is either on the verge of concluding an agreement with Marseilles or has already done so. Lord Snow, who was a reliable moderate, has been frozen out of the final discussions. The king himself, and a handful of his cronies, have handled the negotiations. If the reports are accurate, and I have no reason to believe they're not, the terms of the agreement are very simple. The king is going to surrender a number of star systems to Marseilles."

Sarah felt the shock ripple around the room. It was one thing to discuss ceding territory to outside powers, but it was another to actually *do* it. The colonials *knew* they were considered little more than pieces on a game board by the Tyrians, but . . . the king was supposed to be on their side. He shouldn't be selling out a number of worlds, even if doing so brought him victory. The border stars hadn't had a chance to vote. She wondered, numbly, if they even *knew* they were being sold. Some of them might be happy with the transaction, others . . . rather less so, being bought and sold like trinkets in a marketplace.

"So far, it's being kept a secret," Governor Rogan warned. "Hardly anyone outside the king's innermost circle knows about the agreement, let alone the terms. They know it will cause . . . problems. I think they're working on ways to present it to the public . . ."

Representative Qing made a face. "Do they think they can convince us to *go along* with it? With selling out the border stars?"

"I don't know what they're thinking," Governor Rogan said. "My source doesn't have access to their innermost discussions. I do know . . ."

Sarah coughed. "How do you know the story's true?"

"My source has never been wrong before," Governor Rogan said. "And there are . . . hints . . . that the king is expecting supplies from Marseilles. They won't be sending missiles and starship components and whatever out of the goodness of their hearts. There'll be a quid pro quo somewhere, public or not. And there isn't much else the bastards would want."

"Or that the king could give up," Qing pointed out.

"Yes," Governor Rogan said. "He's running out of cards to play."

There was an awkward silence. Representative Quinn broke it. "Assuming the report is true, and I'm not willing to take that for granted, what do we do?"

Governor Rogan let out a breath. "A handful of us have been conducting negotiations with Tyre, searching for a way out," he said. "You all know that's true. Agreements we made with the king are of strictly limited value, particularly now. We don't want to hitch ourselves to a cause that's about to go off the rails or crash headlong into a brick wall."

Sarah blinked in surprise, then wondered why she was so shocked. Governor Rogan hadn't called them here for drinks and chitchat. She knew he was an effective politician, one who'd played a major role in shaping the Colonial Alliance before it had joined forces with the king. He had friends and contacts on Tyre, friends and contacts who'd remained on the planet and stayed close to the House of Lords. There was plenty of room for covert discussions. In hindsight, she would have been more surprised if there weren't under-the-table discussions. Both sides had a certain interest in not fighting the war to the bitter end.

"The House of Lords has made us an offer," Governor Rogan continued. "It isn't perfect, it isn't what we want, but it's better than nothing. If we leave the king, either by declaring neutrality or switching sides, they'll accept us."

"That's very vague," Quinn said. "What are the specifics?"

Sarah nodded. "What are they offering us?"

"If we switch sides, they'll basically forget the interest on any money we owe them," Governor Rogan said. "We'll return to the status quo ante bellum, with a handful of minor changes. The Commonwealth will resume its originally planned course towards greater economic development, technological enhancement, and, eventually, political unity. You can review the documents if you like, or check out their broadcasts, but that's pretty much the best we're likely to get."

"So we put our head back in the noose," Qing said, "and in return they'll graciously forgive us for taking our head out of the noose in the first place."

"They've agreed to a handful of safeguards," Governor Rogan said. He showed a flicker of irritation. "The blunt truth is that we might well lose this war. If the House of Lords punches out the navy and physically occupies our worlds, we will have nothing to bargain with and no way to keep them from extracting our resources to repay our debts. If the king's descent towards autocracy turns to outright tyranny, we'll find ourselves his slaves. I think we have to acknowledge, right now, that we have to take preemptive steps to secure our position, to secure something we can bargain with."

He looked around the room. "I've had my people running simulations," he added. "They've been trying to predict the course of the war. So far, reality has inconveniently failed to live up to our predictions"— there was a handful of chuckles—"but the overall course of the conflict is clear. The king *may* manage to recover Tyre, giving him the chance to win the war outright. However, the longer it takes to do so, the greater the chance of him losing instead. Indeed, if our predictions are even roughly accurate, we'll lose the war within a year if we don't win within the next few months."

"You can't be serious," Representative Hammond said. "The Tyrians don't have the stomach for a long war—"

"Their industrial base is considerably larger than ours," Governor Rogan said, cutting him off. "Given a year, they will have somewhere between a hundred and two hundred superdreadnoughts under their command, as well as literally thousands of supporting elements and millions of missiles and everything else they need to keep their fleet operational. They'll have enough trained manpower to run it too. They'll roll over our defenses here"—he waved a hand upwards—"and land troops. And that will be the end."

"Shit," someone said quietly.

"I can show you the projections, if you like," Governor Rogan said. "They're not comfortable reading."

Sarah could believe it. She knew the House of Lords had an advantage, but . . . *that* great an advantage? Her stomach churned as she ran through everything she knew about Tyre and the loyalist worlds. They *could* build and man a massive fleet. They'd done it before, during the last war. And this time, they wouldn't be constrained by the Gap. The colonials would have to take out at least three or four times their own tonnage in each engagement to have a hope of holding their own. Her heart sank as she realized the truth. Governor Rogan was right. Their window of opportunity was rapidly closing. If they couldn't win the war within the next few months, they were doomed.

"So you want us to switch sides, as a body," Qing said. "I'm sure the king will accept our defection."

"No, he won't." Governor Rogan's voice was completely devoid of humor. "We're going to have to arrest him and take control of the fleet."

"Which will be difficult," Sarah said. She remembered Soto and frowned. "The king already has people on our ships."

"I notice there's no one from Caledonia here," Quinn put in. "Do you foresee them siding with the king?"

"I think they have little choice," Governor Rogan said. "If we don't take out the king quickly, he could trigger another civil war."

"Yes," Sarah said. "Do you know how hard it will be to secure even a fraction of the fleet?"

"They're not all loyal to the king," Quinn insisted.

"Many of them are loyal to Kat Falcone," Sarah pointed out. The king's admiral was a bona fide war hero. The officers who disliked or distrusted the king would still respect her. "And if we failed to take the fleet in the first few moments, she'd start organizing a counterattack."

"And she'd know what to watch for," Hammond said. "She had a mutiny on her ship, didn't she?"

"It wasn't *her* ship," Sarah corrected. "But yeah, she would pick up the warning signs."

"And she's loyal to Hadrian," Governor Rogan said. "She would probably refuse to join us."

"Probably," Sarah agreed. She didn't know Kat Falcone that well. "It would be better to move when she's somewhere else."

"Quite," Governor Rogan agreed. "We can deal with her after we're in control."

"We'd be taking one hell of a risk," Hammond said. He looked terrified, as if he was on the verge of fainting. "Is there no way to talk the king out of fighting to the bitter end?"

"He has everything to gain and everything to lose," Governor Rogan said. "The best he can hope for, if he loses the war, is to be sent into comfortable exile somewhere. I don't think the House of Lords will be so generous, not after everything he did. And everything he's supposed to have done. They'd probably shoot him on the spot and worry about impeaching him later."

"Or simply not bother at all," Qing said. "Their evidence is a little scanty. They wouldn't want their descendants worrying if they did the right thing."

And there's not much point in impeaching a dead body, Sarah reflected as the discussion turned to the practicalities. *And if we don't pull this off in the first few moments, we'll be screwed no matter the outcome.*

CHAPTER TWENTY-TWO

CALEDONIA

"It was a great victory, Admiral," Sir Reginald Grantham said as he led Kat through a maze of corridors. "The media broadcasts have been hammering home our message from the moment we got word."

Kat resisted the urge to tell the king's fixer precisely what she thought of him *and* the media broadcasts. The king's spin doctors were insisting that she'd wiped out a giant enemy fleet, something that simply wasn't true. The recon reports stated she'd killed three superdreadnoughts during the cruise. Perhaps more, if the damaged ships were deemed beyond repair. But that wasn't enough to tip the balance in the king's favor, and she knew it. Anyone who knew anything about naval combat would know it too. She hoped—she prayed—that the *king* would know it.

Caledonia was changing—and not for the better. More troops were on the streets, more heavy weapons emplaced around the palace and the remainder of the government complex. The planet felt as if it was on the verge of chaos. She'd seen a couple of celebrations that had been going on during the drive through the city, but something seemed *forced* about them. The partygoers had been partying to keep their minds off . . . what? She suspected she understood the truth. They knew as well as she did that their victory was a sham.

"Kat," the king said. Hadrian was sitting on a sofa, Drusilla sitting next to him. There was something oddly touching about their pose, even though it was strikingly demure. "Thank you for coming."

"Your Majesty," Kat said formally.

She took the seat he offered her, studying them both as Sir Reginald retreated. The king looked happy but tired. Beside him, Drusilla's face was an unreadable mask. Kat had never really warmed up to the princess, even though Drusilla had done the Commonwealth a huge favor. There was something about her that put Kat's teeth on edge, something she *really* didn't like. Drusilla had grown up in a very different environment, with very different rules.

And you're being stupid, Kat told herself sharply. *What sort of person would you be if you grew up in a hellhole like that?*

"You can call me by my name, you know." The king sounded expansive. "We're friends."

"Hadrian," Kat said. She shook her head. "I'm sorry. I don't see any grounds for celebration."

The king raised his eyebrows. "You won two battles in quick succession."

"I cheated, both times," Kat said. "I shot myself dry, to the point the entire fleet could have been destroyed if the engagements had been prolonged. Things could have gone badly wrong."

She met his eyes. "And I destroyed the lives of thousands of people, the ones I didn't kill," she added. "Please excuse me for feeling a little guilty about it."

"They could have come here," Drusilla said. "By staying there, they aligned themselves with the wrong side."

Kat shot her a sharp look. "They chose to stay out of the fighting," she said. "And we brought the war to them anyway."

"We'll help them to rebuild, after the war," the king said. "And you *can* call me by my name."

Kat met his eyes. "Hadrian."

It felt . . . *wrong*, as if something had been lost over the last few weeks. This was almost a kind of forced intimacy, an attempt at pretending nothing had changed even when they both knew there was no point in pretense. The war was bogged down, waiting for one side to do something that would take it to victory or send it crashing down in defeat. She knew the stalemate wouldn't last forever. She hoped the king knew it too.

She felt something twist deep in her heart. The cause—the king's cause—was changing, warping and twisting into something else. And . . . She winced, remembering the rumors spreading through the fleet. Jenkins and his ilk had done a lot of damage just by suggesting the king didn't trust his people any longer. The days when he could walk the streets without an escort were long gone. Indeed, they had never really existed. Kat mourned, deep inside, for everything she'd lost. Oh, if her father had lived. *He* would have found a way to bridge the gap between the sides . . .

"Kat," the king said gravely. "There have been developments."

Kat looked up. "Indeed?"

"I signed a treaty with Marseilles." The king's lips curved. "They'll be supplying us with missiles and . . . everything else."

"Really." Kat met his eyes. "What did you concede?"

"The border stars," the king said. "They're to be handed over in a matter of weeks."

Kat blinked. "And the House of Worlds just . . . went along with it?"

"They don't know, not yet." The king frowned. "They might be a problem."

"Yes, Hadrian," Kat said. She felt torn between the urge to laugh and the urge to cry. "That *might* be a problem."

She leaned back in her chair, thinking hard. "The Colonial Alliance isn't going to like the idea of surrendering . . . how many? Five? Ten? Twenty? How many?"

"Nine," the king said. "They're all in my possession."

"Their inhabitants might feel differently," Kat said. "And the Colonial Alliance certainly *will* feel differently."

"If we don't win the war," Drusilla said, "does it matter?"

"No," Kat conceded. "But they're not going to like the idea of just . . . selling the locals out."

"We've demanded protections for them," the king said. "And we'll take anyone who wants to leave."

"Such protections are rarely worth the paper they're written on," Kat said. She remembered something her father had once said and stole it. "Did you write the treaty on toilet paper? It would be good for *something* if you did . . ."

The king's eyes flashed fire. "Do you have any better ideas?"

Kat frowned. The sudden change was worrying. The king had been drinking the last time she'd seen him . . . She wondered, suddenly, if he was still drinking. Or if he'd moved on to something stronger. Or . . . There was nothing she could do about it. She had less influence these days. The king was surrounding himself with yes-men.

"No," Kat said finally. "Are you sure they can supply us?"

"The freighters are already on the way," the king said. "They should arrive within the week."

"You're cutting it fine," Kat commented. "The House of Lords is probably already swearing revenge."

"They'll have to choose a target first," the king said. "And so will you. We have to hit them again."

"We're running out of targets that can be hit," Kat reminded him. "And the more soft targets we hit, the more we unite them against us. Hadrian . . . you're not universally popular."

"Not inside the House of Lords," the king said. "But outside . . ."

"You didn't have as much popular support on Tyre as you thought," Kat said. "If they really loved you, they would have risen up in your name. Instead . . . your supporters are keeping their heads down while the population is either supporting your enemies or waiting to see who comes out ahead. And the recent attacks, particularly the one on Rosebud, haven't helped. I daresay we made you a few million more enemies."

"They can join the line," the king said. "How do you intend to win the war?"

Kat sighed. "I've been looking at our options," she said. "We can hit a number of tougher targets, but that'll cost us. We *could* raid the infrastructure at Tyre . . ."

"Out of the question," the king said. "We're going to need that infrastructure."

"And yet, as long as it stays in their hands, it's a dagger pointed at our heart," Kat countered bluntly. "The only other option is to find a way to destroy Home Fleet."

"Then do it," the king said.

Kat looked back at him. "Do you have a few extra superdread-noughts in your pocket?"

"No," the king said. "And I don't think we could convince our allies to join us in a strike on Tyre."

"No," Kat agreed. The House of Lords *might* turn a blind eye to weapons shipments if they didn't alter the balance of power significantly, but they would take action if foreign ships and troops joined the king. Marseilles would have to be crazy to take the risk. "They're hoping to keep us off-balance as long as possible. They want time to absorb the border stars, not get yanked into our war."

She felt sick. Objectively, she understood the king's logic. She understood he had no other choice. There was *no* other way to get missiles and supplies. The logic was simple. If they didn't give up the border stars, they wouldn't get any supplies; if they didn't get any supplies, the war would be within shouting distance of being lost. And yet, subjectively, it felt like a betrayal. It felt as if they'd condemned the planetary inhabitants to slavery. There was certainly no way to ensure Marseilles kept its word. The locals might find themselves trapped behind an iron curtain.

And even if we win this war, she mused, *what will it make us?*

"We'd have to find a way to lure part of Home Fleet out of place," she said carefully. "And then we'd have to deal with the remainder of the fleet and land troops before it returned."

She considered a handful of options. None of them seemed particularly good. The prospects for outright disaster were terrifyingly high. And yet, if they were short on good options, they might have to risk a bad option and hope for the best. It would hardly be the first time in human history that a military force in a desperate position had been forced to attempt the near-impossible. Armchair admirals might scorn, but they were commenting from the safety of their homes. The officer on the spot had to do the best she could with the resources at her command.

"We *could* use Caledonia itself as bait," she mused. "If we strip the defenses to the bare minimum, relying on the fixed defenses to protect the system, we *could* aim a major fleet at Tyre. It would give us our best chance of winning the war outright, particularly if they launch their own fleet at Caledonia. You'd be switching capital worlds . . ."

The king laughed harshly. "I'm sure it would be quite a shock for them to reach my world and then discover that I've taken *their* world."

"It would," Kat agreed. She'd read a story, once, where one side had launched a naval operation to conquer the other side. The *other* side had sent its army to cross a seemingly impassable desert and invade the *first* side's territory. In the book, they'd had to shamefacedly organize a swap. She doubted the real world would be so obliging. "And they'd set out at once to recover Tyre."

"Unless they came to terms," the king said excitedly. "Which they might, if I was in control of Tyre."

"It would depend," Kat warned. "If we took heavy losses in the battle, which we would even if we faced *just* the fixed defenses, they might be able to boot us back out of the system . . . which would leave us completely isolated from just about everywhere. We wouldn't be able to recover Caledonia, and it might be useless even if we did. They'd take pains to destroy as much as they could of the infrastructure. They wouldn't want to keep it."

"No," the king said. "But this might be the only workable plan we have."

"Might," Kat echoed.

She looked at her hands. She was no stranger to risk, but gambling everything on one throw of the dice sounded insane. And yet, she could see some advantages. No one would expect the maneuver, for a start. Even William wouldn't expect her to stake everything. She frowned, wondering if that was actually true. William had watched her risk her career, repeatedly, to do what she felt to be right. He might have contingency plans for an all-out attack on Tyre.

But having contingency plans isn't the same as being mentally ready for them, she told herself. She'd seen some of the contingency files the navy had drawn up over the years. They'd looked at wars with any or all of the nearby interstellar powers, but also at things as unlikely as alien invasions or losing the ability to jump into hyperspace. And no one in their right mind genuinely thought that any of those things would happen. *William could hardly prepare himself for something he thought I'd never do.*

"I'll have my people look at the options," she said. A plan that depended on someone else doing precisely what she wanted them to do was doomed. She'd been told that at Piker's Peak, then learned it repeatedly during her career. "But we may not be able to lure them out of place."

"Then find ways to double your firepower," the king said. "You did rig a number of freighters to carry missiles."

"That was one punch," Kat said. "They couldn't sustain such a rate of fire for long, Your Majesty."

"Hadrian, please," the king said.

"And they'd know to watch for it now," Kat said. "We need to find a game changer."

"Just gambling might be enough," the king said. He sounded as if he was trying to convince himself. He knew there were limits to how far they could get on luck alone. "Or . . ."

Kat shook her head. "You know we could lose everything?"

"That's always been true." The king's voice was calm, but there was a nasty edge to it she didn't like at all. "I've always done the best I can for my people. I know I have to look to the long term. I've always borne in mind that I have to lay the groundwork for my successor, just as my father did for me. I know . . .

"The others are small-minded, wherever they are. They look for personal advantage and ignore the bigger picture. The House of Lords dismisses the colonials because they're not strong; the Colonial Alliance dismisses the House of Lords because the aristocracy has lost the ability to see into the future. They have no *vision*. They see short-term problems and come up with pettifogging objections to anything designed to build a better future. They have no . . ."

He stopped himself with an effort. "And now we have something of *ours*," he said quietly. "They don't want to lose it. They're plotting against me. I know it."

Kat's eyes narrowed. "Who?"

"Everyone who thinks he has something to lose," the king said. Beside him, Drusilla took his arm. "And that's just about *everyone*. Who can I depend on *now*?"

Me, Kat thought. She didn't say it. She wasn't wholly convinced the sentiment was true. *But who else can he depend upon?*

Sir Reginald and his ilk had nowhere else to go. They'd support the king because . . . because they had no choice. But the others . . . Kat wondered, suddenly, just how many of the king's supporters were looking for a way out. She could, if she wanted. She could go back home . . .

Sure, her thoughts answered. *Go back home and get sent into exile for treason.*

She almost smiled. Peter would have some *real* problems deciding what to do with her. Put her on trial for treason? Lock her up on the estate, like a character from a movie set in a half-forgotten era of dresses and perfume and two worlds, one aboveground and one belowstairs? Or simply send her into exile, with strict orders never to come back? Or quietly arrange an accident? Or . . .

But returning home would mean betraying the king, she thought. *And breaking my word.*

"I'll speak to my officers," she said, "and see if we can find a way to put an end to the war."

"Good," the king said. "My child will be born into a happier world."

Kat blinked. "You're pregnant?"

"I'm pregnant." Drusilla grinned. Her face lit up. "But he *did* help, a little."

"Just a little." For a moment, the king looked *years* younger. He reached out and touched his wife's belly. A remarkably gentle touch. "Our little one will be the next ruler."

He glanced back at Kat. "There aren't many people who know, yet," he said. "I'd be grateful if you kept it to yourself."

"As you wish," Kat said. She wondered, suddenly, what would have happened if she and Pat had actually managed to get married. Would they have had children? Her heart fell. She could use his DNA to bear his children, if she wished. It was against the bioethics code to do so without his consent, but she had the power to override the regulation. Yet . . . it wouldn't be the same. "My congratulations."

"We'll try to win the war before he's born," the king said. He looked proud, yet his tone was calculating. "I dread to imagine what the House of Lords would say."

"Quite," Kat agreed. The House of Lords had never liked Drusilla. No, that wasn't entirely true. They'd liked her as long as she was a retired heroine, not when she'd married into the king's family. The thought of her children being the heirs to the throne . . . "We'll try to make sure of it."

But she knew, as she took her leave, that was a promise she might not be able to keep.

CHAPTER TWENTY-THREE

CALEDONIA

"The new missiles are good," Kitty said as she stepped into Kat's office. "Not *quite* up to modern standards, but good enough."

"Good," Kat said absently. She didn't look up from the datapad. "Have the warheads been checked for unpleasant surprises?"

"The techs checked their programming," Kitty assured her. "They found nothing."

Kat frowned, unconvinced. The warheads were fiendishly complex. It would be easy to hide a couple of lines of code within the programming, ones designed to shut down or detonate the warhead upon command. She had no reason to assume the Marseillans were setting them up for a fall, but she rather suspected they'd fear the king turning on them. Rumors of his deal with Marseilles had already started to leak out. They had to realize the king might seek to renounce the arrangement, even to deny it had ever been made, when he returned to his homeworld. The missiles might wind up being aimed at their manufacturers.

"I hope they're right," she said. A nuke going off inside the super-dreadnought would be bad enough. An antimatter warhead detonating inside the armor would vaporize the entire ship. "How do they compare to *our* warheads?"

"They seem to have the same basic characteristics as the Mark-VIII missiles, according to the techs," Kitty said. "Their warheads are more powerful, but their targeting systems are weaker. The Marseillans may not have solved some of the guidance problems . . ."

"Or they haven't given us top-of-the-line missiles," Kat finished. She would have been astonished if the Marseillans *did*. Mark-VIII missiles weren't *bad*, but they were seriously outclassed by Mark-IX and Mark-X. The House of Lords would have a sizable advantage if Tyre went to war with Marseilles, if Mark-VIII missiles were all Marseilles had. "They'll try to maintain deniability as long as possible."

Kitty didn't look convinced. Privately, Kat was inclined to agree. The missiles weren't refurbished UN or Theocracy crap. They had to come from a frontline power, and there weren't many who had both the motives and the means to interfere. Rumors or no rumors, there was no way Marseillan involvement would remain unnoticed. The real question was how the House of Lords would react.

They'll know soon enough, if they don't know already, Kat mused.

She had a feeling the Marseillans were counting on the king to win, which was the only way they'd get to keep their gains. And . . . the king was presumably counting on them upping the ante, if things continued to get worse for his cause. They were committed now. Either they backed the winner or, after the House of Lords won, the Marseillans faced their wrath. Kat could see some of the fire-eaters on Tyre calling for war, promising that it would reunite the battered Commonwealth. Peter wouldn't go along with the demands, she was sure, but he might be outvoted. And who knew what would happen then?

It probably won't be my problem, she thought as she took the datapad. *I'll be dead by then.*

"Keep working on the tactical plans," she ordered. "And let me know if anyone in the department makes a breakthrough."

Kitty nodded, then turned and left the compartment. Kat looked at the datapad, paging through the report without actually reading it.

She didn't need to read the report to know the plan to attack Tyre wasn't going to get off the ground, let alone into orbit, unless something changed. The more she looked at the details, the more her staff officers worked through the permutations, the more she started to realize that too much could go wrong. No, *would* go wrong. The best she could do was factor the variables into the plan, leaving herself plenty of room to back off if the enemy refused to cooperate.

And if they realize what I'm doing, they may cooperate long enough for me to give them the rope to hang me. She put the datapad to one side, promising herself that she'd review it later. Kitty had done her best, but Kat needed to assess the new missiles before she took them into combat. *They'll want to catch me with my pants down too.*

She chuckled at the silly thought, then forced herself to stand and pace the deck. Her brain wasn't working quite right, as if she'd pushed herself too hard. She rather thought she had. There was no way to change the facts, not without surrendering to wishful thinking and self-delusion. Her father had told her repeatedly that she had to accept reality, for reality would quite happily slap her in the face if she tried to deny it.

"And not always metaphorically," he'd said. She'd been young enough to think he was joking at the time. She'd learned hard lessons since. "It's cheaper to listen to reality when it demands your attention."

The intercom bleeped. "Admiral," Kitty said. Her tone carried a hint of irritation. "Commodore McElney requests the pleasure of your company."

Kat blinked. William? Reality asserted itself a second later. No, not William. *Scott.* The smuggler chief had insisted on dealing with her the last time they'd met. Kat understood, better than she cared to admit. Scott wouldn't want to get too close to the king, not when Hadrian might lose. His enemies would swoop on him like flies on shit if he was suddenly charged with treason. Or giving aid and comfort to the enemy. But then Scott McElney had always tried to play both ends against the middle.

"Odd choice of words," she observed dryly. "Is that what he told you?"

"Yes, Admiral," Kitty said. "Those were his exact words."

Kat allowed herself a moment of irritation. "Then have him shown to my office," she said. The rumors would be all around the ship by the end of the shift, damn it. "I'll deal with him personally."

She sat back at her desk and checked the updates from System Command. Commodore McElney had been in and out of the system a dozen times over the past three months, bringing war material and supplies from all over the Commonwealth and beyond. He didn't seem to have found anything particularly vital, but Kat wasn't too surprised. The prewar stockpiles had been drawn down sharply, when they weren't heavily guarded by one side or the other. Scott McElney would have been lucky to find *any* mil-grade components, let alone weapons, this side of the Gap.

Her heart twisted as Scott McElney was shown into the compartment. He looked like William, close enough that she might have mistaken one for the other if she hadn't known them both. There were ten years between them, if she recalled correctly, but it was easy to think they were twins. But then, they'd both had access to rejuvenation technology.

"Admiral," Scott said. He shook her hand firmly. "It's a pleasure to see you again."

Kat nodded, then gestured him to a chair. "And you," she said. It wasn't entirely true, but she would have welcomed almost any distraction. "I notice you've been bringing us more supplies."

"What little I could find," Scott said. He looked up as the steward entered carrying two mugs of coffee. "Everyone who has military hardware these days wants to keep it."

"So I hear," Kat said.

"There's a bunch of worlds that are trying to gear up their defenses as quickly as possible," Scott added. "They're not involved in the war, officially, and they want to stay out of it. They've placed large orders for ships and orbital defenses from Tyre, but the House of Lords is dragging its feet on actually meeting their demands. They think the ships will eventually end up being given to the king."

"I haven't heard anything about it," Kat said. "But I'd be astonished if the House of Lords actually sent the ships."

Scott smirked, as if he knew something she didn't. "Me too."

Kat sipped her coffee. "And they probably need all the war material they can get for themselves these days," she added. "They can't fight wars with money."

"But you can't fight wars without money either," Scott said. "You *do* know the king's credit has been dropping sharply, don't you?"

"No." Kat frowned. "I never paid much attention to high finance."

"Shame," Scott said. "You could have warned the king that his accounts are somewhat overdrawn."

Kat shrugged. Technically, the king had access to vast resources. Practically, the monies, supplies, and workforces on Tyre were denied to him. He had relatively little to live on, let alone fund the war effort. And yet, as long as there was a possibility he'd win the war, his creditors would be reluctant to pounce. If they tried to cut him off at the knees, he'd be sure to cut them out after he returned to Tyre.

And if he loses, the creditors will be out of pocket anyway. Kat smiled coldly. *Serves them right.*

She met Scott's eyes. "It's nice to see you again," she said. "But I am a very busy person."

"You do know that you and William have quite a bit in common?" Scott reached into his pocket and produced a slip of paper, which he passed to her. "You've picked up some of his mannerisms."

"Quite," Kat said.

She unfolded the paper and read it quickly. Scott had written a single line. CAN WE BE OVERHEARD? Kat opened her mouth to respond in the negative, then frowned. Jenkins and his staff had been very intrusive over the past few weeks. They hadn't eased off *that* much since she'd read him the riot act. Her blood ran cold. Would they have the nerve to bug her office? She tried to tell herself that it wouldn't happen, but she didn't know. They seemed to think their authority came from the king himself.

"That's a compliment," she said evenly. She reached into her drawer and produced a pair of privacy generators. Pat had taught her, years ago, that one privacy generator could be spoofed, with the right equipment. Running two in unison made breaking through a great deal harder. Or so she'd been told. Pat wouldn't have lied to her, but technology advanced in leaps and bounds. "There are worse people to learn from."

"Or to copy." Scott watched her with unblinking eyes. "Or did he copy you?"

Kat felt her ears pop as the conjoined privacy fields fell into place. "We should be safe now," she said. The bugs would report that she'd used the fields . . . if, of course, there were bugs. She wondered if she should call a countersurveillance team from Marine Country. There was no way she'd be able to find them with the naked eye. "Why do you ask?"

Scott looked unconvinced. "How do you know the generators haven't been tampered with?"

"There could be a bug in one generator," Kat said. Pat had pointed that out to her too. It was the easiest way to subvert countersurveillance technology. "But the other generator will deal with it."

"And arouse suspicion in the process," Scott pointed out. "How exposed are you, up here?"

Kat's eyes narrowed. "Scott . . . what do you want?"

"I spoke to William, shortly before you attacked Perfuma and Rosebud," Scott said. "He wants to meet."

"What?" Kat wasn't sure she'd heard right. "He wants to meet me? Here?"

"I don't know where," Scott said. "He seemed to think you'd have some trouble getting off the ship without being observed."

"True." Kat shook her head in disbelief. "He, a senior enemy commander, wants to meet me, face-to-face? And secretly?"

"Yes." Scott flattened his hands. "I'm not sure how to work it. But he asked me to let you know so you could work on the problem."

Kat looked down at her pale hands. "I don't know," she said. "Could you bring him here? To the spaceport strip?"

"Maybe." Scott didn't look very certain. "Getting him down to the planet without setting off a bunch of alarms would be tricky. Getting him back into orbit would be even harder. They've been tightening up entry and exit controls, even for people who just want to visit the spaceport. I had a couple of people held for questioning after they passed through the biotech scanners."

Kat grimaced. "And even if he did get down to the surface, arranging a meeting might be tricky."

"Yeah." Scott shrugged. "Do you *like* running the Golden Mile?"

"I never did," Kat said. She felt an odd little pang for the days of her youth. "I was an officer candidate. We weren't allowed to wear lipstick, let alone go on pub crawls."

"Spacers have far fewer restraints," Scott said. "Going from pub to pub and drinking a beer is a great bonding activity."

"I'm sure it is," Kat said. "Explaining a hangover to the officer on watch is *also* a great bonding activity."

She chuckled. "I could take a room at a hotel," she said. It would be easy enough, if she was prepared to sacrifice her dignity. "But we might be watched."

"Perhaps," Scott agreed. "I *might* be able to get him into the system. Or *a* system, depending. Would you be able to meet?"

"Perhaps," Kat echoed. She was the fleet's commander. Normally, she could do whatever she liked. But with Jenkins and his colleagues aboard . . . she felt oddly exposed, even though she didn't know if Jenkins was actively watching her. She could be paranoid. And yet, once she'd had the thought, it refused to go away. He might start asking questions and coming up with the wrong—or right—answers. "Why?"

"I don't know." Scott let out a breath. "But he felt meeting was important."

"It would have to be," Kat said. The idea of a fleet commander putting himself in a place where he could be kidnapped, or worse, would horrify anyone who took a moment to think about the possible outcomes. Kat could kidnap William, if he came so close. The king would certainly order her to kidnap William, if he knew. She let out a long breath, realizing that she was about to do something the king would see as treason. "And I assume I'm not meant to tell anyone about this?"

"I believe not," Scott said. "William wants you to keep it to yourself."

Kat nodded, slowly. "And if this gets out . . ."

"Feel free to blame everything on me." Scott laughed harshly. "I make a very good scapegoat."

"It won't work," Kat said. She knew she had enemies on the planet below. They'd take a hint of disloyalty and use it to brand her an outright traitor to the king. Admiral Ruben, wherever he was, probably wanted to take command of the fleet. Again. He'd make sure the king heard the worst possible version of the tale. "You're not a big enough scapegoat."

Scott pretended to cry. "That's the nicest thing anyone has ever said to me."

Kat glanced at the privacy generators, frowning. "If you can bring him here, or to wherever the fleet goes next, we should be able to arrange a meeting. And then . . . we'll see."

The king really won't be happy, her thoughts warned. *And he'll suspect the worst.*

"Understood." Scott stood. "I'll have to make use of the StarCom. Don't worry. We have an unbreakable code."

"I hope you're right about that," Kat said. "And Scott . . . do you have an *official* story for this meeting?"

"I came here to protest the detention of two of my people." Scott gave her a droll smile. "And I really *would* like it if you pulled strings on my behalf. I can't keep coming here if my people think they'll be arrested at any moment."

"I'll do what I can," Kat said. As cover stories went, she supposed it had the advantage of being reasonably simple. "No promises, but I'll do what I can."

"As will I." Scott stood. "William is looking forward to seeing you again."

"Me too," Kat said. She held up the generators, ensuring he knew they were being switched off. "I'll get back to you as soon as possible. I'm sure His Majesty will understand."

Scott smiled wryly. They both knew the king *wouldn't* understand. Or, perhaps, that he'd understand a little *too* well. Kat dismissed him with a nod, then tapped her terminal and searched through the files for Scott's people. The arrest records were clear enough. They'd been arrested on the grounds they were traveling with forged papers. Their DNA had been linked to people who'd left Tyre before the Theocratic War. It was enough to get them held until the investigation was completed.

And that could be a very long time, Kat thought. *Scott has every reason to be annoyed.*

She keyed her terminal. "Kitty, get me a private line to Sir Reginald," she said. "Put him through the moment he answers."

"Aye, Admiral."

Kat had to smile at her aide's confusion. She knew Kat didn't like Sir Reginald. The king's fixer was an oily little man, someone who'd tried to bend Kat to his will. Kat grimaced. He'd be delighted to do her a favor, never realizing that she was using him to cover her tracks. Kat was sure he'd want something in return, but whatever it was, she'd deal with it.

Right now, all that matters is arranging a meeting, she thought as she waited. *And finding out, finally, what William wants.*

CHAPTER TWENTY-FOUR

TYRE

"You got here just in time," Peter said as William was shown into his office. "You missed the meeting."

William had the grace to look embarrassed. "I *did* offer to attend via hologram."

"It's important to touch base and press the flesh from time to time," Peter said, indicating a chair. Face-to-face meetings were less comfortable than holographic conferences, but they did tend to be more honest. It was certainly harder to hide behind a mask without holographic filters. "That said, there was little real debate. Everyone wants to hit back as soon as possible. If not sooner."

"I know," William said. He sat. "I believe the Grand Admiral was looking at a handful of options."

"War is too important to be left to the admirals alone," Peter said. His father had said that from time to time. "There are political implications as well."

"Yes, Your Grace," William said. "What do you have in mind?"

"There's a decent possibility that Quist will switch sides," Peter said. "We've had a number of meetings with their ambassadors over the past couple of weeks. Things *were* put back a little by the recent engagements, but overall . . . Quist has had enough of the king. They'll switch sides if we meet their price."

He watched William narrowly. "What do you make of it?"

"Quist is far too close to Caledonia for my peace of mind," William said slowly. "The king could have a fleet there within a handful of days, perhaps less if he's prepared to risk burning out their drives."

Peter nodded, pleased. "Quite," he agreed. "The Grand Admiral raised the same concerns."

He scowled. Grand Admiral Rudbek had been a lot more assertive since the Battle of Perfuma, disrupting patron-client relationships that had been carefully built up over the past few decades. Duke Rudbek was giving him a very hard time indeed, pointing out that the grand admiral hadn't put the interests of his family first and foremost. Peter understood the logic, but he also understood the importance of winning the war. Not, he supposed, that he'd do any differently if Falcone interests were challenged. His family would seek to remove him if they felt he wasn't defending them properly.

"He's devised a plan to launch a feint at Fotheringay," Peter explained. "That will, hopefully, keep the king from raiding our worlds while we gather the power to smash him flat. If Quist changes sides, as planned, you'll be in the area with enough firepower to protect the population. Hopefully, that will convince the rest of the colonials that they can switch sides freely."

"Hopefully," William echoed. "Is there any particular *reason* why Quist is switching sides?"

"Economic damage appears to be the main reason, as far as we can tell," Peter said. "The king is apparently placing huge demands on them, for relatively little purpose. Or so we believe. There are other possibilities."

William leaned forward. "It's rare for a colonial to switch sides like that," he said. "It would mean breaking their word openly. They'd be very reluctant to break their word unless the king broke his *first*. Did he?"

"We don't know," Peter admitted. "Our spies have passed on all sorts of rumors, but, as you know, sorting the wheat from the chaff is a difficult task."

He scowled. He'd grown up among the highest aristocracy. He knew how easy it was for a rumor to mutate into something thoroughly absurd. He knew how easily a simple story could become something so complex that no one could make head or tails of it—or believe it, if they sorted the story into something reasonably comprehendible. The king was planning to sell the colonials to the highest bidder, the king was planning to turn Caledonia into his personal garden, the king was planning . . . Peter shook his head. So many rumors swirled around that it was hard to believe that any of them might be true.

But something happened to convince Quist to take the plunge, Peter thought. William was right. A reputation for breaking their word would haunt them for the rest of eternity, particularly if they didn't have a good reason for selling out for the best they could get. The king might still win. *What happened on Caledonia?*

"You may find yourself being lured into another trap," he warned. "If so, you have full permission to act as you see fit."

William looked surprised. "Your Grace?"

"There were some people who wanted to blame you for losing Perfuma," Peter said honestly. "But it was pointed out that you *had* asked for a third superdreadnought squadron, which was denied. And you *did* recover the world."

"After Kat abandoned it," William said. "And then she gave me another bloody nose."

Peter nodded. "Right now, we don't have time for a protracted struggle. Not again. We need you to take the fleet to Fotheringay and give them hell."

William lifted his eyebrows. "And if they choose to join us?"

"Do what you can for them," Peter said. "You have wide latitude. If you think you can hit Caledonia, feel free."

He met William's eyes. "Did you hear anything from your brother?"

"Not as yet," William said. "I don't know how easy it'll be for him to meet Kat."

"Then proceed on the assumption she won't be meeting you," Peter said. "Admiral . . . we need this victory. We need it very badly."

"I understand." William stood and saluted. "I won't let you down."

Peter watched him go, then looked down at his terminal. William couldn't be blamed for his defeat at Perfuma and the bloody nose he'd been given at Rosebud, but the twin engagements had shaken public confidence. The economy had taken a serious blow. Minor, in the long run, but . . . right now, people were openly wondering if there was going to *be* a long run. Peter had read the projections. The defeats were minor, but collectively they posed a serious threat. There was a prospect, a very serious prospect, that the aristocracy, collectively or individually, would start serious talks with the king.

And then we'll discover, again, that neither side can make enough concessions to satisfy the other. In one sense, it was good news. There was no point in trying to debate the issue when the king would clearly never give them what they wanted, no matter what they offered him in return. In another sense . . . He scowled. If the damage got too bad, they'd either concede whatever the king wanted, and effectively lose the war, or simply watch helplessly as the economy collapsed anyway. *This isn't going to end well.*

He keyed his terminal, bringing up the latest reports. The intelligence officers had pointed out that someone was spreading rumors on Caledonia, but why? Were they trying to unseat the king? Drive a wedge between Hadrian and his colonial supporters? Or discredit the truth by broadcasting lies no one would actually believe? Peter was no stranger to the way things worked, but they were hundreds of light-years from Caledonia. There was no way they could figure out the truth until after the war was over.

But there must be a reason for the fabrications, he mused. One could tell a great deal about what was really going on by what someone chose to lie about. If someone was spreading lies about the king selling the colonial worlds to the highest bidder . . . was the king actually selling some of the worlds? Possibly. *And if the colonials knew the truth . . .*

"They wouldn't believe us, if we told them," he muttered. "They didn't believe the king started the war."

Yasmeena entered, looking as unflappable as ever. "Your Grace, you have a meeting at four o'clock. You asked me to remind you."

"Thanks," Peter said. He glanced at the terminal. He had just enough time to splash water on his face and eat something before the meeting. And then . . . He wondered if he'd be able to go home, or if he'd be sleeping in the office. Again. His wife was practically a stranger. "Do you want to forget next time?"

"I thought I got paid to remind you," Yasmeena said. "Not reminding you costs extra."

"In more ways than one," Peter said. If something came up and he missed the meeting, people would understand. *Most* people would understand. But if he was late because he'd forgotten, or he couldn't be bothered attending, it would be a different story. People would think he was losing his grip. They'd start bringing out the knives. Probably literally. If the king had assassinated his father . . . "Damn it!"

Yasmeena blinked. "Your Grace?"

Peter rubbed his forehead. "Sorry," he said tiredly. "Not your fault. Just . . . I'm angry."

"I understand," Yasmeena said. "Do you want me to cancel the meeting?"

Yes, Peter thought.

He scowled at the window, looking out over the towering skyscrapers that dominated the city. He lived a life of unabashed luxury. He could order everything from a six-course meal from the finest restaurant on the planet to the services of any number of escorts and no one would say anything. Not openly, at least. Still, they'd notice if he gave himself over to sybarite luxury. And . . . he knew his duty. He couldn't put it down, not until he had an heir. There were some possible candidates among the next generation, but none were *ready*. He couldn't rest until they were.

No wonder so many of us go off the rails, he thought. *We have so much, and yet we can't do anything with it.*

"No," he said, turning to face her. "I'll see him when he arrives."

◆ ◆ ◆

The orders were remarkably vague, for something drawn up by Grand Admiral Rudbek. William read them carefully, noting just how many weasel words and CYA paragraphs had been written into the document. The grand admiral hadn't drafted the orders himself, naturally, but he would have signed off on them before they were sent to William. His staff had known the grand admiral wanted to avoid any further blame. They'd done a damn good job.

But they also gave me the leeway to ensure the mission is carried out properly. William disembarked from the shuttle. *And the fleet train to make sure I can continue chopping away at their worlds, perhaps even hitting Caledonia itself, without having to fall back on a naval base to rearm.*

He keyed his wristcom as he headed to his cabin. "Staff meeting, twenty minutes," he said. "Contact the newly assigned squadrons and inform them that I want their commanders to attend too."

"Aye, Admiral," Yagami said.

"And make sure they know that we'll be leaving within the next few hours," William added. He'd ensured the fleet was prepped for a rapid turnaround after he'd returned from Rosebud, but there would be problems if he didn't make it clear they would be leaving. The crews wanted shore leave. Hell, the officers wanted shore leave. "I don't want any delays."

"Aye, Admiral."

William closed the channel as he stepped into his cabin, hastily removing his dress jacket and replacing it with his daywear. It wouldn't look perfect, but his officers were smart and experienced enough, now, to know that it was better to be good than merely *look* good. He snorted as he splashed water on his face. They wouldn't care if he commanded battles in the nude, as long as he won.

He sat at his desk, his eyes widening as he saw the single message from Scott. His brother's message was encrypted, with a civilian code that had been cracked long ago. The message path showed that it had passed through a dozen StarComs, bouncing from station to station until it had finally reached William's terminal. A dozen chances for it to be intercepted and read . . . William let out a long breath. It hardly mattered. The encryption might be broken, but there was no way to pull the true meaning out of the text. Unless Scott had fallen into enemy hands . . .

Kat wouldn't betray him, he told himself. *But the mere fact he's connected to me might betray him.*

The message opened at his touch, without even a pretend-delay for decryption. William scanned the words, his lips twitching as he read the bitching about entry procedures at Caledonia and the risk they posed to free movement of goods. Scott had always specialized in running banned goods to people who wanted them—goods they wanted, at least in part, because they were banned. William suspected that was the *real* thrill. He'd tested a few things that had been banned on his now-dead homeworld when he'd joined the navy. They'd been decidedly unimpressive.

He picked out the important phrases among the chatter. *He met Kat. She agreed to meet. They don't know where. Not yet. He's still in orbit, waiting for my reply.*

William sat back, thinking hard. Kat was a . . . conscientious naval officer. She'd sided with the king, at least in part, because she took her duties seriously. If he sent her a message that hinted he might be coming in her direction, she'd do . . . what? Tell the king? Prepare for attack? Guess his target and lay an ambush? She knew him well enough to guess which world he might attack; she didn't know, really, that he *hadn't* chosen the target. Or . . . did the king have spies watching the fleet?

He took a moment to compose the message. Scott couldn't remain at Caledonia indefinitely, not when he'd be burning money for no return. But . . . William sketched out the encoded words, asking Scott to stay close. They'd be able to link up, once William reached Fotheringay. And then . . . William studied his hands. There would be no end of problems in actually getting Kat and himself together. He didn't think they'd be easy to overcome, but they could do it.

The intercom bleeped. "Admiral, the meeting is about to begin," Yagami said. "I—"

"I'll be there." William cut him off. "Give me a moment."

"Aye, sir," Yagami said.

William finished the message, wrapped the code phrases in meaningless drivel, and sent it on its way. The king's counterintelligence specialists *shouldn't* be able to pluck meaning—the wrong meaning, that is—from the words. They'd probably be reassured by the very basic encryption, if they bothered to think about it. William hoped that was true. Scott was probably under close observation. A smuggler would hardly be considered a paragon of loyalty, not as long as he needed money. The king's people would fear being outbid by the House of Lords.

But Scott is doing it for me, William told himself. He'd always been able to depend on his brother, even though he'd never really trusted the man Scott had made of himself. *He won't let me down.*

He put the question aside and stood, brushing down his jacket as he headed to the hatch and stepped through. The superdreadnought was humming with activity as her crews prepared to leave the system, crewmen and yarddogs hurrying from compartment to compartment as they finished the repairs and stocked up on everything from missiles to fresh fruit and vegetables. They looked young, so young, and it was hard to believe that many of them had fought in the last war. William felt his heart twist again. People were not meant to live so long.

And you shouldn't be complaining, he told himself sarcastically. The average lifespan on his homeworld had been very low, even before the Theocracy had turned it into a radioactive nightmare. *You'd be worse off if you were dead.*

The holograms were waiting for him as he strode into the briefing room, overlapping each other as they turned to face him. William glanced from face to face as he walked to his seat and sat down, silently giving them his blessing to sit too. He knew most of them from the last few months. The ones he didn't know came well recommended. Home Fleet was no longer the shambolic wreck that had barely won the Battle of Tyre. It was one of the best-trained fleets in the known universe, and perhaps the best equipped.

"We're taking the offensive," William said. His words hung in the air. "We're launching a strike into the heart of enemy territory."

He was careful not to name the target. He'd planned to keep it to himself until they were deep within enemy space. The king's agents, if they heard his words, would believe that Caledonia itself was the target, an assumption that should keep the king's ships pinned down long enough for William to strike, then hold position. If nothing else, the king and his fleet would be reacting to *William* for a change.

"This time, we're going to make them jump," he said once he'd outlined what little he could reveal. They'd remain annoyed at the secrecy, but they'd understand. "If they come after us with a small force, we're going to kick its ass. If they come after us with a large force, we're going to make them wear out their equipment chasing us. Simple. Deadly."

He smiled. Complex plans were asking for trouble. "Any questions?"

There was a pause. No one spoke. "To your ships," William said. "We leave in five hours. And I want to be ready."

CHAPTER TWENTY-FIVE

FOTHERINGAY

William had feared, more than he'd ever admit to anyone, that *something* would go wrong during transit. Fotheringay was nearly three weeks from Tyre, even if they pushed their drives to the limit. Grand Admiral Rudbek and Home Fleet—the remains of Home Fleet—had worked hard to conceal the fleet's departure, but there were limits to how much they could do. Sooner or later, someone would notice that officers and crew who should be on shore leave were nowhere to be seen. Or someone would be puzzled, then alarmed, when they sent a message to their relatives on naval service and received no reply. He was relieved beyond words, as the fleet approached its target, that nothing had gone spectacularly wrong.

Which means they could be lurking in cloak, ready to spring an ambush, he thought coldly. *Kat could be baiting a trap if she guessed my target.*

He scowled. The House of Lords had been generous. They'd given him *four* superdreadnought squadrons, although one of them was composed of ships snatched out of the repair yards or hastily yanked out of the naval reserve and pressed back into service. Their training wasn't the best, but he'd drilled his crews hard during the journey in hopes of smoothing out the worst of their imperfections. Kat would find herself outgunned, unless she threw the king's entire fleet at him. And, if she did, the war would practically be decided overnight.

"Admiral," Yagami said. "Emergence in five minutes."

William nodded tersely. There were no orders to be issued, not now. His crews knew their duties. They were already at battlestations, counting down the seconds until they encountered the enemy. For some, it would be their first taste of combat. William could feel the mixture of anticipation and fear as they braced themselves, relishing the challenge even as they accepted the prospect of dying in the next few hours. It had been a long time since William had felt anything of the sort. He knew that he could die too, but . . . He shook his head. The only thing he could do was wait.

And brood, he thought. Scott had left Caledonia, according to the last report. He was going to another world, then heading back to the king's capital. It was a shame William hadn't dared suggest he go straight to Fotheringay, but the risk was simply too great. They'd just have to hope they could meet up once William invaded Fotheringay and occupied the system. *It will be interesting to see how quickly the king responds.*

He glanced at the starchart. Fotheringay was just over a day from Caledonia, assuming the king's forces set out at once. He'd have some of his ships on QRF duties, ready to leave at a moment's notice, but the majority of his fleet would be stepped down. QRF duties put so much wear and tear on the equipment that the king wouldn't need William's forces to attack to lose the war. And yet, Kat couldn't send anything less than three or four superdreadnought squadrons herself. William would have sold his soul to run into two enemy superdreadnought squadrons. Four against two would hardly be an even match.

"Emergence in ten," Yagami said. "Nine . . . eight . . ."

William leaned forward as the countdown reached zero. The display lit up, revealing a handful of starships and orbital installations surrounding Fotheringay. They'd come out of hyperspace too far from the planet for a meaningful blockade, ensuring the enemy warships and freighters had a chance to run before his ships entered weapons range. William knew there'd be armchair admirals questioning the wisdom of allowing the enemy a chance to flee, but he knew what he was doing. His ships would have plenty of room to maneuver or jump back into hyperspace if they were flying into a trap.

He felt an odd little pang as the fleet shook down and glided towards its target. Fotheringay wasn't anything like as developed as Tyre or Caledonia, but it was on the way. Given time, and a little more investment, it would join the first-rank worlds . . . or would have, if he wasn't about to devastate the system. He watched the enemy ships forming into a ramshackle line of battle, torn between respect and contempt. He outmassed them so badly that he could fight with both hands tied behind his back and still come out ahead. They should have run. They knew, didn't they, that their world would be treated gently? He was damned if he'd bombard civilian targets to force the planet to surrender.

But they don't want to seem cowards in front of the watching world, he thought. He'd seen enough of that when he'd been an adolescent. People too foolish to back down, preparing to fight while secretly hoping someone with authority would come along and put a stop to the fighting before it got out of hand. *There's nothing to gain by getting themselves blown to atoms.*

He glanced at Yagami. "Send the surrender demand," he ordered. "And reduce speed."

If Yagami was surprised at an order that was *odd*, to say the least, he didn't show it. "Yes, sir."

William waited, wondering if the enemy ships would see sense and run. They honestly had nothing to gain from fighting, nothing at all. They'd be better off slipping into hyperspace and lurking at the edge of the system, raiding his fleet train and waiting for relief to arrive. But they were too stubborn to retreat. They were colonials, just like him. The thought brought him no peace. He'd been too stubborn, once upon a time, and then he'd grown up. And he wasn't sure he liked the man he saw in the mirror.

"Admiral, the enemy fleet is locking weapons on our hulls," Yagami said. "I—"

He broke off as red icons flared into life. "Missile separation! I say again, missile separation!"

"The point defense is to engage as soon as the missiles enter range," William ordered. "Hold the decoys back, for the moment."

Yagami's back stiffened. "Aye, Admiral."

William wanted to grin. Yagami wasn't practiced at hiding his emotions. He thought his admiral had made a bad call. Or, worse, that he'd deliberately *allowed* the enemy ships to take a shot at his hulls. But the enemy missiles weren't modern missiles. There weren't even very many of them. A few hundred warheads weren't going to get through the point defense web, let alone the shields. The salvo was impressive for such a small cluster of ships, but wasn't good enough to stop a single superdreadnought. They'd need to fire upwards of a thousand missiles, backed up by decoys and remote targeting systems, to have a fighting chance.

And they didn't know we were coming, he thought as the enemy missiles closed on his superdreadnoughts. *They could have pre-positioned missile pods if they'd known.*

He watched as the enemy missiles flew into his point defense network and evaporated. They just weren't advanced enough to survive, not long enough to get to his ships. The enemy ships fired a second, much-reduced salvo, then opened vortexes and jumped into hyperspace. William was almost relieved. The brief engagement hadn't ended in slaughter. Hell, they'd have done more damage by forcing him to expend missiles than anything else. His lips curved into a smile. His fleet had won without having to exterminate the enemy.

"They're gone," Yagami reported. "They could be going anywhere . . ."

"What's important is that they're not *here*," William said. He watched the remainder of the orbiting freighters fleeing in all directions, then turned his attention to the planet. "Raise Fotheringay. Inform them that they have a choice between surrender, with their installations garrisoned until the end of the war, or watching helplessly as we take out the installations before withdrawing."

"Aye, Admiral," Yagami said.

William nodded as the range closed, hoping that someone smart was in command of the planet below. He understood the urge to fight, but the worst the planet could do was little more than kicking and scratching on the way to the gallows. Still, there were enough stories about what had happened at Tarleton, ranging from the believable to the frankly insane or easily disprovable, for him to worry about the planet's future whoever won the war. It didn't help that he couldn't stay. If Quist changed sides, William would have to take his fleet there.

"Targets locked," Yagami said. "Ready to fire on your command."

Don't be a fool, William pleaded silently. *Give up. Surrender. You'll live. Your planet will live.*

"Admiral, I'm picking up a response," Yagami said. "They want to speak with you."

"Put them through," William ordered.

A face appeared in front of him. William studied the planetary leader curiously, noting the telltale signs of genetic enhancement and modification. The man was a little *too* perfect, just like Kat. He had light-brown skin, and his dark hair was strikingly bold, cut in a pattern that had been fashionable a few decades ago. It probably was *still* fashionable on the planet below. The colonials had made a big deal about not following fashions set by Tyre.

"Admiral," the speaker said. A line of text identified him as First Councilor Palaver. "What are your terms?"

"My terms are very simple," William said. He'd heard of Palaver. He'd been one of the founders of the Colonial Alliance, back when it had been nothing more than another pressure group. The poor bastard had to be wondering if he was about to be arrested for treason. "You are to shut down your remaining planetary defense installations and order your troops to return home. You are to evacuate your orbital installations so they can be occupied for the duration of the conflict. My intelligence staffers will land and inspect your communications terminals and StarCom nodes for actionable intelligence. Beyond that . . ."

He met Palaver's eyes, willing him to understand. To believe. "Beyond that, your world will remain untouched. There will be no bombardments, no reparations, no retributions. Certain of your political leaders will be expected to retire from public life, but otherwise . . . there will be no punishment."

Palaver frowned. "And these demands come directly from the House of Lords?"

"Yes," William said. "They will be honored, as long as you do likewise."

"Fine." Palaver made a dismissive gesture. "We accept your terms."

"Thank you," William said. "My troops will board the installations in one hour."

He smiled, thinly, as Palaver's face vanished from the display. The man didn't *believe* the promise of no retributions, at least not when it came to the Colonial Alliance's movers and shakers. Palaver had to expect the worst. There was no shortage of people on Tyre with excellent reason to demand his head, with or without his body attached. But Duke Peter had made it clear that they'd follow a policy of conciliation as long as the former rebels behaved themselves, which would hopefully make it harder for fire-eaters to demand they continue the war.

"Keep the fleet in high orbit, ready to leave at a moment's notice," he ordered. "The marines can deploy when the deadline expires."

"Aye, Admiral," Yagami said. He frowned. "Permission to speak freely, sir?"

"Granted." William had a very good idea what Yagami was about to say. "What do you want to ask?"

"You worked hard to avoid killing them," Yagami said. "Those ships, the ones that fled, we're going to see them again, firing missiles at us. Why did you let them go?"

William took a moment to consider his answer. "You're right. I *did* let them go. I could have destroyed their ships or forced them to surrender, but I let them go. Right?"

"Yes, sir," Yagami said carefully.

"On one hand, those ships are largely worthless," William said. "They're not going to add anything to the king's fleet unless they have a lot of them. They'll certainly need to be rearmed before they can do anything more than soak up our firepower. Ideally, the king will waste missiles rearming them instead of giving the missiles to his superdreadnoughts. And if not . . ."

He kept his eyes on the display. "On the other hand, there's no point in slaughtering them. And yes, it would be slaughter. We'd be smashing them from well beyond their effective range. It would lead to more and more bad feeling on the planet below, making it harder for them to accept peace after the war. There'd be people wanting revenge and setting up insurgencies or terrorist campaigns. We don't really want another Cadiz."

Yagami didn't look convinced. "Sir . . . they hate us anyway."

"Yes, they do." William nodded. There was no point in trying to dispute it. "But we can at least *try* to change their minds."

He frowned as he studied the display. "And as we're not going to be staying here for long," he added, "it's probably in our interests to make sure they don't see us as murdering bastards."

◆ ◆ ◆

Kat dreamed.

She hadn't slept well in the nights since Scott had come to her. The mere thought of being watched by unfriendly eyes was enough to bother her, even though, as a naval officer, she had no expectations of privacy. Jenkins had been as slimy and unpleasant as ever during their brief talks, his attitude enough to convince Kat that he was watching her. The reports from the rest of the fleet suggested that the political commissioners had long since worn out their welcome. One unlucky commissioner had suffered a horrific accident in an airlock that no one believed had been remotely accidental. But, so far, the person behind the "accident" hadn't been found.

The dream was shadowy, a threat she couldn't place, a deafening noise . . .

She jolted awake, lying in a pool of her own sweat. The intercom was bleeping loudly, so loudly that she was half convinced the planet was under attack. She started upright, brushing her hair out of her face as she reached for the terminal. The screen lit up, revealing Kitty's face. Kat was silently relieved the cabin was so dark. She probably looked as far from an admiral as it was possible to be.

"Admiral," Kitty said. "We just received word. Fotheringay is under attack by a major enemy fleet."

Kat rubbed her forehead. "How many ships?"

"The last report stated over thirty superdreadnoughts," Kitty said. "The planetary defenses don't have top-of-the-line gear. I mean, they *didn't* have it. I . . . those superdreadnoughts could be fakes. They didn't fire missiles, just point defense."

"Curious." Kat stood. "Have the records downloaded to the tactical department, then signal His Majesty. Tell him . . ."

Kitty glanced at something off-screen. "He's already calling you, Admiral," she said quickly. "Should I put him through?"

Kat grabbed for a robe and pulled it on. Her body ached, as if she hadn't really slept at all. She turned on the lights as soon as she was decent, then nodded to Kitty. The king's face appeared in the display a second later. He looked as if he'd been woken up too.

I should have been told first, Kat thought crossly. Her fingers danced across the terminal, putting the fleet on alert. She'd need to muster at least three superdreadnought squadrons if she wanted to counterattack, unless . . . *How many of those enemy superdreadnoughts are real?*

"Kat." The king sounded wretched. "This offensive cannot go unanswered."

"I understand," Kat said. "However, it could easily be a feint to draw us out of position."

The king stroked his unshaven chin. "They've got us, either way," he said. "If we don't respond, we look weak. If we do, we run the risk of them launching a massive attack on Caledonia."

"Yes." Kat frowned. "We don't know how many of those super-dreadnoughts are actually real."

"You mean some of them could be nothing more than sensor ghosts?" The king met her eyes. "Are you sure?"

Kat shook her head. "The analysts will have to see what they make of the records," she said. Whoever was in command might be smart enough to play a shell game with his superdreadnoughts and decoys, the same sort of game she'd played herself. Getting it wrong could be catastrophic. "But they might not be entirely sure."

"They never are," the king told her. He pursed his lips, thinking hard. "Very well. You will take your fleet to Fotheringay. If the enemy is weaker than we thought, you can give them the boot. Drive them back out of the system, then deal with any traitors . . ."

"Not again," Kat said flatly. She had no intention of going through *that* again. "We don't need another Montfort."

The king's eyes flashed fire, just for a second. "Very well," he said. "Proceed as you see fit. And if you can't boot them out, retreat at once. No point in trying to win an impossible battle."

"Understood, Your Majesty," Kat said. William was at Fotheringay. He *had* to be. And that meant . . . what? A chance to meet, or yet another chance to kill each other? She didn't need to look at the records to know Scott wasn't in the system. "I won't let you down."

"I know it," the king said. "Hold the line, just long enough for us to get the new weapons into play. And then we can retake Tyre and win this war."

Kat took a long breath as the king's face vanished. "Kitty, alert the fleet," she ordered curtly. "We'll depart in two hours."

"Aye, Admiral," Kitty said. If she had any doubts about an impossibly short departure time, she kept them to herself. "How many superdreadnoughts?"

"Three squadrons, if they'll let us," Kat said. "And two if not."

"Aye, Admiral."

CHAPTER TWENTY-SIX

FOTHERINGAY

Fotheringay, Kat thought as the fleet flew through hyperspace, was an odd choice of target. It was too close to Caledonia for the planet to be attacked, occupied, and properly looted before reinforcements could arrive, yet too far away to give the enemy fleet a chance to attack Caledonia itself. Sure, they *could* launch themselves at Caledonia, but Kat would have plenty of time to send a warning and hurry back to join the defense. It would be the worst of all possible worlds for the attackers.

She glared at the latest report from the analysts, wishing, again, that they could commit themselves. They weren't sure how many of the enemy superdreadnoughts were real. None of the enemy ships had fired a major salvo, something that couldn't be faked; the jury was still out, it seemed, on the question of if their point defense fire could be faked. The analysts were confident there were at least two enemy superdreadnought squadrons orbiting Fotheringay, unless they'd moved in the last few hours, but they weren't sure if there were two *more*. Kat hoped the former and feared the latter. She'd be happy to meet the enemy on even terms, but four against two was a guaranteed disaster.

Unless the new missiles really are good, she thought as the timer ticked down to zero. *It will be interesting to test them before we stake everything on one last roll of the dice.*

She braced herself as the fleet opened vortexes and flew back into realspace. The display blinked and updated, four enemy superdreadnought squadrons taking shape near the planet. A handful of smaller ships orbited the planet itself, but the remainder were well clear . . . as if they wanted to flee at the first hint of trouble. Kat frowned, puzzled. They might be playing more shell games, if half the superdreadnoughts were nothing more than sensor ghosts, or they might be trying to lure her into an ambush. Her drives whined as they cycled back up, ready to yank the entire fleet back into hyperspace if they ran into something they couldn't handle. Kat smiled, despite herself. If nothing else, the chance to test the new missiles could hardly be wasted.

"Long-range sensors are picking up four enemy superdreadnought squadrons, plus sixty smaller ships," Kitty warned. "It's unclear if any or all of them are sensor ghosts."

"Launch probes," Kat ordered. They were short of probes—they hadn't been able to buy any from *anyone*—but there was no choice. "And then take us in on attack vector."

"Picking up a signal from the planet," Lieutenant Hamilton called. "They're saying the enemy occupation force is bugging out."

It can't be a very big occupation force, Kat thought. *They wouldn't have landed thousands of troops unless they were confident they could hold the high orbitals.*

Her gaze shifted to the display. The enemy superdreadnoughts were coming to life, flowing into formation as they swept her ships with tactical sensors. They looked ready for a long-range engagement rather than preparing themselves to steer towards her and trying to close the range as much as possible. Her eyes narrowed as she felt a hint of cold satisfaction. They had to be bluffing. The opportunity to trap and destroy two of the king's irreplaceable squadrons could hardly be ignored. If, of course, they had the power to take advantage of the opportunity . . .

"The probe reports are inconclusive," Kitty reported. "The superdreadnoughts look real, but they're running away."

"Yes." Kat studied the raw data for a long moment. It *was* odd. The superdreadnoughts looked real—they were certainly emitting sensor pulses that suggested they were real—but they weren't acting real. They were like cats fleeing mice. They should have turned on her and taken advantage of their supremacy to crush her ships. "They might have scattered their squadrons . . ."

She stroked her chin as the range continued to close. They could be trying to spread out their ships in the hope of adding real sensor pulses to a fleet of sensor ghosts, but that only weakened them. They had to know it too. Unless . . . She wondered if there had been four superdreadnought squadrons originally, but two had departed to parts unknown. The House of Lords wasn't short on targets. They could cause a great deal of trouble if they rampaged around Caledonia without ever hitting the king's capital itself. They could . . . so why weren't they?

"Admiral, we'll be entering missile range in two minutes," Kitty said. "Your orders?"

"Lock missiles on target," Kat ordered. "Fire when we enter standard range."

Her eyes narrowed as the range continued to fall. She would have preferred to hold her fire until the range closed still further, but she didn't dare get into a close-range missile duel with four enemy squadrons. It was simply too risky. And yet, firing at extreme range would give the enemy plenty of time to prepare their point defense *and* give them insight into the new missiles too. They wouldn't be that much of a surprise when the decisive engagement was fought and won. But . . . She shook her head. It couldn't be helped. If those superdreadnoughts were real, she'd have to turn tail and run as soon as they revealed themselves.

"Entering missiles range," Kitty reported. "Admiral."

Kat nodded. "Fire."

◆ ◆ ◆

I'm going to be fired for this. It wasn't really a joke. William had been taught to be aggressive, and the chance to obliterate two enemy super-dreadnought squadrons wasn't one he was supposed to pass up. *They'll be expecting me to close the range and open fire.*

He shook his head as his fleet continued to head away from the planet, luring the enemy fleet into a pursuit course. He could see a dozen ways to lure them closer, to keep them fat and happy until they entered point-blank range and discovered, to their horror, that all four of his squadrons were real. But he didn't want to blow them away, not when he needed to keep them guessing. The chance to meet Kat was merely the icing on the cake.

If Scott makes it to the RV point in time, he reminded himself. There'd been no reply. There was no way, even, to know Scott had gotten the message. The king's counterintelligence officers might have twigged to him, might have arrested him . . . William had no way of knowing what had happened until it was too late. *He might already be on his way, or he might be dead.*

The display sparkled with red icons. The enemy superdreadnoughts had opened fire. William's intelligence analysts had sworn blind the enemy was running out of missiles, that they were expending far more than they could hope to replace, but . . . it looked as if the analysts had forgotten to tell the enemy. If Kat was short of missiles, surely she would have sought to close the range as much as possible. She would have needed to ensure that all shots counted, despite the risk of running into a trap. William smiled as the missile vectors updated again and again. His point defense would stop most of them in their tracks.

"Admiral," Yagami said. "The missiles are nonstandard."

William looked up. "In what way?"

"They're close to Mark-VIII missiles, but not exact copies." Yagami looked up from his console. "I'd say they were bootleg versions if there weren't so *many* of them."

We thought the king was trading with foreign powers, William mused. *I guess we've just found the proof.*

His mind raced. He knew his crews could handle Mark-VIII missiles. The enemy missiles, on the other hand, might be harder to predict. Their targeting systems might be better than expected, or worse; they might be armed with nukes or antimatter or some weapons system he'd never imagined until Kat hit him with it. No, that wasn't too likely. He'd be astonished if *anyone* sold the king top-of-the-range weapons, no matter what they stood to gain. There would be too great a risk of the weapons falling into unfriendly hands. Hell, Hadrian himself might turn unfriendly. A man who'd plot to start a war and assassinate his closest allies would hardly hesitate to plot another war.

"Stay the course," he ordered quietly. They'd get some good data, although it would come at a price. "Let them close the range."

Yagami looked uncomfortable. William understood. They could—should—be returning fire. They could have given Kat a scare, even if she was smart enough to run rather than let him batter her ships to bits. But instead he was letting her get closer. There was nothing to be gained by opening fire, not now. Better to close the range.

And we don't want to keep the planet below. That makes it a little bit easier, doesn't it?

He cleared his throat. "Have the landing parties returned to their ships?"

"Yes, sir," Yagami said. "The locals made no attempt to impede them."

"Then tell them to depart now," William ordered. "They can link up with us at the RV point."

"Aye, sir," Yagami said.

William nodded, watching coldly as the enemy missiles finally entered point defense range. His ships opened fire as one, the sheer weight of fire dispelling any illusions about sensor ghosts and ECM tricks. Kat knew, now, that his vessels were real. He wondered, idly, what she'd do as her tidal wave of missiles started to evaporate. The missiles, wherever they'd really come from, were good . . . but not *that* good. A handful made it through the point defense, only to expend themselves uselessly on sensor decoys, their targeting systems not up to scratch.

But they were fired at extreme range, he reminded himself as a couple of enemy missiles made it through the web and threw themselves onto his ships. *They didn't have time to pick their targets carefully before their drives burned themselves out.*

"*Nelson* took two hits, both nukes," Yagami reported. "Her shields handled it."

"Good." The range continued to close. Kat hadn't slowed, surprisingly. She had to be *very* confident that she could jump out before he smashed her ships to rubble. He wasn't going to try. "Are we ready to jump out?"

Yagami glanced up. "Yes, Admiral."

William heard a dozen unasked questions in the younger man's tone. Why wasn't William pressing their advantage? Why wasn't he dealing a second blow to the king? William promised himself that he'd explain later, if there *was* a later. The dukes had signed off on the plan, despite their doubts. It all depended on factors outside their control, but the plan was designed to give them room to maneuver if things didn't go as he hoped.

"Open the vortexes," he ordered. "Take us out of here."

"Aye, Admiral," Yagami said. He keyed his console. "Vortexes opening . . . now!"

◆ ◆ ◆

"Admiral," Kitty reported. "The enemy fleet is retreating!"

Kat stared, unable to believe her eyes. She'd been wrong. All *four* enemy squadrons were real. The enemy commander had a decisive advantage, if he wished to use it. And instead . . . he'd just buggered off, without even bothering to fire a shot? It made no sense. Her gaze slipped to Fotheringay, a blue-green orb floating in the display. The planet's skies were clear. The enemy fleet that had held the high orbitals had fled too.

Her thoughts ran in circles. Whoever was in command had to be an idiot. Except . . . the House of Lords didn't give commands to idiots. It would be William or . . . She couldn't think of anyone who would give up a two-to-one advantage. He'd be in deep trouble when he got home. It wasn't as if he had reason to believe he was outgunned. Kat hadn't tried to convince him that she had a decisive advantage. She was fairly sure he wouldn't have believed her if she'd tried.

Maybe he just wanted to force us to expend our missiles. Shoot ourselves dry so we couldn't put up a fight when they attacked Caledonia.

Fotheringay was practically immaterial, as far as the war effort was concerned. The House of Worlds would be demanding action, action the king couldn't take without weakening Caledonia's defenses . . . Maybe that was the point. Give the king a taste of his own medicine without risking a battle that could have gone either way. But it couldn't have gone either way. She knew she'd been seriously outgunned. The enemy shouldn't have passed up the chance to smash her ships. She wouldn't have let the opportunity slip away if *she'd* been in command.

"Reverse course," she ordered. "Take us to the planet. Once the StarCom is powered up, get me a direct link to the king."

"Aye, Admiral," Kitty said. She glanced at Kat. "We won, didn't we?"

"I don't know," Kat said. The king's PR specialists would turn the engagement into a glorious victory. She knew better. The enemy had practically let them win. No, there was no *practically* about it. They'd retreated rather than risk an engagement. Her thoughts ran in circles. No matter how she looked at it, there was no logic. "Keep the fleet ready to depart at a moment's notice. They might be on their way to Caledonia."

"Aye, Admiral."

◆ ◆ ◆

William was gloomily aware of the perplexed mood in the CIC as the fleet dropped back out of hyperspace. The RV point was only a couple of light-months from Fotheringay, but it might as well have been on the other side of the galaxy as far as the planet's long-range sensors were concerned. Tyre's network of deep-space sensors might pick up a fleet that close to the planet, but Fotheringay didn't have the resources to monitor interplanetary space, let alone interstellar space. They wouldn't know the fleet was lurking nearby.

Unless they followed us through hyperspace. But they'd have to be very lucky.

He smiled rather thinly. Most people wouldn't consider finding the fleet to be luck, unless they had a bigger fleet under their command. His fleet hadn't even fired its missiles. He was as ready as ever to fight, while the enemy fleet had already expended its external racks. And that meant . . . he could go back if he wished, go back and recapture the planet. But Fotheringay really wasn't that important.

"Send a signal to Tyre," he ordered shortly. "We've completed Phase One."

"Aye, Admiral," Yagami said. "Sir . . ."

William felt his smile grow wider. "What's the point? It depends. It really depends."

An alarm bleeped before he could explain. "Admiral, we have a freighter inbound," Lieutenant Mumbai said. "She reads out as *John Galt*."

"Good," William said. Scott had arrived. "Hail her commander. Inform him that his ship is cleared to dock, then get me a link to Commodore Tyco. He'll be taking command of the fleet in my absence."

Yagami looked even more puzzled but obeyed. William sat back in his chair, wondering if he stood on the cusp of victory or total defeat. Total personal defeat, he supposed. He had a high opinion of himself, but not *that* high. The House of Lords had a multitude of officers who could be promoted into his seat, if necessary. Commodore Tyco was hardly incompetent. He could handle the remainder of the operation if William didn't make it back.

"Commodore," he said when Tyco appeared in the display. "Phase Two is about to begin. Do you understand me?"

"Yes, sir." Commodore Tyco was the only other person on the fleet who knew the complete plan. "I'm ready."

William's lips twitched. "Take command of the fleet. If you don't hear back from me in twenty-four hours, or if you come under attack, assume the worst. Take the fleet to a random location, then report to Tyre and await orders. Do *not* try to retrieve me."

"Aye, sir," Commodore Tyco said. "I . . . good luck, sir."

"Thanks." William stood. "Once more into the breach, dear friends."

"Consign their parts most private to a Rutland tree," Commodore Tyco countered. "Or would that be a mistake?"

"Probably, at least here," William said. If the mission turned to violence, it would have failed. And he'd probably be dead. "I'll see you in twenty hours or so."

He handed squadron command to Captain Cavendish, then headed to the hatch. Scott would take him into the system, with the codes necessary to ensure a meeting with Kat. And then . . . William felt unsure of himself, no matter how much he tried to hide it. Kat was stubborn, just like her oldest brother. She'd be reluctant to admit a mistake. He stepped into his office, retrieved the datachips from his safe and pocketed them. Duke Peter had given him copies of the evidence. He'd just have to hope Kat didn't dismiss them as obvious lies.

And if she does, I won't be coming home, he thought. He took one last look around the office before walking down to the airlock. *It could all end very badly.*

"William," Scott said. "Are you sure you want to do this?"

"Yes," William said stiffly. He didn't have time for Scott's attitude, not now. His brother didn't know what was at stake, beyond the war itself. William hadn't risked telling him the full truth. "It has to be done."

Scott snorted as he closed the airlock. "You'll go down in history," he said. "But will it be as a great hero? Or history's biggest boob?"

"I'll do my duty," William said. "And history will say what it damn well likes."

CHAPTER TWENTY-SEVEN

"Admiral," Kitty said. "A freighter just dropped out of hyperspace. Her captain is asking for you, by name."

Kat blinked as she saw the IFF. *John Galt?* Scott McElney's ship? Had the entire engagement been nothing more than an excuse to lure her away from Caledonia, to arrange a meeting well away from Jenkins and his ilk? The man himself was down on the planet, reassuring the planetary leadership they had nothing to fear from the king and his government. Kat had been rather hoping they'd be recalled to Caledonia so quickly that she'd have an excuse to leave him behind.

"Clear him to dock," she ordered. The *John Galt* was tiny compared to the massive superdreadnought. Smugglers preferred speed to size, at least when they were operating along the fringes of civilized space. Scott would have no trouble docking his ship to hers. "And inform him that I'll come aboard once he's docked."

Kitty looked surprised but did as she was told. Kat was the admiral. Scott McElney should have come to *her*, not the other way around. But Kat was fairly sure Scott's ship would be free of bugs. Her marines had carried out a handful of searches and discovered a number of unauthorized bugs scattered throughout the ship. Jenkins would be in real trouble, under normal circumstances. But things hadn't been *normal* for years.

Kat passed command to her second, then headed through the ship to the airlock. A pair of marines stood on guard, as per standard procedure. Kat wished, again, that Pat had lived. She knew General Timothy Winters and his subordinates fairly well, but they'd never been intimate. There was no way to know which way they'd jump if the shit hit the fan. They'd stayed with the king . . . or had they stayed with *her*? It was hard to be sure these days. She braced herself, nodded to the marines, and tapped the airlock. It opened, blowing a gust of air into her face. It smelled . . . different.

Too many people in too close proximity, Kat thought as she stepped through the airlock. *And perhaps too many orbital habitats.*

The ship's interior looked . . . civilian. Kat peered around with interest. The ship was a mess, although her experienced eye could pick out that it wasn't a *true* mess. Scott might not keep his ship in perfect shape, but he wasn't cutting corners either. The man himself stood by an inner hatch, indicating a small compartment. Kat stepped up to him and looked inside. William was there, waiting for her . . .

She felt her heart skip a beat. William had come to her, he'd *trusted* her . . . Her mouth was suddenly very dry as she realized the true magnitude of the risk he'd taken. She should arrest him. The king would order her to do so, if he knew William was on her ship. And there was no way in hell William would have taken the risk, would have done something that would have earned him a court-martial even if she didn't arrest him, without permission from higher authority. Had Peter signed off on the mission? Or . . . She found it hard to believe William would have launched peace talks, particularly in such a manner, without clearance from the House of Lords.

"I'll leave you two to get on with it," Scott said. "I'll be on the bridge."

Kat glanced at him, then looked back at William. He looked older somehow, despite a series of rejuvenation treatments. He held himself like an old man. His face seemed lined, even though the wrinkles existed only in her imagination. And his gaze was severe as he studied her in return. She wondered what he saw. She wasn't the jumped-up aristocrat she'd been, back when they'd first met. A lot of water had passed under the bridge.

"Kat," William said. "I . . . I don't know what to say."

Kat had to laugh. "Me neither," she said. She indicated the blast chairs. "Should we sit down?"

"Good idea," William said. "You know, I tried to think of what I should say. I went through it, time and time again. And yet, here you are, and my mind has gone blank. Utterly blank."

"Mine too," Kat admitted. William had always been open with her, once they'd learned to trust one another. It felt good to know they still had each other, even if they *were* on opposing sides. "It's good to see you again."

William sobered. "You might not feel that way in an hour or so," he said. "I wish there was another way to do this."

Kat's eyes narrowed. "Are you here to ask me to take a message to the king?"

But she knew, even as she spoke, that William had something else in mind.

He didn't need to engage in subterfuge if he wanted her to take a message to Hadrian. He certainly wouldn't have worked hard to ensure she could talk to him without anyone knowing what she'd done, let alone . . . She tried to imagine how much the brief engagement had cost him and shuddered in horror. Whatever Peter had said, whatever he'd promised William, it might not be enough to make up for the bucket of crap that was about to land on his head. Every armchair admiral in the known galaxy was about to condemn his handling of the recent battle, if battle wasn't too strong a word. And, for once, they'd be right.

"No." William held her eyes evenly. "I wanted to bring a message to you."

Kat looked back at him, reminding herself that she'd fought and won a dozen battles. She had no reason to be nervous, no reason to feel a mad impulse to turn and run or . . . She composed herself, resting her hands in her lap. She could handle whatever he had to say. She could.

"I don't know where to begin," William admitted. "Can I start at the beginning?"

"A very good place to start," Kat said. His words didn't make her feel any better. "I'm listening."

William looked down at his hands, then met her eyes again. "When the king fled, the House of Lords captured his palace, his bunker, and a number of installations that didn't appear on any official record. Since then, they've had investigators going through the king's files and trying to put together a picture of what he was actually *doing* before the war broke out. It's been a very slow process. A number of datacores were destroyed. Others were missing or seemingly incomplete."

Kat frowned. "And . . . ?"

William produced a handful of datachips from his pocket and held them in his hand. "We know, now, that the king deliberately conspired to lure the Theocracy into attacking Cadiz," he said. "The timing was good, good enough to allow the Theocracy to score a victory without doing any real damage to the Commonwealth's war-making power. Admiral Christian's redeployment was intended, we believe, to ensure the Theocracy didn't do more damage than the king wished."

"The king has already discredited that claim," Kat pointed out. She had an uneasy feeling in her stomach. Hadrian's statements were logical, but she knew and trusted William. "Why would he need to *bother*?"

"Even fanatics can be convinced to stay their hand, if they believe they'll get their asses kicked," William pointed out. "The king, we think, didn't want to take chances. Admiral Morrison's orders were to keep the defenses down, so the Theocracy wouldn't think they'd lose. The only thing he didn't expect was Morrison being captured instead of killed. That's why he was killed on Tyre, when you brought him home. He knew too much."

"Impossible," Kat said. "You're talking treason."

"Yes," William said. "The king didn't care about Cadiz. He didn't care about Hebrides or any of the other worlds that got attacked. He wanted a war and he got one, a war that allowed him to consolidate his position and make a grab for supreme power."

Kat took a breath. "That's a basic conspiracy theory," she pointed out. "And it relies on everything going right. It assumes there's an angel in the whirlwind, directing the storm . . ."

She shook her head. "It's absurd."

"Is it?" William tapped one of the datachips. "You can study the proof for yourself, if you like."

"I will," Kat said. She had a feeling they weren't done. William had nothing to gain and everything to lose by bringing her a discredited conspiracy theory. "Why . . . ?"

William seemed to understand. "There's something we didn't make public," he said quietly. "The king was operating black ops units on Tyre. They carried out missions for him, ranging from assassinating Admiral Morrison to attacking the House of Lords, when the shit really hit the fan. Kat . . ."

He met her eyes. Kat looked back at William, bracing herself. There was nothing but compassion in his eyes. She knew she wasn't going to like what he was about to say, that there was no way for him to sugarcoat his words.

"Kat," William said quietly. "They assassinated your father."

Kat felt the bottom drop out of her stomach. She wanted to be sick. It was impossible. Unthinkable. It was . . . Her stomach churned as she realized it *was* all too thinkable. If the king was prepared to start a war, if he was prepared to manipulate his way to power . . . her thoughts spun in circles. Duke Falcone—her father—and the king had been allies, hadn't they? But the duke had been trying to find out who'd backed Admiral Morrison right from the start. He'd held the purse strings during the war. And . . . Her legs trembled. If she'd been standing, she would have collapsed. Her father had been assassinated by the king . . . ?

She tasted bile in her mouth as the pieces fell into place. Her father had worked with the king during the war, but . . . he'd never been one of the king's servants. He had a power base of his own, a network of clients that made him independent . . . and loyalties to a class in direct opposition to the king. The House of Lords had wanted the wartime economy to be dismantled as soon as the war came to an end, and her father would have done it, if he'd lived. Instead, he'd died and policy had drifted . . . giving the king a chance to take control. And he'd taken the chance and run with it and . . .

He wasn't wrong, she thought, desperately. She knew, even as she thought, that she was trying to rationalize her decisions. Her instincts were telling her William was being honest. Her intellect was connecting the dots. And yet, she didn't want to believe it. *He wasn't wrong to insist we keep our debts of honor.*

She shuddered, realizing now just how thoroughly she'd been manipulated. How *everyone* had been manipulated. The king had used the Colonial Alliance as a tool, nothing more. He'd used the liberated worlds as an excuse to keep the wartime economy in being . . . an economy that placed vast powers in his hands. And he'd killed her father. She could understand his position. She could *sympathize* with his position. But she couldn't overlook her father's death. She *couldn't*. She wanted to believe it wasn't true. She couldn't even do that!

Her hands shook, helplessly. How many people had died, under her command, because she'd led them to the king? How many people had she killed, fighting for the king, because they were on the wrong bloody side? Except it was the right side . . . Her thoughts churned. The king hadn't been entirely wrong, damn it. She knew that was true.

But he'd also killed her father, the one man who might have prevented outright civil war . . .

William touched her shoulder, lightly. "I'm sorry . . ."

"Not your fault." Kat felt tears in her eyes. She blinked them away angrily. No time for crying. Or anything. "I . . ."

She wanted to believe he was lying, but . . . The weight of her sins crashed down on her, threatening to *crush* her. She was a traitor. She'd served the enemy. She'd . . . She wondered, morbidly, if she'd be hung, drawn, and quartered or simply hung. She felt an urge to run, combined with a sense she'd never get away. That . . . she *shouldn't* get away. The mess she'd created wasn't wholly her mess, but . . .No, it *was* her mess. And she had a responsibility to clear it up.

"Fuck it." She clenched her fists, but there was nothing to hit. "Just . . . fuck it."

She blinked, hard. She didn't have time to collapse into a ball. She had to do *something*, anything, to fix the mess before things managed to get worse. And then . . . take whatever punishment was aimed at her. She'd do it, somehow. She'd cope. She'd . . .

"Thank you for telling me," she managed. Kat wished, suddenly, that she'd paid more attention to her mother's lessons on deportment. She was able to deliver and receive bad news with equal detachment, even if the news was truly disastrous. "I . . ."

She met his eyes. "What are you going to do?"

"I don't know," William said. "The House of Lords was . . . *reluctant* . . . to let me know their long-term plans."

Just in case I decided to keep you prisoner. She wasn't sure that was true. William might not know, officially, but he was smart enough to make a few guesses. She dismissed the thought with a scowl. It didn't matter. She wasn't going to arrest him. She was . . . She wasn't sure what she was *going* to do, but she wasn't going to do *that. You have to go back while I figure out a way to clear up the mess.*

William passed her the datachips. "There're copies of all the files here," he said. "Be careful who you show them to."

"Of course," Kat said. "I do have *some* experience at hiding incriminating datachips."

She laughed, humorlessly. She'd taken illicit datachips into the academy, like almost everyone else. This . . . *this* would be a great deal worse. Jenkins would blow a fuse, if he found out. She wondered what he'd do, if he knew the truth. Turn on the king or . . . or stay with him? Perhaps the latter. There was no shortage of clients who would prefer to change patrons but were too dependent on their current patrons to make the jump. The king had had plenty of patronage to distribute, once upon a time. And now there was no way anyone who'd fought for him could hope to find safe landing on the other side.

"Be careful," William warned. "Really."

"I will." Kat felt an insane urge to giggle, mingled with an awareness that she didn't have time. "William, I . . ."

"I understand," William said. "I need to return to my fleet now."

"I'll do what I can," Kat said. She glared at the datachips. She'd go through them, of course, but . . . she knew William was telling the truth. And Peter . . . Her brother might be a pompous ass, but he wouldn't lie about their father. Even he had standards. "And I'll get in touch, when I can."

"Things are moving fast," William said.

"You probably shouldn't have told me that," Kat said, although she knew it wasn't *that* helpful. She already knew the four superdreadnought squadrons under William's command couldn't be that far away. They probably had orders to shoot the hell out of her fleet, or Caledonia itself, if he didn't make it home. "I'll see you afterwards."

William frowned. "What are you going to tell them? I mean . . ."

Kat grimaced, then raised her palm to her mouth and kissed it repeatedly. It would smudge her lipstick, just a little. She'd heard the rumors. Let Jenkins think she and Scott were in a relationship. Let

him hear the rumors and report them to the king. Let him think . . .
Someone brighter might suspect the truth, but by the time they did
she'd be ready. And then she'd deal with the king.

"I'll think of something," she said. "Good luck."

"And to you," William said.

Kat opened the hatch, nodded to Scott as she walked out, and
stepped through the airlock. The superdreadnought felt welcoming,
yet . . . there was a faint sense of *threat* hanging in the air, an awareness
that it was no longer her territory. Her mind spun, her thoughts chasing their tails as she made her way back to her cabin. The datachips felt
heavy. She was almost tempted to drop them in the recycler instead of
studying the files.

She frowned as she reached her cabin, closing and locking the hatch.
Her original crew had been loyal to her personally, but now . . . the
combination of colonials and the king's loyalists could prove dangerous.
She considered the problem as she found a datapad and carefully isolated
it from the ship's communications network. It was technically against
regulations, but no one would press charges against *her*. She checked,
just to make *sure*. If someone found the datachips, charges concerning
jailbroken datapads would be the least of her worries. Jenkins would
probably have her assassinated, rather than risk having rumors get out.
The conspiracy theorists would have a field day.

And if I don't find a way to take back control, she thought as she
started to read, *the king might just get away with everything after all.*

CHAPTER TWENTY-EIGHT

Caledonia/Interstellar Space

"Governor?"

Governor Bertram Rogan frowned as his secretary tapped on the open door and peered into the office. He'd been expecting trouble ever since he'd started preparations to take control of the fleet, preparations that had been badly disrupted by the occupation and liberation of Fotheringay. The king and his admirals were moving officers and crewmen around with a frequency that worried him, suggesting that they had a vague idea of what he had in mind. If they knew the truth . . . The only thing that kept him from panicking, from launching a desperate bid for total victory or total defeat, was the simple fact that he hadn't been arrested already. The king, whatever else one could say about him, was not the sort of person to let the grass grow under his feet. He would have arrested Bertram already if he knew the governor was the one behind the plot.

Unless he's hoping to ferret out the remainder of the plotters, Bertram pondered as he looked up. *That makes a kind of sense too.*

"Yes?" Bertram kept his voice level. There were contingency plans, but he preferred not to use them. "What is it?"

"A message from the king, sir," his secretary informed him. "The inner council has been summoned."

"I see," Bertram said slowly. "Did he say why?"

"No," his secretary said. "But a car is already waiting for you."

Bertram nodded. "I'm on my way," he said. "I'll be back in time for tea."

I hope, he added silently as he walked up the stairs and onto the roof. The aircar looked nice and normal, but the pair of armed flyers holding position above it were worrying. *This could be a trap.*

He calmed himself as he climbed into the craft. The driver took off, steering a course between the towering skyscrapers directly towards the palace. There were surprisingly few vehicles, either in the air or on the ground. The streets below were lined with protesters, troops, and reporters, the latter gleefully filming the other two. The population hadn't heard, yet, that the king had already liberated Fotheringay. Bertram wondered, sourly, why no one had told them. The engagement might have been a bit of a damp squib, but it *had* ended in victory. The king should be gloating to the entire universe.

The aircar tilted, dropping towards the palace. There were more armored vehicles on the streets, from antiaircraft platforms to tanks and personnel carriers. Bertram wondered what the planetary government thought of it all. The king had practically taken over the inner city. Maybe they felt they couldn't resist. Caledonia had been the king's pet project for so long that he probably owned the entire government. He'd certainly had no trouble convincing them to take him in.

He braced himself as he landed, the hatch opening to reveal Sir Reginald. The king's fixer dropped Bertram a deep bow—a sign, perhaps, that Bertram wasn't in trouble—and led him down the stairs to the innermost chambers. The king himself was standing by the head of the table, flanked by his wife and Admiral Lord Garstang. Bertram frowned as he bowed to the king, then took his seat. Lord Garstang wasn't a bad sort, for a nobleman, and his logistics talents were undisputable, but he was the king's man, through and through. He just couldn't be trusted completely. *No* aristocrat could be trusted completely.

"Kat Falcone isn't here," Lord Gleneden said. "Should we proceed without her?"

"There's no time," the king said. His voice was low, but Bertram could hear an underlying note of anger. "We have to proceed immediately."

Bertram winced inwardly as the remainder of the council took their seats. The king himself stayed standing, leaning on his chair as if he wanted to pace the room or lash out at an unseen enemy. Kat Falcone couldn't be trusted, but . . . he frowned as he surveyed the room. She was a rationalist, like Lord Gleneden—and unlike most of the inner council. Earl Antony was a fire-eater, Lord Snow seemed to believe that supporting the king was the only option . . . Bertram was mildly surprised *he'd* been summoned. He'd opposed the king often enough to be firmly on his enemies list.

"We received a message forty minutes ago," the king said. "From Quist."

"Quist?" Lord Gleneden looked worried. "I thought they were—"

The king spoke over him. "They have formally withdrawn from both the war and the Colonial Alliance," he said. His eyes rested on Bertram for a long moment. "I imagine"—his voice was laden with sarcasm—"that their message to the House of Worlds has yet to arrive."

"No," Bertram agreed. He forced himself to think. Quist wasn't *that* important, in the grand scheme of things . . . No, that wasn't true. The world had a sizable industrial base. Tiny, compared to Tyre or Caledonia, but large enough that losing it would hurt. And yet, he wondered just what offer the House of Lords had made to convince the planetary government to drop out of the war. Or, perhaps, to switch sides. "We haven't heard anything."

"My agents inform me that they intend to *join* the House of Lords, as soon as enemy ships arrive," the king said. "This treason cannot be allowed to stand."

"They have the right to withdraw," Lord Gleneden said carefully. "Your Majesty . . ."

"They do *not* have the right to change sides," the king said. He glared at the dovish lord. "And even if they *do* have a legal right to do whatever the hell they please, why the fuck should we condone it? Why should we let them do something that will hurt us?"

Bertram blinked in surprise. He was no stranger to foul language. The Colonial Alliance preferred blunt-spoken men to polished politicians, and if that meant a little profanity around the discussion table . . . well, he'd heard worse. But it was odd to hear the *king* swearing like a drunken spacer.

"I'm dispatching Admiral Ruben with orders to secure the system, take control of the planetary defenses, and seize their industrial base," the king continued. "If they don't resist, well and good. If they do, they will be punished. Let there be no doubt, now or ever, that treason will not go unpunished. Justiciar Montfort will accompany the squadron, with orders to ferret out the traitors and drag them back in chains . . ."

"Your Majesty," Bertram said. Montfort? The man the king had promised would never serve in a position of power again? "I understand your feelings, but we must not act hastily. We must—"

"Act fast, before someone else jumps ship," the king said. "How many other worlds would switch sides if they thought they could get away with it?"

"And that they wouldn't be punished by the House of Lords, afterwards," Earl Antony purred. "Perhaps we should leave them alone. Their punishment will come if their new side wins the war."

The king snorted. Bertram hid his surprise with an effort. Earl Antony . . . on *his* side? It didn't seem quite right, somehow. But the fire-eater wanted to take the war to Tyre, to recover the estates he'd lost or die trying. He didn't want a diversion to Quist, not when he wanted the fleet heading to Tyre. He'd complained enough about sending Kat

Falcone to Fotheringay. Who cared about a tiny little world when Tyre was ripe for the plucking?

Bertram leaned forward. "Your Majesty, public opinion won't stand for it."

"Who cares?" The king started to pace the room. *"Public opinion"*— he made the words a curse—"was prepared to sell you all out, just for a few extra years of peace. The public doesn't understand what has to be done. We have to act fast."

No, Bertram thought. *We—us—have to act fast.*

He groaned, inwardly, as the king continued to rant about treason and ungrateful bastards in high places. Admiral Ruben was loyal to the king, completely loyal. If the king ordered him to commit an atrocity that would make the Theocracy blanch, Admiral Ruben would do it without a second thought. And Justiciar Montfort? If there was anyone more unpopular among the Colonial Alliance than Montfort, Bertram had never heard of him. The king had to be out of his mind. A heavy-handed response to Quist departing the alliance would unite everyone against him.

And there's no way to talk him out of it, Bertram thought. Their plans would have to be moved up, fast. They'd have to hope they could take control of enough ships and platforms to force the king to surrender, if they couldn't trap or kill him on the ground. And then . . . they'd have to see what terms they could get. *We have to move now or lose everything.*

"We will not let this pass," the king said. "Dismissed."

No, Bertram agreed as he headed to the door. *We won't.*

◆ ◆ ◆

"There have been some . . . mutterings . . . about how you conducted the battle," Duke Peter said. "They think you should have gone for the kill."

"We expected as much," William reminded him. He felt his heart twist again. He'd been uncomfortable ever since he'd returned to his ship. "And you know what we had in mind."

"Yes, but the others don't." Duke Peter steepled his fingers. "We can delay things long enough for the plan to work, in which case you're a genius, or for something else to happen."

"And in that case, I'm a complete idiot," William commented. He smiled. The great commanders of human history had often been considered mad before they pulled off something conventional wisdom said couldn't be done. "We'll see."

"Yes, we will." Duke Peter let out a breath. "The Grand Admiral will forward you your official orders in a moment, but, whatever happens with Kat, you're going to Quist."

William leaned forward. "They joined us?"

"Not quite," Duke Peter said. "Officially, they've withdrawn from the war. They're filing their departure from the Colonial Alliance even as we speak. Unofficially, they'll change sides once we have a fleet in place to protect them. You need to be there as quickly as possible."

"We can be there in five days," William said. Quist should have waited. Or given him more advance notice. It was going to be close. "We're going to have to circle around Caledonia, unless we want to risk blazing through the system."

"Do as you see fit." Duke Peter's eyes suddenly sharpened. "How did she take it?"

"I think she believed me," William said. "But I don't know what she'll be able to do about it."

"She's smart," Duke Peter said. "She'll think of something."

William wasn't so sure. Joel Gibson, damn him to hell, had *years* to plan his mutiny. Kat had a few days, at best. And, after the first mutiny, the navy had taken precautions to prevent another one. They hadn't been good enough to keep a significant percentage of the active-duty fleet from joining the king, but they might be good enough to keep

Kat from plotting a mutiny of her own. He scowled, knowing just how distant an admiral was from his crew. Kat's first crew would have followed her into hell itself. Her current crew might not be so sure where their loyalties lay.

Particularly as they won't give a damn about Duke Falcone, William thought. He found it hard to care about Duke Cavendish, who'd vanished with *Supreme*. If he hadn't known Kat's father, he wouldn't have been too concerned about his death either. *The colonials may even think the king did the right thing.*

"I'm sure she'll come up with something," William said. He wished Pat Davidson hadn't died on Ahura Mazda. If Kat got the marines on her side, securing the fleet would be a piece of cake. "And even if she doesn't, there are other plans."

"Quite," Duke Peter said. "I'll keep you informed of developments here."

William nodded as the duke's hologram vanished. Kat would be on her own, at least for the next few weeks. He knew he couldn't help her. He had his orders. If Quist had declared independence, the king was likely to do something drastic in hopes of putting them back in their box. William doubted it would end well.

He keyed his terminal. "Commander Yagami?"

"Yes, sir?"

"Inform the fleet," William said. "We're heading for Quist. Maximum speed."

"Aye, sir," Yagami said. "Sir . . . do you want to risk brushing past Caledonia?"

William frowned. Theoretically, the fleet would remain undetected as long as they didn't drop out of hyperspace. There should be no danger. But if he was wrong . . . He sucked in a breath. He had to get to Quist as quickly as possible. The risk was unpleasant but could be borne—would *have* to be borne.

"Yes. Take us on the quickest possible course, maximum speed."

♦ ♦ ♦

Kat knew, without false modesty, that she wasn't an intelligence expert. She wasn't skilled enough to spot a detailed deepfake, particularly when the deepfake was in a field she knew nothing about. But she did know enough about orders and mission specifications to spot anything that didn't quite add up . . . and there was nothing. She hadn't expected any blatant mistakes, not when the deepfake would be inspected by people who knew precisely what to look for, but there weren't any small inconsistencies either. The lies were either completely perfect . . .

. . . or they weren't lies.

She sat on her sofa, feeling tears prickling at the corners of her eyes as she worked her way through the files. The king *had* planned the war, or at least created an opportunity for the Theocracy to launch their first attack. In hindsight, she wondered just how much the king had planned and how much he'd simply worked into his plan as it had happened. Plans tended to work better if they weren't rigid. She winced as she read the files concerning her father, concerning his final day . . . If they were faked, they were very *good* fakes. And she didn't think that was possible.

"I'm sorry," she said. She wasn't sure who she was apologizing to. Her father, who'd been murdered? William, who'd never liked or trusted the king? Peter, who had clashed with her once too often? Or everyone who had died in the last few months? "I'm sorry."

She put the datapad aside and forced herself to think. There were options. There *had* to be options. But there were fewer than she wanted to admit. The ship wasn't *her* ship, the fleet wasn't *her* fleet . . . Someone would object if she led an attack on Caledonia, even if they weren't personally loyal to the king. And then . . . what? She'd be shot in the back, probably. She couldn't take control of a whole superdreadnought by herself. Admiral Junayd had done that, back during the war, but he'd been planning to jump ship and leave his crew to die in a hyperspace storm. And he'd succeeded.

I've been a damned fool. She wanted to smack herself, hard. *If I'd listened to William or even to Peter . . .*

She looked back over the last few years, knowing it would make no difference. She'd done as she'd seen fit, as always. She'd thought the king had the best interests of Tyre, the Commonwealth, and the remnants of the Theocracy at heart. She'd thought the rumors about him to be little more than a conspiracy theory, an absurd tissue of lies meant to cover up the House of Lords' collective incompetence. She'd thought . . . She'd been wrong, damn it. She'd been wrong.

Shaking her head, she picked up another datapad and brought up the crew roster. It was supposed to be complete, but who knew these days? Too many officers and crew had been moved around . . . In hindsight, the king and his loyalists clearly didn't want his subordinates comparing notes or plotting coups. And she'd gone along with it because she hadn't realized what he'd done. She really *was* an idiot. She'd practically waged war on her own family for the man who'd murdered her father. Damn her to hell.

You can't change what you've done. The voice in her head sounded like her father. *All you can do is try to make up for it.*

She keyed her terminal. Jenkins was still on the planet, thankfully. His subordinates were probably abusing their authority by playing voyeur or something equally despicable. As long as they weren't paying attention to her . . . She smiled coldly, wondering if they'd noticed her smudged lipstick. Let them think she'd been abusing her authority. Given what she'd actually done, having a semilegal relationship was minor. They'd probably be pleased at such wonderful blackmail material. It would keep them from wondering what *else* she might have been doing.

"Kitty," she said. It was hard to keep her voice under tight control. "Contact General Winters. I need to see him. Immediately."

"He's currently reviewing the planetary defenses," Kitty said. "I can get him to you within the hour."

"Do so," Kat ordered. Hopefully, Jenkins wouldn't want to leave the planet *just* yet. "Is the planetary StarCom active yet?"

"No, Admiral," Kitty said. "They're saying it won't be powered up again for at least two more days."

How terrible, Kat thought. Her lips twitched. A day ago, it *would* have been terrible. She was out of touch with Caledonia. Anything could happen in the time it would take to send a message to the king and get a reply, anything at all. *But it comes in handy right now.*

"Tell them I require priority use of the system, when it's back online," Kat said. Jenkins was probably too ignorant to notice, but it was well not to take chances. "And prep a courier boat for dispatch. I'll need to send messages to the king."

But not the messages I want to send him, she told herself. *I'll be delivering those in person.*

CHAPTER TWENTY-NINE

QUIST

Admiral Henri Ruben prided himself on his loyalty to the king. It had been King Hadrian who'd picked him out of Piker's Peak and offered him patronage, in exchange for loyalty. It had been King Hadrian who'd ensured a smooth ride through the ranks to ship, squadron, and finally fleet command. Henri knew—he felt no urge to dissemble, in the privacy of his own head—on which side his bread was buttered. He was a king's man, and proud of it. He'd do *anything* for His Majesty.

He leaned forward in his command chair as the display rapidly updated. The planet was surrounded by industrial nodes, from giant facilities funded by the king's planetary development charities to smaller structures assembled by the local corporations and government. *Quist has benefited hugely from its association with the king*, he thought sourly. Hatred curdled in his breast as he contemplated the depth of their treachery. The king had given them everything, from mining hubs and factories to naval installations and corporate fueling stations. Quist had been well positioned to take advantage, once the king returned to Tyre and took back control. Instead, the planetary government had betrayed their benefactor and sided with the hated House of Lords.

They'll pay. Henri had spent enough time with the aristocracy to know he hated them. The king was the sole exception. But then, the king actually had power and responsibility. The other aristocrats he'd met spent their days eating, drinking, abusing their clients, and talking down to anyone who didn't meet their exalted standards. Now Quist would find itself in deep shit, whoever won the war. *They'll pay for what they've done.*

"Admiral," the tactical officer said. "The planetary defense force is scrambling."

"Open communications," Henri ordered. He hadn't bothered trying to be subtle. His ships, two battlecruiser squadrons and supporting elements, had punched their way out of hyperspace dangerously close to the planet. "This is Admiral Henri Ruben, speaking for the king. You are ordered to stand down your defenses and prepare for occupation. You are . . ."

He spoke on, outlining the demands the king had told him to make. Henri was fairly sure the planetary government would refuse to accept, but it didn't matter. If they conceded, well and good; if not, they'd get a savage lesson in what happened to people who deserted their cause and stuck a knife in their former allies. He thought cold thoughts about the missiles in his tubes, ready to fire at the planetary defenders. If they refused to surrender, the fight was going to be very short and sharp.

And there's no time to do more than sweep up the planetary government, he reminded himself. *We might have to leave in a hurry.*

The thought ground at him, even though he was experienced enough to know there might be no choice. There was an enemy fleet lurking nearby, although he had no idea where. If Quist had swapped sides, the chances were good the enemy fleet was racing towards the planet already. They'd want to take control, both to protect the locals and to make it clear that Quist wouldn't be allowed to swap sides again. Henri couldn't remember who'd said that turning one's coat tended to be habit-forming, but he believed it. The House of Lords practically operated on the principle of turning coat whenever it seemed advantageous. They were so treacherous themselves that they'd expect perennial deception from others. They never seemed to realize the king was a man of honor.

"Admiral," the communications officer said. "They're ordering us to clear their space."

Henri glanced at Montfort, sitting at a disused console. The planetary government had to be insane. Quist was better defended than most colonial worlds, but not defended enough to stand off his fleet. They *had* to know he could blast them to hell at will. Unless . . . He frowned as he contemplated the vectors, wondering where the enemy fleet was lurking. If the planetary leaders were expecting it in the next few hours, they might just try to hold out long enough to be rescued. His eyes narrowed sourly. They were in for a nasty fright.

"Repeat our message," he ordered. "Clear for action."

The battlecruiser *thrummed* as the range continued to close. Quist had put together a sizable defense force for a planet of its size, but nowhere near big enough to stop him. A handful of midsized, outdated warships, backed up by several dozen converted freighters . . . They were doomed. They had to know they were doomed. Any modern warships would have been summoned to join the king's fleet long ago. His gunners were going to use the enemy fleet for target practice.

"No response," the communications officer said.

"Weapons locked," the tactical officer put in. "The enemy fleet is activating its drives, preparing to come at us."

Henri nodded. The king had made it clear that Henri wasn't to hesitate. They *couldn't* let the colonials get the idea that they could leave without punishment, not when mass desertions would spell the end of the king's cause. The House of Lords would punish the bastards in due course, Henri was sure of it, but by then it would be too late. By the time the colonials came to regret their treachery, the king would be dead and his cause would be lost. Henri braced himself, confident he was doing the right thing.

"Fire," he ordered.

The battlecruiser shuddered as she unleashed her first salvo. Henri leaned forward, watching as the missiles raced towards their targets. The enemy fleet didn't hesitate. They lunged forward, freighters moving into attack formation as if they were battlecruisers or superdreadnoughts. The formation was odd. Henri couldn't recall seeing anything like it in a tactical manual, save perhaps for the handful of object lessons in what *not* to do. They were closing the range with terrifying speed, but . . . they were flying *towards* his missiles. Suicide. He liked the thought of his enemies committing suicide when they saw him coming, a joke that dated all the way back to Old Earth, but he didn't believe it. They were up to something.

He frowned as the enemy ships opened fire. They'd loaded their freighters with point defense, everything from phased pulsars to modified mining lasers. Their targeting wasn't great, but they were pumping out so much fire that it hardly mattered. Dozens, then hundreds, of his missiles vanished from the display. He blinked in astonishment as he realized what they were doing, using the point defense freighters to shield their warships as they worked frantically to close the range. Their outdated missiles would be worse than useless, *unless* they were fired at close range. He would have saluted them, if he hadn't been so angry. They weren't content with betraying the king. They'd led their people to destruction.

"Target the enemy freighters," he ordered. "Continue firing."

The enemy freighters started to vanish. They were tough, but more focused on covering the warships than protecting themselves. *A mistake on their part*, Henri thought. The ships might be operating remotely—there was a certain lack of flexibility to their movements, suggesting they were being controlled from the ground—but they were still important. Their point defense was all that was keeping the enemy warships from being summarily destroyed. And, with each freighter that vanished, those warships were becoming more and more vulnerable.

"Admiral," the tactical officer said. "The enemy warships have opened fire."

Henri frowned as red icons sparkled to life. The enemy missiles were as outdated as their warships, lacking both the drives and seeker heads to pose a significant threat to his ships . . . if, of course, his ships hadn't been flying right *towards* them. But the enemy had fired a little too soon. His point defense was already going live, sweeping vast numbers of enemy missiles out of space. And their motherships were taking a pounding. They were being destroyed, one by one . . .

"They're still coming," someone breathed. "They're mad."

Henri shrugged. The bastards had closed the range too much now. They *couldn't* turn and run without being shot in the back. God knew he wasn't going to let them go. Kat Falcone was a fine naval officer, but she was too merciful. Tarleton should have been soundly spanked for even daring to think of switching sides, whatever pressure was brought to bear on her government. Henri would show her how it should be done. By the time he was finished, no one would dare raise a hand against the king.

And we'll return home in victory, he promised himself. *And . . .*

"Admiral," the tactical officer snapped. "They're making suicide runs!"

"Bring all weapons to bear on them," Henri ordered, knowing his crews were already doing so. They were trained to deal with would-be kamikazes. "Take them down . . ."

He felt his heart pound as the enemy ships closed to point-blank range, overloading their drives in the hopes of slamming themselves into his battlecruisers before it was too late. Red icons flared up, warning him of radiation surges that had probably killed the enemy crews if compensator failures hadn't gotten them first. Their ships were coming apart, but too late. He watched four of them die in quick succession, a fifth lasting long enough to slam itself into a battlecruiser. Both ships vanished from the display.

"Sir," the tactical officer said. "*Justinian* was lost with all hands."

Henri stared, feeling something cold and unpleasant within his gut. A battlecruiser was gone. A battlecruiser, taken out by a ship so outdated . . . His head spun, knowing he was going to be in deep shit when he got home. The enemy had lost their entire fleet, but they'd still come out ahead. It would be a long time before the king was able to replace the battlecruiser, even if he won the war. The colonial shipyards couldn't churn out anything larger than a heavy cruiser.

"Target the high orbitals," he ordered savagely. "Sweep them clear."

The tactical officer hesitated, as if he wanted to say something but didn't quite dare. Henri watched coldly as the officer keyed commands into his console, directing the fleet to fire on the planet's orbital installations. They'd probably have been evacuated the moment they saw his fleet, but if they weren't . . . He told himself firmly that the locals had to pay a harsh price for their sins. They were going to pay through the nose for betraying the king. And if that meant blowing away a few hundred thousand trained personnel . . . well, they shouldn't have picked the wrong side. Quist was supposed to be a democracy. They'd voted for a government that had betrayed its allies and nearly cost them the war.

Cold hatred surged through him as the planet's orbital installations died. Messages flared up on the display, begging and pleading and offering everything from a truce to unconditional surrender. He ignored them. They'd had their chance. They could rejoin the king, after they'd been punished for their crimes. Until then . . . he was going to make damn sure they understood the price of what they'd done. The fleet closed on the planet, sensors picking out the handful of defense bases on the surface. Those bases were probably being evacuated, if they hadn't been evacuated long ago. He'd seen the plans. They might have been devised for an entirely different attacker, but the basic concept remained the same. Any target on the surface that drew attention to itself would be smashed from orbit.

And no one is going to worry about civilian lives. They're going to pay for what they've done.

"Bring up the targeting program," Henri ordered. "Prepare to start striking the planet."

"Aye, Admiral."

"Take us into high orbit," Henri said. "Fire at—"

"Admiral!" New icons appeared on the display. "Vortexes! Behind us!"

"Shit," Montfort breathed.

Henri ignored him as the enemy ships flew into the system. It was a fleet out of nightmares, a fleet that could smash his battlecruisers as if they were made of paper. A single superdreadnought squadron would be more than enough, but . . . the enemy had *four*. He tried to tell himself that the ships weren't real, yet he was too canny to believe such delusions. There were just too many superdreadnought-sized vortexes. The ships might not have opened fire during the previous engagement, but it didn't matter. The formation they'd adopted spoke of a cold certainty they didn't need to be clever to win.

"They'll enter engagement range in twenty minutes," the tactical officer said. "Admiral . . ."

Henri thought fast. The enemy ships could have come out of hyperspace a lot closer to Quist or his fleet. That they hadn't suggested they hadn't expected to encounter him, not yet. They'd chosen to emerge far enough to give the planet a chance to get a good look at them, without coming out so far away that they had to mess around with hyperspace rather than make the transit in realspace. It was sheer damned luck they hadn't arrived an hour or so ago, when they could have baited a trap. He'd have flown right into the teeth of thirty-six superdreadnoughts before he realized how badly he'd fucked himself.

"We can still take the planet," Montfort said. "We can—"

"No," Henri corrected. Battlecruisers were designed for hit-and-run raids, not for sustained combat with superdreadnoughts. Pinned against the planet, their speed advantage minimized if not eliminated entirely, they'd be rapidly and cheaply smashed to atoms. "Taking the planet is out of the question."

His eyes narrowed as the enemy fleet shook down. Whoever was in command *definitely* hadn't expected to encounter him. They'd assumed a formation designed for reassurance rather than combat. They were correcting their mistake now. Too late. They'd dropped out of hyperspace too close to the planet to make it easy to return to hyperspace and close the gap, yet they were still too far to prevent his ships from leaving. He had time to act, unless they decided to risk hyperspace anyway. And there was only one thing he could do.

"Tactical, bring up the Hammer-III Program," he ordered. "Activate on my command."

The tactical officer looked up, sharply. "Admiral, the Hammer-III—"

"Is to be activated at once." Henri reached for his pistol, bracing himself. If the tactical officer refused to carry out his orders, he'd have to be relieved from his post. And that might spark all kinds of problems. He'd chosen the crew for loyalty to himself, but there'd been limits. No one knew if someone would be mindlessly obedient until the order was issued and it was time to choose. "You have your orders."

He watched as the tactical officer keyed his console. The Hammer-III program was extreme, even by the Theocracy's standards. It was nothing less than the total destruction of the enemy's capital city, along with every governmental installation, military base, and planetary infrastructure target on the surface. It would ensure the deaths of hundreds of thousands, perhaps millions, of people immediately, with millions more dying in the weeks and months to follow. The planners who'd devised the concept had assumed it would never be used except in the most extreme circumstances. Their imaginations had been sorely lacking.

"Missiles away, sir," the tactical officer said. His voice shook. "Impact in thirty seconds."

"Bring us about," Henri ordered. The enemy ships were picking up speed—too late. They wouldn't be able to come into missile range in time. "Jump us out as soon as the drives are ready."

"Aye, Admiral."

Henri nodded, watching as the missiles started to explode. The enemy capital vanished in an eye-tearing blast of light. The KEWs followed, systematically wiping out the planetary infrastructure. Quist was going to fall all the way back to the Stone Age, a harsh lesson for anyone who dared betray their oaths to the king. It was their fault, he told himself again and again, for electing a treacherous government. A smart population would have kept its word.

And everyone else will take heed. They won't be plotting any longer, not anymore.

♦ ♦ ♦

"Dear God."

William came to his feet, watching helplessly as atomic fire consumed a city. A straight fusion warhead, according to his sensors. There would be no radiation clogging up the atmosphere, not like Hebrides. Anyone who wasn't killed outright by the blast would have an excellent chance to survive, if they could get out of the city. If . . . He shuddered as he realized, in his heart, just how many people had been killed. And how many would die in the next few months.

"Admiral," Yagami said. "The enemy fleet has jumped back into hyperspace."

William clenched his fists. He wanted to hit something, but there was nothing to hit. He was no stranger to horror, yet the war had been relatively civilized . . . *had been*. Hadrian had gone mad. There was no way in hell the colonials, and even half his courtiers, would go along with mass slaughter. If they'd refused to bombard Tyre, they'd certainly be outraged at the bombardment of Quist.

If they find out about it in time. The planetary StarCom was gone. *They might not know before the king has a chance to put his own spin on it.*

He keyed his terminal. "Get the PR teams down there," he ordered. The House of Lords should technically make the call, but he had wide authority. And if they didn't move quickly, they wouldn't be able to move at all. The king could not be allowed a chance to shape the narrative and blame everything on the House of Lords. "I want the entire galaxy to know what happened here. Total disclosure."

"Aye, Admiral."

CHAPTER THIRTY

CALEDONIA

The intercom bleeped, urgently.

Ambassador Francis Villeneuve rolled over in bed, brushing against his sleeping mistress as he reached for the terminal. He'd had a long day, talking with Hadrian and his cronies and plotting ways to assist the king in his war while setting up matters so his homeworld would come out ahead. The king's recent setbacks had made him more dependent on his innermost circle, a group Francis hoped to enter. The king would never trust him completely, but, as long as Francis was delivering the goods, it didn't matter.

"What?" His voice sounded thick in his ears. "This had better be important."

"It is." Admiral Giles Jacanas spoke with quiet urgency. "You'd better get out here."

Francis scowled, then stood and reached for his dressing gown. It was barely 0400, local time. His internal clock was insisting, loudly, that he should go back to bed. He took a longing look at his mistress, wishing he had the stamina to wake her before deciding he simply didn't have time. Whatever it was, it had to be urgent. Francis's staff would have handled it if it was something that could wait until a more civilized hour.

He pulled the gown on and buckled the belt, then walked through the door. There were four guards on duty outside his suite, two more than usual. His eyes narrowed as he paced down the corridor. If the security commander had ordered the troops to go to alert—a very quiet alert—it meant trouble, yet . . . what *sort* of trouble? Francis knew he'd have been told to go to the emergency bunker or the aircars if the shit had *really* hit the fan. Anyone attacking the planet should know the embassies were off-limits, but accidents happened. He wouldn't have been too surprised if the embassy had been targeted deliberately. Tyre would want to make it clear that they knew where the missiles had come from, without making it so obvious that they had to go to war.

Admiral Giles Jacanas was sitting in the office when Francis arrived, drinking a mug of military-grade coffee. The secretary's assistant, a young woman on her first posting, poured a second mug and passed it to Francis, then left without saying a word. Francis tried not to stare at her retreating back, reminding himself sharply that she had friends and family back home who'd secured the posting for her. Had she picked the posting for herself, assuming it would be a springboard to something greater, or had her family assumed she'd be safe on Caledonia? If the latter, they might be in for a shock. The entire planet might be on the verge of becoming a war zone.

"Admiral." Francis dragged his attention back to his subordinate. "What happened?"

"We . . . *intercepted* . . . a message from Quist," Jacanas said. He sounded badly stunned. "It was sent by Tyre's relief fleet, broadcast on all StarCom channels . . . by now, it will be all over the galaxy. Everyone will know what's happened."

Francis felt a lump of ice congeal in his heart. "What happened?"

"The king's fleet attacked Quist," Jacanas said. "The enemy fleet arrived in time to prevent them from occupying the planet. The king's fleet retreated, but as they left they fired on the planet itself.

Ambassador . . . they destroyed an entire city. They hammered an entire planet. The death toll is believed to be in the millions."

Francis, for a moment, didn't catch what Jacanas had said. "They . . . they destroyed an entire city?"

"That's what the broadcasts say," Jacanas said. "I have no independent confirmation, not yet, but it isn't the sort of lie that can be maintained for long. There are . . . there *were* . . . over two million people in the capital city alone. It was practically a magnet for people who wanted to leave the farms and find work elsewhere. They might all be dead."

"And if they're not dead now, they may be wishing they were." Francis sipped his coffee, grimacing at the taste. "Dear God. What *happened?*"

"I don't know," Jacanas told him. "But I doubt it was an *accident.* People don't throw nuclear-tipped missiles around by accident. I'd believe a KEW strike could go wild and hit a school or a marketplace or somewhere where there were lots of civilians, but a nuke? That had to be deliberate. The broadcasts make it clear that it wasn't a stray shot that missed its target and hit the planet itself."

"Assuming the broadcasts can be trusted," Francis said. He fought to keep his voice under control. "Can they?"

"So far, we haven't caught them in any lies." Jacanas sounded pessimistic. "Like I said, it isn't the kind of deception that can be sustained for long. Every reporter in the sector will be racing there, hoping to be the first to broadcast even more gruesome images of death and destruction. A single freighter could collect enough evidence to prove the atrocity happened . . . or didn't happen. Quist isn't *that* far from Caledonia. The king could dispatch a fly-through mission now and get results in a couple of days. The lie wouldn't last past that point."

Francis stared at the black liquid. "Which means the reports might be accurate."

"Substantially accurate," Jacanas corrected, pedantically. "They could have made them a little worse."

"Hah." Francis felt no real humor, just a chill that sank into his bones. "I don't see how they could have made it any worse. Assuming, of course, that the attack actually happened."

There was no real conviction in his voice. He'd read the news broadcasts, both the puff and propaganda pieces and the more objective reporting from media outlets based hundreds of light-years from Tyre and Caledonia. Both sides had smeared each other as much as they could, but they'd drawn the line at implying genocide. No one would have believed them, not really. Smear campaigns had been a fact of political life since humanity had evolved governing structures more complex than warlordism. But . . . No, the reports had to be true. The king would be delighted if he caught his enemies in such a big lie . . .

He took another sip of his coffee, thinking hard. In one sense, nothing had changed. The king was still a useful tool, nothing more than a tool. Francis had his orders. He was to keep the king's cause alive as long as possible, ideally long enough for the fighting to weaken the Commonwealth and the Border Nine to be occupied without resistance. If both sides started carrying out atrocities, the Commonwealth would be wrecked beyond repair. Francis admitted, privately, that such an outcome was greatly desired.

But, in another sense, *everything* had changed. The king would have real problems keeping his side together. His delicate balancing act between his courtiers and the colonials would collapse if both sides were shocked and appalled by the atrocity. Neither would want the war to turn savage, not when it might convince the House of Lords to take the gloves off and repay the atrocity in spades. It was terrifyingly easy to render a planet completely lifeless. A handful of strikes would be more than enough to shatter the Colonial Alliance, sparking off a series of atrocities and counteratrocities . . . Francis felt sick. His people would find themselves implicated in mass murder and outright genocide. They hadn't encouraged the king to carry out atrocities. They certainly hadn't ordered him to slaughter vast numbers of his own people. But they'd find themselves bearing a share of the blame . . .

"Merde," he breathed. "What do we do?"

He sipped his coffee, thinking hard. His superiors had given him wide latitude, although he was honest enough, at least with himself, to admit that they'd also arranged matters so he'd take the blame if things went spectacularly wrong. He hadn't minded that at the time. He'd known success would take him to the very highest levels, while refusing the mission would see his career permanently stalled. But now he was on the cusp of being pushed to exceed his authority. If he tried to encourage the king, or talk sense to him . . . either way, he needed permission from higher up the chain. And if he chose to abandon the entire mission . . .

"I need to speak to my superiors," he said. He finished his coffee and put it to one side. "They'll have to decide what to do."

"That might not be possible," Jacanas said. "The StarCom has been"—he made quotation marks with his fingers—"taken down for maintenance."

Francis swore. "So quickly?"

"I believe so," Jacanas said. "The king must have had a contingency plan in place."

"I see." Francis forced himself to think. "Has word got out? Yet?"

"I'd be surprised if it hasn't," Jacanas said. "The king couldn't clamp down on the broadcast in time. I think it'll be all around the planet by now."

"I see," Francis said again. "You put the guards on alert?"

"Yes." Jacanas met his eyes evenly. "Mr. Ambassador, this could turn very nasty."

"Prep the staff to evacuate the embassy if necessary," Francis ordered. In theory, the embassy was impregnable to anything less than a full-scale assault. In practice, he didn't want to test it the hard way. "I'll try to speak to the king."

"I doubt he'll want to speak with you, not now," Jacanas said. "All hell could be on the verge of breaking loose."

"I know," Francis said. "But I have to try."

◆ ◆ ◆

"The reports are, of course, total nonsense." The king sounded convincing. Very convincing. "I've ordered the StarCom taken down to ensure the reports don't spread further before we have a counternarrative in place."

Governor Bertram Rogan kept his face under tight control. He didn't believe a word of it. No, that wasn't quite true. He believed the king hadn't known the atrocity was coming—the simple fact he hadn't prepared better for bad news suggested it hadn't been planned—but he didn't believe the story had been made up of whole cloth. The House of Lords was a snake pit of overprivileged aristocrats who'd been born with silver spoons in their mouths . . . he used a cruder analogy when addressing his people . . . yet they weren't *stupid*. They wouldn't tell a lie that would be disproven very quickly if it wasn't true.

"I trust you'll be sending a starship to Quist to find out what actually happened," he said, knowing he couldn't trust whatever answer he received. The king would have to be out of his mind to admit to such a crime, yet there was no way he could escape blame. "We need answers before the public goes mad."

"It will be done," the king assured him. "I trust that you will calm your hotheads before it's too late."

It was a statement, not a question, but Bertram chose to pretend otherwise. "I'll deal with them personally," he said truthfully. "And I expect you to make a broadcast as quickly as possible. The people will need to be reassured."

He tapped the console, dropping out of the holographic conference. The meeting room faded away, to be replaced by his office. He stood and strode to the windows, peering into the sky. Dawn was breaking, slowly but surely. And yet . . . He looked down. He could see people forming mobs on the streets even at this early hour. He'd half hoped the king had succeeded in suppressing the news by shutting down the StarCom. Mobs were dangerous. Bertram was all too aware that he might be blamed for the atrocity, along with the king himself. He had spoken in the man's defense over the last few months.

And I can't pretend otherwise, not any longer. Bertram had planned for trouble, he'd planned to betray the king, but . . . the thought of breaking his word gave him an uneasy twinge. No one would trust him again, ever. They might agree, in private, that he'd done the right thing, but they'd never trust him. And why should they? *It's time to go.*

He studied the mobs for a long moment, then walked back to the desk. The news report glowed on the terminal, mocking him. He wanted to believe that the report was all lies. He wanted to believe that the House of Lords had carried out the atrocity. He knew better. Of course he knew better. The king had been angry, and Quist had paid the price for daring to think its vote counted for something. A storm was about to break over the Colonial Alliance and he . . . he had to take control or get out of the way.

"I can accept dishonor," he told himself, "if it saves my people."

He keyed the terminal, bringing up a communications chain he'd planned weeks ago, when he'd first started discussing treason. The network was designed—cunningly designed—to impede, delay, or simply *eat* messages sent by the king's enemies. A person could be shadowbanned, cut out of the system without ever *knowing* he'd been cut out, until it was too late. And yet, there were gaps in the system, chinks that could be exploited. Caledonia had never been as developed as Tyre. The locals had worked hard to maintain a degree of freedom the Tyrians lacked.

The message glowed in front of him, seemingly utterly harmless. It would jump from his account to another account, then propagate itself to its final destinations. No one would know what it meant unless they'd already been briefed, unless they already knew what to do. He shuddered, wondering if anyone would jump the gun. The communications network couldn't be trusted. He'd scattered cells and assets all over the planet and fleet, yet . . . he was already cut off from the outside universe. The plans to take control of the remainder of the alliance were doomed. Unless . . .

He tapped a key, sending the message. His pocket terminals bleeped a second later. Sending a copy of the message to himself, to both his public and private terminals, was a risk, but it was the only way to be sure the message had gotten out. Unless they knew his private address and had made sure to copy the message there . . . He shook his head, telling himself there was no more time for second-guessing. The die was cast.

His secretary, Cathy, opened the door. "Sir, you've been summoned to the palace."

"A little late." Bertram opened his drawer and removed a pistol, pinning it to his belt. "It's time to go. Are you ready?"

Cathy paled. "I'm ready, sir."

Bertram nodded. Cathy had many advantages, not least an astonishing talent for looking completely harmless. Bertram had lost count of the number of men who'd turned into babbling idiots just by having her sit next to them. They never saw the sharpness in her eye because they were looking elsewhere. And she was very good at taking advantage of their distraction.

"Go now," Bertram ordered. "Take your bug-out bag and *don't* look back."

Cathy met his eyes. "Good luck, sir," she said. "See you on the far side."

She turned and left. Bertram felt a twinge of guilt, even though he *knew* Cathy was far from helpless. In theory, she shouldn't have any trouble getting to the spaceport and booking travel on a courier boat. Bertram had absolutely *no* doubt that the combination of money and undisputed charms would override any qualms the boat's commander might have. He'd take her straight to the nearest star system with a StarCom. And she could spread the word.

And who knows? Bertram cursed himself. *She might just bring help back in time to save us if things go badly wrong.*

The intercom bleeped. "Sir," someone said. "The king's agents are demanding to speak to you."

"I'll be down in a moment," Bertram lied. If the king was demanding his presence . . . he knew. Or suspected something. It didn't matter. "Tell them to take a seat and wait."

His people had their orders. They'd been putting the contingency plans into effect ever since they'd seen the broadcast. The king's men were going to find out, sooner rather than later, that the entire building had been abandoned. *By the time they raise the alarm, it will be too late.*

He kept one hand on his pistol as he hurried out of the office and down to the elevator shaft. The doors opened on his approach, revealing an empty chamber. He pushed his fingers against the scanner, ordering the lift to descend into the underground bunker. His staff had spent *years* preparing their line of retreat, fearing the House of Lords would one day move against the Colonial Alliance. Bertram had been careful to keep his precautions from the king. It would only have upset him.

His terminal vibrated. He pulled it from his belt and glanced at the screen. A handful of messages, all seemingly innocuous. No one would think twice about a message advertising sexual services, even if they were physically impossible. It would be just spam. But the mere fact the messages had been sent to him was a very real tip-off. The plan was about to begin. All hell was about to break loose.

And then we'll find out just how good our planning actually was, he thought as the doors opened. The tunnel was ahead of him, the hatch already gaping open. The passage was connected to the sewers, a complex mess of tunnels that would confuse anyone who hadn't spent years exploring them. *And just what the king has in mind to deal with us.*

CHAPTER THIRTY-ONE

FOTHERINGAY

Kat had expected, as she sent messages arranging a meeting between herself and some of her most trusted officers, that Jenkins would have demanded to be included—or, more likely, lodged complaints about the deactivated StarCom. Kat hadn't dared issue orders to slow the power-up sequence, not when she didn't know who could be trusted to carry them out without question. The more she looked at it, the more she realized she was largely on her own. The king and his courtiers might not have intended to prevent a second round of mutinies, but they'd succeeded magnificently. Kat hadn't felt so frustrated since her father had bought her promotion to command rank. The memory made her heart ache.

Her anger had turned to ice, a cold determination to exact revenge. If she'd been on Caledonia, she would have stormed the king's palace personally—she was allowed to carry firearms, even into the king's presence—and shot him before his guards could react. But the short distance from Caledonia in which she found herself might as well have been an impassable gulf. It gave her time to plan, to lay the groundwork for doing . . . *something* . . . about the king, yet it also limited her options. She needed to be a great deal closer to him before she could do *anything*.

She looked up as the hatch opened, revealing General Timothy Winters. The marine met her eyes questioningly, searching for answers she wasn't ready to provide. Not yet. She felt her heart twist in pain, remembering Pat . . . Wherever he was, he had to be disappointed in her. Her *father* had to be disappointed in her. She'd gone to work for his murderer! She felt the urge to hit something—anything—boiling up in her. Her tutors had lectured her, more than once, about her temper. She'd learned to control it, after her father had pointed out how easy it was to lose respect from one's peers. But now she wanted to wrap her hands around the king's neck and squeeze as hard as she could. She wanted him to suffer. But she'd settle for putting a bullet in his brain.

"Hang on," she said, as the hatch opened again. "There are a couple of others still to come."

Lieutenant Kitty Patterson stepped into the compartment, followed by Captain Tony Procaccini and Commodore Fran Higgins. Kitty looked a little intimidated by being in such high company, although, as Kat's aide, she'd worked closely with all of them. Fran seemed perplexed, clearly wondering why she'd been summoned in person. She was, perhaps, the only person who might guess what Kat had in mind. She'd been part of the conspiracy to save 6th Fleet, back before the Battle of Cadiz. It seemed so *different*, now she knew the king had planned to start the war. Or, rather, *allow* it to start.

Kat's lips twitched. The people who wrote the history books would be very annoyed. They'd have to rewrite practically everything they'd written and published since the war began.

The steward appeared with mugs of coffee and handed them out before retreating as silently as he'd come. Kat felt her heart pounding loudly, knowing she was about to cross the Rubicon. If she'd misjudged any of her guests, she was in deep shit. She had a vague idea of how she might escape the superdreadnought, but she knew there was scant hope of it actually working. She'd drilled her crews too well. It was funny, she reflected sourly, just how something that normally worked in her favor could turn into a major liability if things were different. She certainly couldn't trust her crews to be loyal to *her*, not any longer. She wasn't their captain.

"Admiral," Winters said. "Can I ask . . . ?"

"One moment." Kat produced the two privacy generators, turned the devices on, and placed them on the small table. "We need to talk privately."

Winters frowned. Kitty looked nervous. The other two showed no visible reaction. Kat wondered what they were thinking, then decided it wouldn't matter. She'd have to act fast if they refused to believe her. She hated the thought of improvising a plan from scratch, but there might be no choice. Her two squadrons could hardly fight if they were being torn apart by internal conflict. She'd spent a lot of time trying to determine if there was a way to take control of Caledonia's orbitals. Nothing had come to mind, not without an unacceptable degree of risk. Kat didn't care if she got killed herself, as long as she took Hadrian with her, but she didn't want to get anyone else killed if it could be avoided. Too many people had already died because of her.

"I had a visitor," she said. She wondered, numbly, if the rumors had reached them. Probably. They were all plugged into the grapevine. "William. Admiral Sir William McElney."

Kitty gasped. "Isn't he . . . ? I mean . . . isn't he . . . ?"

"On the wrong bloody side," Fran said evenly. She *knew* William. They'd been friends, once upon a time. She knew him well enough to know William would hardly risk visiting enemy ships for a lark. "Admiral, what happened?"

"William brought a message," Kat said. She picked up the terminal and held it out. "And"—it hurt to say the words—"we're the ones on the wrong side."

She passed the terminal to Winters, then ran through the whole story. Kitty paled, noticeably. Winters seemed impassive. Procaccini and Fran . . . They both looked as if they believed her, without question. Kat hoped that was true. If they had the wit to hide their disbelief until they could leave the room, they could stop her in her tracks. She tried to keep her churning emotions to herself as she brought the story to an end. The die was very definitely cast.

"Jesus," Procaccini said when she'd finished. "Are you sure . . . ?"

The words hung in the air. Kat said nothing, unsure what she could say. She'd never been one for grand speeches. She'd certainly never been forced to attend elocution lessons, let alone been pushed to compose her own statements and deliver them. The navy had taught her how to argue her case, but that was different. She needed to convince her peers, and she wasn't sure how.

"Yes," she said quietly. "I'm sure."

"The data looks accurate," Winters commented. "And there are no obvious flaws."

"But that doesn't mean anything, does it?" Procaccini sounded like a man who was clutching at straws. "They'd know how to make a deepfake that would fool us, right?"

"William wouldn't cooperate," Fran said coldly. "He'd never do anything like . . . like *that*."

"Then they didn't tell him," Procaccini said. "He might have thought he was telling the truth."

"As far as I can tell, the records are *real*." Kat felt a stab of pain in her heart. "We sided with a mass murderer. A man who got millions of people killed."

"He might not have been in the wrong," Winters said. "The Theocracy *was* a deadly threat."

Fran glared at him. "I was at Cadiz," she snapped. "The fleet was hung out to dry. We would have been slaughtered effortlessly if Admiral Falcone hadn't laid her plans. The living would have envied the dead. I don't care *what* excuse he puts forward. He shouldn't have done it and . . . and we bloody well shouldn't be helping him."

"No," Kat agreed. "We made a mistake."

"Many of us came because of *you*," Kitty said very quietly. "Not because we supported the king."

Procaccini opened his mouth, perhaps to rebuke her, but Kat spoke first. "I know," she said. "I made a mistake and . . . I led you into making a mistake too. The fault is mine."

"You couldn't have known," Fran said. "This is treachery on an unimaginable scale."

"It wouldn't be the first time someone provoked a war in the hopes of using it to bolster his position at home," Winters said. "And he managed to bring most of it off."

"And then he started a civil war, when the House of Lords refused to go along with him," Kat said. She scowled at her hands. There was blood on them. The fact it wasn't *real* wouldn't make it any easier to wash off. "And I made things a great deal worse."

Procaccini let out a long breath. "If this is true . . . fuck it." He laughed, harshly. "If this is true, what do we do?"

"We have two options," Kat said. "We can take the fleet to William and surrender. Or we could take the fleet to Caledonia and remove the king."

"You mean kill," Fran said. "He's not getting out of this alive."

"Probably not," Kat agreed. She intended to kill the king personally. And yet . . . Drusilla was pregnant. Was that true? Or was it just more manipulation? Hadrian had wanted to delay the announcement . . . "I . . . I think we have to deal with him before he does something terrible."

"There *is* a third option," Winters said evenly. "We do nothing."

Kat stared at him. "Whose side are you on?"

"Right now, that's probably a dangerous question," Winters said in the same dispassionate tone. "Point is, the king was not wholly wrong. Not when he planned to give the Theocracy a chance to start the war and not when he called out the House of Lords for playing petty politics while postwar space burned down and the colonials started to *hate*.

His methods are unacceptable, but his motives are not. We do have the option of doing nothing."

"He killed my father," Kat said sharply.

"Admiral, your father was not universally beloved," Winters said. "There were many on the colonies, even the world below us, the world we just saved, who cheered his death. He did great good, but also great evil. And they won't rise up in his name."

Kat balled her fists, then forced herself to calm down. "That might be true, on the surface," she said, tightly. "But the king's ultimate goal was *not* to make a new heaven and a new earth for us. It was to take power, supreme power. He wants the kind of power that no one, not even the House of Lords acting in concert, could have. I don't believe he cares anything for us, not once we stop being useful. And even if he did, autocratic governments tend to decay sharply. His kids will be weaker than he is and his grandkids weaker still."

She took a breath. "We do not have the option of doing nothing."

"William will be glad to see us, no doubt." Fran spoke calmly, although Kat could hear tension underlying her voice. "But will the House of Lords?"

"The fault was mine," Kat said. "I led you to the abyss."

"They won't accept that argument," Procaccini said. "You gave illegal orders, technically speaking, and we followed them. We're not going to be given a slap on the wrist and generally let off."

"No." Kat knew he was right, no matter how much she sought to take the blame. There would be more than enough of it to go around. "I intend to . . . *deal* . . . with the king. Afterwards, I will surrender to the House of Lords and take whatever punishment they feel I deserve. If you want to leave before I surrender, I won't try to stop you."

"Understood," Procaccini said. He looked around the compartment. "How many people can be trusted?"

"Not many." Winters spoke with cold certainty. "Right now, we only have a single platoon of marines on each of the superdreadnoughts.

The remainder of the berths are filled with colonial troops. They'd assume we were betraying the alliance and turn on us."

"And Jenkins will be looking over our shoulders," Kitty added. "His men are armed and presumably dangerous. They'd be loyal to the king."

"We could deal with them," Winters said. "The real problem would be getting the troops under control before they started an uprising. It isn't *easy* to seal off sections completely . . ."

"No," Kat agreed. "And we don't know how many can be trusted to help."

She winced, inwardly. There were two thousand crewers on the superdreadnought, most of whom didn't know her personally. They hadn't had time to get to know *Procaccini* personally. And enough of them were colonials that she knew they could take the ship, if they wished. She'd be surprised if they didn't already have contingency plans. In hindsight, it had probably been a serious mistake to allow officers and crew to carry weapons. She'd only gone along with the setup because the king was trying to curry favor with the colonials.

And we can't disarm them without setting off all sorts of alarms. Even if we did, taking control of the ship would be almost impossible.

"William presumably has troops under his command," Fran pointed out. "We could ask him . . ."

"We'd be sunk if we tried," Kat countered. She knew it wouldn't be easy to link up with William without raising too many alarms. The colonials were already uneasy. They might do something stupid, setting off a civil war within the civil war. "Do we have any other options?"

"Not unless you want to slaughter the crews," Winters said. "Sleepy gas is unreliable. The chances are good that most of the colonials are immunized already. Venting the ships would work . . ."

"No." Kat shook her head. "I'm not going to slaughter people who made the mistake of listening to me."

"You thought you were doing the right thing," Winters said. "You'd hardly be the first person to make such a mistake."

"I know," Kat said. "That doesn't make it any easier."

Winters straightened. "I'll speak to my men," he said. "We could take Jenkins and his band of commissioners, then put the ships into lockdown. We've been running drills for so long that we could probably portray it as yet another exercise, at least until the hatches are firmly closed and bolted shut. Given time, we could probably secure most of the fleet. The remainder . . ."

His eyes hardened. "We might have to fire on them."

"Not if it can be avoided," Kat said.

"You might not have a choice," Winters warned. "Then . . . once you have command, you link up with William. Game over."

"After we see what we can do to the king," Kat said. She didn't want to just give up, not when she wanted to deal with Hadrian herself. "If we went back to Caledonia . . ."

"It might be impossible to take the planet," Winters said. "The system *is* heavily defended."

"We couldn't." Kat shook her head. She'd helped design the defense plans. "Two squadrons of superdreadnoughts won't be anything like enough."

"Then we're screwed," Procaccini said. "Admiral, perhaps we *should* simply surrender the fleet."

"I could get to the king," Kat said. A desperate plan was starting to look like the best of a set of bad options. "If we go back and get into orbit, with no one having any reason to stop us, I could go down to the planet and kill him."

"And then what?" Winters raised a hand before Kat could answer. "I don't doubt you could do it, Admiral, but there'd be no orderly transition of power. They'd kill you. The king's courtiers and the colonials would fight over what little scraps were left, triggering a full-scale civil war. The damage would be immense, no matter who won. I shudder to think how many people would be killed."

Kat snorted. "For some strange reason, plotting coups was never taught at the academy."

"I can't imagine why," Winters said dryly. "They *were* taught at OCS, as lessons in coup-proofing the regime. The king learned his lessons well, although I don't recall him ever attending any sort of formal training. His regime is fairly well balanced. Anyone with the means and motives to launch a coup couldn't possibly be unaware of the chaos that would follow in its wake. The only way to avoid it would be to have so *many* people involved that detection would be certain. I don't think the courtiers and the colonials will be making common cause against the king any time soon."

"No," Kat agreed. "I don't think they have enough in common to band together against the king."

She finished her coffee, putting the mug to one side. There weren't many options. She briefly considered a kamikaze mission for herself, but the hell of it was that Winters was right. She might kill Hadrian, only to set off a rolling wave of chaos that would take out everything else. There was no way William could put an end to the fighting in time to save Caledonia. The probability of someone accidentally *hitting* the planet was terrifyingly high.

"We plan to take the fleet," she said. It was all she could do, right now. If nothing else, removing eighteen superdreadnoughts from the king's order of battle would give the House of Lords a decisive advantage. "And then we make our move."

"Aye, Admiral," Winters said. "I'll speak to my men. They can speak to the other platoons."

"And hope no one has a crisis of conscience," Fran said. Her voice was very cold. "Or simply says the wrong thing to the wrong person."

"Yeah." Kat looked from face to face. None of them looked pleased, even if they had the bare bones of a plan. Kat didn't blame them. In the space of a few short minutes, she'd turned their universe upside down. "For what it's worth, I'm sorry."

"You did what you thought best," Winters said. "I cannot blame you for that."

"Thanks." Kat shook her head. "But I'll spend the rest of my life blaming myself."

CHAPTER THIRTY-TWO

CALEDONIA

Captain Sarah Henderson had been concerned when the entire command network had gone to priority-only status. It wouldn't have been a surprise if the enemy had launched an invasion while Admiral Falcone was away, but her sensors revealed no sign of enemy activity. And yet, the planet seemed to be going on alert. It wasn't until the emergency alert was forwarded to her from *another* ship that she'd realized the shit was about to hit the fan. Governor Rogan was about to launch his coup.

She looked around her bridge, silently grateful that she'd been able to fiddle with the shore leave roster so a sizable percentage of the king's loyalists were off the ship. The move had been chancy, given that her people were very sensitive to discrimination, yet it had apparently passed unnoticed. Mr. Soto and his men were still on the ship, unfortunately, but they were alone and isolated. There weren't many people they could deputize if . . . when . . . all hell broke loose.

"Captain," Lieutenant Honshu said. "There's a priority-one signal coming in, aimed at Mr. Soto."

Sarah frowned. The king presumably had contingency plans of his own. Mr. Soto definitely had authority to take control of the ship, if nothing else. He and his team were armed to the teeth. They *could* take control. They'd have to be stopped.

"Mr. XO, implement the lockdown procedure," she ordered. She raised her voice, addressing the bridge. "The king can no longer be trusted. I'm taking control of the ship in the name of the Colonial Alliance. If any of you have a problem with this, step away from your consoles now. You have my word that you will be returned to loyalist forces as soon as reasonably possible."

A long pause followed. No one left their console. Sarah hoped that meant her bridge crew were loyal, to her if not the colonies. A single person in the right place could do a lot of damage. Sarah thought she knew her bridge officers, but too many of them had been moved into their posts on short notice. They didn't know her well enough to give her unconditional loyalty. If word of the atrocity on Quist hadn't already spread through the fleet, they might have sided against her or stepped to one side.

"Captain, Soto and his men have broken the lockdown," Commander Clinton Remus reported grimly. "They overrode the hatches and are heading this way."

"Secure the bridge," Sarah ordered. Soto wouldn't be able to use the intership cars to move around, not during lockdown. He'd have to use the tubes. It would take him longer than he thought, even if he'd brought hacking tools. Hopefully, he wouldn't know the way. "Put suited personnel on guard outside the hatches."

"Aye, Captain," Remus said.

Sarah nodded, studying the near-orbit display. A handful of ships were breaking orbit, clawing their way into interplanetary space. The planetary defenses themselves hadn't come online, yet, but it was just a matter of time. The majority of the fleet was far too close to the orbital defenses for comfort. They'd be blown away in seconds if the defenses opened fire before they raised their shields. And yet, there was no way to bring up the shields without raising the alarm. She had no way to know what was happening on the other ships.

The communications channels are down, she reminded herself. She knew who else was involved in the bid to seize the fleet but couldn't contact them without revealing that *Merlin* was in rebel hands. Again. Soto might have managed to get off a warning before he made his bid to recapture the ship . . . *We have to assume the worst.*

"Bring up the drives," she said. "And be ready to snap up the shields at a moment's notice."

"Aye, Captain," Remus said.

Sarah gritted her teeth, feeling the seconds crawling by. The display showed a handful of internal hatches opening and closing, suggesting that Soto and his men were heading straight to the bridge. They were well trained, she noted, but not *experienced.* Someone with genuine starship experience would have realized that it would be easier to take the engineering or life-support departments, then force the crew to surrender. A handful of gunmen could render the entire ship powerless if they discarded all hope of recapturing her.

She looked at Honshu. "Establish a laser link to *Vigilance,*" she ordered quietly. "Send my codes to Captain Wu and ask him . . ."

"Emergency alert," Remus snapped. "The planetary defenses are powering up!"

"That's torn it!" Sarah snapped. "Bring up the shields, then take us out of orbit!"

The display seemed to explode with icons as the universe went crazy. A handful of starships raised their shields and opened fire, targeting the planetary defenses. The orbital fortresses seemed sluggish, slow to react even as missiles and energy weapons pummeled them from point-blank range. Two superdreadnoughts shut down their drives completely, falling out of formation. One drifted towards the planet itself, thousands of tons of metal and antimatter that would do immense damage if it hit the surface. The remainder of the superdreadnoughts brought up their shields and weapons, emergency transmissions flashing in all directions. Sarah stared at the display, watching as the tactical programs tried to determine who was on what side. The results were inconclusive. There seemed to be no fewer than *five* different sides, much to her surprise. How many plotters had there been?

No one knows who is fighting for whom, she mused as a superdreadnought appeared to switch sides. *And we're out of contact with the rest of the fleet.*

"Captain, they're breaking into Officer Country," Remus snapped. "They'll be here in a moment."

"Vent the access corridor," Sarah ordered coldly. If Soto hadn't thought to carry masks and life-support gear, it would put an end to his countercoup before it even got off the ground. "Tell the marines to fall back to the bridge."

And put their masks on. A low rumble ran through the ship. A grenade? How many weapons had Soto and his men brought aboard? *This could end very badly.*

"They're hitting the hatch," Remus warned. "Captain?"

"Helm, put as much distance as possible between us and the orbital fortresses," Sarah said. "And be ready to shift command to engineering, if they take the bridge."

She drew her pistol. "And prep the datacore for shutdown," she added. "If they capture the ship, I want her to be useless."

"Aye, Captain."

◆ ◆ ◆

"The people aren't happy, Mr. Ambassador," the driver said. "I have to advise you . . ."

Francis understood the driver's point and his unspoken concern for their safety, but he shook his head. He couldn't delay visiting the king, not now that reports were spreading through a planetary communications network that was supposed to be shut down. The colonials had clearly spent a lot of time preparing for this day, even if they hadn't realized who they'd be fighting. The network was erratic, but it was still functioning. His intelligence officers believed it couldn't be shut down completely.

Not that it matters, he thought as the aircar flew over the city. *Word of mouth is carrying the message everywhere it needs to go.*

He scowled. Dawn was breaking over the city, shedding light on an ever-growing crowd of angry protestors. His officers, monitoring the police bands, had warned him that cops were being called in from all over the planet to reinforce the locals, but he couldn't see any law enforcement on the streets. The police themselves probably had mixed feelings, he figured, being colonials themselves. The reports that the king had ordered an entire planet scorched might be exaggerated, but who knew? There was no *quality* reporting from trusted media figures . . . as if they even *existed*! The locals believed the story, and that was all that mattered. The king and his government were heading towards catastrophe.

The aircar passed over the troops defending the palace and dropped towards the landing pad. Francis felt sweat prickling his back as he spotted the HVM teams, hastily deployed to protect the palace from aerial threats. If they decided he was hostile . . . He shook his head again as the aircar landed with a *thud*, rocking gently as the hatch opened. He could hear shouting and gunshots from outside the perimeter. Smoke was rising in the distance, suggesting that the brewing riot had already turned nasty. The colonials were probably intent on causing as much trouble as possible. He peered at the towering skyscraper, Governor Rogan's headquarters, and wondered what the man was doing. His intelligence officers had never managed to get someone into the governor's lair.

He clambered out of the aircar and submitted, meekly, to an intensive pat down from the guards. It was unusual for guards to search ambassadors, instead of merely scanning their bodies before allowing them to enter, but he supposed the guards were on edge. There was enough firepower surrounding the palace to wipe out a marine division, yet . . . there was no way to tell if the soldiers would actually fire. They might turn on the king, if they were ordered to slaughter the crowd. Who knew what would happen if things *really* got out of hand?

"Ambassador." Sir Reginald looked terrible. His pallid face was sweating so badly that Francis half expected him to faint on the spot. "Thank you for coming."

Francis nodded, stiffly. "My pleasure," he lied. His security officers had protested in a body when he'd insisted on visiting the king. They'd pointed out that no one, not even the king himself, could guarantee his safety. The entire city was about to explode. "I trust His Majesty is well?"

Sir Reginald gave him a cutting look, then led the way into the building and down a long flight of stairs. They passed through two more guard posts, each one insisting on a full search before allowing them to proceed. Francis was tempted to ask if the guards would be buying him dinner later, but swallowed the impulse before it could get him into trouble. He had diplomatic immunity, but that wouldn't protect him from bullets. His government could hardly retaliate against a foreign government that no longer existed. Hell, they'd have hard questions to answer about what Francis had been doing there in the first place.

And that could get embarrassing. They wouldn't want to answer those inquiries.

The king looked tired, tired and worn, as Sir Reginald showed Francis into the war room. He was surrounded by holographic displays, each one showing images from the streets outside or the high orbitals. Francis was no military expert, but even he knew that friendly ships firing on each other was not a good sign. The king's forces appeared to be collapsing into chaos. A superdreadnought was drifting towards the planet, spewing lifepods in all directions. Francis hoped the planetary defenses would blow the ship to atoms before it hit the planet itself.

"Ambassador," the king said. He sounded tired too. Princess Drusilla sat next to him, her hand resting on the king's hand. "I am surrounded by traitors."

Francis didn't bother to dispute the statement. "What actually *happened?*"

"They're lying about me," the king said. His voice rose. "They're saying I killed an entire world!"

"So I hear," Francis said. The king should have realized that shutting down the communications network—worse, unsuccessfully *trying* to shut down the communications network—would only give credence to the rumors. It might have been better if he'd mocked the stories, like he'd mocked the charge that he'd started the last war. "What actually happened?"

"I gave orders to punish the planetary government, nothing more," the king snapped. "And now my people rebel against me!"

His voice grew louder, but there was a nasty edge to it Francis didn't like. "I'll punish them all. I'll make sure they never rise against me again!"

Francis nodded, keeping his face as blank as possible. The king was losing it. His cause had taken a major blow, perhaps even a mortal blow. If his fleet was racked by civil unrest, it wouldn't be able to put up a fight when the House of Lords launched its long-awaited attack on Caledonia. The displays flickered and updated, revealing that one of the superdreadnoughts was trading fire with an orbital fortress. It wouldn't be long until the remainder of the fleet took sides and opened fire.

And that leaves us with a problem. Can we still make use of the king? Or should we back off now?

He looked up as Lord Gleneden and Earl Antony entered, the former looking badly shaken and the latter grimly determined. They were the king's dove and hawk, he recalled, if the files were accurate. He knew from bitter experience that the dossiers might be completely wrong.

"Your Majesty," Lord Gleneden said. "We must seek terms."

"Treason," Earl Antony snapped. "We cannot surrender!"

"Right now, the entire planet is revolting," Lord Gleneden insisted. "The fleet is falling apart at the seams. You have to come to terms or . . ."

"I will not surrender. I will *certainly* not surrender to liars and betrayers and . . ."

He stood, pacing the room as he ranted. Francis watched him, realizing, deep inside, that the king might have outlived his usefulness. The man was coming apart, right in front of him. And yet . . . there was still something to be gained by supporting him. If nothing else, they could secure the border stars and dare the House of Lords to do something. The Commonwealth couldn't keep fighting without risking everything . . .

And they already know the dangers of fighting a war to promote unity, he mused. *They won the last war, and it left them with more problems than ever before.*

"We cannot surrender, not now," Drusilla said. She touched her abdomen. "My child will not grow up in exile."

Lord Gleneden glared at her. "With all due respect," he snapped, "the situation is dire. Your child will not grow up at all if we don't seek terms! Now!"

He looked at the king, dismissing his wife. "Your Majesty, we need to speak to Tyre," he said. "I can talk to some of my contacts, get you terms . . ."

The king spoke, very quietly. "You'd like that, wouldn't you? Sell the cause out . . . sell *me* out . . . for whatever you can get. You'd like that. You could go home to your estate and spend the rest of your days in comfort, while I . . ."

His voice grew stronger. "I am surrounded by betrayers and traitors and . . ."

Francis flinched as the king produced a gun and shot Lord Gleneden through the head. He was no stranger to the theory of violence, but he'd never seen a man killed right in front of him. He stepped back as the body hit the ground, blood staining the carpet. Lord Gleneden had been a good man, according to the files. Francis barely knew him, but . . . Francis didn't think Lord Gleneden deserved to die. Not like that. Not shot down by his master.

"We will not surrender," the king said. The building shook, gently. Alerts flashed up on the displays. "We will *not* give in."

◆ ◆ ◆

"I think they're screwed," Lieutenant Allot said. "They're firing on each other."

Captain Sonny Greenbank nodded in agreement. The spy ship had been holding position several light-minutes from Tyre, where they could monitor the enemy fleet without straying into detection range, but they were close enough to see all hell breaking loose. Starships were firing on each other or flying away from the planet and dropping into hyperspace. He could see a dozen merchantmen crawling away, trying desperately not to be noticed as they put as much distance as possible between themselves and the warring parties. A couple of them had already been blasted out of space, in passing. The two sides were fighting at point-blank range. They didn't have time to be sure of their targets before they opened fire.

"Power up the StarCom," he ordered. "Let Admiral McElney know."

He smiled, coldly. Their orders were clear. They were to alert the admiral the *moment* something, anything, happened that might give the fleet a clear shot at Caledonia. It was a risk—the moment they powered up the StarCom, they'd set off alarms right across the system—but there was no choice. An enemy civil war was greatly to be desired. By the time Admiral McElney reached Caledonia, the enemy fleet might have destroyed itself.

And then he'll put an end to the war, Sonny thought. *It will be the end.*

"Got two squadrons of battlecruisers and supporting elements dropping out of hyperspace, sir," Allot warned. New icons flickered onto life on the display, a single light-minute from the planet. "They look pretty pissed."

"As long as they're not targeting us," Sonny pointed out. He frowned as he studied the display. The enemy ships looked as if they'd redlined their drives, trying to get back to Caledonia before . . . before what? They had no way of knowing all hell had broken loose on the planet. The StarCom had been shut down hours ago. "We'll let the admiral know, and then we'll go into hiding."

"And we'll have a front-row seat to Armageddon," Allot said.

Sonny shot him a sharp look. The intelligence corps was notoriously informal, but there were limits. "That isn't a good thing," he said. An enemy ship vanished from the display. "A lot of people are about to die."

CHAPTER THIRTY-THREE

CALEDONIA

"Report," Bertram said as he reached the makeshift OP. "What's happening?"

"Our forces are in position, sir," Colonel Hector Yuan said. He was a tall man, a colonial militia officer who'd led an insurgency on an occupied world before joining Bertram's staff. "So far, the king hasn't made any visible reaction."

Bertram looked at the map made from paper, astonishingly primitive by modern standards. It couldn't update automatically, although he knew from experience that wasn't always a bad thing. The modern displays were so good that it was easy to forget the fog of war blanketing the battlefield, the grim truth that whatever the displays showed might not be remotely accurate. A red marker had been used to draw out the king's position, a handful of notes representing his known and suspected forces . . . a handful of blue marks sat outside the defensive line, waiting for the order.

"The police had been trying to clear the streets," Yuan added. "So far, they've been unsuccessful."

"Not too surprising," Bertram said. The angry crowds pressing against the king's walls were in deadly danger, even if they didn't know it. "And the rest of the targets?"

"The assault forces are in position," Yuan said. "But we haven't had word from the fleet."

"We'll have to hope for the best," Bertram said. "If we can capture the king, we can force him to order his forces to stand down."

He let out a breath. "Give the order," he said. "Begin the assault."

And may God forgive me, he thought. His people were more practical and pragmatic than the Tyrians. They might forgive him for launching an assault that would ensure the deaths of thousands of civilians, even if the citizenry ran the moment the assault force started shooting. They'd understand he hadn't had a choice. But he'd never forgive himself. *If this goes wrong . . .*

He put the thought aside as Yuan picked up his handset and started to issue orders. They were running out of time. God alone knew who'd win the battle for the high orbitals. It was alarmingly clear that the king had either launched his own plan to seize the fleet or activated contingency plans for a colonial attempt to do the same. Whoever won, the fleet was going to be in tatters. Bertram *had* to be in control of the planet—and the king—before the House of Lords came knocking. It was his only hope for negotiating a surrender that wouldn't be completely unconditional.

And if we lose, the entire planet will burn, he reminded himself. *We must not lose.*

♦ ♦ ♦

Lieutenant Jackie Richton had never really questioned the king, not even when he'd been given the flat choice between traveling to Caledonia with the rest of the king's personal guard or remaining on Tyre. The king and his officials had been good to Jackie and the rest of the personal guard, ensuring that they received everything from promotion prospects to paid leave and educational opportunities for their children. Jackie himself had been looking forward to a tour with the

Grenadier Guards or one of the other frontline formations when his time with the personal guard ended, although *that* was probably dead in the water now. It was something that would have to wait until they returned home . . . if, of course, they ever did.

He shuddered as he heard the sound of angry marchers screaming for justice. The mob looked terrifying, even to experienced soldiers. Jackie wasn't sure what he'd do if his superiors ordered him to fire on the crowd. There would be a very quick slaughter and then . . . He shuddered again, unable to deny the reality of what he was contemplating. He was loyal to the king. He'd put his life between the king and an assassin, even if it meant his children would grow up without a father. And yet, he drew the line at mass slaughter. He couldn't fire on a crowd. He'd kill hundreds of people in less than a minute.

His heart sank as he surveyed the defenses. The palace hadn't been built for defense, and it showed. The walls were too low to keep the crowd out, even though they were designed to stand up to anything smaller than an antitank plasma cannon. They probably already had ladders, if someone with a bright spark hadn't thought of simply driving vehicles to the walls and using them to scramble over and into the palace grounds. The skyscrapers nearby provided plenty of perches for snipers, allowing them to fire into the compound without much fear of retaliation. And the armored vehicles sitting on the grounds themselves wouldn't be that useful when it came to crowd control. There was no way they could handle the crowd gently.

"The crowd is pressing closer," the CO said. "Watch the walls."

"Yes, sir," Jackie said. The CO was in the palace itself, relatively safe. "Can the local police not do anything?"

"They're caught on the outskirts," the CO said. "They're too scared to move."

Jackie scowled. He'd heard horror stories of postings to uncivilized worlds, where foreign ambassadors were seen as hated intruders, but Caledonia was supposed to be relatively civilized. And yet, the locals were convinced that the king had ordered an entire planet wiped clean of life. Didn't they *know* it was better to check rumors before actually rioting? Jackie had heard through the grapevine that 99 percent of rumors about senior political leaders were either lies or simple exaggerations. The king wouldn't order an entire planet destroyed. Jackie refused to believe such madness.

"Sir, the crowd is growing bigger," he said. "They'll be pushing down the walls by—"

He glanced up, sharply, as he heard the telltale *crump-crump-crump* of mortars. The laser point defense stations came to life a second later, beams of light flickering through the air and detonating the mortar shells before they could crash down in the palace compound. More followed, lighting up the air in a grotesque fireworks display; he heard someone barking orders for counterbattery fire, despite the near certainty of hitting and killing civilians. The big guns rotated and opened fire, hurling shells back towards the mortars. Moments later, he heard explosions in the distance.

A dull rumble echoed through the crowd, followed by an explosion that picked him up and threw him against the wall. The impact was so hard, despite the body armor and helmet, that he thought for a moment his sanity had been impaired. The wall in front of him, at the bottom of the grounds, was nothing more than a smoking crater. He stared in horror, barely able to see the dead bodies surrounding the ruins. There had been hundreds, perhaps thousands, of people pressed against the walls. Now they were dead or injured or . . .

He snapped back to himself as a line of soldiers appeared, hugging the edge of the crater as they flowed into the palace grounds. Orders reverberated through the tactical combat network, commanding the armored vehicles to engage the newcomers. Jackie raised his rifle, snapping shots at the enemy troops as they took cover. A streak of light blazed through the air, striking one of the vehicles and turning it into a massive fireball. Bullets pinged off the armor, one of them coming far too close to Jackie's head for comfort. He looked at the distant skyscrapers, knowing he didn't have a hope of picking the sniper out against the dull exterior. He didn't have the slightest idea in fact which building housed the sniper. Perhaps they *all* held snipers.

"We're being attacked from all sides," someone said. The communications network was hissing, suggesting someone was trying to hack or jam it. "They're coming at us . . ."

The ground shook, again. Jackie turned just in time to see a massive fireball blasting up on the far side of the palace. The walls had fallen . . . A third explosion sent pieces of debris crashing to the ground, clattering against windows and walls that had been designed to take impacts up to and including direct missile strikes. He sucked in his breath as he saw another line of enemy troops pressing their advantage as they flowed towards the palace. Behind them, he saw more mortar shells rise into the air. This time there was no counterbattery fire.

Surrender might not be an option, he thought. The attackers looked like soldiers, colonial military probably, but the mob behind them was angry. Very angry. Anyone who was going to flee, if they still *could* flee, would have done so already. The mob would tear the king's defenders and the king himself limb from limb if they caught him. *We dare not try to escape.*

He gritted his teeth. He'd heard plenty of horror stories about embassies that had come under attack. Their only hope was local forces arriving to save their bacon. Here, he was grimly certain that the local forces were the ones doing the attacking. There was no point in screaming for help when there was no one who *could* help. And he doubted they could escape if they fled the palace. By now there'd be roadblocks on all the major roads.

"Get back into the building," he ordered. The strategy wasn't much, but it was the best he could do. The king could talk to the attackers, perhaps negotiate . . . Whatever had happened, the colonials would be reluctant to kill their king. He hoped. The rumors had *really* spun out of control. "And slam down all the blast doors."

The communications network hissed. Jackie swore as he ordered his troops to use grenades to cover their retreat, making life difficult for the attackers. Whoever was in charge, back in the palace, should *still* be in charge . . . damn it. The CO was well trained, but if the communications network was down, the poor bastard wouldn't have the slightest idea what was really going on. His orders would be worse than useless, if he could issue them in the first place. Jackie tried to be optimistic as they piled their way into the palace, an instant before the remaining blast doors slammed into place. The building was tough. They could hold out long enough for sanity to assert itself . . .

"Take up sniping positions," he ordered the remnants of his squad. The CO hadn't made an appearance, not yet. The local network was down. "And be ready."

A dull *thud* echoed through the building as a mortar shell struck the walls. That wasn't a problem. Jackie would be quite happy to let them waste ammo by trying to blast down an impregnable sheet of armor. But they'd have plenty of time to come up with something more effective if they got control of the high orbitals. Hell, they could just starve the king out. The bunker below the palace wasn't self-sustaining. How could it be?

The intercom crackled, but all he heard was a low hiss. He felt his heart sink still further as his people took up their remaining positions. Without the command network, they were screwed. And then . . .

We have to hold out. It's our only hope.

◆ ◆ ◆

"How bad is it?"

Bertram asked the question, knowing with a grim certainty that he wasn't going to like the answer. Colonel Yuan and his fellow planners had insisted that the palace had to be taken as quickly as possible despite the certainty of civilian casualties. It was starting to look as though their estimates of how many people would be killed or wounded had been absurdly low.

"We hold the palace grounds," Yuan said. "But the defenders have retreated into the building."

He nodded at the map. "We have overwhelmed the remainder of our targets," he added after a moment. "The planetary defense installations are in our hands. Our message has already started to go out over the airwaves."

"Good." Bertram let out a breath. "But you don't have control of the StarCom?"

"No." Yuan grimaced. "The structure is still in lockdown. Right now, we're fighting to take control of the fortresses—or destroy them, if they remain loyal to the king. We might not have been able to take out the king's communications links to the fleet either."

"But the fleet is being torn apart too," Bertram said.

"Yes, sir," Yuan said. "We're unsure what the final outcome will be."

Bertram looked up at him. "Is the secondary assault force ready to go?"

"Yes, sir," Yuan said. "We've prepped weapons to burn through their armor."

"Then send them in," Bertram ordered. He'd always prided himself on being able to make the hard decisions. He knew, now, that he hadn't really understood what a hard decision actually *was*. "Capture the king. Now."

"Yes, sir."

◆ ◆ ◆

"Admiral Ruben has returned, Your Majesty," a young naval officer said. Francis didn't know her name. "He's requesting orders."

"At least his fleet is loyal," the king growled. He was still pacing the room, holding his pistol in one hand. "Tell him . . . tell him to take control of the high orbitals."

Francis winced, inwardly, at the expression that crossed the naval officer's face. There was no way a handful of battlecruisers could regain control of the high orbitals, not when superdreadnoughts and orbital fortresses were locked in mortal combat. Admiral Ruben would be well advised to stay clear of the planet, at least until loyalist ships could be separated from rebels. But there was no way anyone could say that to the king. His mood kept oscillating between a gritty determination to keep fighting, even when the end was in sight, and a deep depression that seemed likely to overwhelm him. He'd said too much about not being taken alive for Francis's peace of mind.

He glanced at the live feed from the display, wishing he could speak to his staff. It was hard to be *sure* what was going on. The reports kept contradicting each other, as if people were trying hard to avoid being the one who had to bring bad news to the king. The superdreadnoughts were loyal. No, they were disloyal. No, the crews were fighting each other, and whoever won would be loyal or disloyal or . . . or what? Francis felt isolated and alone even though he was in a crowd. He should leave, but he knew it was pointless. Even if the king let him go, the attackers were unlikely to permit him to pass through their lines.

"Fortress Seven has dropped out of the command network completely," another aide called. "I think they're withdrawing from combat."

"Blow them away!" The king's voice rose again as he turned to address the speaker. "Crush them!"

"Yes, Your Majesty," the aide said. "I'll pass the orders at once."

"They're prepping another assault," General Ross said. He indicated the displays, showing a handful of militiamen readying themselves. "Your Majesty, we should move to the bunker!"

"No," the king said. He shook his head firmly. "I will not run."

You should, Francis thought. An idea crossed his mind. *If we were to go elsewhere . . .*

"Call Admiral Falcone," the king said, seemingly unaware that it was infeasible. He didn't even seem to realize that it was *his* orders that had made contact impossible. "Tell her to bring her fleet here."

"The StarCom is down, Your Majesty," the young naval officer said. Francis admired her nerve, even though she was clearly terrified. "We can't send messages outside the system . . ."

"Then power it up," the king snapped. "Now!"

You don't have time, Francis thought. The king could issue orders all he liked, but they couldn't be carried out. *By the time Admiral Falcone gets here, you'll be dead.*

He cursed. The king had few options left now. *And unless you listen to me, I'll die right next to you.*

◆　◆　◆

Jackie frowned as a sudden quiet fell over the building. Even the incessant bombardment stopped. He glanced at his terminal, cursing as the link to the network failed, reasserted itself, and failed again. They were reduced to sending messengers from place to place, as if they'd been sent back in time to the prespace days . . . He shook his head in irritation as he wiped sweat from his brow. Jackie wanted to think the king was talking to the attackers, trying to come to terms, but he wasn't sure. His instincts told him the quiet was just a pause in the storm.

He surveyed the lobby, feeling cold. The solid blast doors were firmly in place, but he knew they wouldn't pose a barrier once the attackers brought up heavy weapons. He'd set a handful of ambushes, positioned men in places where they might . . . might . . . be able to hurt the bastards, but it was just kicking and scratching on the way to the gallows. No one would fault the king for surrendering now, not when his defenses were so badly weakened. But would surrender be accepted?

A messenger popped up beside him. "Sir, they're readying another attack."

Jackie gritted his teeth. He'd thought as much, but it was still irritating to have his fears confirmed. "Any word from the king? Or the general?"

"Hold to the last," the messenger said. He shrank back as Jackie glared at him. "I . . ."

A low rumble ran through the building. Jackie glanced up just in time to see a chandelier detach itself from the ceiling and plummet to the ground. It didn't even have time to smash itself on the floor before the blast doors glowed red and exploded, pieces of superheated metal flying in all directions. Jackie saw, just for a second, something very bright moving towards him . . .

. . . and then the world went away in a brilliant flash of light.

CHAPTER THIRTY-FOUR

CALEDONIA

The bridge hatch exploded inwards.

Sarah ducked behind the command chair as a pair of shock grenades exploded, sending arcs of blue-white light crackling in all directions, then popped up and opened fire. The bridge pressure dropped alarmingly as air rushed into the vented section beyond, pushing the attackers back as the bridge crew shot them down. Sarah felt her ears pop, but she ignored the stab of pain as the last of the attackers fell. A handful of her crew had been caught by the grenades and were lying on the deck, moaning in pain, but the remainder were safe. Sarah breathed a sigh of relief. It was sheer damned luck that Soto had been smart enough not to risk using real grenades on the bridge.

He probably didn't know how to take command from engineering. She forced herself to stand. The bodies looked as if they'd been shot repeatedly. They probably had. Her crew knew how to use their sidearms, but they were hardly experts. *And now his men are dead.*

She found Soto himself and checked his body, then returned to the command chair. Her crew were taking their places, as if shootouts on the bridge were routine. The thought chilled her. There had been no shortage of shootouts during the last round of mutinies, including a number that had ended with the ship effectively wrecked. Mutiny was becoming a habit . . .

"Report," she ordered.

"We're clear of the fortresses," Honshu stated. "And we have solid laser links to a handful of other ships."

"Assemble a command datanet," Sarah commanded. "And figure out who's in charge . . ."

Alarms howled. Red icons appeared on the display. Sarah stared, torn between relief and a sinking sensation that told her the war was over and they'd lost. Four superdreadnought squadrons and flanking elements, heading straight towards the planet. The House of Lords had attacked at the worst possible time. The fleet was in no state to mount a defense, even if it wanted to fight. The Battle of Caledonia was going to be a walkover.

"Captain, the incoming fleet is hailing us," Honshu said. "The entire system will hear them."

"Put it through," Sarah said calmly.

". . . Is Admiral McElney," a voice said. "You are ordered to stand down and prepare to be boarded. Crews that surrender will be treated as POWs, detained until the end of the war then allowed to return home. Ships that refuse to surrender will be regarded as hostile and destroyed without further warning. This is . . ."

"The message is repeating," Honshu said. "Captain?"

Sarah glanced at Remus. The incoming ships would pass within firing range well before *Merlin* could power up her drives and jump into hyperspace. They didn't have a hope of escape, let alone standing in defense of Caledonia. The command network was shattered beyond repair. And she didn't know how many of her crewers could be trusted. God alone knew what they'd do if they learned what was happening.

Sarah was no coward. She knew she was no coward. But she had no intention of throwing her crewers into the fire for naught.

"Stand down," she ordered reluctantly. "Take us out of the fight."

◆ ◆ ◆

William ignored the series of alarms and complaints from his engineers as the fleet advanced on Caledonia, into a scene out of nightmares. He'd redlined his drives to reach the planet before someone, anyone, took control and rebuilt the defenses, but it was starting to look as if he needn't have hurried. The enemy fortresses had battered themselves practically into scrap or depowered themselves or . . . He sucked in his breath as his tactical staff struggled to impose order on what they were seeing. It looked as though there were a dozen different sides, all wrapped up in their own struggle even as his fleet bore down on them.

"A number of ships are surrendering, sir," Yagami said. "But I can't raise the planet itself."

"They might have destroyed their own command and control network," William said. It would be irritating as hell if the rebels, whoever they were, had killed the only people who *could* order a surrender. He stared at the display, as if looking closer would bring him the answers he lacked. "Where is the king?"

"Unknown, sir," Yagami said. "I can't locate a command post."

"Then keep us heading towards the planet," William said. Once he took the high orbitals, the king and his allies—and enemies—would no longer be a major factor. "We'll engage any defender who refuses to surrender when we come into range."

"Aye, sir."

◆ ◆ ◆

"That's confirmed, Your Majesty," the naval officer said. "The House of Lords has attacked!"

"Treachery," the king shouted. "I am betrayed by everyone!"

By the universe itself, Francis thought. The timing wasn't perfect. Apparently, the House of Lords had merely taken advantage of the uprising rather than planning and directing it from Tyre. There was no way to be sure, but he'd been in politics long enough to know the signs of someone directing the storm. The timing would have been better, he was sure, if the House of Lords had planned the insurgency from the start. *You simply got unlucky.*

Another rumble ran through the building. "They're pressing in from the north," General Ross said. "Your Majesty, we need to get down to the bunker."

The king's eyes were wide and staring. Perfect. He couldn't believe what was happening. Francis's plan took shape. A window of opportunity had appeared if he had the chance to use it. But . . . that wouldn't be easy. Too many other factors were at play for him to be *completely* certain of success. And yet, if the ploy worked, it would boost his career to the highest levels.

"Your Majesty," he said gently. "You *do* have another option."

The king rounded on him, hope dawning in his eyes. "What do you suggest?"

"You take your loyalists to the border worlds," Francis said. "You set up a base there, under our protection. And you could plan your reconquest of Tyre and the Commonwealth . . ."

"Exactly." The king turned to his staff. "Prepare all personnel on the alpha list for transit to the shuttles. We'll join Admiral Ruben and travel to the border."

"The skies aren't clear," General Ross warned. "Your Majesty . . ."

"It's that or die!" Earl Antony slammed his fist into his palm. "We have to go now."

"Quite," the king said. "And Admiral Ruben can clear the way."

Francis frowned inwardly. He would have preferred the king alone, with perhaps a handful of ships. There was no way to know how many starships and crews would follow Hadrian to the border. If there were too many, they might become a problem that neither Tyre nor Marseilles could easily overlook. But . . . He pasted a calm expression on his face, trying to look benevolent as the king's courtiers looked at him with new hope. They didn't have any other options. The best they could expect, if they fell into enemy hands, was spending the rest of their lives in exile. Somehow, after whatever had happened at Quist, Francis doubted the House of Lords would be so kind.

"Send Ruben the targeting data," the king ordered. "And tell him to put it into effect at once."

"Yes, Your Majesty," General Ross said. "And now, if you don't mind, we must go."

The king grinned. "Of course, of course . . ."

◆ ◆ ◆

Admiral Henri Ruben felt sweat trickling down his back as his fleet slid into high orbit, carefully keeping their distance from the handful of disloyal fortresses. The enemy ships were right behind him, trying to trap his ships against the planet . . . He gripped his palms to keep them from shaking as the range continued to close. The king's orders had been quite explicit, leaving no room whatsoever for creative interpretation. And yet . . . Henri knew they would have bare seconds, if that, to pull it off. The enemy fleet would close the range very quickly once Henri stopped running.

"Admiral." The tactical officer sounded uneasy. "We have weapons lock."

Henri nodded. "Fire."

A series of shudders ran through the battlecruiser as she unleashed a full spread of KEWs, targeted on the city below. He tried not to think about the impact, about the skyscrapers that would be toppled and the underlying buildings that would be smashed to rubble when the kinetic projectiles slammed home. The king was under attack, and it was the duty of all loyal men to come to his aid, even if it meant slaughtering the innocent along with the guilty. He told himself, time and time again, that they deserved it. *They deserved it.* The guilty had risen against their king and the innocent . . . they weren't really innocent at all, because they hadn't tried to defend their king. *They deserved it . . .*

"Impact in ten seconds," the tactical officer reported. There was a hitch in his voice as he spoke. "Sir . . ."

"Recycle the drives," Henri ordered. "I want to be out of here as soon as the king is aboard."

"Aye, sir."

◆ ◆ ◆

"Shit!"

Bertram spun around. "What?"

"They dropped KEWs!" Yuan sounded shocked. "They fired on the city!"

"Who fired?" Bertram realized, to his horror, that they were almost certainly doomed. The House of Lords had attacked in force. Caledonia was going to be occupied, even if she refused to surrender. "Who . . . ?"

"Admiral Ruben," Yuan said. "Sir, he . . ."

Bertram turned to stare out the window. Streaks of light were falling down all over the city, the pattern steadily marching towards him. The ground shook, time and time again, as the KEWs hit the ground. He saw a giant skyscraper shiver, then start to topple like a house of cards. It struck its neighbor, starting off a series of dominoes that tore across the entire landscape. The sound hit his ears, the force of the impact shattering windows and shaking the entire building so heavily he *knew* they were done for. The walls started to crumble, the floor collapsing into a black hole . . .

He fought down an urge to laugh as he plunged towards the ground, plummeting to his death. They'd made a dreadful mistake. They'd backed a madman, someone who had led them to utter destruction.

And yet, they'd needed the king. They'd been manipulated because they'd *needed* the king. A truly dreadful mistake.

And then the ground came up and hit him.

◆ ◆ ◆

Francis could *feel* the ground shaking as the KEWs crashed down, setting off a series of earthquakes that sent cascades of destruction running through the palace. He tried not to think about what was happening outside as they were hurried up the stairs and into the emergency shuttles, about the dead and dying and everyone else caught in the storm. His people might be dead now, he realized as he was pushed into the shuttle and told to buckle up. The embassy was close to the center of the city but far away enough to keep it from being part of the government complex. The structure could have been smashed to rubble by now.

He told himself that it wasn't *his* fault. He hadn't ordered the king to fire on his own city. It wasn't *his* decision to destroy the embassy . . . something that was going to cause all sorts of problems if the king became dependent on support from Marseilles. God knew how the government would react. Blame it on the House of Lords? Or demand that the king make a show of punishing his rogue admiral? Who knew?

A child started crying as the shuttle lurched, then threw itself into the sky. Francis pushed his fears away and forced himself to peer through the porthole, looking out over a vision of hell itself. The city lay in ruins, the crumpled remains of hundreds of skyscrapers lying broken and shattered on the ground. Plumes of smoke rose from dozens of fires that burned out of control. They were already too high for him to see anything as small as a body, but he was all too aware that there would be *millions* of dead in the rubble below. The devastation stretched as far as the eye could see. He wondered, morbidly, if the king had destroyed the entire world.

The shuttle shook again, the gravity field fluctuating as it slipped into orbit. The displays had shown a chaotic nightmare gripping the high orbitals, but he couldn't see any sign of it with the naked eye. Everything seemed so *peaceful*. He gripped the armrests, feeling terrified for the first time in years. A single missile could obliterate the shuttles in passing, no one knowing who they'd eliminated. He looked towards the front of the shuttle, where the king was sitting with his wife. Did he understand how quickly he could be killed? Or did he simply not care? Francis had no idea.

His heart twisted as the battlecruiser came into view. The ship looked invincible, completely unstoppable . . . He knew it was an illusion, but he clung to it anyway as the shuttle latched onto the airlock. The gravity twisted again, an unpleasant sensation churning in his stomach as the battlecruiser readied itself to depart. The ships had refused the chance to surrender. Francis was all too aware there wouldn't be a second, not after whatever had happened at Quist. And Caledonia, now. The House of Lords wouldn't let the ships escape.

"Your Majesty," a voice said. "We are ready to enter hyperspace."

"Thank you, Henri," the king said. He sounded more in control, of both himself and events. "Signal the fleet. The loyalist ships are to jump out and link up with us at Sycamore. We'll proceed to our final destination from there."

Francis frowned. Sycamore? There was nothing there, save for a handful of settlements and . . . He remembered what *else* was there. A StarCom. The king needed to signal his remaining loyalists, including Admiral Falcone. He'd be able to order her to meet up with him—or something—instead of returning to Caledonia and flying straight into a trap. Good to see the king was thinking again, he supposed. Who knew? As long as the situation wasn't quite hopeless, it might bring out the best in him.

And we might have problems dealing with him, afterwards. Whatever else happened, the king was going to go down in history as a mass murderer. Very few others had thrown so many of their own people into the fire, sacrificing countless lives to save their own. *A hot potato.*

But it didn't matter, Francis told himself. As long as the king was useful, his . . . *issues* could be overlooked. And, once he was no *longer* useful, he could be quietly tossed aside.

A shudder ran through the ship, a sense of unease that seemed . . . *unearthly.* "We have entered hyperspace," Henri's voice said. Henri Ruben, Francis guessed. "We're dropping mines as we flee."

And that will make it harder for them to chase us, Francis thought. *It might just give us time to get away.*

◆　◆　◆

"Admiral, they're dropping mines in hyperspace," Yagami reported. "The forward pursuit elements are already reporting energy storms."

"Cancel the pursuit," William ordered. There was no point in trying to give chase, not with the king deliberately agitating hyperspace. He was running a serious risk, but he *was* desperate. If he was caught now, he'd be lucky to survive long enough to stand trial. "Order the advance elements to take control of the high orbitals."

He let out a long breath as the roar of battle slowly died away. Caledonia had gone silent. His long-range scans revealed that the planet's capital was nothing more than a pile of rubble. The king's ships hadn't struck *many* targets outside the capital itself, but what they *had* done was quite enough. They'd aimed to destroy as much of the planetary government and infrastructure as possible, and they'd succeeded. William had no idea who was in charge down there, if anyone was. It was quite likely that a lowly councilor might be the senior surviving government official. No one was left, as far as he could tell, with the authority to order the planet to surrender.

"Admiral," Yagami said. "The marines are taking possession of the surrendered starships now."

"Very good," William said. "Once the ships are secure, and the crews transferred to Caledonia, the marines are to provide what help they can to the locals."

He turned his attention to the starchart, rubbing his chin as he considered his options. The king could have gone anywhere, but . . . his logistics chain had been shot to hell. Was he trying to link up with Kat? He was in for a nasty surprise if he did. Or . . . or what? There was no way he'd be able to get back to Tyre now. He only had a handful of ships under his command, and they'd all been through hell. Perhaps he would go to Kat. *She* would put an end to this.

"Power up the StarCom," he ordered. "Contact Tyre. Inform them that we have secured Caledonia."

"Aye, sir," Yagami said. "Is it over?"

"Not until the king is dead," William said. Perhaps Hadrian would head into unexplored space and try to set up a colony. Ideal, he supposed. The king simply didn't have the resources to establish an industrial base. Given time, his own people would overthrow him. But William knew better. It really wasn't over. "And now we have to track him down, before he finds a way to strike back."

And Scott might have to take a message to Kat. She has to know what happened here before she hears it from the king.

CHAPTER THIRTY-FIVE

FOTHERINGAY

"This is impossible," Jenkins said. "Admiral . . ."

Kat nodded, concealing her own astonishment as best as she could. She'd run out of excuses to keep the StarCom powered down eventually, but it had worked out better than she'd ever dreamed. Caledonia had fallen, the king was on the run . . . and he'd issued orders for her to take her ships and join him. It was abundantly clear, all too clear, that he was making a run for the border.

Not that he has anywhere else to go. The news broadcasts had made that clear too. *The Colonial Alliance is in open revolt, and Tyre will welcome him back with a hangman's noose. His only hope is to head to the border and pray the House of Lords doesn't feel like starting a third interstellar war.*

She cursed as the king's scheme took shape in her mind. He'd already sold the border stars to Marseilles. If he turned them into a vest-pocket empire, a client state . . . the Marseillans might be quite happy to bring him under their wing. Or they might recoil in horror. They had a fig leaf of legality when it came to claiming the systems for themselves, but they had no cover at all if they wanted to protect the king. They might simply take him prisoner and return him to Tyre. But . . .

Father could have made the politics work, she thought morbidly. *The king doesn't even begin to have his political skill.*

No matter, she told herself firmly. The king was not going to get away, even if she had to kill him personally. She'd follow orders, up to a point. And . . . She smiled inwardly as the rest of the pieces fell into place. The king had given her the tools she needed to stick a knife in his back.

The intercom chimed. "Admiral, *John Galt* has entered the system," Kitty said. "He's requesting permission to . . ."

"Later," Kat said. She saw a knowing look in Jenkins's eyes and felt a flash of amusement. Let him think badly of her for a few hours longer. "Tell them to hold station and wait."

She looked at Jenkins. "We cannot allow word of this to get out," she said. "Half the crew is colonial. They'll turn on us in an instant if they hear that the king and the Colonial Alliance have fallen out."

Jenkins paled. "Do you think they can *take* the ships?"

"They can certainly do a great deal of damage," Kat said. She wanted to roll her eyes at his ignorance. The colonials certainly *could* take the ship. She rather suspected they had a contingency plan to do so. There had to have been *some* preplanning, well before Quist had become something more than an icon on a starchart. "We can't let them take control of the fleet."

She pressed her fingertips together, trying to sound as reassuring as possible. "We'll put the entire fleet into lockdown," she continued. "You and your men . . . I assume they'll remain loyal?"

"Of course." Jenkins puffed up. "They're loyal to His Majesty."

"Good," Kat lied. "I'll announce a lockdown drill in twenty minutes. Go back to your men and ready them for action, then take them to the shuttlebay. I want to move fast if any of the ships drop out of the command network. We don't want them bringing up their weapons and firing on us at point-blank range."

Jenkins frowned. "I only have fifteen men under my command . . ."

"It will have to do," Kat said. "There's no other way we can keep the ship under control."

She dismissed him with a wave, wondering if any of his men would see the looming trap. They couldn't be as ignorant as their commander, could they? If their orders were to take control of the ship, if the colonials revolted or Kat herself turned on the king, they'd have to know how to do so. Right? But Jenkins had never struck her as the kind of person to listen to dissent from his subordinates. It helped that Kat's orders were completely reasonable, if one didn't know she intended to mutiny. Jenkins's men might *have* to take control of the other superdreadnoughts.

And then we'll have to secure the rest of the fleet, Kat thought. There'd been no way to hold an in-person command conference, not without arousing suspicion. They were in a war zone. There was no reason to hold a face-to-face meeting when holograms would suffice. *And then proceed directly to Willow.*

She tapped her console, sending a message to Winters. The marines had their own communications net, one isolated from the remainder of the crew. Winters had been convinced Jenkins couldn't hack it—and that, if he tried, it would set off all kinds of alerts—but Kat wasn't so sure. Jenkins might not be a complete idiot. Her father had told her, more than once, that he'd encountered hundreds of very slippery characters who pretended they couldn't count past ten without taking off their socks. An appearance of idiocy made it easy to underestimate them. Kat had never cared for the tactic herself—she'd spent too long dealing with people who thought she'd bought her way into all of her posts—but she saw the value of it now. Jenkins could be biding his time while readying his forces to take control of the ship.

Over my dead body. Kat's lips quirked. That was *exactly* what Jenkins would have in mind if he'd realized she'd turned against the king. *Let's see who strikes first.*

She checked her sidearm automatically, wishing she'd spent more time on the range. She'd enjoyed shooting, once upon a time. But she'd never taken it seriously . . . not as seriously as she *should* have. She unbuttoned the holster, cutting down the time it would take to draw the weapon. She was pretty sure she couldn't outdraw the commissioner's men, if they turned on her, but it was better than nothing. Smiling, she stepped through the hatch and walked into the CIC. The space was nearly empty. The only officers on duty were ones who knew what had happened . . . and what she had in mind.

And if any of them were going to betray me, they missed the ship.

She took her chair and glanced at Kitty. "Did the communications embargo hold?"

"I believe so, Admiral." Kitty looked pale. "The messages weren't automatically dumped into the communications network."

Kat nodded. There'd been a backlog of messages from the last few days, ranging from automatic updates that were now hopelessly out of date to personal messages that probably, almost certainly, contained concealed messages to colonial and aristocratic crewmen. The king himself had sent her a dozen messages, messages she hadn't had time to view. She keyed her console. The king's final message was the only one that mattered. He might suspect something, given that her fleet had dropped out of contact for a few days, but Hadrian had no choice. He needed her if he wanted to defend his pocket state.

"All hands, this is the Admiral," she said. "Lockdown drill is in effect. I say again, lockdown drill is in effect."

A dull drumbeat echoed through the giant starship as the crew hurried to their lockdown posts. Kat watched progress on the display, feeling a hint of pride combined with the grim sense it no longer mattered. She'd drilled her crews extensively over the last few days, working hard to ensure that the right people were in the right place at the right time. Jenkins had been monitoring the drills, she was sure, but how could he spot the dangerous moments amid the flurry of movements?

An experienced officer wouldn't have worked out she was planning a coup of her own, unless he was paranoid as hell. And Kat was sure she'd be dead by now or fighting for her life if Jenkins suspected something.

Kitty looked up. "Admiral, the commissioners have taken up position in the shuttlebay," she said. "They're requesting permission to power up two assault shuttles for deployment."

"Tell them to hold position and wait until the ship itself has gone into lockdown," Kat ordered. The remnants of her crew were rushing now, trying to get to their places before the hatches started slamming closed. They'd be too badly scattered and isolated to mount a counter-coup. She hoped. "We might need them."

She looked at the display, feeling numb. So far, only a handful of her officers knew about her plans. The timing had been terrible. The ones in the know could secure their ships and should be doing it now if everything had gone according to plan, but the others would have to be kept in the dark, at least until she could be assured of their loyalties. She kicked herself mentally for allowing her original squadrons to be broken up, ships and crew scattered across the remainder of the fleet. In hindsight, Hadrian had been trying to prevent a second round of mutinies. And he might well have succeeded.

Not well enough, she thought as hatches started to seal themselves. *And he won't live long enough to correct his mistake.*

Kitty cleared her throat. "Admiral, the lockdown is in effect," she said. "All crew are accounted for."

"Good." Kat let out a breath. "Pass control of the shuttlebay to my console."

"Aye, Admiral."

Kat nodded as her console bleeped, bringing up the shuttlebay control systems. The shuttlebay could be isolated from the remainder of the ship, if the people on duty knew they needed to pull out the communications blocks before it was too late, but Jenkins hadn't bothered. Her lips curved into a predatory smile. He hadn't known he *needed* to bother, damn him. His men milled around the shuttles in shipsuits, not spacesuits. That was careless of him. They'd have masks, she was sure, but the vacuum would get them well before they could find an emergency chamber or airlock. The shuttlebay was supposed to be safe, but she had the codes to make it very unsafe indeed.

She scanned the live feed from the shuttlebay, counting heads until she was *sure* all sixteen of the commissioners were inside. Kitty had told her that everyone was where they were supposed to be, but Kat hadn't been particularly reassured. There *were* ways to spoof the sensors, if one had time to make preparations. The king's men knew how to do it too, which was how so many of his clients had been able to take control of their ships and fly them to Caledonia. She wondered, sourly, just how many of them had come to regret their choice. There were limits to loyalty. They wouldn't all go along with effective genocide.

"Contact Winters," Kat ordered. "Tell him to move now."

She inputted her codes into the datacore, isolating the shuttlebay and commanding the hatch to open. The commissioners looked astonished, then relieved as they realized the forcefield was still in place. There was no real danger, not yet. A handful started to make their way to the shuttles, as if they expected to be able to use them. Kat locked down the shuttles, just in case, then deactivated the forcefield. The atmosphere vented with terrifying speed. Figures were yanked off the deck and pulled into vacuum before they had a chance to magnetize their boots. She wondered, as she counted wriggling shapes falling into the darkness, if Jenkins had realized what was happening. If he'd had a chance to grab a mask . . .

"Shuttlebay vented, Admiral," Kitty said. "One commissioner is holding on to a shuttle. The others are gone."

Kat nodded, feeling a twinge of guilt. The poor bastards didn't have any protective gear. They would suffocate or freeze well before they could be rescued. No one even knew they were in trouble. The other ships might notice something, but venting the shuttlebay *was* a well-established emergency drill. They might not spot the tiny figures until it was far too late.

"The shuttlebay is to remain sealed," she ordered. "In thirty minutes, the bay can be repressurized and the body removed."

"Aye, Admiral," Kitty said.

Kat turned and studied the display. Thirty minutes was excessive. She'd never had any reason to think the commissioners had enhancements that would allow them to survive in a vacuum for more than a few minutes. Their entire bodies would need to be rewritten if they wanted to *thrive* in a vacuum. And yet, she was feeling paranoid. The king had had access to the very cutting edge of personal enhancement. He could have enhanced his guardsmen beyond all reason, if he'd wished. No one would have asked awkward questions.

"Keep the fleet in lockdown," she commanded. "Add a second priority access user to the StarCom, then forward the details to me."

"Aye, Admiral," Kitty said.

"Then inform the fleet that we'll be breaking orbit in twenty minutes," Kat added. "The lockdown will remain in place until we're on the way."

She sucked in her breath. She'd have to tell the crews *something*, if only to keep their imaginations from filling in the blanks. Lockdowns rarely lasted long, unless it was a genuine emergency. But . . . the sheer lack of information would grate on the isolated crewers, pushing them to eventually do something stupid. She forced herself to consider the issue, knowing she didn't dare tell them the truth. Both sides would rise up against her if they knew what was really going on.

A shame we can't sedate everyone, Kat thought. It would take five days to reach Willow, and that was if they redlined the drives. *But that would put their lives at risk.*

She stood. "I'll be in my cabin," she said. "Inform me when the fleet is ready to depart."

"Aye, Admiral."

Kat heard the doubt in Kitty's tone, but she ignored it as she stepped back into her cabin and closed the hatch. The terminal was bleeping, alerting her to an urgent message. Kat sat down and checked the list. Scott was trying to contact her, using priority codes he shouldn't know existed. William must have given them to his brother. Kat pressed her palm against the scanner. William would be in deep shit if someone decided to make an issue of it. He might wind up sharing her prison cell.

The thought sobered her. She was doomed. Whatever happened, her career was over. And . . . there was no way she could be sent quietly into exile. She'd betrayed more than just the family. The entire planet would want her dead. She touched her sidearm, wondering if suicide would be better than facing the hangman. But . . . it would be too much like giving up.

Scott's face appeared in front of her. "Kat," he said. "Have you heard the news?"

"From Caledonia?" Kat pushed as much conviction into her voice as she could. "I have."

She pressed on before he could say a word. "The king wants me to meet him at Willow. I intend to do so, and kill him. Inform William that he is to meet me there and"—her lips curved into a humorless smile—"you might want to be a little more diplomatic."

"Of course, Your Highness," Scott said dryly. "It will be my pleasure, Your Supreme Eminence."

"And hopefully we can put an end to it," Kat said. "I'm giving you priority access rights to the StarCom"—she keyed her console, forwarding the codes to Scott—"so you can get the message to him quickly. Wait until we're gone to send it."

"Hyperspace near Caledonia is fucked," Scott warned. "I don't know how long it will be before William can set sail."

Kat grimaced. "Tell him to set course as soon as possible," she said. She should have seen it coming. The king had plenty of incentive to trigger hyperspace storms to cover his retreat, even though they were dangerously unpredictable. William's fleet might be able to leave in an hour . . . or might be becalmed for weeks, if not months. "If not . . . I'll do whatever I can do."

Scott tossed her a jaunty salute. "Good luck, Your Vengefulness."

"I'm also forwarding a pair of messages," Kat said, ignoring his mockery. She'd taken the time to record them after overcoming her guilt for sending messages when her crew couldn't do the same. "I'd appreciate it if you delivered them to their destination. You'll be paid on delivery."

"Good thing I'm already being paid through the nose," Scott grumbled as she sent the messages. "Your brother had better keep his word."

"I'm sure he will," Kat said. Peter might be unimaginative, but he wasn't stupid. A reputation for breaking his word, even to a smuggler and mercenary, would follow him for the rest of his life. No one would ever trust him again and rightly so. The family would eventually dismiss him from his post, after his reputation started to ruin them. "And you have a perfect opportunity to go straight."

"We'll see," Scott said. He winked at her. "You never know, do you?"

His image vanished from the display. Kat let out a breath, then stood. There was too much to be done before the fleet could link up with the king. And . . . she had to think past his death, damn it. She owed it to her people. The ones who had followed her hadn't known what they were doing. They'd thought they were fighting for the right side.

And if that means paying the price for leading them into treason, she told herself, *you can damn well pay the price for them.*

CHAPTER THIRTY-SIX

In Transit

HMS *Implacable* was not a happy ship.

Francis was no military expert, as he'd reminded the king more than once, but he could feel the grimness pervading the hull. The crew might be loyalists, yet they hadn't signed up to be exiles. Admiral Ruben had made all sorts of promises and posted guards all over the ship, but he hadn't been able to stop the rumors. Quist had been destroyed. Caledonia had been destroyed. Tyre itself had been blown to atoms by a previously unknown planet-cracking weapon. And no one, no matter what they said or did, had been able to disprove them.

It didn't help, Francis reflected as he lay on his bunk, that the ship was crammed with exiles. The king's closest allies had fled Caledonia, bringing their families and friends with them, displacing the ship's senior officers from their cabins. Dozens of officers were bunking with the crew, something that wouldn't do wonders for morale either. Resentments were threatening to tear the crew apart, particularly when half of the exiles seemed convinced they could get good terms if they turned the ship around and surrendered to Admiral McElney. Francis wasn't convinced of that. There was nothing left for any of the exiles on Tyre.

And we're isolated from the outside universe. That doesn't help either.

He sighed, inwardly. The fleet had made a brief stop at Sycamore, long enough for the king to send orders to his remaining followers and Francis to send a message to his superiors, then slipped back into hyperspace. The crew and passengers had no way of knowing what was going on back home, neither on Tyre nor Caledonia. The handful of updates they *had* downloaded hadn't been particularly reassuring. Caledonia was occupied, the Colonial Alliance effectively defunct and the House of Lords pretty much the victor by default. The king's fleet had shrunk to forty warships, not counting Admiral Falcone and her fleet. He no longer had any reasonable hope of winning the war.

But that doesn't stop him talking about his plans to return home. There were times when he wondered if the king knew his fleet was heading *away* from Tyre. He made it sound as though they'd drop out of hyperspace and find themselves at Tyre . . . Francis had been so alarmed, the first time he'd heard the rant, that he'd checked the ship's navigational data. They were quite definitely heading towards Willow. *And he's not thinking about the future.*

He scowled. He'd had a lot of time, over the last few days, to consider everything that had happened. His staffers were probably dead. Admiral Jacanas and his officers would have put everyone in the bunker, once the shooting started, but they hadn't reckoned on mass planetary bombardment. The bunker hadn't been designed to stand up to an assault powerful enough to wreck the entire city. And even if they had survived, somehow, they'd be trapped, waiting helplessly for the power to run out. Francis tried not to think about his people starving or suffocating underground, but the thought had a habit of haunting him when he didn't manage to distract himself. Guilt gnawed at him as he remembered the last time he'd seen Jacanas. He could have told the admiral to evacuate the embassy long before the bombs started falling.

And your career is doomed, unless you convince the king to work with you. He thought he heard Admiral Jacanas laughing at him. Or maybe it was one of his old rivals, one of the men he'd climbed over to get the posting to Caledonia. *The government will need a scapegoat, and you're elected.*

He forced himself to think, hard. No point in simply giving up. He wouldn't be *allowed* to withdraw from public life. And the king wouldn't give up. The situation had to be managed, unless some kindly soul put a bullet in Hadrian's brain. Francis had no choice. He *had* to manage the situation, somehow. It was his only hope of salvaging something from the utter disaster his career had become. And who knew? If it was successful, he might still reach the very top.

There was a tap on the hatch. Francis sat upright and keyed the bedside terminal, unlocking the portal. No point in trying to claim diplomatic immunity, not now. The cabin was hardly an embassy. Besides, his government might have already revoked his credentials. Thankfully, the king would be as ignorant as Francis himself. It might just give Francis a chance to steer him in the right direction.

The hatch hissed open, revealing Sir Reginald. The king's fixer was sporting a nasty-looking black eye. Francis raised his eyebrows, wondering who'd dared lay hands on the bastard. He understood the impulse to beat the toadying scumbag into a pulp, but the king would punish anyone who dared. Sir Reginald was loyal because he had nowhere else to go. But now . . .

"Mr. Ambassador," Sir Reginald said. "The king would be pleased to see you in his cabin."

"Of course." Francis stood, brushing his borrowed tunic into some semblance of respectability. His suit and tie had been ruined during the escape. "I'd be delighted."

And that is a lie, he told himself as he followed the king's fixer out the hatch. *I don't want to see him at all.*

He grimaced as they made their way down the corridors. They were lined with makeshift beds, piles of mattresses and blankets hastily assembled to give junior crew and exiles places to rest their heads. Francis could *feel* eyes boring into his back as he walked, resentful crewmen silently hating him for taking one of the precious cabins for himself. He'd been lucky to get a compartment large enough to swing a cat in. Others hadn't been so lucky. The king's ragged fleet was in no state to stop and reorganize. Some ships were crammed to the gunwales with unwanted passengers, while others had empty berths. A shame that most of the exiles were civilians. They couldn't be put to work to save the day.

If anyone can. Five guards stood on duty outside Officer Country, two more than he'd seen yesterday. They patted him down thoroughly before calling the duty officer to open the hatch, allowing him access. *The king cannot continue the war without help.*

Sir Reginald led him into the king's cabin. The air smelled . . . *funny*, as if the life-support system wasn't fully working. He felt as if he were walking into the lair of a dangerous and desperate animal. The king himself sat on the sofa, his wife clinging to his arm as if she feared he'd vanish if she let go. Francis felt his eyes narrow briefly, wondering just what the relationship between the king and his wife actually *was*. The House of Lords detested her, for no reason he could see. Drusilla could hardly be blamed for her unfortunate relatives.

"Your Majesty," he said. He had no idea if the king could be addressed as a monarch any longer, but there was nothing to be gained by denying him the title. The king was surrounded by allies and servants. If he wanted something to happen to Francis, something would happen. Marseilles would never know they needed to punish the insult. "Thank you for summoning me."

The king poured himself a glass from an unmarked bottle. "Shipboard rotgut," he said as he took a swig. "Do you want some?"

"No, thank you." Francis had attended enough tedious formal balls to have a high tolerance for alcohol, but he'd never liked getting drunk. All too easy for one to get tipsy and make a complete fool of oneself. Or say something one really shouldn't. "I've heard vile things about ship-brewed alcohol."

"This one probably breaks a few laws on chemical weapons," the king said. A joke, Francis thought, but it was hard to be sure. "One sip will do horrible things to your gut."

"Charming," Francis said. The morbid side of him wondered just how many problems would be solved, how many lives saved, if the king accidentally killed himself. "Might I suggest, Your Majesty, that we concentrate on affairs of state?"

"I'll be returning to Tyre," the king said. He took another sip. "And that's the end of the matter. Once Admiral Falcone joins me . . ."

"You still won't have enough ships to retake Tyre," Francis pointed out. It wasn't what the king wanted to hear, but what he *needed* to hear. "You must think about the future."

He pressed his eyes, noting the flash of comprehension in Drusilla's eyes. "You cannot win a straight fight, not now. And you cannot hope to lure their fleet out of place. They can just sit tight and wait for your fleet to decay into uselessness."

"And so we have to fight!" The king glared at him. "It was your idea to fly to Willow!"

"Yes, it was." Francis met his eyes evenly, wondering if he dared suggest the king take a sober-up pill. When he was thinking clearly, the king could plot and plan with the best of them. When he was drunk . . . he came up with ideas like throwing forty-odd starships into a meatgrinder. He might as well have hurled *eggs* at the enemy fleet. "And it is your only hope for survival."

"Really," the king said. He lifted his glass, eying the translucent liquid. "What do you have in mind?"

Francis sighed inwardly. The king already knew much of what Francis had in mind. Had he forgotten? Or convinced himself it wasn't important? Or . . . was he just enjoying making Francis dance to his tune? A man who'd lost power might try to assert it again, even if he *couldn't*. Not really. Francis realized that it might have been the *king* who'd struck Sir Reginald. He might have grown sick of the toady's toadying. Francis could hardly blame him for *that*, even though it weakened his position. A man who thought he had nothing to lose had nothing to keep him from turning on his former master.

"When we reach Willow," he said, "you declare independence. The border stars will be yours. Marseilles will, of course, recognize you at once. My government will send ships to defend your kingdom. The House of Lords will hesitate to invade when it might trigger a *third* interstellar war."

The king let out an unfamiliar, chilling sound. "And if your people refuse?"

"Your Majesty, we need those stars detached from the Commonwealth," Francis said evenly. "We do not mind who holds them, as long as the Commonwealth *doesn't*. And it will give us political cover for resupplying your ships and, eventually, giving you a chance to return to Tyre as its ruler. It's your only hope."

And that's true as far as it goes, he added silently. The king would have his statelet, but he probably wouldn't be allowed to continue the war. Marseilles wanted time to develop the border stars and open up hyper-routes to the Rim, not get entangled in an endless proxy war with Tyre . . . or, for that matter, a full-scale interstellar war. *But you'll be alive and well and safe. Who knows? Maybe you'll be invited back to Tyre.*

"You seek to take advantage of me," the king said. "Don't you?"

"Yes, Your Majesty." Francis wouldn't have been so blunt, normally, but his instincts told him to be honest. "We do want advantages, yes. I won't try to deny it. But there are advantages to you too. You'd be safe. You'd be in a position to rebuild your fleet and, when you're ready, resume the war."

"A few years of the House of Lords in complete control and they'll be begging me to come back," the king said. "Wouldn't *that* be funny?"

"Yes, Your Majesty," Francis said, playing along. He highly doubted it would happen considering the severity of Hadrian's crimes, but . . . who knew? The Commonwealth really hadn't been very good at dealing with the consequences of the *last* victory. Another couple of victories like that and it really *would* be ruined. "But you have to be a person of consequence if you want to retake your throne. You have to conserve your power until you can make a decisive move."

He waited, resisting the urge to glance at Drusilla. He had a feeling she was going to work on the king in private, to convince him to see sense and accept Francis's plan. The king would listen too, as long as it didn't make him look weak. He was no stranger to manipulation techniques. He was starting to think that Drusilla was just as good as he was, if not better. She had access to the king he couldn't hope to match. His stomach churned. He was bisexual and had to admit the king was handsome, but he was highly undone by what he saw behind that man's eyes. The king would do *anything* in pursuit of power.

And as long as he does what I want him to do, it doesn't matter. Carving a little statelet out for the king is my only hope of survival.

"I'll consider it," the king said finally. "I'll let you know when we reach Willow."

"I'll have to send a message as soon as we arrive," Francis warned. "We must have fleet elements in place to protect you, Your Majesty."

Drusilla suddenly spoke. "Why don't we go deeper into your space?"

Francis blinked, surprised by the question. He'd never heard Drusilla speak out of turn before. He reminded himself, sharply, that she wasn't stupid. A woman who could escape from the heart of the Theocracy, a state that regarded women as chattel, was hardly *stupid*. The odds were she was a lot more ruthless than her husband. She'd known what could, what *would* have happened to her if she'd slipped just once.

"We could," he agreed. "But my government would have to intern your ships the moment they arrived. We couldn't turn a blind eye to your presence, nor could we provide overt support. There would certainly be no hope of acknowledging His Majesty as a person of consequence. We wouldn't hand him over to the House of Lords"—*probably,* he added silently—"but we couldn't support him either. It would be the end."

"And that could not be borne," the king said. He nodded to the hatch. "We'll speak soon, Ambassador."

"Yes, Your Majesty." Francis stood. "That we will."

◆ ◆ ◆

William was not given to brooding. He'd spent most of his life on worlds and starships where there was *always* something to do, even if it was just basic maintenance. Even when he'd reached flag rank, there had been work to do. The shortage of staff officers—*trustworthy* staff officers—had made sure of it. And yet, now . . . he brooded. He knew he might well be on the verge of making a terrible mistake.

"Scott was telling the truth," he said to himself. "But he might have been lied to."

He shook his head. Kat wouldn't stay with the king, not now that she knew the truth. And yet, if she failed to take control of her fleet, or take out the king, all hell was going to break loose again. He couldn't disagree with her assessment of the situation. The king was going to link up with Marseilles and defy the House of Lords to do something about it. William knew, all too well, that he might just pull it off. The House of Lords didn't want another war. They'd be happy if Marseilles simply interned the king and his fleet.

But the king won't want that. He'll want to take control of the border stars for himself.

The intercom bleeped. "Admiral, we're redlining the drives. Again." Yagami sounded badly worried. "*Monster* is signaling that she might have to drop out of formation. Do you want to slow the fleet . . . ?"

"No." William shook his head, although he knew Yagami couldn't see him. "My orders stand. The fleet is to redline its drives all the way to Willow."

And hope we get there in time, he thought grimly. He'd run the simulations, but they hadn't given him any decent answers. It depended on what assumptions he made about the king's intentions. And . . . there were just too many variables. He had no idea where Marseilles had placed its fleet, or what orders its commanders had if they found themselves on a collision course with Tyre. *We have a window of opportunity, but it's closing fast.*

"Sir." Yagami hesitated. "Four more ships are having drive problems too."

"I am aware of the dangers," William said. The bean counters would bitch and moan about repair costs, even if he'd won the war. "But if we don't get to Willow quickly, everything we've done will be for nothing."

"Yes, sir," Yagami said.

William nodded as the connection closed. He understood the younger man's doubts, but there was no choice. They had to get to Willow before it was too late or the war would continue, perhaps dragging in other interstellar powers. And who knew where it would end?

The Theocratic War was bad, he thought. Humanity's first major interstellar war had been nasty but confined to a relatively small section of the galaxy. *This will be worse.*

CHAPTER THIRTY-SEVEN

WILLOW

Kat let out a breath she hadn't realized she'd been holding as the fleet opened vortexes and plunged back into realspace, sensors scanning for potential threats. The Willow System had never been particularly important—the planet hadn't received much in the way of developmental aid, either from the king or the big corporations—but it *was* right on the border with Marseilles. She frowned as her sensors picked out the king's fleet, holding position near the planet. No Marseillan ships kept formation with them, as far as her sensors could tell. *That* was a relief. The presence of foreign ships would have made matters a great deal harder.

She glanced at Kitty. "Send the message," she ordered. "And keep the fleet in lockdown."

"Aye, Admiral," Kitty said.

Kat braced herself. Five days of lockdown hadn't done wonders for anyone, although she'd been able to open a few compartments and recruit crewmen who had reason to suspect the king would turn on them as soon as possible. She'd been lucky to avoid another mutiny, and she knew it. Thankfully, the king would understand her reluctance to unbutton her ships. Who knew *who* could be trusted, these days? The

StarCom orbiting Willow was a mocking reminder that Hadrian's cause was dead in space. He didn't have a hope of regaining control.

Kitty looked up. "Admiral, he's agreed to meet you in person," she said. "He's inviting you to *Implacable*."

Pity he didn't want to come here, Kat thought. She'd issued the invitation more in hope than any real expectation the king would take her up on it. *It would have been so much easier if we'd been able to grab him the moment he stepped aboard.*

"Tell him I'll be over as soon as possible," she ordered. "And inform General Winters that we're about to begin."

She touched the sidearm in her holster, feeling cold. She'd made sure to spend some of the last few days in the shooting range, running through a handful of simulations. She was better than she'd thought, but . . . if she got into a shootout with the king's guards, she'd lose. There was a good chance they'd take her weapon before letting her into his presence . . . She'd tried to think of a way to carry a concealed firearm, but nothing had come to mind. The guards would *definitely* scan her, even if they didn't search her physically.

And then they'd start wondering why I was trying to hide a weapon, she thought as she stood and braced herself. *And then all hell would break loose.*

She studied the console for a long moment, silently counting the handful of ships that had remained loyal to the king, then keyed her terminal. "Captain Procaccini, you have your orders?"

"Aye, Admiral," Procaccini said. "If we don't hear from you in two hours, or if they bring up their shields and weapons, we're to open fire at once."

"Good." Kat let out a breath. "Either way, this ends today."

She strode down the corridor to the nearest exit. The shuttle was already waiting for her, the drives powering up. She'd made sure to choose her personal ship, hoping and praying that it would be cleared to dock at the airlock closest to Officer Country. If it wasn't . . . she had contingency plans, but none of them were particularly reliable. The king's guards could ruin her plan simply by insisting she land in the shuttlebay, where the shuttle could be inspected with the naked eye. It would be hard to hide the marines clinging to the hull if they flew into the battlecruiser.

We've used the trick before, she reminded herself. *Will they watch for it now?*

She took her seat as the shuttle undocked and glided into open space. Kat felt her heart starting to pound as she inspected the king's fleet, although she knew it was no longer strong enough to pose a serious threat. Four superdreadnoughts, two heavily damaged; eighteen battlecruisers, powerful enough to cause trouble, but not strong enough to do more than annoy their victims; and, beyond them, twenty smaller ships. They could become an impressive pirate fleet, she supposed, but little more. The superdreadnoughts would rapidly start to degrade if they were denied access to shipyards. The king would be wise, if he wanted to go into piracy, to abandon the capital ships. There was no way he could keep them alive.

But he thinks my ships are loyal. He may think he still has a chance.

"We're receiving orders to dock at the officer's hatch," the pilot said. "Should I proceed?"

"Of course," Kat said. "No point in delay."

She wondered why the king hadn't moved to one of the superdreadnoughts. Well, it wasn't her problem. She wasn't about to look a gift horse in the mouth. That would just make life easier for Winters and his marines when they started to sneak into the ship and take control. A superdreadnought would be a far tougher target.

And their crews might be on the wrong side, Kat reminded herself. A dull thud, followed by a hiss, echoed through the shuttle as it docked with the battlecruiser. *Who knows what rumors have been flying through the fleet?*

She stepped through the hatch, her nostrils tightening as she caught a whiff of too many humans in too close proximity. She'd been on pirate ships that smelled like toilets, literally, but she'd never boarded a *naval* starship that reeked so bad. Even *Uncanny* had been in better shape. But . . . Her heart fell as she saw the makeshift sleeping arrangements, feeling a twinge of pity for the exiles. They had to think themselves in hell. They'd probably never liked the idea of sharing their bedrooms, let alone being crammed in corridors and holds and . . .

"Admiral." Sir Reginald looked as if he'd lost an argument with a door. "His Majesty is delighted to see you."

"I'm sure he is," Kat said, concealing her concern. Sir Reginald sounded like a man who'd simply given up. "Take me to him?"

He nodded and half stumbled down the corridor. Kat followed, trying to keep her face under tight control. She was no stranger to horror—she still had nightmares about the exodus from Hebrides and the refugee camps on Ahura Mazda—but the sight in front of her gnawed at her thoughts. She knew it could be worse, yet . . . some of the people lying listlessly on mattresses were her *peers*. They shouldn't be running like common . . .

She shook her head. She was being stupid. And selfish. They'd believed the king's lies, and it had cost them everything. She'd believed them too, but at least she knew the truth. They didn't. A hot surge of anger nearly overcame her. They were lying on their backs, doing nothing while she tried to set things right and . . .

"You'll need to surrender your weapon." A set of guards stood in front of the hatch, their expressions blank. "It will be returned to you . . ."

"I am a privy councilor and a knight of Tyre," Kat said, drawing herself up to her full height. She drew on all her lessons for speaking to subordinates as she met their eyes. "By command of His Majesty himself, I *cannot* be disarmed."

The guards hesitated, clearly unsure how to proceed. Beside her, Sir Reginald twitched uncomfortably. The correct thing to do was to contact the king, to ask if she *could* be disarmed, but . . . she had a feeling none of the guards wanted to risk disturbing their monarch. They could try to disarm her anyway, yet they'd expect her to file complaints with His Majesty. As long as he hadn't specifically ordered them to do anything, they had some wiggle room.

"Keep it, until His Majesty says otherwise," the guard said finally.

Kat barely managed to keep the sneer off her face as they patted her down, then opened the hatch. She was carrying a loaded weapon, for crying out loud! Their touch was professional, yet . . . they hadn't disarmed her. Sir Reginald led her into Officer Country, then down to the admiral's cabin. Admiral Ruben was probably on the bridge, issuing orders that wouldn't make any difference at all. The fleet had come to the end of the line.

The hatch opened, revealing the king. Kat felt a surge of blind hatred she had to fight hard to keep off her face. He was as handsome as ever, yet his face was twisted into something dark and shadowy. She wondered how he'd been able to hide the monster inside for so long. There was no sign of anyone else, not even Princess Drusilla. Kat remembered Sir Reginald's dead-eyed look and shivered. The king might be the only one who still believed he could win the war.

"Kat." The king sounded tired but happy. Pleased to see her. "I'm glad you made it out."

Kat nodded as she surveyed the compartment, making sure they were alone. Drusilla might be in the next compartment, the bedchamber . . . She kept a wary eye on the hatch as she took the seat in front of the king. Time wasn't quite up. The marines would get to their targets or . . . or the alarm would sound, and she'd have to do what she could to retrieve the situation. It wouldn't be easy. There was a very good chance that Captain Procaccini would blow the battlecruiser to hell along with everyone on it. Kat told herself to be calm. She owed it to her conscience to take some risks.

"We've made contact with Marseilles," the king said. "We'll be setting up a kingdom out here, a springboard to take back Tyre itself. Their fleet is already on the way."

They must have positioned the fleet close to the border, Kat thought. *Readying themselves to take possession of the border worlds.*

"Good," she said, trying to keep the horror out of her voice. How long did she have? She didn't know. A little voice in her head was screaming at her, telling her to move . . . to move now and to hell with the marines. "How long until their fleet arrives?"

"Not long." The king smiled brightly. "The enemy won't find us until it's too late."

William is on his way, Kat reminded herself. *He already knows where to find you.*

She stood and started to pace the room, silently counting down the last few seconds. "Do you think you can win?"

"Of course," the king said. "I always come out ahead."

Kat's wristcom bleeped, once. It was time.

"Tell me something," she said, allowing some of her anger to bleed into her voice. "Why did you kill my father?"

The king blinked. "What?"

Kat drew her sidearm. "My father," she said. "Why did you kill him?"

"Put the gun down." The king's voice rose, alarmingly. A dull quiver ran through the starship. "Kat . . ."

Alarms started to howl. Kat glanced at the display, just for a second. It nearly killed her. The king threw himself at her, slamming into her body and knocking her to the deck. The pistol flew through the air, crashing into the bulkhead and landing on top of the desk. Kat grunted as he drew back his fist, twisting just in time to keep him from punching her in the throat. His affable mask was gone. His face was consumed with madness as he drew back for another punch.

Kat gritted her teeth, then headbutted him as hard as she could. The king's body had all sorts of genetic enhancements, but there were limits. Blood trickled from his nose, splashing onto her face. He wasn't used to pain. She yanked herself forward, out from under him, and brought her knee up as hard as she could. The king screamed in agony, his entire body spasming violently enough to throw him off her. Kat rolled over, grabbed a datapad that had fallen on the deck, and brought it down on his head as hard as she could. His body shook violently, then lay still. Kat hit him again, just to be sure. The files insisted the king didn't have any real training, but she didn't really take it on faith.

She stumbled to her feet and grabbed the pistol as the hatch opened, bringing it about to bear on Sir Reginald. "Keep your hands where I can see them," she snapped. She wanted, needed, to pull the trigger. "What happened?"

Sir Reginald stared at her in shock. Kat waved him aside, then closed and sealed the hatch. It would take time for the king's supporters to burn it down, time they didn't have. The battlecruiser's crew had too many other problems. She glanced at the display and swore openly. A fleet had arrived. She couldn't tell *which* fleet.

"You." She jabbed the gun at Sir Reginald, who cringed back. An unpleasant odor filled the air. "Who's arrived?"

"The House of Lords," Sir Reginald said. "They've found us!"

Kat's wristcom bleeped. "Admiral," Winters said. "We've taken control of the bridge."

"And I've got the king," Kat said. "Order the fleet to surrender. It's over."

She ignored Sir Reginald's splutters as she turned to look at the king. Alive? Dead? She honestly wasn't sure until she saw his chest move, just slightly. Rage boiled up within her, demanding that she kill him on the spot. He'd led her into betraying the navy, her family, and her father . . . She wanted him dead.

And yet, she knew she needed him alive. *Someone* had to take the blame for the civil war. Someone had to pay.

"Sit down," she ordered quietly. "You'll be dealt with soon enough."

Sir Reginald found his nerve. "So will you," he said. "Do you think they'll let a traitor like you just walk away?"

"Probably not," Kat said. "But at least I did what I could to fix things."

"Or maybe not," Sir Reginald said as new icons appeared on the display. "I think the king's reinforcements have arrived."

◆ ◆ ◆

"Admiral!" Yagami looked up, sharply. "Long-range sensors are detecting unknown ships on attack vector!"

William cursed, inwardly. He'd lost four ships during the headlong rush to Willow, four ships that had dropped out of formation and had been left behind to lick their wounds and wait for rescue. Four ships he'd miss desperately if yet another interstellar war was about to begin. He studied the display, silently assessing the unknown fleet. Marseillans. They had to be Marseillans. Who else could they be?

"Tactical analysis suggests four squadrons of superdreadnoughts, plus supporting elements," Yagami said. "They're charging weapons."

"Hail them," William ordered.

He forced himself to think. He had three squadrons of superdreadnoughts . . . five, if Kat's ships were in any state to fight. He doubted it. Her message had warned that she'd put her entire fleet into lockdown, ensuring that no one could rise up against her. William had the nasty feeling that her crews were too confused to fight anyone. He frowned as his marines continued to take possession of the king's ships. In theory, he had the numbers. In practice . . .

"They're responding," Yagami said.

"Put them through," William said. "This is Admiral Sir William McElney, Royal Tyre Navy."

A face appeared in front of him. "This is Admiral Joan Vendee, governor-general of Willow," she said. "You are ordered to withdraw from our space at once."

William deliberately took a breath, taking a moment to compose his arguments. "Admiral. King Hadrian is under arrest. His fleet has been secured. His government no longer exists. He no longer has the power to hand the border stars over to you, if indeed he ever did. And we, not you, are in possession of the stars. You're intruding on our territory."

There was a long, chilling pause. William kept his face blank, silently calculating the odds. Four squadrons against three was hardly an even fight. Kat's superdreadnoughts *might* make up the difference or they might not. Cold prudence told him to withdraw. But he knew he couldn't, not without conceding the border stars. If they'd been asked, if they'd chosen to transfer themselves to Marseilles, it would have been different. But they hadn't. They'd been sold for a handful of missiles and God alone knew what else.

"We paid for the systems," Admiral Vendee said.

"They weren't his to sell," William said. He pushed as much conviction into his voice as possible. "Admiral, I understand your position. I also understand that you entered our space accidentally, under the impression that you were doing the right thing. And if you choose to leave now, we'll say no more about it. We won't even register a formal protest.

"But if you choose to press the issue, we will have no choice but to fight. We won't abandon these systems to their fate. We don't want a war, Admiral, but if you do it will begin here."

Another pause. It grew longer and longer. William waited, silently praying the enemy admiral would see sense. And then Admiral Vendee's face vanished.

"Admiral, the enemy fleet is reversing course," Yagami said. "They're retreating."

"Good." William felt a flicker of sympathy for the enemy commander. If she'd arrived a few hours earlier, William would have had a much harder time driving her out. Hell, *he* might have been the one who started the war. "Have the king's ships been secured?"

"Yes, Admiral," Yagami said. "The king himself, and Admiral Falcone, are on their way here."

"Then power up the StarCom and contact the Admiralty," William ordered. "And tell them, when the connection is established, that the war is over."

"Aye, sir," Yagami said. "We won!"

William smiled. "Yeah," he said. He felt . . . relief. And fear, for the future. "We won."

CHAPTER THIRTY-EIGHT

TYRE

Peter took his place among the remainder of the dukes and watched as the king, the *former* king, was marched into the chamber. He looked surprisingly well for someone who'd spent two weeks in a starship brig and a further week in a reasonably luxurious cell on Tyre, but there was something shadowy and unpleasant in his gaze. He wasn't trying to hide what he was any longer, Peter decided. The monster behind the king's smile was finally in the open. And yet . . .

We stand in judgment, he thought. *And none of us have any doubt about the sentence.*

The king was going to die. Everyone knew it. His death was the price for ending the war on reasonably civilized terms, for extending amnesty to just about everyone who'd followed him into hell. Not everyone was safe—Admiral Ruben faced an array of charges for crimes against humanity—but the vast majority of his followers would have a chance to rebuild their lives. Peter had argued that they should simply order the king shot, without bothering with a kangaroo court. The remainder of the dukes had overruled him.

We want to prove we put him to death justly, Duchess Zangaria had stated. *Or, once he's dead, people will try to defend him.*

The king was half pushed into the center of the chamber. There was no chair, not for him. The chamber was designed to cloak the judges in shadow, to give an impersonal sense to the whole affair . . . Peter doubted it would work. Not really. The king knew who'd be judging him. He stood in the center, his hands clasped behind his back. He looked . . . unafraid. Peter wondered, despite himself, if the king had one final trick up his sleeve. Even now, after the end of the war, after an extensive security procedure that bordered on naked paranoia, it was impossible to be sure. There were dukes and politicians who agreed with Peter, who wanted to execute the king immediately, without bothering with a trial. They feared what he might do.

Israel Harrison spoke into the silence. "Hadrian. You are called before us to answer charges of treason, crimes against humanity, and various lesser offenses. How do you plead?"

Peter waited, wondering what the king would say. He'd refused the offer of legal representation, refused suggestions that might have given him a better chance of surviving the next few weeks. It was hard to tell, really, if the king had given up or if he was waiting for one final throw of the dice. The psychologists swore blind the king was unlikely to give up, not completely. He wasn't the sort of person who could surrender to the inevitable. Peter supposed it was one thing he'd inherited from his father and grandfather. Their lives would have been very different if they'd given up at the first hurdle too.

The king smiled, as if there was one final card left to play. "I do not recognize this court's legitimacy."

Harrison looked irked. "You have been formally impeached," he said, "and stripped of your rank, titles, and family name. This court has every right to try you."

"For an impeachment to be legal, I must be impeached in person," the king said calmly. "And I was not."

"You were offered a chance to mount a defense," Harrison pointed out. "And you refused."

"The point is moot," Duke Rudbek growled. "Whatever the legalities of the situation, we have the ability and *will* to put you on trial. You will not be allowed to delay matters with pettifogging legal arguments. Your guilt has been well established."

"So this is just a kangaroo court?" The king smiled again, as if he'd won a point. "Or is that too generous?"

Yes, Peter thought. The matter would be debated endlessly over the next century, once the recordings were released to the public. *But you're not going to get out of this alive, and you know it.*

"You have had the opportunity to read the charges," Harrison said. "How do you plead?"

"Not guilty."

Peter leaned back in his chair. Harrison outlined the case for the prosecution. Admiral Morrison's secret orders. Admiral *Christian's* secret orders. The grab for power, following the declaration of war. The preparation of entire armies of secret clients. The assassinations of at least a dozen people, including the previous Duke Falcone. An attempt to murder the entire political class and seize power by force. Mass slaughter of a planet and city, effective genocide. And, last but far from least, leading a war against his own people.

"What a long list," the king observed, when Harrison was done. "You forgot to include jaywalking."

Harrison scowled. "Flippancy will not help your case."

The king straightened. "No," he agreed. "To all of these charges, I plead not guilty."

He let the words hang on the air for a long moment, then smiled. "I wish to make a statement. I believe I have *that* right, do I not?"

"You do," Harrison confirmed.

"Thank you," the king said.

"I do not deny that I have done terrible deeds," he continued. "There is no one here who has not done, or ordered, terrible deeds of their own. But everything I did, I did for the Commonwealth. I did my duty, as prince and king, to serve the greater interests of my people. It was—it *is*—my duty to protect them. And everything I did was in their name.

"You accuse me of starting the Theocratic War. Anyone who knows anything about the Theocracy will know that war was inevitable. There was no way to avoid it. I manipulated events to make sure the war started at a time and place of my choosing, a time and place that would be best for the Commonwealth as a whole. And I was largely successful. I made sure the war's outcome would never be in doubt.

"But my duties were far wider than merely defending my people against a foreign threat. It has always been the role of the monarchy to protect the people against their aristocratic overlords. I sought to protect my new subjects from exploitation, from corporations and interstellar banking services that would strip them bare and reduce them to penury. I pushed for investment, right across the Commonwealth, to make sure that the colonials would eventually take their place among us. I believed in the Commonwealth. I sought to make it *work*, when so many others regarded the colonials as servants at best and inconveniences at worst. You cannot condemn me for fighting for my people.

"My father had a vision for the Commonwealth. I have worked hard to uphold it, despite opposition from the aristocracy. Could you not see, gentlemen and ladies, the horrors wrought by your *failures*? The people whose lives were destroyed, the worlds that were devastated . . . in many ways, your lack of concern was *worse* than outright malice. You played games here, in the halls of power, while people suffered on the colony worlds. And then you wondered why so many colonials hated you."

He paused for a long, chilling moment. "I sought power, not for myself, but to fix the evils you unleashed. I sought power to ensure a more even distribution of wealth and resources, to provide investment and protection for the colonials—and the liberated worlds—until it was no longer required. And you seek to condemn me, not for anything I might have done, but for daring to stand in your way. I did everything for my people. You know nothing of the long term, nothing of the importance of planning for the future. You are so concerned about short-term profits that you cannot look to the future. I did. And I worked for it."

The king eased into an eerie smile. "Everything I did, I did for you. You can condemn me for it, if you wish, but it changes nothing. I had a vision of the future and worked for it. And if I had won, if I had returned to Tyre in victory rather than defeat, you would all be groveling at my feet, begging for forgiveness. You didn't even have the courage of your convictions. There isn't a single one of the ducal families that *didn't* send messages to Caledonia, readying themselves to switch sides if I won the war. You are not condemning me because I was wrong. You're condemning me because I was *right*."

His face became stoic. "Now, why don't you put an end to this farce?"

Peter frowned. The king *did* have one final trick up his sleeve, one no one had expected. The files would be released, sooner rather than later. The public would hear the king's final statement and . . . some of them, he supposed, would think he was right. It would be *easy* to think it, with the king himself safely dead. Who knew? Peter shrugged. His father had always said that the ends didn't justify the means. The means *made* the ends. The king had meant well, perhaps, but it didn't matter. He'd allowed himself to fall from grace long ago.

Harrison clearly agreed. His voice was thick with anger. "You did not work for anyone but yourself. You passed up countless opportunities to work out compromises that would have solved the problems you noted, without leaving you with power. You exploited political and military crises to gain power and hold it. And when you were threatened with losing everything, you resorted to violence. You've long since abandoned all claim to being on the *right* side. You fought a war to impose yourself and lost.

"Your supporters were the dregs of society; the power-hungry, the desperate, the *lost*. You cared nothing for them. Millions of people died in the occupied zone, after the war, because of you. Millions more suffered over the last year as the civil war swept through the Commonwealth like an avenging fire. And millions more perished in the attacks you authorized on two colonial worlds. And, when the war was clearly lost, you sought to establish a pocket statelet under foreign protection. You could have fought and died in defense of your ideals. That you fled tells us everything we need to know about your character."

The king shrugged. "Am I always to be surrounded by ankle-biters?"

Harrison spoke with cold fury. "You have chosen to waive most of your legal rights, despite the seriousness of the charges leveled against you," he said. "Do you have anything else you wish to say before we pass sentence?"

Peter leaned forward, curious. They *were* rushing things. He had no doubt future generations would say as much, even though they *had* to be sure the king was safely dead. The charges against him were proven, thankfully. The king hadn't tried to mount a real defense. It might have worked if he'd won the war, but . . . the king wasn't going to survive the next few days. And he knew it.

"I have only one thing to say," the king said. "My wife is pregnant with my first child. My *only* child. That child is the legal heir to the throne. I ask that you place my son on the throne."

"We'll consider it," Harrison said stiffly. "Your unborn son is an innocent. He will not suffer for the sins of his father."

"Thank you." The king bowed. "That's all I ask."

Peter frowned. It was going to be an interesting legal battle. The king and Drusilla hadn't been legally married, not by Tyrian Law, but the child *was* the king's. He—Peter assumed the king had chosen the child's gender—*was* the legitimate heir. There weren't many others with a claim to the throne, certainly no one so *close*. And yet, the House of

Lords would be reluctant to crown the king's son. They hated the poor kid's father too much.

It might be better to give the child up for adoption, where he would grow up unaware of his identity, Peter mused. *Or arrange for him to be fostered in an aristocratic household.*

Harrison took a breath. "You have been found guilty of all the charges leveled against you," he said. The decision had been made a long time ago, although the king's refusal to answer the charges and put forward a defense had spared them a long and utterly pointless trial. "It is the judgment of this court that you will be taken from this room to a place of execution and put to death. You may write a final statement, if you wish, or spend your final hours in prayer and contemplation. May God have mercy on your soul."

The king swayed, just slightly, but said nothing. Peter watched as the guards appeared from the shadows, escorting the king back to his cell. There would be a final meal, whatever he wanted to eat, and pen and paper if he wanted to write letters to his wife and family. And a priest, if the king wished to call for one. Peter had never thought the king to be particularly religious, but death *was* coming for him. Who knew? Maybe he'd find comfort in a priest's words at the end of his life.

"Well," Duke Rudbek said, once the lights had come up. "That's the end of that."

"I'll wait until we see his body dangling from the gallows," Duchess Zangaria said. "He may have one last trick up his sleeve."

"Maybe," Peter said. "But we've covered all the bases."

"We think," Duke Rudbek said. "We never knew he was building an army under our noses either."

Peter nodded. In hindsight, the signs had been clearly visible. The king had raised soldiers, trained them for a year or two, then sent them into the reserves to wait until they were called. In hindsight . . . He scowled. Whoever took the throne, after the king's death, wouldn't have anything *like* the same freedom of action. The ducal families were already taking steps to separate the monarchy from its corporate power base. The next monarch would be nothing more than a figurehead, with no power to influence events beyond his words.

"You read my proposals," he said calmly. "Do I have your support?"

"Smacks of letting most of the bastards off," Duke Rudbek commented. "Do you really *want* to set such a precedent?"

Peter looked back at him, evenly. "Do *you* really want to restart the war a few decades down the line?"

"No," Duke Rudbek said. "But rebellion should be punished."

"It isn't as if they're going to get away with it," Peter said. "Not completely. The ones who are guilty of outright atrocities—Admiral Ruben, for example—will face justice. But the ones who did nothing more than believe what they were told . . . they'll have a chance to go home and slip back into society. Mercy will serve us better than harsh punishments."

He looked around the chamber, silently gauging support. The war was effectively over. The ducal families were already resuming the competition for power. He'd have to pay a price for their backing, both for dealing with the king's unwitting supporters *and* the ones who'd known what they were doing when they joined the wrong side. If the war had gone the other way, *he* would be on the wrong side. Might didn't make right, as his father had pointed out time and time again, but it *did* determine what *happened*.

"And your sister is a problem you'll have to solve," Duchess Zangaria said. "I like your thinking though."

"It would be awkward to hang her, after she ended the war for us," Peter pointed out. "And she probably saved us from *another* interstellar war."

"True," Duke Rudbek said. "But we're going to have to ready ourselves to fight anyway."

"All the more reason to lay the king's side to rest as quickly as possible," he said, finally feeling as if he'd grown into his father's role. "Do I have your support?"

"I believe so," Duchess Turin said. "You can handle it as you see fit."

Thank you, Peter thought sourly. He wasn't blind to the implications. If he failed, or if the policy produced unwanted consequences, he'd get the blame. But there was no way to avoid it. *I'll just have to make sure the results are satisfactory.*

"That does leave us with the problem of Drusilla," Duke Rudbek said. "What do we do with her?"

Peter let out a long breath. The king himself had kept his silence, but some of his supporters had pointed the finger at his wife. They'd claimed that Drusilla had made the king worse. Much worse. Peter didn't buy it. The king had started scheming for power long before he'd known Drusilla even existed, let alone fallen in love with her. Drusilla hadn't said much of anything either. The doctors had confirmed that she was pregnant, but nothing else.

"Send her into exile, if she wishes." Peter knew what the Theocracy would have done, but he liked to think Tyre was a little more civilized. "There's probably little to be gained by punishing her."

"Particularly after she has the kid," Duke Rudbek growled. "What do we do with the king's brat?"

"A question for another time, perhaps," Peter said. His terminal bleeped. "I have a meeting with Admiral McElney. I'll see the rest of you tomorrow?"

"Of course," Duke Rudbek said. "I wouldn't miss the hanging for the world."

"Speak for yourself," Duchess Turin said. "There's something distasteful in watching a man die."

You gave orders that sent people to their deaths, Peter thought coldly. He'd done it too, time and time again. *And yet, all of those people were just numbers to you. Weren't they?*

He dismissed the thought. The war was over. And now they had to win the peace.

If William and Kat help me, it should be possible. And if they don't . . .

CHAPTER THIRTY-NINE

TYRE

There had been a gallows in the center of Kirkhaven, the closest town to his village on Hebrides. William had watched three people die as a young boy, two men and a woman who'd been convicted of serious crimes and sentenced to death. His tutors had told him to watch and learn, perhaps thinking it would scare him and the other children straight. Now . . . he studied the metal gallows, in the center of a large metal room, and shuddered. There were no crowds jeering and hurling moldy vegetables, but otherwise the chamber felt very much like the gallows he recalled. The handful of watching aristocrats and the former ambassador from Marseilles were very quiet. They didn't quite believe it was over.

The king was marched into the chamber. His hands were cuffed behind his back, his feet shackled to make it difficult to walk and impossible to run, but his head was uncovered. William had been told the king had rejected the offer of a blindfold, even though he knew he was walking to his death. The king looked calm, composed, his face a picture of martyrdom. He was deliberately shaping his own legacy, as much as he could. The recordings might just change the public's perception of him after they were released.

Maybe, William thought sourly. *Or maybe they'll see him as a fool.*

The king walked up the steps to the gallows and stood placidly as the noose was fixed around his neck. He'd had a chance to file an appeal, or request a different method of execution, but he'd done neither. William wasn't surprised. Given how much the king had done, and how much more was already being blamed on him, there hadn't been any doubt about his fate. His execution warrant had been drawn up well before the final battle, just awaiting the names in the right places. But he could have delayed things a little longer . . .

"It's time," the executioner said. "Do you have anything you wish to say before your sentence is carried out?"

"I did my duty," the king said.

William kept his face under tight control as the trapdoor opened. The king fell, the noose tightening around his neck with terrifying speed. There was a snapping sound as it broke, his body dangling like a sack of potatoes over the abyss. The executioner waited, counting the seconds. In theory, if a man managed to live through his intended execution, he had to be allowed to go free. In practice . . . William had never heard of it happening, not in real life. And here, of all places, there would be no mistakes that would force the House of Lords to let the king go.

Don't bet on it, he thought. *The king might have one last card to play.*

The executioner scanned the body. "He's dead. It's over."

William heard a rush of air as everyone exhaled at once. The executioner ignored them, carefully cutting down the body and placing it in a sealed coffin. Members of the royal family were traditionally buried on a hill overlooking their country estates, but this time . . . he had a feeling the body would be cremated and the ashes dumped at sea. There would be no burial ground someone might turn into a center of opposition, now that the king was safely dead.

Duke Peter stepped up beside him as the remainder of the audience left the chamber. "Did you think about my offer?"

William nodded stiffly. There'd been rumors he'd be promoted to grand admiral, particularly after Grand Admiral Rudbek had ended up with egg on his face. There would be people who'd insist he'd been deprived of his reward, although he hadn't wanted to be promoted into a desk job. The grand admiral wasn't allowed to command ships, lead men into battle, or fly anything more exciting than a desk. There was a peerage, if the grand admiral wasn't already an aristocrat, but it wasn't enough to make up for being permanently grounded. He intended to suggest that policy be changed, if the House of Lords was still listening to him now the war was over. A grand admiral who lost touch with the realities of naval warfare was a grand admiral who'd be worse than useless when the shooting restarted.

"I did," he said. "It would mean a demotion, but . . . I'll take it."

Duke Peter smiled. "I'll be sending you as many of the king's former supporters as possible," he said. "I think . . . if there's anyone who can bring them back into the fold, it's you."

"Thanks," William said. "I suppose the real question, Your Grace, is how much power and political support you're willing to give me. May I ask . . . ?"

"I've discussed it extensively with the others," Duke Peter said. "Your formal written orders will be upheld, to the hilt. You'll have extensive authority, at least until the StarCom network is up and running. And you'll be assured of the fleet deployment for at least five years."

"Because the ships and personnel will be drawn from the remnants of the king's fleet," William said. He had to admit it was a neat solution. On one hand, those who'd supported the king would be permitted to work their way back to favor; on the other, they'd be unable to cause real trouble if they started to plan a second revolt. "And supplies and suchlike?"

"You'll have everything you reasonably need," Duke Peter said. "I trust this won't cause problems with Asher Dales?"

"They've probably already replaced me," William said. "There wasn't any shortage of prospective officers before the civil war and . . . well, there isn't any shortage now."

"I suppose not," Duke Peter said. "I have to visit Kat this afternoon. I'd speak to you after then, if you don't mind."

And if I do, it doesn't matter, William told himself.

He considered the offer again for a long moment. He'd been knighted. His pension would keep him afloat if he wanted to retire. Or . . . he could stay in the navy. They could hardly fire him after he'd won the war. He could keep command of Home Fleet or request assignment to the border stars. God knew what Marseilles would do in the next few years. Things might simmer down or explode into war. He'd seen the plans for border defenses. If anything, they were more elaborate than anything the king had planned. But then, Marseilles would be a more serious enemy than the Theocrats. The war could get very unpleasant indeed.

And yet, going to the liberated sector would be one hell of a challenge. And *someone* had to do it. And William knew, without false modesty, that he was the most qualified officer for the role.

"I'll do it," he said, again. "When do you want me to depart?"

"Depends on Kat," Duke Peter said. "But within a week, no more."

He shrugged. "We're clearing your personnel as fast as possible. Captain Sarah Henderson appears to be the senior surviving officer . . . at least, among those who didn't commit suicide or flee if they weren't killed in the final battle. She'll probably be your second. How much trust you want to rest in her is up to you."

"Understood," William said, with the rather cynical thought he'd get the blame if Captain Henderson proved unworthy of his trust. "I'll speak to her before departure."

"And I'll speak to Kat," Duke Peter said. "Good luck, Admiral."

William bowed. "And to you, Your Grace."

◆ ◆ ◆

Francis hadn't expected to feel quite so numb when, as a semiwilling guest, he'd been forced to watch King Hadrian being marched to the gallows and executed. The king had been teetering on the brink of madness well before the final battle, well before Kat Falcone had boarded his ship and brought his reign to an end. Francis had been all too aware that the king was growing increasingly unstable, that he might prove to be a dangerous puppet if things went badly wrong . . . In some ways, Francis was relieved the matter had ended so quickly. Marseilles had been able to extract itself from the morass without being dangerously exposed. The House of Lords knew what Marseilles had done, but . . . the matter hadn't become public. They weren't going to be pushed into war.

He kept his thoughts to himself as a pretty dark-skinned woman led him away from the execution chamber and up into a small office that was so bare and barren of any personality that he *knew* it wasn't in regular use. The chairs were comfortable, but functional; the desk naked, without papers or datapads or anything else the owner could fiddle with in the hopes of putting his guests in their place. Francis was experienced enough to read the underlying message, the grim warning that he was on thin ice. A *friendly* meeting would be handled by the foreign officer in nicer surroundings. This meeting was going to be very unfriendly indeed.

"Mr. Ambassador," a voice said. "Thank you for coming."

Francis turned as Duke Peter strode into the room, heading straight for the desk. Francis's eyebrows crawled up his forehead as he wondered why the duke had come in person rather than delegate the task to a subordinate. An ambassador could be disowned, if he got his planet into trouble; a duke, one of the most powerful men on the planet, had far less freedom to maneuver. Francis wasn't blind to *that* message either. Whatever he was about to hear had come straight from the dukes, from the leaders of Tyre and the Commonwealth. There would be no going back on it.

"Your Grace," Francis said. He'd never really expected to meet the dukes. "I . . . thank you for inviting me."

Duke Peter sat, resting his elbows on the hard metal desk. "This will be a short meeting," he said bluntly. "First, as I'm sure you're aware, the king's government has been declared illegitimate right from the start. The deals he made with you have no legal validity, and the Commonwealth will not honor them. Even if that *was* the case, selling the border stars to you was illegal under the Commonwealth Treaty. The border stars themselves have protested the king's attempt to trade them away in the strongest possible terms.

"That said, we accept that you were . . . *misled* on the issue. We believe that you believed you had a valid claim when you attempted to occupy the systems. We will not press the issue of you laying claim to the stars. In exchange for this, we want you to abandon your demand for payment for services rendered. The king's government had no legal right to enter into any treaties with you, and we are certainly not obliged to pay his debts. The remaining missiles and spare parts you sent to his fleet will, of course, be returned to you."

After your techs have had a good look at them, Francis thought. *That will not go down well back home.*

"Second, we protest, again, in the strongest possible terms, your government's decision to interfere in our internal affairs. We have no doubt that *your* government would be furious if we were to support separatist groups on *your* side of the border, which we could easily do. We demand a formal apology for your actions and a complete account of everything that transpired between you, the king, and his allies. If this is not forthcoming, we will have to reconsider the multitude of trade deals between my government and yours."

Francis's eyes narrowed. The trade deals weren't that important, but losing them would be painful. Worse, Tyre would start aggressively pushing into Marseillan-dominated markets and exporting its products farther corewards. Who knew what that would do to the government's balance sheet? Marseilles had more enemies than Tyre. They wouldn't hesitate to take advantage of a sudden shift in the balance of power.

"Finally, it has become clear that you, you personally, overstepped the bounds of diplomatic protocol and gave more encouragement and support to the king than anyone, including your government, is prepared to countenance. Accordingly, you are hereby declared persona non grata, with orders to remove yourself from Tyre by the end of the week and Commonwealth territory by the end of the month. You may not return. Your government may do whatever it likes with you, but you are no longer welcome in our space as a diplomat or private traveler, and if you are caught you will no longer have the protection of diplomatic immunity."

Francis kept his face impassive with an effort. It was clear, now, that the fix was in. His government would blame everything on him, giving them political cover to step back from a war. They'd backed him every step of the way until . . . He scowled, promising himself that it was *not* over. He had friends and allies on Marseilles. He could push back, given time. He could salvage something from the disaster, if he acted fast. But . . .

"I understand." The words tasted like ashes. "I'll return to the embassy, then book transport tonight."

"Good." Duke Peter stood. He didn't offer to shake hands. "I look forward to meeting your replacement."

Hah, Francis thought.

"I'm sure you will enjoy the experience," Francis said crossly. He didn't try to hide his anger. "And if you'd lost the war, you'd be begging yourself."

"Perhaps." Duke Peter smiled, although there was no real joy in the expression. "But we didn't lose, did we?"

"No," Francis agreed. "You won."

For the moment, he added, silently. He'd seen the reports. The Colonial Alliance had shattered, but the problems that had birthed it were still there. The House of Lords was doing nothing more than papering over the cracks, as far as he could tell. Sure, they were making noises about doing the right things, but . . . were they? Francis wasn't so sure. And if they didn't make any real changes, they might wind up refighting the war. *Your victory may turn to dust in your hands.*

He bowed. "Thank you, Your Grace," he said. It was hard to say the next words, but . . . there was nothing to be gained by spitting in the duke's face. He had a career to rebuild. "My congratulations on your victory."

Turning, he strode out of the room.

◆ ◆ ◆

Captain Sarah Henderson—who wasn't sure if she was still a captain, particularly now her ship was in enemy hands—paced the brig, wondering what would become of her. Governor Rogan was dead, most of his allies were dead . . . the *king* was dead. She'd been denied access to the datanet, but she'd been permitted to watch entertainment channels and news broadcasts. The word was already spreading. The king was dead. So far, no one seemed to be his successor.

She wondered, not for the first time, if she'd done the right thing. The king had been mad, yes, but . . . if she hadn't led a mutiny against him, who knew what would have happened? Surely . . . She sighed. The king had killed millions of people on Quist and millions more on Caledonia. The news broadcasts insisted the death toll was still rising, as more and more bodies were pulled from the debris. No one had yet found a trace of Governor Rogan or his fellows. Some were already speculating they were still alive. Sarah would have liked to believe it, but she knew better.

The outer hatch opened. She stilled herself, knowing it didn't matter. There was no privacy in the brig, even though she was alone. She was under constant observation. The guards rarely spoke to her, even when they brought food. She had the distinct impression that they didn't know what to do with her. Their ultimate superiors probably hadn't made up their minds.

She lifted her eyebrows as she saw William McElney, feeling an odd surge of emotions. Respect, anger . . . even a hint of hatred. William was a colonial, yet he'd fought on the wrong bloody side. She found it hard to understand why he'd thrown away his chance to lead the colonials to victory . . . Perhaps he'd simply never liked or trusted the king. Or . . . things would have been different, she supposed, if his homeworld hadn't been destroyed. His people had taken no side in the war.

"Admiral," she said. She stepped up to the forcefield and peered through the faint haze. "What can I do for you?"

William studied her for a long moment. "First, there's a general amnesty for anyone who wasn't guilty of crimes against humanity," he said. "You qualify. There will be a brief check to make sure you're *not* guilty, but . . . if so, you're free to go."

Sarah's eyes narrowed. It was a good offer. Too good. "What's the catch?"

"You have two choices," William said. "On one hand, you can accept dismissal from the navy. You can return to your homeworld and enter civilian life. On the other . . . you can stay in the navy, but you'll be under my command—and, to some extent, in exile—for the next five years. I think you'll enjoy the work, but . . ."

"It won't be command," Sarah said. She missed her ship, more than she could say. She was *born* to command. "They won't give me a ship."

"We'll see." William surprised her. He tapped a switch, deactivating the forcefield. The haze vanished. "I'll tell you what I have in mind, Captain. And then you can tell me what *you* have in mind."

CHAPTER FORTY

TYRE

The luxury suite was a prison cell.

Kat had spent the first few hours of her imprisonment—and it *was* imprisonment—searching the suite thoroughly, picking out the surveillance devices and proving, to her satisfaction, that she could neither leave the room nor send messages without having them held in a buffer and read first. There was only one way in or out of the suite and it was locked, locked so securely that there was no way she could get out without permission. She'd allowed herself to relax, just a little. She'd had a bath, then climbed into a sinfully comfortable bed, but as she'd waited she'd known, all too well, that her fate was being decided. Her family had probably already disowned her. God knew she'd screwed up so badly she couldn't hope to save herself.

She sat on the bed, holding a datapad without actually reading it. Tears prickled at the corners of her eyes. It didn't matter. Nothing mattered. She'd made a terrible mistake and . . . everything she'd done, since she'd realized the truth, didn't make up for what she'd done before. She wondered, bitterly, what the family would decide. Exile? Death? Or would they hand her over for a public trial? The entire *universe* knew she'd sided with the king. The entire universe knew she'd fucked up so badly . . .

A dull click echoed through the suite. The outer hatch was opening. Kat looked up, then shrugged and stayed where she was. If they wanted her, they could come *get* her. She heard a single person pacing across the floor, then stopping just outside the bedroom door. There was a single loud knock.

"Are you decent?" Peter. It was Peter. "Can I come in?"

"Yes," Kat said, as if she had any choice in the matter. Her brother already knew she was up and dressed. "You may as well."

Peter pushed the door open and stepped into the room. He'd always taken after their father, but now . . . the resemblance was uncanny. Kat felt her heart skip a beat as she saw him. Peter had grown up, somehow. The boring, pedantic adult she'd known right from birth had turned into a man of wealth, influence, and power. Kat wondered, idly, what Peter's wife made of it all. She had to be proud. Or maybe not. Peter wasn't the man she'd married any longer.

Not that it matters. Kat stood slowly, brushing down her slacks. *Peter could be as ugly as sin and sinful as hell itself and people would still be lining up to marry him.*

"Peter," she said. It was hard to keep her voice steady. "What can I do for you?"

Peter took a chair and perched on it. "Why did you support the king?"

Kat looked down, unwilling to meet his eyes. "I thought he was in the right."

"I see," Peter said. "Even though I was opposed to him?"

Kat let out a breath. "You weren't on Ahura Mazda," she said. "You never visited the liberated zone. You didn't see the suffering. You didn't see how much I couldn't prevent because you kept taking ships and troops away from me. You weren't there."

She forced herself to look up. "I suppose it doesn't matter now," she said. Anger slid into her voice, anger and a bitter hatred directed at herself. "I fucked up. Dad died at the hands of a monster, a monster I thought was doing the right thing. I supported him . . ." She shook her head. "If it wasn't for me, he would never have escaped Tyre."

"Perhaps not," Peter agreed. "But you were deceived."

"I should have known," Kat snapped. "I should have realized the truth *before* I got thousands of people killed!"

"You didn't," Peter said calmly. "You were not the only one to be fooled."

"But I was the most significant," Kat said. "I thought . . ."

Peter held up a hand. The gesture was so much like their father's that Kat stopped dead.

"You weren't the only one," Peter said quietly. "Very few people knew the truth. The colonials, the naval officers and crew . . . most of them believed they were fighting for the right side. They thought . . . Yes, they were wrong, but they genuinely believed they were fighting for the right. You are not alone."

Kat glared at him. "How many of them got their fathers killed?"

"You *didn't* get Father killed," Peter said. "I read the files. Father was going to decentralize the economy and demobilize much of the military, once the war was over. The king killed him to prevent him from even *starting*. You are not to blame for his death. You thought the Theocrats had done it and . . . so did everyone else, until recently."

He met her eyes. "And when you *did* find out the truth, you turned on him. You took him prisoner, at great personal risk. You ended the war before it could get much worse, when the Marseillans tried to claim what the king owed them. Yes, you made a mistake. But you did everything in your power to fix it."

"Too late for the dead," Kat said. "Peter, I thought . . ."

She looked to the floor, all the tangled thoughts and emotions bubbling up in her mind. She'd been prepared to overlook a *lot*, because she'd thought the king was doing the right thing. She'd been a bloody fool, time and time and time again. Peter was being nice to her . . .

He should be dragging her, kicking and screaming, to the gallows. She deserved no less.

"Peter," she said. "What happened to the king?"

"He was executed this morning." Peter looked embarrassed. "Sorry. I thought you had a terminal here."

"There's nothing more than a library," Kat said. "Tons of entertainment, from bland and boring books to porn, but nothing from the outside world."

"I'm sorry," Peter said, again. "I can send you the recordings . . ."

"Never mind," she said. She'd think about Hadrian's death—and what it meant to her—later, when she was alone. "What now? What about me?"

"There's a general amnesty for everyone—well, almost everyone—who sided with the king," Peter said. "Those guilty of crimes against humanity, crimes outside the laws of war, will be charged and punished. Everyone else . . . There are some special arrangements for a handful of people, but the remainder are free to go. We'll discuss that later, if you wish."

"Maybe," Kat said. "Am I free to go?"

"In a manner of speaking." Peter looked at his hands. "There was a *lot* of debate about it. Your public image is still pretty good. You fought for the wrong side, but you're still seen as a hero of the last war, and you're credited with turning on the king when you discovered the truth. And you aren't charged with any real war crimes. You are not to blame for the king's slip into madness."

"Really," Kat said sourly. "And that's the *family's* opinion?"

"The family is conflicted," Peter said. His lips quirked. "Have you ever known our aunts and uncles to agree on *anything*?"

"No." Kat let out a breath. "Exile, then?"

"In a manner of speaking," Peter repeated. "They want you punished. At the same time, they don't want you *too* punished."

Kat rolled her eyes. "What do they expect you to do? Put me over your knee?"

Peter didn't smile at her terrible joke. "We're putting together a fleet to patrol the liberated zone, given that we were partly responsible for the chaos that swept through the sector during the early occupation. A sizable chunk of the king's naval supporters—his *former* supporters—and their ships will be assigned to the fleet. Admiral McElney has agreed to take command for the moment. He won't have any superdreadnoughts under his command, nothing larger than a battlecruiser, but he'll have enough smaller ships to carry out his mission. We'll also be investing in a number of the liberated worlds, in the hopes of them either joining the Commonwealth at a later date or, at the very least, becoming allies."

"In other words, you're doing exactly as I wanted you to do," Kat said. "Exactly as the *king* wanted you to do."

"I'd keep that opinion to yourself, if possible," Peter said dryly. "It wouldn't be very politically correct."

Kat snorted, rudely.

"We'd like to assign you to the fleet," Peter said. "You'd be in exile, effectively speaking, for the first five-year deployment. After that . . . it depends on politics. Things might settle down here, they might not. I won't make you any promises I won't be able to keep. You may be able to come home, you may not."

"I get the picture." Kat smiled as a thought stuck her. "I'll be under William's command?"

"Yes." Peter sounded inflexible. "The others didn't want to give you a whole new command, after everything."

"I understand." Kat nodded. "At least William got the recognition he deserves."

"Yes." Peter leaned back in his chair. "I don't know how things are going to work out. We have the economy stabilized, but . . . it'll take time to recover from the war. People are still out of work, collecting government benefits and food supplies rather than trying to get reemployed. The jobs just aren't there. And the colonials . . . Yes, we've come to an agreement on debt forgiveness. But I don't think that'll solve *all* their problems."

"Probably not," Kat agreed. "It'll be a start though."

"Yeah." Peter met her eyes. "Kat. Katherine. I need a decision fairly quickly. I want you away from the system before people start asking awkward questions. And looking for scapegoats."

Kat wasn't surprised. "What are my other options?"

Peter shot her a reproving look. "Right now? You can be dismissed from the navy and . . . effectively isolated from the family. You'll be disowned practically, if not legally. I don't think your enemies have enough votes to make it legal, but it won't matter. Or . . . you could cash in your trust fund, buy a ship, and go exploring. Or do whatever you want, as long as it's nowhere near us. Or you could hang around long enough for some enterprising political asshole to start pressing for your trial and punishment."

I deserve it, Kat thought bitterly.

"You can do some good in the liberated sector," Peter said. "Or you can go into exile."

"That's no choice at all," Kat said tiredly. She ran her hand through her hair. "I'll go with William."

"I thought you would," Peter said. He stood too. "I asked him to wait. I'll send him to see you, then . . . We'd prefer you stay here until William's flagship is ready to leave."

"I thought as much," Kat said. "How many people out there"—she jabbed a hand at the wall—"blame me?"

"Fewer than you seem to think," Peter said. "But enough to be dangerous, if they see you."

He turned and left the bedroom. Kat followed him, oddly unsure of herself. It felt good to be free, to feel as though a sword was no longer hanging over her head, but . . . she still blamed herself. She'd beaten the king, she'd stopped him, she'd made sure he'd be executed, yet . . . she felt as if she was still at fault. What had happened would haunt her for the rest of her days.

Peter stepped through the hatch. A moment later, William stepped in.

"Kat," he said. His voice was awkward. "Are you . . . ?"

Kat had to smile, despite their shared awkwardness. "I think I need to salute you," she said, suiting action to words. "When are we leaving?"

"Soon," William said. "I'm glad it worked out."

"So am I," Kat admitted. She promised herself that she'd catch up with the news broadcasts and reports as soon as she was on the way to William's flagship. She'd lost track of what was happening in the liberated zone since the civil war had broken out. "The future will just have to take care of itself."

"We'll take care of it," William corrected. "Together."

AFTERWORD

If you've been following my career, you'll have noticed that I seem to like writing about civil wars, rebellions, and insurrections. In this, I am following in the footsteps of such greats as Robert A. Heinlein (*The Moon Is a Harsh Mistress*), David Weber/Steve White (*Insurrection*), and a multitude of other writers who have mined history for inspiration. Indeed, many of those writers got me into studying real history instead of history getting me into those books! Truth—historical truth—is often stranger than fiction.

In one sense, all civil wars are different. In another, they are often very alike. There are, in general terms, only *two* types of civil war. The first might be defined as a War of Secession, where a region of a country, perhaps one culturally distinct from the remainder of the nation, fights for its independence. The second might be defined as a War of Revolution, where one side seeks to gain control of the levers of power and use them as it sees fit. The latter tends to veer between battles for the throne—putting someone else on the throne without threatening the structure of monarchy itself—and outright revolutions, which aim to reform or destroy the governing system itself. This is never as easy as it sounds. People are naturally conservative, perhaps in fear that what might replace the old system will be worse. This is not an unreasonable fear. The Russian and French Revolutions destroyed the monarchist governments, which were awful, but they were replaced with governments that were inarguably worse. In both cases, the losers made their lives harder by reminding the people who threw them out precisely *why* they threw them out.

The origins of civil wars, therefore, can be hotly disputed. The winner, whoever that happens to be, has an interest in portraying the losing side as negatively as possible, if only to discourage others from following in their footsteps. The American Civil War, for example, had a number of separate causes, but most studies tend to focus on the slavery issue alone, both because slavery is seen (and rightly so) as a great evil *and* because it is relatively *simple*. This does tend to raise the question of why so many poor white Southerners fought for a system that was weighted *against* them—slavery was hardly an asset to those who owned no slaves, who struggled against a warped economy—and leads to all sorts of nasty allegations, ranging from racism to simple stupidity. The fact that the South had good reason to resent and fear the North is generally overlooked.

Indeed, the American Civil War is odd because the *losers* shaped so much of its early mythology. The Myth of the Lost Cause, a belief the South lost because it was utterly outgunned rather than morally in the wrong, lingers on.

Throughout Anglo-American history, there have been *three* civil wars of staggering significance. The American Civil War (attempted War of Secession) is obviously one of them. The American War of Independence (successful War of Secession) is also one of them. But there is a third, the *English* Civil War (War of Revolution), and its semicontinuation, the Glorious Revolution (War of Revolution). The English Civil War is far less well known, particularly in America, even though it swept across all *three* British kingdoms and touched the early American colonies. In some ways, the winners sought to bury the truth and vilify their enemies. In others, the origins and course of the war are confusing, unlike the relatively simple, and later, American War of Independence.

The English Civil War was hardly the first civil war in Britain, nor was it the first to reshape the political and social landscape, but it was, perhaps, the most significant. Put simply, the dispute between King Charles I and Parliament was over who *really* called the shots. In theory, the king possessed near-absolute power; in practice, the king's powers were limited by long-standing customs and legalities, including the need to go to parliament for funds. In some ways, Charles inherited a mess from his father and Elizabeth Tudor. In others, Charles blundered from mistake to mistake until he found himself committed to war against his own government. The resulting civil war seesawed backwards and forwards for several years until Parliament developed the New Model Army, came to terms with the Scots, and crushed Charles's army. Even then, they were unsure what to do with him. It wasn't until Charles, who had already developed a reputation for double-dealing and outright treachery, finally overstepped himself that they put him on trial (itself a legal headache, as previous dispositions tended to wait until matters were beyond recovery) and beheaded him.

This may seem odd, from our point of view, but Parliament was not at first interested in tearing down the *entire* social order and starting again. Parliament wanted to reform the system, not destroy it. The king had a vital role in the prewar constitution—the collection of laws, understandings, and suchlike that govern Britain—and simply chopping off his head was not, for many of them, an understanding. To us, the idea of *negotiating* with someone who had nothing to negotiate *with* seems absurd. To them, the king still had something to offer. Weirdly enough, there was a considerable degree of continuity between Charles I, Oliver Cromwell (who became Lord Protector, king in all but name), and Charles II. The English Civil War was a War of Revolution, but not *too* much revolution.

But it did change things, more than ever before. Parliament's supremacy was largely unchallenged. Charles II, upon his Restoration, knew the risks of pressing too hard. (This didn't stop him risking everything on a secret understanding with France, which, luckily for him, remained undisclosed until after his death.) The steady weakening of the royal supremacy ensured that James II, when he took the throne upon Charles II's death, could be simply and bloodlessly removed in the Glorious Revolution. Indeed, the English Civil War and the liberties it enshrined in law can be seen as a precursor to the American War of Independence.

Such wars, however, come with extreme risks. The French Revolution did not lead to a stable, postmonarchical form of government. Instead, Napoleon eventually took power and unleashed an endless series of wars across Europe until he was defeated and exiled in 1814. The monarchists were returned to Paris, but rapidly proved they'd learned nothing from their exile, giving Napoleon a chance to make another bid for power in 1815. The Russian Revolution started promisingly, at first, but collapsed into a nightmare when the communists took power and imposed their own order on the country. On one hand, this was different from the monarchy. On the other, it was far worse.

In the modern world, it must be noted, civil wars can be brutal. The collapse or perversion of government power, in which the government sides openly with one of the factions, can rip society to shreds, shattering what little social trust remains. It becomes impossible to either separate peacefully or escape, thus ensuring a war that rapidly leads to an endless series of atrocities. This is very human—people who feel they cannot escape have a flat choice between submission or fighting and often choose to fight—but disastrous. Once the cycle of revenge gets underway, it cannot be stopped easily. The collapse of Yugoslavia, the civil wars of Iraq, and the chaos that gripped British India as the British withdrew and the Raj separated into India and Pakistan stand as a stark warning of how bad things can become.

There has been much talk recently, from America, of civil war. This is, in one sense, hardly a new phenomenon. America was born in a civil war—the only reason the American War of Independence is not generally counted as a civil war is that the rebels *won*, turning the conflict into a successful War of Secession—and there were outbreaks of violence almost from day one. The Whiskey Rebellion, for example, sowed the seeds for much to come. On one hand, it showed the newborn government *could* exercise effective control in its territory; on the other, it showed the government was prepared to impose taxes on people who lacked representation. The fear of the federal government growing so powerful it could not be stopped is not a new thing. Donald Trump's "drain the swamp" battle cry is merely the continuation of a struggle as old as America itself.

But the American Civil War was *relatively* civilized, by the standards of the time. The Confederate States of America did not seek to overrun, occupy, and reshape the United States. They lacked the power to do so, even if they had the will. They merely sought independence, which seemed, to many in the North, to be an entirely reasonable request. And this could have been granted, without causing immense hardship to the North. The South, both poor whites and blacks who were enslaved, would have had serious problems as industrial development continued, but those would have been the results of a system already in place. They would not have been imposed by outside powers.

A modern-day American Civil War would be far worse. There would be no clearly defined "nations," no unified command-and-control systems . . . the military would be torn apart, battles would be fought over every state government and capital, food distribution networks would break down, and the economy would collapse, causing mass starvation that would bring the cities to their knees. Whoever won would have to cope with a legacy of bitterness that would pervade every layer of society, from the high to the low. It would be a nightmare beyond calculation, one that would cast a long shadow for decades to come.

The only way to stop such a catastrophe is to seek compromise. But our modern-day societies are increasingly averse to compromise. And that bodes ill for the future.

ABOUT THE AUTHOR

Christopher G. Nuttall is the author of more than a dozen series, including the bestselling Ark Royal books, as well as the Embers of War, Angel in the Whirlwind, Royal Sorceress, Bookworm, Schooled in Magic, Twilight of the Gods, and Zero Enigma series. Born and raised in Edinburgh, Scotland, Christopher studied history, which inspired him to imagine new worlds and create an alternate-history website. Those imaginings provided a solid base for storytelling and eventually led him to publish more than one hundred works, including novels, short stories, and one novella. He moves between Britain and Malaysia with his partner, muse, and critic, Aisha. For more information, visit his blog at www.chrishanger.wordpress.com and his website at www.chrishanger.net.